Amy Elizabeth Saunders

I Can't Help Falling in Love

*To my family, who have never had a Norman Rockwell
Christmas, and special thanks to the wonderful flying Evli
of Las Vegas, Nevada, who graciously consented to making
a fictional appearance in my story.
Merry Christmas to all.*

Chapter One

Every year, they begin their Christmas pilgrimages to the grave of the King. They are the fervent, the devoted, the faithful. Many believe that he still lives and walks among us.

G. Charles Van Dusen reread the paragraph, frowned, deleted the word *fervent*, hesitated, and then put it back.

"More coffee, sir?"

He glanced up at his waitress long enough to notice that she had dark hair, made a quick motion that indicated assent and dismissal at the same time, and turned back to his laptop computer.

Christmas in Bethlehem? Jerusalem? No, it's Christmas at Graceland, and when you say "the King" in Memphis, you're talking about Elvis.

He took a sip of the coffee, barely registering the taste, and went back to his article.

7

"Do you mind if we share this table?"

Irritated, he glanced up. A cursory glance around the room told him that every other table in the airport restaurant was, indeed, full. Normally, at two in the morning, an airport coffee shop was a silent, almost deserted place—one of the reasons he preferred to travel at night.

But with only two days till Christmas, it seemed that everyone who could pack a bag was either coming to, leaving, or passing through St. Louis International Airport. Holiday travelers were crowding for room at the tables, and lining up at the cash register: mothers balancing sleeping babies and strollers, students with backpacks and skis, red-eyed businessmen rushing home to their families.

"Go right ahead." He didn't even bother to look up at the man as he spoke, and felt, rather than saw, the intruder pushing his way into the booth beside him. He was already typing again, back in the bizarre world of Elvis Presley's devoted fans.

True, the article wasn't due until July, when the editors at *Today's Psychology* would be putting together next December's issue, but Gabriel Charles Van Dusen kept meticulously to his own schedule—no last-minute deadlines for him. And it was a good article. It would be an entertaining and welcome diversion amid the magazine's usual Christmas offerings—articles about unrealistic holiday expectations, overeating and drinking, and familial guilt.

He clicked the screen on his laptop over to review the timetable he had written for himself. *Still to be done—find and interview an Elvis fan.* There should be no shortage of those in Memphis. It would fill the article out nicely—interspersing his carefully gathered facts and observations with the story of a genuine fan on pilgrimage. He pictured her as he spoke. Her name would be something like Eula Mae, and she would be from Arkansas, or Alabama, or some equally godforsaken place. She would be fiftyish, and—

"Attention, passengers. Due to snow accumulation, all Delta Airlines flights are temporarily canceled."

Thank God he wasn't flying Delta. He switched back to his

8

article, and kept writing, ignoring the dismayed chorus rising around him. He barely took notice of the man next to him leaving the table, jostling his elbow as he went. The din of chatter, piped-in Christmas music, and clattering silverware faded into the background.

What brings them here, filing past the grave of their "King" like medieval pilgrims leaving flowers and gifts, lighting candles at the shrine of a saint? Some claim to have seen him since his reported death, miraculously alive. . . .

He carefully typed, "Insert commentary from Eula Mae here," and wrote on.

The darkened windows behind him mirrored the chaos of the restaurant, the crowds, and his own reflection—a well-dressed, good-looking man with pair of wire-framed reading glasses resting on his aquiline nose as he typed on, oblivious to the snow falling onto the dark runway beyond, the planes lumbering out to the end of the landing strips and then turning and crawling back, like huge, defeated steel dinosaurs.

". . . the St. Louis International Airport will be temporarily closed to all arriving and departing flights until further notice."

The calm, well-modulated voice on the loudspeaker succeeded in getting his attention. He stopped typing and stared out the window.

The runway was covered with a glowing blanket of white, and sparkling shards of white snow fell from the dark sky, cold and glittering under the brilliant runway light. Baggage carts stood still beside the silent jets, baggage handlers with gloved hands leaning idly against them.

"Damn." He would have to drive, snow or not, and renting a car in this mob of thwarted travelers would be a major inconvenience. He shut down his laptop, closed it with a snap, tucked his reading glasses into his shirt pocket, and reached for his tweed jacket.

It was gone.

The booth next to him showed an empty expanse of crumb-covered brown vinyl, and an empty cracker wrapper.

Alarmed, he looked down at the floor. More crumbs.

His leather carry-on bag, gone. His Burberry overcoat, gone. His wool jacket, with his wallet, identification, boarding passes, and charge cards carefully tucked into the inside breast pocket . . . vanished.

His stomach gave a sharp rumble, and he thought of the package of antacids resting next to his wallet. He searched his pants pockets. One paper clip, the receipt for the antacids, and two dollars and sixty-three cents—mostly in change. In his back pocket was the small notebook he used when his laptop was inconvenient.

"Will there be anything else for you?"

The waitress again. He looked at her face for the first time that night. She had pale skin and bright blue eyes, and was thirty, at the most. Very dark, very curly hair was pulled carelessly back into short ponytail festooned with sparkling Christmas ribbons. Her slender figure was garbed in an atrocious uniform of mauve polyester.

She was quickly adding up his bill—four cups of terrible coffee at the inflated airport price of a dollar and a half each.

"Could you call security? I've been robbed."

She stopped writing and looked up at him with bright, startled eyes. "What? Just now?"

"I'm not sure. Since I've been here, obviously. I arrived at exactly twelve forty-six."

She looked at her watch—a pink leather band, with an oversize clock. Elvis's face, of all things, was in the center of the dial. The second hand was a little guitar.

"Wow. So, in the past three hours?"

"Apparently. Could you please call security?"

"Sure." She hurried away, the black curls dancing beneath the gold Christmas ribbon, while he waited impatiently, berating himself for having been so careless.

She was back almost immediately. "They're on the way. It might take a few, though. Things are pretty hectic tonight."

She was clearing the table as she spoke, piling empty dishes into a gray plastic tub.

"Did you happen to notice the gentleman sitting next to me?" he asked her.

She stopped, considering. "Pecan pie," she answered finally, "and tea. Two cups, with cream."

"Wonderful." Charles didn't really care that he sounded sarcastic. "Did you notice anything else, by chance? What he looked like, what he was wearing? His age? Any companions? One head or two? Something helpful, perhaps?"

She stopped wiping the table, and lifted one dark brow. "Yes. I did notice something."

"Well?"

"He was polite. Very, very polite. He said 'please' and 'thank you.' Unlike some customers, who can't be bothered to remember that waitresses are human."

She gave the table a final wipe with her white towel, scattering the last of the crumbs. "Would you like another cup of coffee?"

He started to agree, and then stopped. "I would, but I'm afraid that our pecan pie aficionado has made off with my wallet."

"Don't worry about it." She spoke quickly, without hesitation, and offered him a quick smile, as if to apologize for her snappy remark about polite customers. He noticed that she had two precise dimples beneath the curves of her cheeks. "Anything else?"

"No, thank you." He sat back down, took out his notebook, and reached automatically for his jacket.

Damn!

"Oh, miss?"

She turned, her smile deepening.

"If I might borrow a pen?"

"Sure." She reached into her apron pocket. "Think fast," she said, tossing the pen through the air.

Though startled, he neatly caught the oncoming missile. He sighed and reached for his notebook, and then, remembering her earlier remark, started to thank her.

11

Amy Elizabeth Saunders

She was speaking to another customer, cooing at the woman's sticky-faced baby. He took note of her name tag, and smiled despite himself. It read, HELLO. MY NAME IS OH, MISS.

Amusing. He clicked the ballpoint pen open, and then looked at it a second time.

Elvis again. It was one of those pens available at souvenir stands, with the upper portion of the barrel filled with water. A tiny, cutout Elvis, guitar in hand, floated up and down past a picture of Graceland.

"My good-luck pen," she commented, carefully placing his coffee on the table. "You can keep it—it looks like you need more good luck than I do tonight."

"Thank you." Charles thought of the pen in his jacket pocket—understated, elegant, and expensive. He had been using that pen for fifteen years, and was used to the way it felt in his hand.

Awkwardly, he adjusted the oversize souvenir Elvis pen in his grip, and began writing his list.

> *Speak to police.*
> *Find telegram office.*
> *Call home—have Mother or Wallace wire money.*
> *Rent car.*
> *Drive to Memphis—find route, est. driving times.*
> *Call the Peabody. Confirm reservations.*

There. He had a plan, a schedule to follow. He felt much more in control of things.

The officer who took his report seemed indifferent to his plight. He dutifully noted the missing items, filled out the report with methodical neatness, and offered Charles little or no hope for the recovery of his possessions.

The waitress, who gave the officer her name as Bailey O'Connor instead of Oh, Miss, was able to offer a little more information than what the man had eaten. He was about forty, thin, wearing a blue coat that zipped. "And the most remark-

12

able thing," she finished solemnly, "was his face. He'd be easy to spot. He looks just like Al Pacino, only not. More like, if Al Pacino and Lucille Ball were married? This guy would look like their child. When he was forty, I mean, and wearing a blue jacket."

Charles noticed that the officer didn't bother writing down that fascinating but ludicrous piece of information. He simply offered the report to Charles to sign, then to Bailey. He offered Charles a duplicate copy, and went on his way, the radio at his hip buzzing.

"How very helpful," Charles remarked, tossing the police report to the table.

Bailey caught it quickly before it fluttered to the floor.

"Gabriel? Like the angel?" she asked, reading his name.

"I never use my first name. I use my second name."

That seemed to amuse her. She gave him a quick, laughing look from her bright blue eyes, and kept reading, as if she had a right to. "Charles? You like Charles better than Gabriel?"

Uncomfortable, he took back the paper, folding it neatly into his pocket. "Gabriel doesn't suit me. It's silly and old-fashioned. Charles is more appropriate."

She nodded. "And stuffy. Gabriel's a much better name for you. It sounds dashing and handsome."

He raised his brows at this compliment, offered without a hint of flirtation. "Thank you, Miss O'Connor. And for the coffee and pen, as well."

"You're welcome. I'm sorry for all your trouble. Were you going home for Christmas?"

"No, actually. I was on my way to Memphis. Graceland, to be precise."

"You're kidding." Her eyes widened, and she leaned forward as if he'd said something of huge importance.

"No. Why?"

"I knew there was a reason I liked you! I mean, even though you're pompous and stuffy—"

"I am not—"

"You're an Elvis fan, too!" she continued, ignoring his

13

indignation. "This is so amazing. I mean, guess where I'm going, as soon as my shift ends?"

"Home?" he suggested.

She laughed, a husky, pleasant laugh. "No. Believe it or not, I'm driving to Memphis. I'm going to see Graceland at Christmas. I've got reservations at the most wonderful old hotel, and I'm bringing my own tree—not a big one—it's in my passenger seat. I'm spending Christmas in Memphis."

"Perhaps I'll see you there," he said. Maybe she was his Eula Mae, the anonymous Elvis fan who could breathe a little more life into his article—younger and prettier than he had imagined, but like as not still a Eula Mae, in her polyester uniform with her pink Elvis watch on her slender wrist.

He rose to his feet, tucking her Elvis pen into the pocket of his shirt, and picked up his laptop computer. "Good-bye, Bailey O'Connor," he said, extending his hand. "And thank you for your assistance."

She smiled her dimpled Vivien Leigh smile, and accepted his handshake. Her fingers were warm and soft. "Good-bye, Gabriel. And if you need anything, I'll be here another forty minutes."

"Thank you. I'm sure everything's under control."

"Hey, I didn't even think. . . ." She was reaching into her apron pocket, pulling out a roll of crumpled dollar bills. "Do you need money? I don't have a lot, but you don't want to be stranded without anything in a strange city."

He was relatively certain that it was the first time a Van Dusen had been offered a loan from a waitress.

"Oh, no. I've only to call home, and someone will wire me money."

"Lucky you." She was already in motion again, wiping down a table, straightening the salt and pepper, checking the level in the ketchup bottle. "There's a Western Union office on the way to baggage claim."

"Wonderful." He opened his notebook, consulted his list, and drew a neat line through *Find telegram office.* "Good luck, Miss O'Connor."

"Good night, Gabriel."

Normally that name irritated him. Only his grandmother and a few musty old aunts insisted on using it. But Bailey O'Connor spoke it with pleasure, as if she liked the sound of it. *Like the angel,* she'd said. *Dashing and handsome.*

Well. Feeling oddly exposed without his coat, he walked purposefully out onto the tiled floors of the concourse, in search of the Western Union office.

Bailey O'Connor watched him go, amused by his obvious discomfort. Great-looking guy, she thought. Too bad there was so much starch in his shorts. And he was out of her league, as well. She had waited on a hundred men like that. They smelled of old money, and wore their wealth as comfortably as their perfectly cut coats. They never really seemed to recognize anyone out of their privileged class as an equal. Their world was divided into "one of us" or "not one of us."

"Oh, miss!"

Automatically, she grabbed the pot of decaf and hurried across the room to the waiting customer. But even as she apologized for her delay, her mind was in Memphis.

Chapter Two

Bailey huried through the main concourse of the airport, rejoicing at the idea of four glorious days off. Okay, she hadn't planned on driving through snow, but she'd handle it. It'd be an adventure. Already the world was a more exciting place.

The airport, usually silent and almost deserted at four-thirty in the morning, resembled some kind of holiday refugee camp. Stranded travelers were sleeping in chairs, playing cards, lined up at phone booths.

And Christmas was almost here. She could see touches of it everywhere—the lights and garland sparkling over the magazine stand, a twinkling tree-shaped brooch decorating the coat of a sleeping woman, the brown paper packages that the travelers were carrying, in addition to their usual carry-on bags.

She pulled her rumpled velvet tam from her coat pocket, jammed it over her dark curls, and searched for her gloves—black wool, with cuffs of fake leopard fur. There, now she felt more festive. She patted her coat pocket, and her car keys jingled like sleigh bells.

Vacation. Four days of freedom. She caught a glimpse of

16

her reflection in a window, and gave herself a smile and a quick wave.

Somebody waved back.

It was Gabriel Van Dusen. Actually, it was less of a wave than the lifting of a weary hand in her direction. He was sitting in a crowded row of plastic-and-chrome chairs, his laptop computer in hand. His hair, which had been perfectly combed earlier, looked rumpled. One disarrayed light brown lock fell across his forehead, giving him a vulnerable lost-puppy look.

"Hey!" Bailey paused, shifting her purse more comfortably over her shoulder. "Did you get everything squared away?"

He didn't return her smile. "Actually, no. I can't seem to get through on the phones. Temporarily out of service, they say."

"Ah." Bailey considered. "Where are you trying to call?"

"Connecticut."

"Well, no wonder. The whole East Coast has been hit by major snow and ice storms. It sounds like the power's down everywhere from New Jersey to Canada." She laughed softly. "Connecticut. I might have guessed. You look like someone from Connecticut. Horses? Country club? Tennis? I bet your mother is a member of Daughters of the American Revolution. I bet your dad's a stockbroker. I bet you went to Harvard."

He didn't appear to find this amusing. "Actually, Miss O'Connor, I went to Princeton."

Bailey stifled a laugh at his obvious displeasure. "Sorry. Seriously, though, are you going to be okay? Those pay phones can really suck up the money. If you need a loan . . ."

The stiff expression faded abruptly from his face, and Bailey noticed again how handsome he was. Healthy skin with a good outdoorsy gold tint. She liked his eyes, too. Brown and wide-set, with a slight downward slope at the corners that gave his face a deceptively lazy look. *Bedroom eyes.* Although, right now, he looked plain lost.

"Hey," she said. "I've got it."

He looked a little alarmed.

"Come with me. You can call from Memphis as easily as here. It'll be fun. More fun than sitting in an airport, anyway.

17

We could be there by nine or ten, if nothing happens along the way. But something always happens along the way, doesn't it? That's what's so fun about road trips. And the car's all ready to go. I have seven uninterrupted hours of Elvis tapes, and Christmas music, too.'' She paused for breath.

He was staring at her with a peculiar expression, half-fascinated, half-appalled.

"Well? Are you coming or not?" Bailey asked.

He looked down at his laptop computer, and then up at Bailey, and murmured something that sounded like "Eula May."

"Excuse me?"

He stood up slowly, smoothing the wayward lock of hair from his broad brow, and smiled at her with a beautiful white smile that transformed his good-looking face into movie-star material. "Bailey O'Connor, I'd be delighted."

"Well, let's go. I've never driven in snow before, and it might take some getting used to."

For a moment, she thought he was going to change his mind.

"Oh, come on, Gabriel! Lighten up. I've driven in snow before. Once."

"What an enormous relief," he muttered, and followed her almost reluctantly out the electric doors of the main concourse, into the snow-covered darkness.

Her car suited her exactly. He found himself wondering if there was an article in that, along the lines of people who resemble their pets, married people who start to resemble each other, that sort of thing. People who resemble their cars . . .

It was a small Volkswagen bug that looked like it had been around at least as long as she had. Small, like Bailey. Slightly off-kilter, like Bailey—the passenger door was dented, which gave him a moment's trepidation.

"Hey!" She was laughing, knocking the snow off the windshield, seemingly oblivious to the cold. "Give me a hand."

Shivering in his oxford cloth shirt, he went around to the diminutive rear window, and began swiping the snow off of

18

the car. A wet bumper sticker appeared. PAGANS FOR A FREE IRELAND, it said. BRING BACK THE SNAKES. He continued on around the car, uncovering the passenger-side windows. The rosy glow of the streetlights revealed an interior crammed with discarded clothing, a Christmas present, an open Happy Meal box—

"You'll have to move the tree," she said, hurrying around to the passenger door.

Of course.

The tree was sitting in the passenger seat, and a burst of fresh pine fragrance wafted out as she yanked the door open. She lifted it out carefully, burying her face in the soft branches and inhaling deeply.

"Gorgeous," she said, beaming at the three-foot noble fir. "What do you think? Is it a Charlie Brown tree, or what?"

"It's somewhat . . . pathetic," he concurred. The snow was settling in his hair, wet and cold, and he was having second thoughts about setting off into unknown territory with this off-kilter navigator.

She was examining the cluttered interior of the car. "No room for the tree. Okay, I've got it! Here, hold this."

Shivering, Charles found himself holding the puny tree, while she clambered onto the passenger seat, digging through the contents of the backseat, giving him a splendid view of her backside that he was too cold to appreciate fully.

"Hurrah!" She came back out, waving a handful of tangled elastic cords. "Okay, you get in. This should only take a minute."

The car wasn't any warmer than the arctic landscape of the parking lot, but at least it was dry. He sat, rubbing his hands briskly as she somehow fastened the tree to the front of the car, like some kind of oversize holiday hood ornament. She laughed at the result as she stood back, snowflakes falling on her red velvet tam. She looked like a deranged Christmas elf.

She banged the door loudly as she settled into the car, then slid the key in the ignition. The car whined, sputtered, wheezed. It seemed to cough, then roared.

"Good girl," she said, in the same voice she would probably use to a dog. "It only takes a minute to warm up," she added to Charles. She leaned over and hit the switch on the tape deck.

Elvis, of course. Singing "Blue Christmas."

She sang the first couple of lines along with the tape. Her voice surprised him—high, but clear and rich. Very tuneful.

She stopped singing abruptly as she noticed him watching her. "Give her a minute more to warm up, and we can go. Fifty-five is clear a little farther south, so we should make good time."

Heat was beginning to fill the interior of the car, rushing out toward his sodden feet.

"Here." Bailey reached into the backseat and retrieved the gaily wrapped Christmas present he'd seen. "Your present. It's not quite Christmas yet, but you could use it now."

"How can it be *my* present, when it was obviously in the car several hours before you met me?" It was beautifully wrapped in red foil paper, with billowing cascades of gold ribbon falling from a central corsage of red silk roses and holly leaves.

"Well, it was mine, at first. I was going to open it Christmas morning, but I'll have time to go shopping again in Memphis."

"You bought yourself a present, and actually went to the trouble of wrapping it?" Her logic, or lack thereof, baffled him.

She lifted a dark brow. "Well, if I hadn't wrapped it, it wouldn't be a present, would it? It would just be something I bought."

Of course. He looked at the tag. It said *To: Me! From: Me!*

He pushed the box back at her. "Really, no. You keep it."

"No, you need it." She shoved it back. "And if you don't take it, we aren't going to Memphis. We'll just sit here all night."

Really. As if there were anything to stop him from walking back into the airport and waiting to get through to his family again. The phone lines wouldn't be down forever. He imagined getting through. His mother would answer. No, she'd be busy out in the kitchen, going over the menus with the staff. His brother would answer. Wallace. Perfect Wallace, with his perfect wife and perfect children, and his perfectly stiff upper lip that would twitch in that ever-so-slight way it did when he spoke to his brother.

"Really?" Wallace would say, and that one word, spoken so casually, contained a million meanings. "Really," when Wallace said it, meant, *Good God, Charles. As if you weren't impossible enough, scribbling your foolish articles for those dreadful magazines, traipsing all about the country, and wasting a perfectly good business administration degree, but you can't even manage to do that without making a mess of it, and how could you be so incredibly stupid as to allow your wallet to be stolen. . . .*

And then Wallace would put his hand over the receiver, but not enough so that Charles couldn't hear, and say, "He's in St. Louis," in the same tone of voice he would say, "He's in prison," or "He's sitting in a sewer," and Wallace's perfect wife, Bitsy, would say "Really?" just like Wallace, and then—

No, he wasn't going back to the airport. Anyway, it would throw his article off schedule.

"Thank you," he said awkwardly, and carefully removed the glittering ribbons from the box.

It was a sweatshirt—black, extra large, with a silk-screened picture of Elvis himself. It felt worn, not new, and unfolding it, he saw why. The lettering beneath the King's face said: NEW YEAR'S EVE CONCERT, PITTSBURGH, PENNSYLVANIA, 1976.

"Isn't it great? Of course, I wasn't there, but it would be great for my collection. The guy I bought it from had a scarf he'd thrown into the crowd—Elvis, I mean, not the guy—and he wanted a fortune for it. The guy, not Elvis."

Charles had never worn a sweatshirt in his life. If he was cold, he threw on a sweater—Shetland wool, perhaps, or an imported Irish fisherman's knit. He stared at the lurid Elvis face, and it seemed to glare at him.

"It's . . . something, all right."

21

"Isn't it fabulous? Put it on."

Awkwardly, bumping his elbow against the too-close window, he struggled into it. An image of Wallace's face, frozen with top-drawer horror, appeared in his mind, and he banished it. He was damp, his Burberry had been stolen, and the shirt was warm and dry.

"Merry Christmas, Gabriel."

"Bailey . . ." He had never felt so ridiculous in his life. He checked himself and began again. "Thank you for the shirt. It's . . . unique. Quite a piece of memorabilia. But could you please call me Charles? Nobody calls me Gabriel."

"No." She smiled her Vivien Leigh smile. "I like saying Gabriel. It makes me think of angels. Puts me in the Christmas mood. Hang on; here we go."

She threw the car into gear, and the VW choked again, roared, and began to move, shaking as it backfired out into the white and frozen night. The windshield wipers swung back and forth with a comforting, rhythmic sound.

"I've always wanted to do this," she said.

"What? Go to Memphis with a perfect stranger?"

"Who told you you were perfect?" she demanded with a teasing smile. Then she hit the brakes, sending the car spinning into spirals across the snowy parking lot.

"That," she added, grinning at Charles, who was clutching the dashboard in preparation for impact.

"Are you crazy?" he asked, when he could speak.

"No. I've always wanted to do that. Come on, it was fun, wasn't it?"

He looked at her, wondering if he should get out now while he still had the chance.

"A little?"

He exhaled, staring straight ahead.

"Well, okay. I won't do it again. Not till we hit the freeway."

"That's it. You can let me out right—"

"I'm kidding! Good heavens, get the starch out of your shorts."

She was crazy. He was driving off into an arctic wasteland

with a crazy woman who wore a pink plastic Elvis watch and a red velvet hat and leopard-trimmed gloves, a crazy woman who offered to lend money to complete strangers and drive them hundreds of miles through winter storms in a rattletrap car with a Christmas tree strapped to the front fender.

"It's an adventure," she said, turning her bright smile toward him.

The streetlights illuminated her profile as she turned her head to watch the road: brilliant blue eyes, a slight elfin point at the end of her neat nose, and those incredible dimples beneath the curve of her cheeks.

He settled back more firmly against the seat. "So, Bailey—why the trip to Graceland? What's the attraction?"

He considered taking his little notebook out of his pocket, and then decided against it. He'd get better material if she wasn't aware of his agenda.

"Well, you know."

An interviewer's least favorite answer.

"Well, I know why I'm going. I want to know why you are."

"Okay." She kept her eyes on the road as she considered her answer. "I've always wanted to see Graceland. And I love Christmas. So why not?"

He thought about how to rephrase his question as the lights of St. Louis grew farther and farther away.

"But why? Why Graceland and Elvis? Why not go visit your family? Turkey and cranberries, chestnuts roasting on an open fire, that sort of scene?"

She rolled her eyes with a pained expression. "As if," she said, a reply that was grammatically dreadful and did nothing to answer his question, but made him wonder how old she was. In the restaurant, he had guessed about thirty. When she'd been spinning her car through the snow of the parking lot, he had lowered that estimation considerably.

"Honestly," she answered, after a few moments, "neither of my parents believes in Christmas. My mother calls it 'the midwinter solstice festival,' and sits around with crystals on her forehead, and then serves this kind of tofu called tofurkey.

23

Kind of tofu lumped into a turkey shape. It's frightening.''

He started to laugh. "You're joking."

"Would I joke about something that twisted? Please. And my father—they're divorced—he teaches philosophy at the University of Washington, and he's married to one of his students—former students—and he doesn't believe in anything that cannot be proven. His idea of a good Christmas is sitting around with his pretentious, intellectually superior friends and saying 'fah-fah' about the wine or the salmon or the latest four-thousand-page book that I couldn't stay awake for, and telling each other how wonderfully clever they are not to buy in to the commercial crassness of the season, blah, blah.''

"You're joking," he said again. "Your father's a professor of philosophy?"

"If you want to give him his title. What he is is an egotistical, self-serving boor. Too smart for Christmas, too smart for religion. Can you believe it?"

She turned an indignant face toward him, and he gestured nervously to the dark highway that stretched before them, snow falling like white shreds of paper in the beam of the headlights. *Thank God for the absence of traffic in these late hours.* They passed only a few moving vehicles. More were parked by the side of the road, abandoned by drivers more cautious or saner than themselves.

"So," she summed up, redirecting her blue gaze to the road, "I like Elvis better than I like my father. And I'm not sitting around with a purple crystal on my head, eating tofurky with bean-curd dressing when I could see Graceland. Do you know that it's all lit up? Thousands of lights, and a life-size Nativity set on the lawn, *and* a life-size Santa and his reindeer. And trees all through the house, exactly like Elvis had, when he was alive—"

"So you agree that he's not alive?"

She gave him a look of withering contempt that killed *that* possible angle of his story. *All right.* He quickly reviewed what little insight she had given him.

"So you say you like Elvis more than your own father?" That would make a nice, ridiculous Eula Mae quote.

24

"Well, not exactly *like*. But admire. As a person, I mean. Elvis was a very nice young man. Gentle. Loved his music. Loved his mother. Believed in God. Not like my father at all. Have you ever considered how absolutely pompous it is to be an atheist?"

He was going to have a hell of a time keeping her on the subject. From Elvis to God to atheism. She spoke quickly, in a bright, animated voice so different from the women he knew. They spoke in soft, well-modulated tones that rarely betrayed excitement of any kind, as if it were beneath them to show emotion.

"Isn't it?" she demanded. "Just pompous?"

"Well, I can't really answer that. It might just be the result of years of careful reasoning, or perhaps the rejection of parental values. Or it could be disillusionment with organized religion. . . ."

"Or he could just be a pompous ass who can't bear the idea of anything greater than himself," she finished, shifting gears with an angry gesture that made him reach for the dashboard again. "Let's not talk about him anymore. The tapes are by your feet. Would you find some nice Christmas stuff, please?"

She kept her tapes in an old Barbie doll case of black vinyl. He rifled through them. Elvis, Elvis, Elvis . . . more Elvis . . . *Home for the Holidays* . . . *Christmas With the Brady Bunch*? *Good God, not that.*

And then, like a silk purse in a pile of sows' ears, he found Handel's *Messiah. Wonderful.* He plugged it in before she could argue, and sighed with relief as the incredible sweetness of strings and woodwinds filled his ears.

Maybe she'd wanted Elvis. He glanced over.

She was smiling, her eyes still on the white road that stretched endlessly into the dark. And then, to his surprise, as casually as she'd sung "Blue Christmas," she opened her mouth and joined the taped soprano, hitting every note with a full and true perfection.

She knew every word to "Rejoice, Daughters of Zion." She was an enigma. She loved Elvis and Handel. She was a better driver than he had expected. She peppered her conversations with expressions he hadn't heard since high school, and then sang along with classical music as easily as she'd said, "Regular or decaf?"

The snowflakes were becoming larger and wetter as they drove farther and farther south, the highway curving along the same path as the Mississippi River, somewhere out there beyond the snow-covered landscape.

He relaxed in the heated cocoon of the car, thinking about which of her remarks would best fit in the context of his article, soothed by the sounds of the music and the richness of Bailey's voice as it danced over the libretto.

"Hey, Gabriel," she said, abruptly abandoning her singing. "What do agnostic, insomniac dyslexics do?"

Startled out of his reverie, he shook his head.

"They lay awake all night and wonder if there really is a dog." Delighted with the punch line, she laughed at herself.

He shook his head, burying his face in one hand. "I know," he suggested. "Let's pass on the jokes, and you just keep singing. Okay?"

"Okay," she agreed, still grinning. "Why don't you put in some Elvis. Pick your favorite."

He grabbed one at random, plugged it in, and the raucous sound of "Jailhouse Rock" blared at him.

She tapped on the steering wheel in rhythm as they traveled down the dark roads, slush flying up to spatter the windshield.

It was going to be a long way to Memphis. He wondered if he'd make it there in one piece, with his sanity intact.

Stick to schedule, he reminded himself.

"So, Bailey, when did you first start listening to Elvis?"

Chapter Three

He wished that he'd brought a tape recorder. She chattered for an hour, as they drove farther and farther south, through small towns and dark stretches of highway.

"Why do we call him the King?" she repeated, as though surprised he had even asked. "It's obvious, isn't it? He changed history in a very major way. Influencing history is usually left to kings and rulers, isn't it? But he did it. He is a king, in a way. Here's a boy, born to very humble, ordinary people, who ascended to incredible heights."

He imagined that quote, in bold letters, by a satiric illustration of Elvis, saintlike, ascending to the heavens. That would work.

"And he changed music forever. What a legacy! He took the very sounds of America—black sounds, white sounds, blues and gospel—and gave them back to us in a way we'd never heard before. Some very old sounds, and the new, revolutionary ones that reflected the world we were becoming. All there, all together. It really was genius, if you think about it."

"So you're saying he was a genius?"

"Define genius," she returned quickly. She had discarded her red velvet hat, and the dark clouds of curls surrounding her face made her skin very pale, almost luminous in the half-darkness of the car. "Try defining the word *genius*. I've tried, and I can't. Everyone's a genius at something, I think. But fate doesn't often give us the chance to show it to the outside world, to write it down for history. He could have stayed an unknown, playing his guitar on the porch for his friends. But for some reason, fate, or God, intervened, and showed his music to the world."

There it was—the Elvis/God connection he was waiting for. His fingers itched for his pen.

"So you believe Elvis was especially loved by God?"

She gave him the same look of withering contempt she had given him when he had asked her if she thought Elvis was still alive.

"No, I didn't say that. I like to think we're all especially loved by God. Do you want some grits?"

The non sequitur startled him. That was Bailey—from God to grits in the same sentence. "Pardon me?"

She was turning off the road, pulling across a parking lot covered with mud and slush. The snow was turning to rain, splattering huge melted flakes across the windshield. She pulled the car between two huge trucks—a baby dinosaur dwarfed by two of its elders.

A neon sign reading DANDY'S HI-WAY DINER blinked red into the dark night. The building itself looked like it had been converted from an old house, with the porch eventually sided to expand the restaurant. Through the windows, Gabriel could see truckers filling the tables, silver garlands decorating the light fixtures and fake wood-paneled walls.

Bailey pulled the emergency brake on, disengaged the key from the ignition, and turned to him with a delighted smile as the car purred to a stop.

"Do you like grits?"

"I wouldn't know. Are we going in there?"

"You're quick, Gabriel. See what I mean about everybody being a genius?"

She was already climbing out of the car, stretching her arms over her head. "Am I cramped! Come on, we need to get out and move our muscles."

He glanced down at himself automatically. He was actually going about in public wearing a souvenir Elvis shirt. But she was right about needing to stretch. The little Volkswagen had been built for someone with shorter legs than his own. He heaved a sigh and pushed the door open.

He immediately stepped in mud past his ankles.

"Wonderful."

Bailey was already opening the restaurant door, and the smell of coffee, tobacco, and frying food wafted into the cold-rain-and-snow scent of the night.

Shaking the excess water from his legs, he followed.

It was warm and loud in the diner. Gene Autry blared from the jukebox—"Here comes Santa Claus, here comes Santa Claus, right down Santa Claus Lane . . ." Broad men in plaid shirts and baseball caps were drinking coffee from dark mugs, huge platters of eggs and fried potatoes before them. A sign on the wall informed the patrons, "We don't want your checks—we still have plenty left over from last year."

A blue jean–clad waitress with an incredible tower of blond hair piled on her head smiled at them. "Y'all just set anywheres," she called, butchering the English language with friendly ease.

Gabriel filed away the scene for possible future use as Bailey led the way to a booth, smiling and nodding at the other patrons as she passed.

"You look like you've been sucking lemons," she told Gabriel as he slid onto the black vinyl bench. "Don't be a snob."

She slid a vinyl-covered menu across the table toward him. Shaking his head, he pushed it back.

"Don't worry about it. I can afford it."

"I really don't want to be indebted—"

"Oh, for crying out loud. You're good for it. Hey, there's

29

a pay phone. Why don't you call your family while we're here?''

"Good idea." He left the booth and crossed the room to where a row of pay phones hung on the wall next to a narrow corridor leading to the rest rooms.

A truck driver on his way back from the men's room gave an incredulous glance at Gabriel's mud-spattered khakis and Elvis shirt, as if he'd violated the dress code at a country club.

He sighed again and picked up the phone. It smelled of cheap aftershave and cigarettes.

He waited for the operator to come on, asked to place a collect call, gave her the number, and waited. He looked across the room. Bailey was turned around in the booth, having an animated conversation with two men in thick plaid jackets. One of them had the Confederate flag embroidered on his baseball hat. He wondered what on earth they were laughing about.

"I'm sorry sir, the lines are down in that area." The operator's voice was hard to hear over the noise of the restaurant and Gene Autry. "There are severe winter storms in the East. If you'd like to try again in a few hours—"

"Yes, thank you."

The blond waitress was at the booth, writing down Bailey's order as he returned.

". . . and two scrambled eggs, with bacon. No, sausage. No, bacon *and* sausage. And grits, please. And a short stack of pancakes. And a chocolate shake. And coffee, please."

Gabriel had to lift his brows at the order, but restrained himself from commenting.

"How about you, hon?" the waitress asked him as he scanned the menu.

"Two eggs. Poached. Toast. Whole wheat, no butter. A small glass of grapefruit juice."

Bailey lifted her brows. "Knock yourself out," she said to him, whatever she meant by that.

The waitress gave him a look that questioned his masculinity, and walked away, shaking her head.

"What? Is there something wrong with poached eggs?"

30

Bailey laughed, shaking her head as she slid out of her black wool coat. *She* wasn't wearing an Elvis shirt, he noted. She was wearing a perfectly acceptable pullover sweater of bulky white wool.

It's not the poached eggs, per se," she answered finally. "It's just so . . . so joyless."

"Oh, for God's sake. How can eggs be joyless?"

That seemed to strike her as funny, too. Her dimples deepened, her blue eyes dancing under her dark lashes. "Not the eggs, Gabriel. You. Such an *austere* breakfast, when I'm sure the food here is fabulous."

"Really?" he retorted, and the minute the word was out, he felt like Wallace. He thought of his brother's stiff face, the prim way he tightened his mouth with displeasure, the too-stiff upper lip that rarely smiled. Was that how people saw him? *Impossible.*

"I'm not joyless, Bailey. I take a great deal of pleasure in life."

"Like what?" She leaned forward, resting her pointed chin on small hands, waiting. "What do you do in life that gives you pleasure, Gabriel?"

"Well . . . for instance . . . my work."

"And?"

"And . . . I like my work very much."

"Work and work. You're a regular party animal. What do you do, anyway? What is this work that's so marvelously fun?"

He hesitated, and then decided to lie. If he said, "I'm a writer," the inevitable questions would follow—what did he write, was he published, what was he working on now? No, if Bailey knew that she was being researched as the quintessential Elvis fan, she might be less spontaneous, or feel used and abandon him here, penniless, in Bumdoodle, Missouri.

"I'm a financial analyst," he finally said.

She laughed as though he'd told her a great joke, stopping only long enough to thank the waitress for bringing their food—three plates for Bailey, and for him, one small plate with two lonely-looking eggs, and another with very dull-looking toast.

"Hey, you're right, Gabriel. That sounds like a real hoot. You must just sing over the graphs and figures."

He wanted to tell her that in his family, he was considered quite the renegade, abusing his trust fund to no end while he traipsed around the world, scribbling articles. Instead, he stuffed a bite of egg into his mouth.

The jukebox was singing something about somebody's grandma getting run over by a reindeer—a Christmas classic that he'd never had the fortune to hear before, he supposed.

Joyless? That hurt. God forbid that he should end up like Wallace, or his father. At any rate, if he had been like Wallace or Dad, he wouldn't be on his way to Memphis in a storm with a beautiful young woman, covered with mud and wearing an Elvis shirt. *A road trip is an adventure,* she'd said, and she was right. That proved it. He wasn't stuffy; he was adventuresome.

"You're very good-looking when you smile," she said, as she cut into her pancakes with pleasure. "You should do it more often."

Was she flirting with him? No, just being Bailey, he supposed.

"Thank you. You're very lovely yourself," he returned.

She smiled with genuine pleasure at the compliment, her cheeks flushing pink. It brightened her eyes to an even more intense shade of blue. "Thank you," she answered simply.

For a moment there was an awkward silence between them, lost in the sounds of the blaring jukebox and clattering dishes and the waitress calling out to her customers. He focused on his eggs, feeling absurdly self-conscious.

"Excuse me, please," she said, after a few more minutes had gone by.

He watched as she crossed the room, smiling at everyone, exchanging greetings as casually as if she knew them all. It was an ease she probably had acquired with her job, he thought, and then immediately rejected the thought. No, that was just her nature. She genuinely liked people and was interested in them.

He watched her disappear into the ladies' room, and continued eating his eggs. He looked across at the remains of Bailey's meal. How could such a tiny woman eat so much? And the shake, too—it was the old-fashioned kind, enough to fill a glass, and more served in the steel cup it had been blended in.

It looked good.

On a whim, he beckoned the waitress and pointed to Bailey's shake. "I'd like one of those, too, please." *There.*

"Live dangerously," the waitress said, and wandered toward the kitchen, notepad in hand and broad hips swinging.

He was halfway through the shake when Bailey returned.

She wasn't alone. She was clasping the hand of an older woman, obviously well into her seventies. She looked like a picture-book piano teacher, with crisply curled white hair and plump, wrinkled cheeks, her lipstick brilliant rose against her pale face. She was wearing a plain blue dress beneath her sensible overcoat, and rubber boots on her feet.

He noticed that Bailey was carrying a suitcase.

"Gabriel, this is LaRay Harper. LaRay, this is Gabriel Van Dusen." She put the suitcase down with a deliberate thump, scooted into the booth, and patted the expanse of seat next to her.

"I'm pleased to meet you, Mrs. Harper." He extended his hand, and LaRay quickly offered him her own. Her fingers felt papery and dry, but her grip was still firm.

"LaRay's bus didn't get through from St. Louis, because of the storm. She's on her way to Memphis, too."

"I have grandchildren there," LaRay informed him. "Seven of them." She fumbled with her large worn handbag as she spoke, and Gabriel waited for the inevitable pictures to appear. To his relief, the old woman withdrew a lipstick-stained hankie and dabbed at her watery eyes. "I was just sitting here crying. Wouldn't be much of a Christmas without them."

33

"No, it would be awful," Bailey agreed, placing her smooth hand over the woman's wrinkled one.

Gabriel was struck by the ease and grace of the gesture, by how easily Bailey was able to take a stranger's hand in her own, and offer comfort.

Though it shouldn't surprise him. After all, she had rescued him, hadn't she, knowing nothing about him at all, other than that he was stranded and broke.

LaRay had her wallet out, and was showing Bailey the pictures. ". . . and that's Ashley, and that's Brittany, and that's Dustin."

"They're beautiful," Bailey said. "Gabriel, would you mind clearing out the backseat? I don't think there's enough room."

Room? For a moment he was baffled, and then it hit him. *Of course.* LaRay was going to Memphis with them. Would Bailey leave a stranded grandmother in a truck stop the day before Christmas Eve?

They were both smiling at him, Bailey's face smooth and luminous, LaRay's creased with a thousand lines. Their hands were still entwined on the table, and any stranger would have taken them for a grandmother and her granddaughter, instead of two strangers who had just met.

"My, my, what a blessing you are," LaRay said. "Just appearing, like in a Christmas story."

"God bless us, every one," Gabriel agreed, and went out into the cold rain.

He was sandwiched in the tiny backseat between suitcases and a huge box, the radio speakers screeching too closely to his ears, his knees drawn up and cramped from the lack of space.

"That's fruitcake in that box," LaRay informed him. "Twenty-three of 'em. I bake them all myself, every year. I tell you, you should see the looks on my family's faces when they see Grandma coming with her fruitcakes."

"I can only imagine," Gabriel said politely. He hoped that

LaRay's family liked her fruitcake so well that she wouldn't dream of parting with any.

"You, young man. You take two of those nice fruitcakes out of there. One for you, and one for your nice girlfriend. That's my Merry Christmas to you."

Your nice girlfriend. Bailey swung her head around and gave him a quick smile, as if to say, *Wasn't that funny?* "You take a bite of that fruitcake, young man, and tell me what you think," LaRay demanded, turning a watchful eye on him.

Repressing a shudder, he obediently unwrapped one of the brick-weight loaves, and managed to fill his mouth with a bite that seemed to last forever.

"Splendid," he lied. He wondered who had ever invented fruitcake, and why. It was one of those Christmas traditions that should die a natural death. Actually, most of them should. Sitting cramped in the backseat, with second-rate Christmas music blaring in his ears, tired and awkward, Charles found it hard to feel the Christmas spirit.

Bailey and LaRay chattered and laughed as if they were completely unaware of him. The car sputtered and coughed its way down the highway. The sky was still dark, but not as deep black as it had been. The rain had faded to a light drizzle.

The last tinny, overenthusiastic notes of "Sleigh Ride" died away, and Bailey sighed.

"I love Christmas," she said. "Don't you, Gabriel?"

Perhaps it was the cramp in his knees that made him irritable.

"No, I don't," he replied bluntly. "I think it's overrated, overcommercialized, and overromanticized. I don't think that it does much more than support the retail giants of America, while people run themselves into frenzies trying to perpetuate traditions that they themselves don't understand. It's a monster day devouring good time and energy that could be better spent elsewhere, while people try to relate to a fairy tale that probably never happened."

She actually hit the brakes. The car stopped dead in the middle of the highway, and Bailey swung around to stare at him, her mouth open with shock.

LaRay turned to him, too, with the face of a piano teacher who'd just been told that no, her pupil hadn't even bothered practicing last week, thank you.

"Are you kidding?" Bailey demanded.

"Is he a Communist?" LaRay demanded, her mouth tight. "He sounds like a Communist."

"No, I'm not a Communist," he replied, leaning back with a tired sigh. What was he doing here, in the middle of nowhere, with these two bizarre women? Better at Mother's overdressed table with Wallace and Bitsy.

"He's not a Communist," Bailey reassured LaRay. "He's just joyless. And a little thick."

"Well, that's better, I guess. I wouldn't have taken a ride if I'd thought there was a Communist in the car."

"I'm not a Communist," he repeated.

"But don't you like any of it?" Bailey asked, her eyes almost pitying. "The magic? The music? The tradition?"

"The magic eludes me, or has since I stopped believing in Santa Claus. The music is like any music—some good, most very poor. The traditions and obligations bore me."

Both Bailey and LaRay stared at him, aghast.

"Maybe he is a Communist," LaRay said. "And I thought he was such a nice young man."

Bailey shook her head. "I did, too."

"You might want to think twice about marrying him," LaRay said. "Wake up one morning, and he'll be preaching atheism and Lord knows what else."

"I'm surprised," Bailey said, ignoring the marriage remark. "Next thing you'll be telling me you don't like Elvis."

He decided not to touch that. "Bailey, have you noticed that we're at a complete standstill in the middle of the highway? My personal disregard for the holidays isn't worth risking our necks over."

Turning around, Bailey eased off the brake and started back down the road.

"He's really not such a bad sort," she reassured LaRay.

"Look," he interrupted, "just because I don't believe in the

36

popular religious mythology and all the hooplah that goes along—"

"Young man," LaRay exclaimed, turning on him with fire in her eye, "I'm a Christian woman. If you have anything more to say, you hush your mouth."

Really.

"So there," Bailey agreed, and he could hear a giggle under her voice.

"I beg your pardon if I've offended you," he said politely, settling back between the suitcases and the twenty-ton box of fruitcakes.

"You have," LaRay said, turning her crisply curled head to stare out into the darkness.

"I'm not offended," Bailey said politely. "I just feel sorry for you. And a little superior."

Really. Sorry for him. She was a waitress. She probably earned less money in a year than his trust funds generated in a month. She was driving a beat-up old car to spend Christmas wandering through the home of a dead pop singer, picking up strangers along the way. She was ridiculous.

"It's all right, Gabriel," she said suddenly, and he saw her incredible Vivien Leigh smile flash in the rearview mirror. "We won't throw you out in the cold, even if you are a Communist."

"Well, I'll try not to fill you with Leninist propaganda along the way," he said, unable to resist smiling back.

"Why, Gabriel," she said happily, "you made a little joke."

She shoved a tape into the deck, and Elvis sang loudly into his ear that he was nothing but a hound dog, who had never caught a rabbit and wasn't a friend of his, whatever that meant. He began wishing for "Jingle Bells."

Chapter Four

Bailey pulled off the highway, the orange neon sign of the gas station guiding her. Morning was coming to this small Tennessee town, gray and pale over the horizon.

She liked small towns. She liked the tidy houses and neat lawns, and she liked to think of the people who lived in them. She liked to imagine that they led simple, tidy, happy lives, but knew that it probably wasn't so. Even so, she liked to imagine it, and to think of all the children who would be waking up in a couple of hours to realize that Christmas Eve had finally arrived. Mothers would be thawing turkeys and making cheese trays—she'd bet her life that nobody here was eating tofu—and fathers would be out doing last-minute shopping—none of them refusing to participate in the "gross commercialization" of the holidays—and grandmothers would be arriving and velvet dresses would be readied for Christmas Eve services.

It made her feel happy to think of the traditional rituals, and a little lonely, too, beneath the happiness.

One day she would be part of it, with a pretty house and a handsome husband to laugh at her jokes.

She left the car running while she stepped out into the frigid morning air. LaRay was asleep, looking older than she did awake. Gabriel, on the other hand, looked younger sleeping. He also looked cramped, his long legs in his mud-stained khakis drawn up to his chest, his arm around the box of LaRay's fruitcakes.

She leaned back into the car and shook his shoulder gently. It felt large and warm beneath her hand.

His eyes opened, and for a moment he looked baffled.

"Happy Christmas Eve," she whispered.

He smiled back, and the lines around his eyes crinkled pleasantly. He looked happy to see her.

"Want to get out and stretch?"

"Where are we?" He climbed out of the bug with awkward legs, looking tousled and worried.

"Only a couple of hours from Memphis, I think. I had to stop for gas. There's a phone over there, if you want to try getting through to your family."

She filled the tank as he went to the pay phone. She watched him dial, and could tell by the way his shoulders fell that he wasn't having any luck.

She replaced the gas cap and went inside the convenience store, smiling at the curious clerk, a young woman with tired eyes.

She bought the usual fare for road trips—to-go coffees, chocolate Ho Hos, spearmint gum for after the coffee, and doughnuts. At the last minute, she threw in a souvenir Tennessee coffee mug, then two more for Gabriel and LaRay. Christmas presents.

"Y'all have a good drive and a merry Christmas," the clerk said, and the *y'all* made Bailey feel that she was in the South now.

"We will, thanks," she said, pushing out the swinging glass door into the parking lot. She carried the paper cups of coffee carefully to the car, balancing them on the roof while she put the plastic bag of junk food inside. LaRay was still sleeping in the passenger seat. Gabriel was nowhere in sight. He was probably in the men's room.

She stood, shivering in the misty morning, looking around. Nobody else was awake at this hour. *No, wait.* Across the road, a pickup truck came swinging off the highway, stopped to drop off a passenger, and drove away toward town.

She watched, interested.

It was a teenage boy, his dark hair standing in gravity-defying spikes, wearing a black leather jacket covered with silver chains and patches she couldn't read from this distance. He looked around, his shoulders slumping, and he crossed the road on heavy black boots, shifting his backpack. He stood by the side of the highway entrance, and pulled a sign from his pack. That she could read clearly.

MEMPHIS.

Bailey pushed back the cuff of her glove and checked her Elvis watch. Barely seven o'clock. He was going to have a long wait.

Taking her coffee, Bailey crossed the damp, dark road and approached him.

"Going to Memphis?" she asked him.

He had large brown eyes that still had a childish look about them, despite the fierce spikes of his hair, the black leather jacket, and the silver ring pierced through his eyebrow.

He checked the sign he carried, as if he wasn't sure.

"Uh, yeah. Memphis."

"Is your family there?" she asked, curious as to what this boy was doing hitchhiking on Christmas Eve. He could only have been sixteen, maybe seventeen.

"No, they're in Seattle. I'm in a band, and I missed the bus."

She wondered if he was a runaway. Did it matter? Whatever his reasons were, she couldn't leave him standing alone on the side of the road.

"We're going to Memphis, too. If you want a ride, come on."

His face lit up, his cheeks turning a childish pink. "Cool."

40

She stuck her hand out. "Bailey O'Connor."

He shook hands awkwardly, a member of a generation that hadn't been raised to observe social formalities. "Ian," he said. "Ian Muldoon."

"Muldoon. That's a nice Irish name," she said pleasantly as they crossed the road to where the Volkswagen was puttering softly by the gas pumps and sending clouds of steam into the damp morning air. The little tree fastened to the front grill looked a little worse for wear, but still stood proudly.

"Yeah, my dad's Irish," he said, in a voice that said he wasn't impressed. End of conversation.

Gabriel was standing on the sidewalk in front of the minimart, one dark brow raised above his searching eyes. His well-shaped mouth was turned down slightly at the corners.

"Here," Bailey said, popping open the door of the car. "You'll have to sit with the suitcases on your lap. Sorry about the close quarters, but it's only for a couple of hours."

"That's cool."

LaRay was awake, peering at the newcomer with worried eyes.

"LaRay, this is Ian. Ian, LaRay."

"Uh, hi."

"Young man," LaRay said, "what on earth is that in your eyebrow?"

"An earring."

"If it was an earring, it would be in your ear. I don't know what the world is coming to. Girls wearing pants, boys wearing earrings in their faces. It makes you look like a farm animal."

Ian looked from Bailey to LaRay nervously, and then smiled. "Oh."

"Back in a minute," Bailey said, leaving them together to debate the proper placement of body piercings.

Gabriel was still on the sidewalk, and he ran a hand through his hair, pushing it off his forehead with an exasperated gesture.

"Dare I ask," he said, "who that is?"

Bailey smiled, hoping he'd smile back, that his aristocratic face would relax. "That's Ian. He's going to Memphis."

"Of course. How silly of me. Who's next? The tin man, or the cowardly lion?"

"Don't get snotty, Gabriel. We can't leave him standing by the side of the road. It's Christmas Eve."

"Bailey, do you always do this? Do you know that some women feel obligated to be rescuers, often to their detriment?"

"You've read too many self-help books. 'Women Who Give People Rides, and the Passengers Who Annoy Them.' Why not? Think about it, Gabriel. It's Christmas Eve. If there ever was a time to show compassion, this is it."

"Well, how about a little compassion for me? There's not enough room in the backseat for me, let alone for Johnny Rotten. We'll go over a bump in the road and I'll be impaled by his hair."

She laughed at that, but he didn't. "Gabriel," she said, finally exasperated by the sour look on his handsome face, "lighten up. Have a heart. Have an adventure. Honestly, if you'd been an innkeeper in Bethlehem, the Holy Mother would have given birth on the side of the road. Good grief, you're an old stick-in-the-mud."

"I'm not. I'm just practical, and my legs are cramped. And you don't know who this kid is. He could be a serial killer."

"He promised to leave his ax and gun at the side of the road. I swear. Now, are you coming to Memphis or not?"

He looked around, as if the minimart might offer some solution. It didn't.

"Fine, let's go."

"Fine," she said, imitating his weary tone.

He shook his head, as if he couldn't believe what was happening. "Fine," he muttered, and followed her to the car, where he climbed into the backseat, shifting suitcases, backpacks, and the box of fruitcakes until he and Ian were wedged as comfortably as possible.

Climbing into the driver's seat, Bailey turned and smiled at them. Gabriel was looking at Ian's jacket, reading the patches. Bailey read them too, and supposed they were the names of bands. HUMPING RHINOS, one said. NOFX and BAD RELIGION, said two more. Ian was looking at Gabriel's souvenir Elvis shirt.

"Nice shirt, dude," he said.

"Thank you so much," Gabriel replied.

"Isn't that that old guy who died on the toilet?"

Bailey turned around, fire in her eyes. "Hold on, fella. Before we go one foot, you'd better know that I am an A-number-one Elvis fan, in no uncertain terms, and that's why I'm going to Memphis, and that's why you're not standing on the side of the road. So get this straight—I will tolerate no disrespect. There's nothing funny about Elvis dying. Death isn't funny. I can tolerate jokes about women, jokes about the Irish, jokes about animals, jokes about anything. But not Elvis dying. Okay?"

"Sorry," the boy said. He glanced at Gabriel, as if expecting another attack. "Sorry, dude."

"Okay," Bailey said. "I'm sorry for snapping. Would anybody like a Ho Ho?" She offered them the plastic bag of junk food.

Gabriel hesitated, then said, "Oh, what the hell," and took one.

Ian said, "Cool," and took two.

LaRay shook her white head. "If I eat cake in the morning, I get all bound up. Just plain constipated."

Glancing in the rearview mirror, Bailey had to suppress a grin at the appalled looks Ian and Gabriel exchanged.

"To Memphis," she called out, and put the car in gear.

"To Oz," Gabriel responded from behind her. She glanced back and saw him scribbling in a little notebook.

The Volkswagen sputtered, shot out some backfire, and chugged down the highway, dragging a little under the unaccustomed weight.

Gabriel liked to remind himself that every person he met was a story. There was always a story in them. It drove his friends crazy, whenever they heard him say it—"Hmm. Maybe there's a story in that."

But it was true. And so, in order to forget about his cramped legs and the fruitcake box stabbing him in his armpit, he watched and listened to his three fellow travelers, learning their stories.

LaRay was originally from the New Orleans area, but had moved to Memphis with her husband soon after they were married. "That was how things were done then," she explained. "You knew what was expected of you. Young women today may have more choices, but they have more worries, too. It was a nice thing, a safe thing, to know what life was going to bring you."

Bailey said that she could understand that, but it must have been difficult for women who wanted something out of the ordinary.

Ian told them briefly about the band he was in, something called Marty the Monkey, though why, he couldn't say. Somebody in the band knew somebody in Memphis who owned a club, and it was their first out-of-state gig. They weren't getting paid. His parents said he could come, as long as he could pay for his own bus ticket, and promised to call every day and not to hitchhike.

He hadn't had enough money to get all the way to Memphis, so he'd gotten as close as he could.

"Young man," said LaRay, "you are a fibber. In my day you would have been taken out to the woodshed and spanked."

"Yikes," said Ian, appearing not at all alarmed and even less ashamed of himself. "That would suck. Unless there was, like, a really cute chick doing it. That would be cool."

No story there, Gabriel reflected. Unless it was about the limited description in modern teenage language. If something was positive, it was cool. If something was negative, it sucked. The end. Short article.

Instead of pursuing that, he took notes on Bailey. He might as well keep his article on schedule.

And she was a character. In all other things, he liked to be neat and orderly, but when simply getting impressions of a person or place, he deliberately scrawled all over the page, noting things in no particular order, and then going back later and organizing by category.

She was explaining to Ian how there would have been no punk rock without Elvis, and no rock and roll as he knew it. Gabriel watched, half listening, scribbling:

Articulate—pauses and looks for correct word. Tiny hands—wiggles fingers for "etc." Laughs at herself when she says something too solemn. Rolls her eyes. Very long lashes, black. Eyes almost electric blue. Skin almost translucent, washed with watercolor rose. Black curl falls from temple, touches cheek—she blows it away, rather than taking time to comb it. Listens to others with almost hungry interest. Cries when LaRay tells of being widowed. Not at all self-conscious. One minute later, eating candy bar. Very small, but eats like a horse. When things are quiet, tells awful jokes. (What did Tarzan say when he saw the elephants wearing sunglasses? Nothing—he didn't recognize them. A horse walked into a bar, and the bartender says, Why the long face?) Sings in front of people—trained voice? Sounds like it. Church choir? Unlikely, given description of parents. Good grammar, no discernible pattern of thought. Quick mind? Disorganized mind? Very charming. Ability to relax others.

What would Mother think?

He imagined bringing Bailey home for Christmas dinner. His mother and Wallace's wife, Bitsy, would have identical expressions on their faces—the politely frozen look. They would see only the plastic Elvis watch, the worn leather of her shoes. They would be perfectly, frostily polite.

It was an art—being absolutely and perfectly well mannered to the point where it was rudeness. He had seen it done a thousand times. Hell, he had probably done it himself.

They would see none of Bailey's charm: the glossy black curls, the brilliant blue eyes, the bright, clear color of her skin. Nobody would be charmed by her laughter, her terrible jokes, her curiosity.

45

And what would Bailey think of them?

He leaned back, closing his eyes, and smiled, lulled to relaxation by the rhythm of the road beneath the car.

She would laugh. They would seem silly and stiff and wooden to her, anchored in generations of dull propriety.

But she would love the house, the old Georgian architecture, the sloping pegged floors and the faded carpets, and the oil paintings of long-dead ancestors: Van Dusens and Maybornes and Fisks. He wondered if she rode, if she would like the horses in the stables, and the riding trails that wound through the dense green Connecticut woods.

He would like to show it to her. If she didn't ride she would willingly try, he had no doubt of it. She'd never turn down an adventure, a new experience. It wasn't part of her psychological makeup; he'd bet on it.

It would be fun to invite her up for a weekend, to show her the countryside and the covered bridges and the quaint, steepled churches in the villages.

It would be fun to watch her take on Wallace and Mother, to have a coconspirator to laugh at their staid and proper stiffness.

The morning was growing lighter, and traffic was beginning to pick up along the highway. It seemed a long time ago since he had boarded his flight in New York. He was exhausted. He must be, to consider inviting Bailey to meet his family.

He might do it, he thought, closing his eyes.

Elvis was singing in his ear again, something sweet and slow about fools rushing in. It was the kind of song that made him think of slow dancing in a smoky room.

He'd like to dance with Bailey. She'd probably feel tiny and fragile in his arms. She'd probably dance well—she was too comfortable with herself not to.

He fell asleep dreaming about dancing with Bailey in a high school gym that turned into a dark forest of pine. She wanted to go look for Elvis, somewhere out deep in the trees, and in his dream, he laughed.

The dream kept changing because that was just like her— you never knew what she'd do next.

46

What she did next was scream.

It was a high, excited shriek that startled him out of his sleep. He jumped, knocking his elbow into Ian's spiky head, and looked about in alarm.

"My land!" LaRay was saying, shaking her head in amazement. "My land!"

"Dude!" Ian exclaimed, rubbing his head and staring out the front window.

And Bailey shrieked again, staring up at the sky. This time the cry was a word.

"Elvi!"

Gabriel, still blinking and dazed, shook his head.

"What did you say?"

"Elvi!" she repeated, in a tone of alarm and excitement. "Elvi! The plural of Elvis. As in, more than one. Several. Look!"

She slammed on the brakes, and Gabriel stared wildly about, wondering if he was still dreaming, if he would see an army of Elvis Presley impersonators storming across the soft green fields.

Ian started laughing. "Look up, guy," he said.

Gabriel looked up at the sky and saw an amazing sight.

Elvis Presley, descending from the sky in a tangled parachute, was falling toward the highway.

And across the field, to the amazement of Gabriel and several grazing cows, another Elvis was coming down, buffeted by the wind, his chute tangling in the treetops.

And there was another, descending toward the highway. And another, coming dangerously close to the power lines.

And another was still too high to see clearly, except for his distinctive white jumpsuit and scarf. And another.

"My land," repeated LaRay, her white curls shaking with disbelief.

Other cars were stopping along the highway, watching, waiting, as the Elvi—as he supposed they were properly called—plummeted toward the earth, some landing gracefully, some dragging as the sharp wind tangled the lines of their chutes. From far away, he heard the sound of a siren approaching.

"Oh, my God," Bailey said, reaching for her red velvet tam. "I don't believe it. They're usually so perfect! They must have gotten caught in a crosswind or something. Come on, let's go see if we can help."

Gabriel stared again. Yes, he was really seeing this.

"Excuse me—did somebody put drugs in my doughnut, or are there multiple parachuting Elvises falling from the sky?"

"Elvi," corrected Bailey, wriggling into her coat and reaching for the door handle. "One is Elvis. Plural is Elvi."

"Dude," Ian said, "you've never seen these guys before? They're famous and stuff."

One was falling toward the car, trying skillfully to untwist the tangled lines of his chute, and it seemed for a moment that he might avoid the power lines that bordered the highway.

At the last minute, a strong gust of wind caught the chute, and it tangled, billowing and puffing as it snared the top of the telephone pole.

"Yeeouch!" Gabriel stifled the empathic exclamation as the Elvis impersonator hit the hard gravel at the side of the road and skidded along one leg.

Bailey was out of the car like a shot, taking her coat off as she went.

"Come on," she shouted back to Gabriel. "Give me a hand here."

"Wow," said Ian. "The Flying Elvi, on Christmas Eve. Who'd have thought it?"

"Who indeed?" Gabriel asked, pushing the seat forward and clambering after Bailey.

Traffic was stopped in both directions, and people were climbing out of their cars. One Elvis lay on the dark highway, holding what looked like a broken arm. Another, farther away, was getting slowly to his feet, supporting himself by leaning on the trunk of a stopped car.

A man and his wife, dressed in holiday finery, were picking their way across the muddy field to help the poor Elvis dangling from the branches of a tree.

The ambulance sirens were getting closer, piercing the peaceful Christmas Eve morning with their wail.

Everywhere he looked, he saw Elvi, black haired and white suited, the morning light shining from silver belt buckles, all downed and injured, all struggling to untangle themselves, being helped by scurrying travelers.

Like Bailey.

He hurried to where she was kneeling next to the fallen Elvis by the side of the road. She glanced up at Gabriel quickly as he approached, and turned back to the fallen sky diver.

"You really shouldn't move until the emergency crew checks you out," she was insisting. "At the very least, you're in shock. And your neck could be injured."

The Elvis shifted a little, managing a smile that looked more like a grimace. "Ah, I've fallen harder. My neck's fine—just scraped my leg a little. Everything was going great till that wind came up. Didn't expect that."

Bailey was taking off her coat, sliding it under the man's shiny black hair. He *did* look remarkably like Elvis, Gabriel noted.

"But you could be in shock, and just *think* you're fine," Bailey was arguing. "People have walked away from accidents on broken legs and done considerable damage."

"Is anybody seriously hurt?" the Elvis asked Gabriel, looking at him over Bailey's shoulder.

Gabriel looked around. "Hard to tell. But the ambulance is here."

"Make you a deal," Bailey said quickly, as the man struggled to rise. "You stay here until you can be examined, and I'll go check and see how the other guys are. Okay?"

Looking too dazed and bruised to argue, the man laid his head back on Bailey's coat and sighed.

"Thank you," he said, in a flawless Elvis imitation. "Thank you very much."

Chapter Five

Among the injured Elvi, Gabriel counted one broken leg, a possible broken arm, and various cuts, scrapes, and bruises. It could have been worse, Gabriel supposed. He watched Bailey as she sent Ian out of the car with the bag of junk food, offering doughnuts and chocolate Ho Hos to sky divers, state troopers, and spectators.

He watched her as she offered her bulky wool sweater to the Elvis who had been rescued from the tree, and smiled as he saw the T-shirt she wore beneath it. It said, GIVE ME AMBIGUITY, OR GIVE ME SOMETHING ELSE.

She caught his eye and smiled at him as she walked between the lanes of parked cars, rubbing her arms in the cold air.

"Merry Christmas," she said. "Did you ever expect something like this?"

He had to laugh. "Bailey, I've never even heard of the Flying Elvi, much less expected them to come falling out of the sky on me."

"I guess they'd been hired to perform at a Christmas party for some big-time record producer. Start off his holiday with

50

a bang. The wind came out of nowhere and blew them way off course, right into our path. I can't believe it."

She shook her head, looking around her at the chaos, her eyes brighter than usual in the lightening morning.

A stretcher went by with an Elvis on it, wincing in pain. A family probably on their way to Grandma's house was offering trays of cookies from car to car, the beribboned and starched children dancing with excitement at this unexpected turn of events.

LaRay was out of the car, talking with a state trooper. She appeared to be lecturing him, about what, Gabriel couldn't begin to imagine.

"Somehow, Bailey, I get the feeling that this is the sort of thing that happens to you all too often," he said, checking his watch. They'd been stalled here for over an hour, and traffic was backing up.

"Oh, I wouldn't go that far. I mean, how often are you almost hit in the head by a falling Elvis?"

"It's a first for me," he admitted.

The state trooper began to direct traffic away from the scene, around the ambulances.

"Well, it's been an experience, but it looks like it's over. Shall we get in the car before you freeze?"

"Sure. Here." She tossed him the keys. "Start her up. I'll go get Dustin."

"Okay." He took two steps, stopped, and turned. "You'll what?"

"Go get Dustin." She pointed at the Elvis who had almost hit the car, who was now on his feet, trying to wad up his parachute. "We're staying at the same hotel, so I offered him a ride."

"Bailey, are you kidding? Is this a joke? How many injured Elvis Presleys can you fit in a Volkswagen?"

She affected a puzzled face. "One?"

He thought about arguing. There was no room. He was already sharing space with a seventy-year-old piano teacher, a punk rocker who resembled a hedgehog, three suitcases, twenty-two and a half fruitcakes, a Barbie case of bad Christmas tapes, and a five-foot, two-inch lunatic with eyes like an angel.

"Do you promise? Only one Elvis? I'm not being uncharitable; I'm thinking of legroom."

"Only one so far," she agreed, her eyes sparkling. "We can make room."

How? he wondered, but didn't ask.

"We look like the clown car at the circus," he observed.

The suitcases, the cardboard box of fruitcake, and the bundle of Dustin's parachute were firmly tied to the tiny roof of the Volkswagen with damaged parachute line; the tree was still strapped bravely to the front fender; LaRay, Ian, and Elvis/Dustin were crammed into the miniature backseat; and Bailey, over her own objections, was enthroned in the relatively roomy passenger seat.

Charles was driving. Bailey needed a break after all the excitement.

A reporter snapped their picture as they drove away from the accident scene, a news crew turned their camera on them, and he hoped that the Flying Elvi were not as famous as Bailey and Ian made them out to be. He could only imagine Wallace's face if he happened to see his brother on the evening news, driving this ridiculous menagerie down the road.

If there was a God, the power was still out in Connecticut.

He laughed despite himself. What a sight they must make. *There's a story in this*, he told himself. *There has to be.*

He looked over at Bailey, who was smiling gently and relaxing. She was wearing the souvenir Elvis shirt she had given him earlier, because she had lost her coat in the excitement. The huge garment made her look smaller than usual, and the black made her pale skin and bright eyes even more startling.

She was chatting with Dustin about the Memphis hotel she had reservations at—the same hotel, by coincidence, where Dustin was staying. It was called, of course, the Original Heartbreak Hotel.

"I'm in the G.I. Blues Suite," he told Bailey. "It's just fine. Nice portrait of the King in his uniform, and some great stills from the movie. Which room are you in?''

"Paradise, Hawaiian Style, I think," Bailey answered. "They weren't sure when I made the reservations. It was kind of a spur-of-the-moment thing."

Surprise, surprise.

"The rooms are named after Elvis movies?" Gabriel asked.

"Named and decorated," Bailey answered with a smile. "It's great."

He had to see this. He wished he weren't driving, and could take notes.

"I can't believe you haven't heard of it," Bailey said. "As big an Elvis fan as you are. Did you watch that special last month, on the Arts and Entertainment channel? They showed it on that."

"I don't really watch television," he told her. He steered the conversation back to Elvis. The whole trip had been so distracting that he didn't have half the notes he'd intended. "So the trip was a spur-of-the-moment thing? You saw the hotel on this special and decided to go?"

"Kind of." She leaned forward and popped open the glove compartment. It was stuffed with papers, a few dead flowers, and what looked like twenty candy bars. "Anyone else?" she asked, waving one.

He shook his head, Elvis/Dustin said, "No, thank you very much," and LaRay declined on the grounds that they hurt what few teeth she had left. Ian took two.

"It went like this," she explained. "I saw the special, and said, 'Wouldn't it be fun to go?' and Dakota said—"

"Who's Dakota?" he asked automatically.

"My boyfriend." She took a healthy bite of chocolate.

He felt as if he'd been hit. *Her boyfriend. Her boyfriend. Just like that. Named Dakota.* Dakota, *for hell's sake.*

"What the hell kind of a name is Dakota?" he demanded irritably. "What kind of people name their child after a state?"

"I don't know. I'll ask my Aunt Virginia," she said carelessly, more intent upon her candy bar than his irritation. "Look! Memphis—twenty-three miles!"

"I saw it," he said, trying not to sound as snappish and

53

deceived as he felt. She had a boyfriend named Dakota.

"At any rate, he said, 'What a stupid idea,' and that he didn't even like Elvis, and that was that."

"You decided to go without him?"

"No, I threw him out." She said it as though the act were a perfectly natural thing to do. 'Oh, honey, I don't like Elvis.' 'Oh, really? Then get out, you scum!' "

"You're joking," he said, for what must have been the twentieth time since he'd met her. He should know better by now. "You threw your boyfriend out because he didn't like Elvis?"

"No. I threw him out because he didn't respect *me*. See the difference?"

"Yes, ma'am, I do," said a voice in Gabriel's ear, and he jumped, remembering that they had Elvis, or a reasonable facsimile thereof, in the car.

"I guess people name their children after states that they're born in," she said thoughtfully, throwing a typically Bailey curveball into the conversation. "Why did they name you Gabriel?"

"After one of my grandfathers. So you decided to go to Memphis, and get rid of Montana?" *Damn!* That sounded more churlish than he had meant it to. *Oh, well.* He had been awake for hours.

"Dakota. It was going nowhere, fast. If there's one thing I can't stand, it's being condescended to. Have you ever met people like that, who think they're terribly clever, but they're not?"

"Entire families of them," he answered honestly. "Now, which exit do we take to the hotel?"

"I'm not sure. There's a map here, somewhere."

She rummaged around on the floor of the car, digging beneath her tape case, an empty plastic bag, and candy wrappers.

"I can't find it anywhere," she explained at last.

"Gee, I'm surprised. Bailey, have you ever considered organizing something?"

"It is organized. Do you need a needle and thread? Look, my sewing kit is under the seat."

"Thank you, Bailey. You're the queen of non sequiturs. No, I don't need to mend my clothes; I need a road map."

She shot him an offended look, then reached back under the seat. "Just a minute. Don't be sarcastic."

"Just head on downtown," Elvis offered helpfully from the backseat. "I think I can find Blues Street from there."

"And here I thought it would be down at the end of Lonely Street."

"Young man," LaRay put in, "you sound crankier every minute. It's probably all that junk food you eat."

"I don't eat junk food. At least, not usually."

"Junk food is cool," Ian put in.

"My digestion," LaRay informed them, "is just not what it used to be. I suffer from horrendous gastritis."

"Yikes," Ian said.

Bailey plugged in a tape of Elvis singing gospel hymns.

Traffic was getting heavier as they approached the city. Gabriel tried to concentrate on driving. He wasn't used to Bailey's car. The stick shift seemed sticky. He hated driving without a map.

Bailey chattered incessantly, about Ian's band, Dustin's injured leg, LaRay's grandchildren. LaRay offered fruitcake. Dustin and Ian tried to shift positions to accommodate Dustin's injuries.

LaRay asked him to pull off at the next exit so that she could find a ladies' room. "I have gastritis, you know," she reminded him.

Good Lord. He tried to glance back to change lanes, saw only Dustin's black pompadour and Ian's spiked hair in the rearview, tried to see out the side mirrors, and decided it was safe.

It wasn't. He swerved wildly to avoid the truck that shot past him, horn blaring.

The driver presented his middle finger out the truck window, and Gabriel blasted on the horn of Bailey's VW.

"Blow me!" he shouted, at the end of his rope.

"Gabriel!" Bailey exclaimed.

Ian laughed, delighted.

"Young man," LaRay said, "there's no need for language like that. On Christmas Eve, yet!"

Gabriel tried to merge into the exit lane again, swearing under his breath.

"Do you kiss your mother with that mouth?" Bailey asked, with suppressed laughter in her voice.

"No, I don't," he snapped. "My mother's a bitch." *So there.* He glanced over his shoulder at LaRay, who had started all this by demanding that he find a ladies' room.

She was staring out the window, her mouth shut as tightly as a mousetrap.

"Gabriel, it's Christmas Eve," Bailey reminded him gently.

"Well, deck the halls. Ho-ho-ho to you and your kin." He shifted down, idling at the end of the exit, searching for a service station. There were none in sight. The area looked more residential than anything else.

He hated not knowing where he was going. He chose a direction at random and set off, the car sputtering through the quiet neighborhood.

"How long have you two been married?" Ian asked.

"We're not married."

"You fight like you're married."

Gabriel rolled his eyes.

"If you decide to get married," Dustin said, "you could hire the Flying Elvi to perform. Why have one best man when you could have ten? We do a lot of weddings in Vegas."

"I don't think she should marry him at all," LaRay said. "He's a Communist."

Gritting his teeth, Gabriel swung an abrupt right on what looked like a more promising street. There had to be a gas station in this godforsaken town. The Volkswagen choked; the gears ground.

"If you can't find 'em, grind 'em," Ian said helpfully.

"Do you want me to drive?" Bailey asked.

"Do you even know where you're going?" LaRay demanded.

"I'm going insane, that's where I'm going," he snapped. No gas station in sight. Just street after street of houses, some

56

with Christmas lights blinking into the gray morning, one with a plastic Nativity set on the lawn.

He turned again, onto a wider street. His head was pounding, and Elvis's voice booming through the speakers wasn't helping.

"I think you're lost," Dustin said.

"Nonsense," Bailey argued, "he's just finding a gas station."

"I don't see one," LaRay said. "And I'm in a hurry."

"This sucks," Ian added.

Gabriel pulled off the road, tires squealing, and slammed on the brakes. He reached out and pushed the eject button on the tape.

The car fell silent.

"There," he said, pointing at a brick building. "Go in there, and find a damned bathroom."

They were all staring at him with shocked faces.

"Gabriel," Bailey said gently, "it's a church."

He glanced impatiently at the sign. SAINT FRANCIS OF ASSISI CHURCH. SATURDAY MASS 5:00 P.M. SUNDAY MASS 9:00 AND 11:00 A.M.

"Well, I'm sure that they have restrooms, don't they? That's it. I'm here. Go ahead."

"It doesn't seem right," LaRay said, her mouth settling into a stubborn line. "Not on Christmas Eve."

"To hell with it," he exclaimed, getting out of the car and flipping the seat forward. "Get in there and go. I'm going to borrow a phone and see if I can't get the hell out of this clown car. I'm sick of Christmas, and I'm sick of driving, and I'm sick of Elvis."

Bailey stared at him, fire in her blue eyes. "You know, Gabriel, I thought you were a nice man. But you're pompous and self-important and snobbish. You're acting just like a . . . like a . . ."

"Like a turd?" Ian suggested from the backseat.

"I'll go in with you, LaRay," Bailey said kindly. "I'm sure it will be no problem."

He watched as Bailey took LaRay's arm, helping her

57

up the brick steps. She pushed the door handle, and they went in.

Ian had climbed out of the car and was leaning on the hood, watching Gabriel. "She's right, dude," he said, lifting his pierced brow knowingly. "You're kind of a jerk."

"Look," said Gabriel, "I'm having a bad day. My wallet was stolen; my coat was stolen. I'm freezing my ass off, I'm trying to get to Memphis on schedule, and we have to stop every two minutes to pick up grandmothers and punk rockers and falling Elvis impersonators, and I'm driving an impossible car and I just want to get my money wired, so that I can get to a decent hotel and finish my story. That's all."

"Bummer."

The phone lines had to be up by now. He left Ian and Dustin with the car and strode up the steps of the church, pushing open the heavy door.

He followed a sign directing him to the parish offices, down a quiet hallway. The door was open, and a pleasant-looking woman was sitting at a desk, leafing through papers.

"May I help you?"

He explained his situation as quickly as possible.

"Well, of all the days to help tired travelers, this is one of the best. Feel free to use the phone." The woman stood, tidy in her striped blouse and navy skirt, and picked up a stack of leaflets. "I'll be right down the hall. Just let me know when you're finished."

"Thank you."

He picked up the phone, connected with an operator, gave his name, and placed a collect call.

"You're connected," the operator said, and the line clicked over.

"Charles? Charles, is that you?"

Wonderful. Wallace's wife.

"Hello, Bitsy. Is Wallace about?"

"It is you. I wasn't sure. The operator gave your name as Gabriel. Isn't that funny?"

"Hilarious." Had he given his name as Gabriel? He must have. "Is Wallace about?" he asked again.

"He's at breakfast. Where on earth are you, Charles?"

"In a church in Memphis. Bitsy, will you please call Wallace to the phone?"

"Fine. Merry Christmas, Charles."

He listened to the background noises. Wallace Jr. was shrieking, and Bitsy's voice was mumbling, and then he heard Wallace pick up the phone.

"Charles? What in heaven's name are you doing in Memphis?"

"Working on a story. Listen, Wallace—"

"Of course. What else would you be doing on Christmas Eve? Certainly not paying your respects to your family."

"Wallace, I've had my wallet and luggage stolen—"

"Good God, Charles. How did you manage that?"

"I couldn't say, Wallace. The thief didn't consult me prior to the incident."

"Did you call the police?"

"No, Wallace, I called for take-out pizza. Of course I called the police."

"Well, one never knows with you. Bitsy tells me you gave your name as Gabriel. Have you changed it? Is it some kind of little writing thing?"

He considered hanging up the phone. "No, just a slip of the tongue. Listen, Wallace, could you wire me some money?"

Wallace gave a low, superior chuckle. "Of course. Why didn't I guess? Of course, Charles, nobody has anything else to do on Christmas Eve but chase around for an open Western Union office. Where should I send it, and how much do you need?"

"Don't sound so put-upon. You know I can pay you back as soon as I get home. As to how much, send two or three thousand. I'll need enough for clothes, hotel, luggage, and airfare home."

Wallace sighed. "Really," he said, and Gabriel cringed. "Where are you staying, Charles?"

"I'm not sure yet. You can leave a message at"—he hated to say it—"the Original Heartbreak Hotel, on Blues Street."

"Really. How quaint. I'll see what I can do. So good to hear from you, Charles."

"I'm sure. Pleasant speaking to you, Wallace. Give Mother and Father my best."

He hung up the phone with a sharp click. How was it that Wallace was always able to make him feel incompetent? He had analyzed it a hundred times, broken it down into categories and lists, believing that once he understood it, saw it in black and white, it would no longer bother him.

But it did. Wallace, the perfect son with the perfect job, the perfect wife and . . . okay, nobody could call that whining little prig, Wallace Jr., the perfect son, but he had no doubt that after a few years, Wallace Jr. would be off to Choate or some other perfect old school, playing tennis and joining the rowing team, and go on to be another perfect Van Dusen.

Was it so wrong to break the mold, to do what you really wanted with your own life?

And had he? Or was he, as Bailey said, pompous and self-important and snobbish? Or, as Ian said, "kind of a jerk."

God forbid. He hated to think he was another Wallace. His mother often said, "breeding will tell." She was usually speaking about people with less than illustrious ancestry, but he suddenly wondered if it was also true about himself.

He left the office, wandering out toward the church entrance. It was quiet and dim, and he heard the faint murmur of voices.

He looked toward the double doors of the chapel, which had been closed when he walked in.

They were all in there: Bailey, Ian, LaRay, and Dustin standing quietly in the first pew before the altar.

He wasn't used to Catholic churches, and looked around quickly, impressed.

It was large, with beautiful old wooden beams arching gracefully across the ceiling. The dim morning light lit the stained-glass windows like jewels. The altar rose high, carved from pale wood and trimmed with gilt along a million Gothic arches and arabesques. To one side, a marble statue of Christ stood, head bowed, one hand raised in a gentle blessing. Opposite stood a statue of the Virgin Mary, her hands resting gracefully at her breast, her eyes lowered. Someone had lain bouquets of white roses at her feet.

It smelled of polished wood and candles and old books. It felt peaceful and mystical and mysterious.

He felt acutely that he didn't belong here. These were not his traditions, this was not his history, and somehow, he felt a stab of regret at not belonging.

The woman from the office was standing, talking softly to Bailey and the rest. He hesitated, then walked quietly toward them.

They were looking at a crèche scene, one of the most elaborate Nativity scenes he had ever seen. The figures were perfectly carved and dressed.

"The church received it as a gift in eighteen fifty-four," the office woman was saying. "It was originally made in Germany in the early seventeen-hundreds. You see that the figure of the Christ child isn't yet in the manger. Our church's tradition is to place the Christ child in his bed at midnight Mass. The father carries him in with the children of the congregation. It's really very beautiful."

He watched Bailey's smile, tender and appreciative. "I can imagine. It's a lovely tradition, Sister."

That startled him a little. It hadn't crossed his mind that the woman in the tidy skirt and blouse was a nun. Briefly, he wondered what, in this modern age, drew someone to such an archaic profession. There might be a story in that.

He looked at the odd group gathered before the altar—LaRay, with her crimped hair and matronly coat, her feet still in rubber boots, and Ian, with his pierced brow and spiked hair, his hands shoved in the pockets of his black leather jacket. Bailey, her black curls hanging in tendrils around her angelic face, her pink watch showing brightly against her slender wrist, and Dustin, the Elvis impersonator, standing quietly to one side, listening respectfully.

They all stood as he was standing, thinking their own thoughts in the quiet mystery of the room, as if unsure what to do next.

And then Dustin lifted his pompadoured head, drew a deep breath, and began to sing.

"O, Holy night, the stars are brightly shining . . ."

He had a voice that could have made angels weep. It was rich and full. He hit each note like a perfectly tuned instrument, and the sounds seemed to swell and fill the quiet holiness of the church.

"A thrill of hope; the weary world rejoices, / For yonder breaks a new and glorious morn . . ."

It was golden and beautiful, filling the room, reaching up past the stained glass and touching the vaulted ceilings. He had heard the song a hundred times, but never sung like this.

"Fall on your knees. Oh, hear the angel voices . . ."

An expectant shiver touched his neck as the rich tenor climbed higher, and still grew in breadth, caressing the notes with joy.

"O night divine. O holy night, when Christ was born."

It seemed impossible that the voice could reach farther, could gain in clarity or richness, but it did, as if it would reach beyond the church, trying to rise to heaven itself.

"O night divine"—how he held that high note, perfect and soaring, before softening into the final gentle echo of the last line—"O night divine, when Christ was born."

It seemed the vibrations of the final note stayed in the church long after the sound had died. Everyone simply stood, silent and awed.

LaRay finally said, "Amen," in a teary voice, and that really seemed to be the only correct thing to say.

Then the office woman began exclaiming with delight, and Bailey hugged Dustin tightly, telling him that he was a marvel, that Pavarotti had better watch his back, and Ian shook his hand, and told him that was "cool."

And Gabriel Charles Van Dusen, self-proclaimed cynic and grinch, stood there watching, shaken by the feeling that had come over him, that elusive and indefinable joy that is commonly called "Christmas spirit."

LaRay was blowing her nose into a large hankie, Ian was mumbling something about needing to call his mom, and Bailey turned to smile at him, the brilliance of her happiness catching him off guard. Dear Bailey, with her laughter and spontaneity and optimism. She was one in a million.

Ian was walking toward him and cast him a quick, mischievous smile. " 'And that,' " he quoted, " 'is what Christmas is all about, Charlie Brown.' "

Chapter Six

He hadn't been quite sure what to expect, but his first sight of the Original Heartbreak Hotel was reassuring. It was solid-looking, six stories of pale brick, with an air of aging respectability about it. It had probably, fifty or more years ago, been a very lovely and elegant hotel.

Next door, however, was a different story. On a vacant lot next to the building, someone had decided to gift them with a living Nativity scene—Elvis style. The players stood around in biblical robes that glittered like sequined majorette costumes, the wise men had Elvis hairdos, and the Holy Mother looked more like Ann-Margret than the Mother of God.

"Good Lord," he muttered, staring in disbelief. "Welcome to Memphis. That has to be the most singularly awful display of bad taste I have ever encountered."

"Isn't it great?" Bailey asked. She carried a small suitcase under one arm, her silly, bedraggled tree under the other. She paused briefly before the double glass doors and dug into her pocket. A red-suited Santa was standing on the sidewalk, ringing a bell, and she dumped a handful of change into his bucket.

"Let's go," she said, smiling. She was tired, too. There were dark circles under her eyes, and her face was paler than it had been. But bright spots of excitement still flushed her cheeks as she pushed open the doors of the hotel.

Gabriel followed her, carrying her other suitcase, his laptop, and LaRay's box of fruitcake; Ian followed him, his backpack hanging from one shoulder and LaRay's suitcase in the other hand; and LaRay and Dustin brought up the rear. She was fussing about his injured leg.

If anybody thought they were an odd-looking group, Gabriel didn't notice. He was busy examining the lobby: good furniture, once expensive but now ready for the attic; lots of vintage thirties stuff; worn carpeting, faded to a nameless color of rose-brown-gray.

He flopped down onto a faded green velvet sofa, and Ian flopped opposite him into a spindly chair that looked as if it had been pilfered from some grandmother's parlor.

Bailey continued on to the desk, leaning her little tree carefully against it as she checked in. LaRay stood next to her, and the desk clerk handed her the telephone, smiling.

He looked to his left, and was startled by the sight of actual paintings on velvet, all of Elvis, all with price tags in the corner. Beautiful. They seemed out of place in the shabby gentility of the room.

But, no, looking around he saw various traces of the King— postcards on a rack by the front desk, Elvis souvenirs in a case. In the center of the lobby was a huge Christmas tree decorated with garish country music memorabilia. And looking straight back, he could see that the hotel restaurant was called the Hound Dog Café.

Of course.

Dustin approached him, limping, dragging the remnants of his tattered parachute, and offered his hand.

"Nice meeting you, Gabriel. You, too, Ian. Merry Christmas to both of you, and thanks for the ride."

Gabriel shook Dustin's hand. "It was a genuine pleasure. Merry Christmas to you."

"Yeah, Merry Christmas, dude," Ian agreed, shaking hands awkwardly.

"Are you going to be all right, young man?" LaRay demanded of Ian as she waddled over to the group, ducklike in her rubber boots.

"Uh, yeah. I, like, called my mom from that church, and she's sending me more money. And I'm grounded when I get home."

"Serves you right. Here, Merry Christmas." LaRay offered him a tightly wrapped fruitcake. "And you, too," she said, handing another to Dustin.

"Well, thank you, ma'am." Dustin hesitated, digging in the pockets of his white jumpsuit. After a moment, he produced three souvenir key rings with the Flying Elvi insignia on them, and gave one each to Ian, LaRay, and Gabriel. "There's a little present for all of you. Oh, and here's one for your girlfriend. She's a heck of a nice girl."

Gabriel accepted Bailey's gift without arguing.

"And if you decide you'd like us to perform at your wedding, the number's right on there. We're in the phone book, in Vegas, if you lose the key ring."

Gabriel laughed, tucking it into his pocket. "No, I think I'll hang on to this. And thanks for the song."

"I'm going to have a nice cup of coffee," LaRay said. "My daughter's on her way to pick me up, so I'll say good-bye."

Bailey hurried over from the desk to join them, hugging LaRay. "I've got your address," she said, "and I'll send you a Christmas card every year."

"You're a lovely girl," LaRay told her. "And you, young man—I guess you're not as big a Communist as I thought."

They all bade farewell to LaRay, and watched as she crossed the lobby to the Hound Dog Café.

A bellman, wearing a uniform straight from a forties movie that looked as if it had been around since then, was loading Bailey's luggage and tree into an equally antiquated elevator.

Bailey frowned at Ian. "You sure you'll be all right?"

"Yeah. My friend Bill is coming to get me, and Mom's sending my bus fare for the way home. Thanks a lot." He scratched his spiked hair, frowning. "Uh, I'm sorry I called you a jerk," he said quickly to Gabriel.

"No problem."

The boy dug in his backpack, and finally offered Bailey a cassette tape. "It's my band. We'll be, like, really famous one day." He was shrugging off his leather jacket as he spoke. He removed a few safety pins, and tugged off a few of the band patches that were tacked on, and then offered the jacket to Gabriel.

"Here, dude. Because your coat got stolen."

Gabriel was taken aback by his unexpected generosity. "I can't accept this, really."

"Hey, it's Christmas. Okay?"

He hesitated and looked at the boy. He was just a kid, despite the affectations of the spiked hair and pierced brow. And he was trying so hard to do the right thing, to help another person who'd been hit by bad fortune.

"Thanks, Ian. I'll keep an ear out for your band."

"Yeah, okay. And thanks for the ride, you guys."

Bailey hugged the boy, to Ian's obvious embarrassment, and told him to be careful and call his mother every day and get home safely. He nodded, pulled away, lifted a hand in farewell, and was gone, out the front doors and into the crowds of holiday shoppers who passed to and fro on Blues Street.

"Well," Gabriel said awkwardly, "I suppose I should check and see if there's a message at the desk for me."

"Don't bother. I already did. Nothing yet."

"Oh." He settled back onto the faded sofa, balancing his laptop computer on top of the leather jacket. What an odd assortment of Christmas presents—LaRay's fruitcake, the Flying Elvi key ring, the used leather jacket.

"It seems funny to say good-bye to them, doesn't it?" Bailey asked. "I mean, they were only part of our lives for one day, but in some ways we felt like . . . a kind of a family."

That made him laugh. "A very bizarre kind of family, Bailey."

"Well, maybe, but you haven't met my family. Now, are you going to hang around the lobby looking lost, or would you like to come up to my room and grab some sleep? We can have the front desk call if a message comes.''

"Bailey, do you always invite strange men up to your hotel rooms?"

"You're not that strange, Gabriel. And for heaven's sake, what are you going to do, tear my clothes off and ravish my body?"

He was startled by how vividly he could picture that—her soft black curls falling over her bare shoulders, the pale, translucent skin glowing in the semidarkness of the room, the feeling of her body, curved and feather soft against his own.

"Don't laugh, Bailey. Maybe later, after I've had some sleep."

"I'll take the risk," she said. Was there a huskiness under her teasing voice? Was it all in his mind, or did her eyes grow a little brighter, even as she laughed?

Put on the brakes, Gabriel. As Ian would say, chill.

"I knew there was some nefarious reason you offered me a ride," he said, picking up his armload of belongings, and following her across the faded carpet to the elevator.

"That's me. Brazen seductress."

They both laughed, but it was awkward. It was the first time the subject of sex had entered their conversation, and however lightly they treated it, there was a new uncertainty between them. He couldn't quite call it uncomfortable. Or was it?

The elevator doors groaned as they shut, and the engines creaked loudly as they began a slow, lumbering ascent.

She sighed, leaning against one wall. "I'm exhausted," she said.

He watched her lids fall over her eyes, shadowed in her pale, fine-featured face. He wished the subject of sex had never come up. He wondered if she made love with as much ease and pleasure as she did everything else. Probably.

Don't think about it, fella.

"You know what I'm thinking?" she asked suddenly, her eyes flying open.

"What?" he asked almost fearfully, wondering if her mind had been following the same path as his.

"Did I remember to pack a string of lights for the tree, or will I have to buy some?"

He exhaled audibly, not sure whether he was relieved or not.

"We'll find out soon enough."

"I guess we will," Bailey agreed, as the elevator ground and lurched to a stop.

"Wake me up at noon," she said, collapsing onto the bed. "I'm going to Graceland." She closed her eyes, her lashes lying in black crescent moons above her pale cheeks. She fell asleep, before he could even draw the curtains. Apparently, she was a lot more comfortable being in a hotel room with him than he was with her.

He wandered around the room aimlessly for a few minutes. It was relatively dull. Just a room, with one window covered by standard dark gold hotel-issue curtains. A bathroom—clean, he observed thankfully—with cellophane-wrapped drinking glasses and those terrible little bars of soap that never seemed adequate. But it was very clean. The little octagonal black and white tiles of the floor were spotless, and the bathtub gleamed.

He turned the light off and went back to the curtained semi-darkness of the main room. He studied the picture that hung over the bed. It was a photograph, perhaps Depression-era, hand tinted—a woman in a faded floral dress, her husband, equally solemn and young-looking, in an open collared shirt and a faded hat tilted back from his face. He looked as if he'd just come from work at a factory. Between them, in a hat very similar to the father's, cherub faced and dark eyed, was a baby in overalls.

Gabriel contemplated the three faces. They had the tired but determined look that one so often saw in photographs from the Depression—tired, down, but not done-in yet. After a moment, he realized that the dark-eyed infant was Elvis. Even in infancy, the swarthy good looks, the distinctive mouth, were recognizable.

He crossed the room to view the picture on the opposite

wall. It was a photograph of a street in a small town, in a worn frame of dark wood. Someone had attached a brass plaque to the frame. TUPELO, MISSISSIPPI, ABOUT 1940.

He opened the curtains and peered four stories down to Blues Street, glanced briefly at the holiday shoppers hurrying along the sidewalk, and then closed them again.

He looked at Bailey sleeping on the bed, one arm thrown up above her head, her T-shirt clinging to her breasts and showing the slender line of her waist.

He looked away quickly and took his notebook from his pocket, leafing quickly through the pages.

There was a small desk against the wall by the window, and he sat down, opened his laptop computer, and began to write.

Eula Mae is on her way to Graceland, one of the faithful arriving to pay homage to the King. She wears a bright pink Elvis watch, carrying the image of Elvis with her like a religious medal.

An exaggeration, but it fit the story.

"I love Elvis more than I love my own father," she proclaims. . . .

He continued on, occasionally glancing at Bailey, sleeping soundly on the rust-colored bed.

"Wake up, Sleeping Beauty."

Startled by the masculine voice next to her ear, Bailey jumped.

For a moment she stared, disoriented, and then she started to laugh. "Gabriel! What have you done?"

He had set up the tiny tree in the wastepaper basket, and draped a string of lights through its branches. The desk, which had been against the wall when she fell asleep, had been moved to the end of the bed, and a feast awaited her.

"What have I done?" he asked, dragging a chair to the

other side of the desk. He sat there, smiling at her, his lazy grin bright in his face. "It was a little late for breakfast in bed, so it's lunch, straight from the Hound Dog Café. I wasn't sure what to order, so take your pick. It looks like your kind of food."

She clambered across the bed, raking her hands through her hair. She could only imagine what it looked like.

"Hey, your brother must have wired your money."

He nodded. "The desk called while you were sleeping, so I went down to the bank and picked it up."

"Wow," she said, surveying the makeshift table. "Did you order one of everything?"

"Only genuine Elvis favorites. The special of the day—pot roast, mashed potatoes, and gravy. Or, if you prefer, fried peanut butter–and-banana sandwiches. The waitress assured me that he was very partial to their cheeseburgers, so I bought one of those. Oh, and the specialty of the house—the hound doggie." He lifted the plate at her, and she stared in amazement at the foot-long hot dog, smothered in relish and onion and mustard. "What do you think? Do your arteries harden just looking at it?"

"It looks fabulous," she said, reaching for a chocolate shake. "But what are you having?"

"Whatever you leave behind." He leaned back, grinning.

She ate a French fry, and grabbed for the fried peanut butter–and-banana sandwich. It was perfect with the shake.

"Gabriel, you *are* an angel. This is pretty wild, for a poached-egg man."

"When in Rome . . ." he said.

"That's how I always feel when I travel," she agreed. "What's the point of going somewhere if you're going to eat the same things you eat at home?"

"Good policy," he said, picking up a giant cheeseburger. "Now, eat up. Graceland awaits."

"Are you as anxious to get there as I am?" she asked, delighted.

He nodded, pulling his little notebook from his shirt pocket. "Okay. This is what I thought. We can get to Graceland, do

71

the tour, look around, and be back on Blues Street by about three. From three to four, we can do Beale Street, soak up some atmosphere, decide where to have dinner. From four to seven, I work. Seven to eight, we change, and then go out for dinner. From eight till—''

"Gabriel!"

Startled, he looked up at her. "What?"

"Put that damned piece of paper away, or I'll burn it. For goodness' sake, you can't schedule fun. And what do you mean, work? You're working on Christmas Eve?"

"Three hours. That's all. Then I'm finished."

"Okay, that I can handle. But no schedules. Schedules are for the workweek, not vacation. Come on, live dangerously."

He hesitated, and then closed his notebook with a snap. "Okay. You win. I'll try it. Except from four till seven. On that, I'm inflexible."

"Agreed. Well done, Gabriel. I think some of the starch is coming out of your shorts."

She watched him over the rim of her glass. He looked happier, more relaxed than she'd ever seen him. She wondered if his brother had sent him enough money for his own hotel room.

She found herself hoping that he hadn't.

Chapter Seven

"Okay, Ebenezer Scrooge," she said. "You slave over your figures. I'm going to run out and do some last-minute shopping."

"Hey, be careful. You're in a strange city." Actually, compared to Manhattan, Memphis could hardly be called a city. It still had a small-town feeling to it. He wondered if the locals were always so friendly, or if it was because of the Christmas season.

"I'll be fine. I'm a big girl, Gabriel."

"Not that big. What do you weigh? Ninety pounds?"

"In my dreams and on my driver's license." She smiled at him, her dimples changing her face from pretty to stunning. "Okay. See you at seven. Don't worry."

See you at seven. It sounded so casual, something a wife would say. He almost expected her to kiss his cheek before she walked out the door.

She didn't.

The room felt too quiet after she left. For a tiny woman, she had a big presence.

"Concentrate," he said aloud to himself, and sat down at the desk. He took up a pen and grabbed a piece of hotel stationery, and started scrawling his impressions down.

Graceland on Christmas Eve. Larger than it looks in the pictures. High fence, winding drive. Bailey, eyes like stars when she crossed the threshold. House very classical Southern—white columns, etc.

Life-size, light-up Nativity on the lawn, clashing with the life-size Santa and reindeer. Hate mixed metaphors. She didn't. She loved it.

Strange feeling in the house. Wandering from room to room felt intrusive—as if Elvis still lived there, and might come walking out of the next room.

Bailey loved the cars. Wants a pink cadillac when she wins the lottery.

She asked lots of questions. Good ones. She loved all the Christmas trees throughout the house. Wants trees in every room of her mansion—again, when she wins the lottery.

He stopped, frowning, trying to remember the other people in the tour group. For heaven's sake, that was why he was there, wasn't it? But all he could remember was Bailey moving lightly from room to room, the way her eyes sparkled with delight, the glowing rose coloring in her cheeks.

"Damn it, Charles," he said aloud, picking up his pen. "Stay focused."

Elvis's grave. Covered with gifts, flowers, teddy bears. Candles left there, like a shrine. Bailey kneeling down quietly, leaving a single rose. Quiet. Eyes like wet morning glories. Said a prayer. Crossed herself. Didn't realize she was Catholic. How did she manage that, with an atheist father and New Age mother? It seems to rest comfortably with her. Not a shallow woman, despite her lightness. Would she expect her husband to convert, when she marries? What would Mother say?

74

He stopped writing abruptly, staring in disbelief at the words that had flowed so easily from his subconscious.

What was he thinking?

"Put the brakes on, Charles," he said aloud. "She's beautiful and charming, but not wife material. As Wallace says, not really 'our kind' of person."

Whatever that meant. Who was "his kind" of person? Someone like Bitsy? Cool and blond, with her luncheons and gardening clubs and charity functions?

"God forbid," he said aloud.

A sparkle of light caught his eye, and he looked over his shoulder. Funny, he didn't remember plugging the tree in. He smiled, looking at it leaning lopsidedly in the little white wastepaper basket. Bailey thought it was beautiful. That was just like her. Always seeing the good, the beauty in everything.

He glanced at his watch, and then down at his notes. Too much Bailey, not enough story.

Concentrate, Charles. Don't think about Bailey. Think about your story. Reinvent Bailey as Eula Mae. Sure, take a few of Bailey's comments, but keep her out of it. Stick to the original theme.

He crumpled up the paper and tossed it aside. He picked up his pen and started fresh, focusing on the details of Graceland, trying to remember the other tourists in the group, trying not to let the image of Bailey's face intrude. *Don't write about her smile, the intensity of her eyes, her tiny wrists and clear laugh.*

When he was finished with the story, he'd show it to her. He hoped that she'd understand his deception.

Focused at last, he turned on his computer, and started to write, quickly, methodically.

At exactly ten minutes to seven, he finished, right on schedule.

"Guess what?" she demanded, pushing open the door. She was bright cheeked with cold and excitement, and tossed several bags to the floor.

"I can't even begin to imagine," he answered.

"You're not wearing pants," she observed, raising her eyebrows at the sight of his modest boxer shorts.

"I know that. I washed the mud off of them." He gestured toward them, hanging in front of the heater vent in the wall. "Is that what you wanted me to guess?"

"No, it's much more interesting than laundry, though you have great legs. This is what: the hotel is . . ." She paused dramatically, pulling off her hat and flinging it to the bed. "Haunted!"

"You're joking."

"Hey, I wouldn't kid you about something like that. Jeanine was telling me—"

"Who's Jeanine, did you rescue her, and did you invite her to stay the night?" he asked, only half joking.

"The owner of the coffee shop, and no, she doesn't strike me as the kind of gal who needs rescuing from anything. She's great. And no, she's not coming for a slumber party. Don't be ridiculous."

"Bailey, if you could fit five people, luggage, twenty-three fruitcakes, and Ian's hair into a Volkswagen bug, I shudder to imagine what you could fit into a hotel room."

She shrugged off her coat and dropped it to the floor, reaching for her suitcase. She opened it and began searching through it, flinging clothes, makeup, books, and shoes as she spoke.

"Now, listen. Jeanine told me that Elvis's ghost has actually been seen here in the hotel by several people. Can you believe it?"

"Honestly, no. Unless, of course, he was carrying a parachute."

"Cynic. Have you no imagination at all? I think it's wonderful. Did anything weird happen while I was gone?"

She was gathering up her clothes and heading for the bathroom.

He decided not to mention the tree turning itself on. "Bailey?"

She stopped and turned.

"Yes, I did notice something odd. Definite poltergeist-type activity."

She waited, breathless, her eyes wide.

"Five minutes ago, the room was absolutely spotless. And then hats and coats and bags and suitcases started materializing and flinging themselves around. Now, amazingly enough, the room looks like the inside of your car."

She rolled her eyes. "Ha ha. You're a card, Gabriel."

She closed the bathroom door with a solid thump.

He waited until he heard the shower running, and then picked up his computer. He took one last run through his story, sorting out the odd word here and there, double-checking for typos.

He stopped and smiled as she began singing in the shower. That didn't surprise him in the least. She sang "The Holly and the Ivy," the first chorus of "Good King Wenceslas," and then switched to "I Can't Help Falling in Love."

He couldn't help imagining her in there, water streaming over her pale body.

"Hell," he muttered. "Get a grip. You're acting like a sixteen-year-old."

He looked around, trying to distract himself. He picked up her coat from the floor and hung it neatly in the tiny closet. He placed her suitcase on the folding luggage rack. He tried not to notice her lingerie, silky sky blue things with lace.

So much for distracting himself. He checked the cuffs of his khakis. Mostly dry. Putting on pants would probably be a good idea at this point.

He heard the water turn off, and tried not to think about her drying off.

"Hey, Gabriel?"

He jumped as her voice came through the closed door.

"Yes?"

"I found a great place for dinner," she called, her voice muffled.

"Wonderful." He was still full from lunch. How did she eat so much, and stay so thin?

"Have you ever had a deep-fried pickle?"

77

He hoped he hadn't heard her correctly. "I don't believe so."

"Do you like blues?"

Non sequitur woman strikes again. "Colors or music?"

"Music, bonehead. We're in Memphis, remember?"

"Sounds great."

He picked up a book from where she'd tossed it. A biography of Ivan the Terrible. He leafed through it. Pretty dry stuff. He picked up another. A romance novel with an impossibly beefy man on the cover, a swooning blonde in his arms.

The bathroom door opened. "What do you think?"

Bailey was transformed. She was wearing a little black dress that clung to her body, dark stockings, and high heels that made her legs look incredible. Her hair was pulled back into a simple sweep, with loose tendrils touching her forehead. The dark color of her dress brightened her complexion, and her eyes were brilliant. She had on glittering earrings. The Elvis watch was gone, replaced by a simple gold bracelet that made her tiny wrist look even more fragile.

She was stunning. She was sexy.

"Well?"

The transformation was so stunning that he was at a loss for words. And then, without thinking, he quoted:

> *"She walks in beauty, like the night*
> *Of cloudless climes and starry skies;*
> *And all that's best of dark and bright*
> *Meet in her aspect and her eyes . . ."*

She stared at him, astounded. The laughter faded from her eyes, and she looked as if she might cry.

"Thank you, Gabriel," she said softly, lowering her eyes. "Nobody has ever, ever quoted poetry to me before. That was honestly the most beautiful compliment I've ever had."

He looked away, embarrassed. What was he doing, quoting Byron like a lovesick college boy? "Well." He cleared his throat. "Well, you're very welcome. You deserve it. You're . . . gorgeous."

78

Her smile was radiant. "I'm going to treasure that forever. Every time I read Byron, I'll feel like that poem is mine."

"It suits you," he said.

They stood, suddenly awkward, looking everywhere but at each other.

"Now, what were you saying about fried pickles? I'm praying that I misheard you."

The spell was broken. She laughed.

"Keep praying, fella, but you heard right. When in Rome, remember?"

"Did I say that? I take it back."

"Too late. Come on. It's Christmas Eve, and I'm in a holiday mood." She looked for her coat, finally found it, and hung it over her shoulders. "It's really cold out there," she warned him. She was holding out Ian's black leather jacket.

"I can't wear that," he protested. "I'll look ridiculous."

"Don't be dumb. You can't freeze."

He hesitated, then sighed. "Okay, I'll try it."

"You look great," she said, when he reluctantly slid it on. "Younger. A little dangerous. It's very dashing."

He glanced at the mirror. Maybe not dashing, but not too ridiculous. He sure didn't look like a Van Dusen. But then, Charles Van Dusen wouldn't be in Memphis on Christmas Eve with a beautiful woman, venturing out to eat fried pickles.

"I get to pick the restaurant next time."

"You're on," she said. She smiled her perfect smile at him, and he had the feeling that he was falling hard and fast, and didn't care.

She was falling in love with him. She knew it from the minute he opened his mouth and started quoting poetry at her. *She walks in beauty, like the night . . .*

She kept hearing the words in her head as they walked along Beale Street, past shops and bars and restaurants.

Maybe it was a mistake. They were too different. It was one of those vacation things. She'd read an article about it once.

79

"Gabriel, do you ever read *Today's Psychology*?" she asked.

He stared at her. He looked a good deal more startled than the question warranted.

"I have," he finally answered. "Why do you ask?"

She stopped, staring in the window of a store called the Collector's Dream. There was an assortment of everything under the sun in the window, from antique watches to tin toys.

"Well, I read this article once, about people on vacation. And how they sometimes behave in ways they wouldn't at home, because it's all part of a big illusion. Getting away from it all. They have affairs, and then go home and forget about it." Her words were hurried and uncertain.

"Ah, yes. As a matter of fact, I remember the very article."

She looked at an old wooden Pinocchio doll, resting on a faded quilt, and tried to choose her words carefully. "Umm, I just wanted you to know that it's not something I usually do." She glanced quickly up at him, and then away.

"Bailey?"

He reached for her hand, and his touch sent a jolt of heat through her fingers. Her pulse raced. His fingers closed over hers, warm and reassuring.

"It's not something I normally do, either."

She didn't know what to say next. The street was still busy, people brushing past them as they stood silently by the lighted window. She felt unreal, like an actress in a movie. Not like Bailey O'Connor, the little waitress in her polyester uniform. She felt enchanted, elegant in her black dress. The kind of woman that someone would quote poetry to.

She looked up at him. He was watching her face intently, his lazy, dark eyes soft and thoughtful. Her heartbeat felt unsteady. She needed to break the silence, cut through the dark tension.

"How many psychiatrists does it take to change a light—"

His mouth covered hers before she could finish.

Warm and sweet, heat flickered through her. She felt his hand on the back of her neck, pulling her deeper into the kiss.

She reached up to touch his face, her hand unsteady against the warmth of his cheek. Oh, she was lost.

He kissed her mouth very softly, twice more, and then leaned back, smiling at her. She stared back, breathless.

"Okay. How many psychiatrists does it take to change a lightbulb?" he asked, brushing a curl back from her temple.

She drew a shaky breath, trying to remember. "One," she finally answered, her voice unsteady. "But the lightbulb has to *want* to change."

He laughed softly. "Okay, Bailey." He shook his head, smiling. "You're nuts."

She blushed, unable to look at his mouth without thinking of the feeling of it over her own. "Look," she said, pointing into the store. "An Elvis collection. Let's go look."

He didn't let go of her hand as they pushed through the door and into the cluttered treasure trove of the store. It smelled of pine and old books and the past.

She made a beeline for the glass display case with the Elvis memorabilia: old albums, a scrapbook filled with movie stills, and a framed, autographed picture of Elvis with Ann-Margret, both signatures perfectly preserved under the glass.

"Wow," Bailey said, pointing into the display case. "Look at that." It was a faded blue denim work shirt. A card was displayed on it. She read aloud: " 'Work shirt worn by Elvis when he was eighteen years old, working at the Parker Machinists' Shop. Gladys's stitches can still be seen where she mended the torn sleeve.' "

"Five hundred dollars," Gabriel added.

"It makes him seem so real, doesn't it? I mean, just a regular kid, working a lousy job and dreaming of something better."

She looked up and saw that Gabriel was not looking at the shirt, but at her. "Is that what you do, Bailey? What do you dream about?"

Someone like you, she thought, but didn't say. "I don't know. Different things. Traveling. Seeing the world. Buying a house."

"Like Graceland?"

"Oh, no. Just a small house. Someplace of my own. A place where I could grow flowers and have children. Someday."

He looked surprised. "That's a pretty conventional dream, for you. I'd be less surprised if you'd told me you wanted to join a Hungarian circus act with trained seals."

She laughed. "Well, Gabriel, underneath it all, I guess I'm pretty conventional. Mostly."

"I don't believe it."

She picked up a snow globe with a plastic replica of Graceland inside. She tilted it, and watched the white confetti swirl. "Well, since I don't have five hundred dollars, I think I'll get this. Then when I'm old and gray, I can remember the Christmas I spent in Memphis."

He watched her walk to the cash register and count out her money for the clerk. A vacation fling? He hated to think it. He'd spent less than twenty-four hours with her, and it felt like forever.

Tomorrow was Christmas—and then what?

She'd have to go back to St. Louis, and he'd be flying back to Manhattan. She'd promise to write, and so would he, and then neither of them would. Maybe a Christmas card every year.

He missed her already.

She was tucking her souvenir snow globe into her purse, and smiled over at him.

"Okay, Gabriel. Are you ready for deep-fried pickles?"

He made a face. "I'm not sure I'm that brave."

She laughed so hard that her rhinestone earrings swayed and sparkled. "Come on, Gabriel. Be brave. Take a chance. Do something unscheduled and insane and totally out of character."

"I might," he said slowly, watching her dimples deepen in her flushed face. "I may do exactly that."

He wasn't thinking about pickles.

Dinner and blues. She took him to B. B. King's, where the owner himself was nowhere in sight. But the music was great, like the barbecued chicken, smoky and dark and rich.

The famous deep-fried pickles were better than he had expected. He had no idea what kind of wine to order with fried pickles. The waiter brought something white and indifferent.

He barely noticed it. He was intoxicated with Bailey. He loved the way she sat, the way she ate, the way her eyes were so clear and bright. He loved her stupid jokes. He loved the way she swayed to the music. He loved the way she spoke to everyone she met, and how they all chatted back, enchanted by her warmth and friendliness.

He bought her a warm brandy after dinner, and laughed at the way her eyes watered when the fumes hit her.

She wanted to dance, so he danced, even though he normally didn't. He wasn't surprised when she turned out to be a wonderful dancer, graceful and completely at ease with herself.

The band played a slow, sultry version of "Have Yourself a Merry Little Christmas," and she wrapped her arms around his neck, and they slow danced, his cheek resting against her clean-smelling hair.

He decided that slow dancing was probably as much fun as anyone could have with their clothes on.

He decided that he loved Christmas. And Memphis. Hell, he even loved Elvis.

The people at the next table were a family of tourists from Georgia, and they talked with Bailey and bought them each another brandy, and they all toasted each other, and exchanged Merry Christmases. The grandfather asked Gabriel if he could dance with Bailey, and he felt an absurd surge of chauvinistic pride when she waited for his answer.

He went off to find the men's room, stopped at the pay phone, and called the Collector's Dream. He told them he wanted the blue Elvis shirt, price be damned. He offered them an extra hundred if they could deliver it discreetly to the restaurant within the next five minutes.

Yes, the owner remembered them. Or more precisely, he remembered Bailey, "the beautiful girl in the black dress."

Gabriel stopped a passing waiter and enlisted his help. By the time Bailey was leaving the dance floor, the waiter was covertly passing Gabriel Elvis's shirt, carefully wrapped in layers of tissue.

Gabriel carefully tucked it into the large pocket of his leather coat. Six hundred dollars for a worn shirt. He must be losing his mind. But Bailey's surprise tomorrow would be worth a million.

The Georgia tourists offered them another drink, which Bailey declined.

"I think I've had enough," she said. "I'm pretty light-headed. Actually, a little fresh air wouldn't hurt."

The air outside was crisp and clean. They walked down Beale Street together, past the old brick buildings and neon signs, past jazz cafés and coffee shops and smart shops and restaurants. The street was quiet now, with only an occasional drift of music wafting from a building as they passed. A Christmas Eve quiet was settling into the night.

"Look," Bailey said softly, pointing at a streetlight.

He looked up, and a flurry of snowflakes swirled through the circle of light.

"Not enough to stick," he commented.

"No, but it's still wonderful. A little token snow for Christmas."

From far away, a bell started ringing, and she stopped to listen to the sound.

"I was in Europe once, on Christmas Eve," he said. "I was in a little village in Switzerland, and at midnight, the church bells started to ring. I stood out there in the snow and listened. I knew that all over the country, all over Europe, all the church bells were ringing at that moment."

It was hard to describe. Perhaps if he'd had paper and pen, he could make her understand what it had been like—the snow, the starlight, the ancient church, the bells ringing from village to village as they had every Christmas morning for more than a thousand years.

"I'd like to hear that," she said softly, her eyes dreamy, and he felt that she'd understood.

"One day I'll take you there."

She said nothing, just walked along with her breath making cold clouds in the air.

"Don't ever lie to me," she said eventually. "Not even to be nice. Promise?"

"I meant it," he protested.

He could see the doubt in her eyes. "Just don't lie to me," she repeated. "I like to know where I stand."

"I won't lie to you."

He meant it. Tomorrow morning he would correct the only lie he had told her. He would tell her about the story, tell her he was a writer. She'd understand. She'd laugh. She'd probably be relieved that he wasn't a financial analyst. He'd let her read the story.

Tomorrow. But tonight . . .

"Bailey?"

She turned around, looking at him with a face that stopped his heart. Her eyes were hopeful and uncertain, and beneath it, he could see the heat in them.

"The truth," he said, "is that right now, I want to make love to you. A lot."

She blushed and looked down. "I want that, too," she said, more softly than he had ever heard her speak.

He pulled her tightly against his chest, kissing her forehead, her cheeks, and finally the sweetness of her mouth, as if he could kiss the uncertainty out of her voice.

When she finally looked up at him, her eyes glowed like cool and distant starlight.

"Let's go," she said simply, and they began the walk through the quiet streets, back to the Original Heartbreak Hotel.

Chapter Eight

The quiet of the night followed them down Blues Street to the hotel. A few snow flurries fell from the dark and silent sky and were gone. Even the Santa Claus who had been at the hotel door was gone, the ringing of his bell already fading into the past.

Bailey thought that the quiet night seemed rich and deep, full of mystery. She wondered if it was simply the magic of Christmas Eve, or if it was falling in love that altered her perception. Everything seemed changed.

She had always believed in following her heart and sorting out the obstacles later.

This time was different.

She knew that she and Gabriel were from wildly different worlds, and that the morning might well reveal the impossibility of any future for them.

But tomorrow wasn't just any other morning, was it? It was Christmas morning, a day of magic and miracles, a day of gifts that were never expected.

She decided to follow her heart, and trust.

*   *   *

As the old elevator lumbered up to the fourth floor, he wondered what she was thinking. It was unlike her to be silent for so long.

He studied her face, trying to read her thoughts there. It was odd how she already seemed so familiar to him. Had he really only met her twenty-four hours ago? What if his stuff hadn't been stolen? He would never have even remembered what she looked like. She would have been another faceless waitress, pouring his coffee till he walked out of her life, leaving a neatly stacked pile of quarters behind.

It would have been a tragedy.

But here he was, already wondering if she would be willing to move to Manhattan, and how his family would like her, and what neighborhoods they would look at when they went house shopping together.

It was insane. It was wonderful. It was enough to make him believe in miracles.

He wondered if she felt the same.

The elevator lurched to a stop, the engine loud in the midnight silence, and he turned to her, offering his hand.

She looked straight into his eyes and offered him a tremulous smile of such hope and trust that he felt his heart actually stop.

He believed in miracles. To hell with clinical explanations of love that cited body chemistry and unresolved personal issues and drivel like that.

It was magic, and it was theirs.

The room was quiet and dark, only the lights of the tree glowing like jewels.

Somewhere in the back of his mind, he thought that it was odd, that he had certainly unplugged the lights before they had gone, but it was only a fleeting thought.

She was kicking her shoes off, and dropping her coat on the floor—one day he would cure her of that habit—and walking across the floor toward him (*She walks in beauty, like the night*) and lifting her slender arms to embrace him, her beautiful, shining eyes meeting his with an expression of love and hope and trust that he was sure nobody had ever gifted him with before.

And all that's good and all that's right meet in her aspect and her eyes . . .

He was hers. She quit thinking about tomorrow, and let herself live fully in the magic of the night. She let her hands explore the hardness of his shoulders, the soft skin over swells of tight muscle, the feeling of his hair, slipping like silk between her fingers. She tasted the place at the bottom of his neck where the pulse beat in the hollow of his throat, and breathed his breath into her own lungs when their mouths touched.

She floated on dark clouds of desire, her body turning and trembling at his touch as naturally as a tree moves at the touch of wind.

Nobody had ever made her feel that way. No mouth had ever felt so perfectly matched against her own, no body had ever complemented her own, like the missing piece of a broken vase sliding into place, and miraculously becoming whole again.

And when he finally entered her, whispering her name warmly into her ear, she almost wept. It was perfection; it was everything new and ancient; it was strength and softness, a promise of love made physical in one moment.

She was his; he was hers.

Together they traveled to the dark and brilliant place where bodies and hearts ignite with joy, and then, shaken, held each other, hearts racing and bodies trembling, silent in the night, until the physical world became real again.

It changed everything. They were lovers now, resting in each other's arms, whispering endearments and trading tender touches with a kind of awed pride.

"Bailey?"

His whisper roused her from the warm lull of sleep. She didn't mind. It was a pleasure to be awake, to feel the heat of his body still entwined with hers.

"Hmmm?" She was too tired to bother with words, too relaxed and deliciously exhausted.

"I have a truth to tell you. Something I kept from you."

He sounded nervous. A sliver of fear intruded into her happiness.

She sat up, staring at him in the half darkness. He looked very dark against the white sheets.

"Oh, my God, you're married." It was the worst thing she could imagine.

"No, no, nothing like that! I'm one hundred percent free and unattached. No, let me rephrase that—I'm one hundred percent yours."

She collapsed with relief, falling with her cheek against his chest, listening to the sound of his heart. "Gabriel, those are the sweetest words anybody's ever said to me. Better than Byron." She exhaled with delight. "What, then?"

"I'm not a financial analyst."

Puzzled, she frowned. "I don't get it. Why say so? What are you?"

"I'm a writer."

She tipped her face back to look at him, perplexed. "So why lie? What's wrong with that?"

"Well, remember when you asked me if I ever read *Today's Psychology*? The article on vacation affairs? I did. I wrote it."

She nodded, remembering his startled look. "I still don't get it. Why not tell me?"

"Well, to be honest, Bailey, I wasn't coming to Memphis to see Graccland. I was, but not in the same capacity you were. I was coming professionally. I'm working on an article for next December's issue, and when you said that you were coming here . . . well, I thought that I could use you in my article."

"Use me?" The sliver of fear became an icicle, large and cold, intruding into the warmth of their embrace.

"Poor choice of words. Not *use* you, but learn from you. Get material for the article."

"Then, all this . . ." Her question was too awful to be put into words.

He pulled her tightly to his chest, his hand moving to her

hair. "All this is true. Learn from you? I've learned more from you than I ever expected. The article has nothing to do with us, I promise. I simply used some of your comments about Elvis, and assigned them to a fictional character. That's all. I only lied because I didn't want you to be self-conscious when I asked you questions. And I'm sorry. I'll never lie to you again."

She was very quiet, thinking. "Gabriel?"

"Yes?" He sounded worried.

"Do you even *like* Elvis?"

"I do now. And I . . . I think that I love you."

"Honestly?"

"Honestly, Bailey."

"You know what, Gabriel?" she demanded, trying hard to sound stern.

His hands tightened on her shoulders.

"What?"

She couldn't help smiling at the nervousness in his voice.

"I think I love you, too," she said, smiling into the darkness.

His breath left his chest with an audible sigh of relief.

"Merry Christmas, Gabriel," she said, closing her eyes and snuggling up to him.

"The merriest," he agreed. "The best ever. God bless us, every one. Elvis and LaRay and Ian and all the Flying Elvi and your tofu-eating pagan mother and even Wallace and Bitsy."

"What's a Bitsy?" she demanded.

"My brother's wife. You'll meet her, unfortunately. Let's not think of them now."

"Okay," she agreed. "What do you want to think about?"

"Us," he said softly, and she wondered if such a small word had ever meant so much.

It was the finest Christmas morning he could remember. The lobby of the old hotel was almost deserted, except for an old bellman, half-asleep in a chair next to the desk, his shabby little hat tipped to one side, and a family carrying their bags out the door. He smiled as he watched them go, the mother and father walking on each side of a little girl, exchanging secret smiles over her head.

That could be us in a few years.

The thought startled him. He'd never considered children before. *Well, why not?*

He hummed as he went into the Hound Dog Café. Even on Christmas morning there were people there, eating their eggs and pancakes in turquoise vinyl booths.

Elvis was playing on the jukebox, of course—the same song Bailey had been singing in the shower, about not being able to help falling in love.

He leaned against the counter, humming along. An aged waitress in a turquoise polyester dress stepped up to help him, a pen stuck behind her ear.

"Merry Christmas, sweetie. What can I do for you?"

"Two coffees to go. Cream and sugar. And . . ." He hesitated. Not too much—Bailey would much rather eat down here, he was sure. "I guess that's it."

"You got it."

He studied the clock above the counter, a gold starburst design that had probably been very fashionable in 1965. It was not quite seven yet.

Bailey was still sleeping upstairs, curled up on her side, with the rumpled look of a disheveled angel. He couldn't wait to wake her, to see the look in her eyes when he handed her Elvis's shirt.

"Okay. Two cups of joe, cream and sugar. That's one-fifty."

He added a dollar to it, and remembered Bailey's remark about people who were rude to waitresses. "Thank you very much. And Merry Christmas."

"You too, hon."

Funny how many people smiled at him. Was it because it was Christmas morning, or because he was smiling at them?

He probably looked like a fool. He didn't care. He smiled as he stopped at the desk to pick up the morning paper; he smiled all the way up the creaking old elevator, the coffee

91

heating his hands through the white foam to-go cups.

He smiled as he balanced the coffee in one hand to turn the key in the door, and pushed it open.

"Rise and shine, it's—" He stopped abruptly, the words dying in his throat.

Something was very wrong.

She was awake, and angry. Not just a little angry, but really angry. Her face was stark white, her brows drawn in two black slashes. Her eyes were glowing with fury, and slightly red.

She was sitting by the desk, dressed only in an oversize T-shirt. It said on it, ALL I ASK IS THAT YOU TREAT ME NO DIFFERENTLY THAN YOU WOULD THE QUEEN.

Behind her, on the desk, his laptop was open, the amber letters glowing on the screen. He tried to remember the last words.

Eula Mae is leaving Graceland, back to her polyester uniform and her future at the lunch counter. But in her mind, she is blessed. She has worshiped at the grave of the King.

"You horse's ass, Gabriel."

He tried to remember if he'd ever heard her swear before. He didn't think so.

"Bailey, it's a fictional character—"

"Oh, yeah. Eula Mae, poor, ignorant, hayseed waitress from St. Louis, so damned stupid that she thinks Elvis is God. So damned ignorant that visiting his shrine is the highlight of her pathetic life."

"Exactly. It's not you—"

"Oh, no, it's not me. She just did what I did, lives where I live, has my job. She uses my words! Only not my words. My words, but taken out of context, twisted and rearranged to make me sound pathetic and ignorant. No, you're right, Gabriel. It's not me. It's a twisted, ridiculous version of me. It's me, turned into a vile, stupid joke."

Her venom, her fury, startled him. The tears in her eyes felt like bullets through his heart.

92

"I didn't mean to make you into a joke. I thought you'd understand. It's just an article."

"It's crap!" she cried, banging her fist on her bare thigh. "It's a snotty, condescending piece of self-important crap. Oh, aren't you clever? Aren't you superior? Looking down your old-money, top-drawer nose at all the poor little ignoramuses who have some respect for a good, decent man, who contributed something good and worthwhile to the world. Isn't it funny?"

"Oh, come on, Bailey. I didn't mean it that way."

She was making him feel terrible. She was almost shaking with fury.

"Don't give me that. You meant it exactly that way. It's condescending and insulting to every Elvis fan in the world. And this whole Elvis-King-God angle. Is that what you think? Is that what you want your readers to think? Not only do you insult my admiration for a fine musician, and make me into an idiotic yahoo, but you have the gall to mock my faith, on top of it?"

"I didn't mean it that way, Bailey. I swear it. I wasn't thinking—"

"Oh, you were thinking," she spat. "You know what you were thinking? You were thinking, 'I'm a snot-nosed, self-important, pompous horse's ass. What can I do next?' *That's* what you were thinking."

"Damn it, Bailey—"

"No, damn you, Gabriel. Damn you and your arrogance and your stupid article and your lies. Get the hell out."

He stood, feeling slapped, clutching the foam cups of coffee. "You don't mean that."

"The hell I don't. Get out. Go back to Manhattan, or Connecticut. Go have a good laugh at the idiots at Graceland. Go marry some cold-assed tennis-playing broad with a tortoise shell headband who went to the right schools. But don't stand there, having made a mockery of everything I am, and everything I respect, and expect me to actually *like* you. Get out, or I'll call the desk and have you thrown out."

93

She threw the laptop computer onto the rumpled bed and turned her back.

He stood there, completely at a loss for words. He tried to remember if anyone had ever actually shrieked at him before. No. People didn't *shriek*, in his world. It just wasn't done.

"It would never work, Gabriel," she said, very softly.

He looked at her back, the dark curls falling over the frayed neck of her T-shirt, the sharp, squared line of her shoulders.

"I'm terribly sorry." It was all he could think of to say.

He waited, and she said nothing.

Carefully, he set the cups of coffee down on the night table, and picked up his computer.

The words *The End* glowed up at him in amber.

He clicked it off, picked up his leather jacket from the luggage stand, and waited.

"I'm sorry," he repeated.

She didn't move.

He left, closing the door quietly behind him.

Chapter Nine

He stepped out into the cold air and turned back briefly to look at the hotel.

The Original Heartbreak Hotel.

He managed an ironic smile. Well. Maybe he could use that one day. Not soon, though. Maybe never.

The street seemed eerie and deserted. Well, what did one expect, at this hour on Christmas? Everyone would be with their families, wouldn't they?

He reached into his pocket, took out his notebook, reached for his pen, and began writing.

> *Go check into the Peabody.*
> *Call home, Xmas greetings.*
> *Call airport, make reservations.*
> *Have lunch.*

The longer he looked at his schedule, the stupider it seemed. *Have lunch?* What was the point of that? Of course, he had to have lunch. When you were hungry, you ate, whether it was on your schedule or not.

"Excuse me."

He looked up.

It was Santa Claus. Or rather, it was the man dressed as Santa Claus who had been standing outside the door ringing his bell since they had arrived.

"I believe you're standing in my spot, sir."

The man sounded like an Elvis impersonator. Or maybe he'd been in Memphis too long. Everyone was sounding like Elvis. Actually, beneath the fake beard, with his dark sideburns showing, this man actually looked a little like Elvis.

Wonderful. Elvis Claus. He needed to get back to Manhattan.

"I'm surprised you're working on Christmas," Gabriel said. "I would have thought you'd be finished for the season."

He wondered why he felt the need to make conversation. Probably avoidance. Anything to keep from thinking about Bailey.

"Not work on Christmas? I'm Santa Claus, aren't I? Can you think of a better day to work?"

"I suppose not," Gabriel answered politely.

"Of course, it's not my idea of work, at all. You put on a Santa suit someday, you'll see what I mean. You hear things, you learn things."

"Really," Gabriel said.

The man was setting his little red bucket on its stand, but he looked up sharply at Gabriel when he spoke, arching a dark brow that contrasted sharply with his fake beard.

"Yes, sir, you do. Like just now, you said, 'Really,' but that wasn't what you meant. You meant, 'Quit your yammering, and spare me your pearls of wisdom, and let me go off and sulk. I'm through being polite.' Something like that."

Well. What could he say to that?

Apparently, Santa didn't really require an answer.

"No, sir," he said, drawing on his fake fur–trimmed mittens, "I don't say too much. Mostly I listen. And I learn. And you know what I've learned about Christmas?"

"I've no idea," Gabriel said, and he meant it.

"It's a miracle. Every year, if you let it. It's about something great coming where you least expect it. Now, there's some never see it. They pass it by. Too busy, too smart, who the heck knows? But I know this—we none of us get too many years. One day it's over. And when you go, what are you gonna regret?"

Gabriel didn't answer.

"It's about life!" Santa said, wiggling his dark brows. "Brand-new, every day! Don't you waste it, friend. Go for broke. Hope, and try, and do whatever it is that you've gotta do, even if it seems like believing in foolishness. Like believing in Santa Claus. Like believing in magic. It's there, if you want it. If not . . ." Santa adjusted his hat, and drew his red bell from his pocket. "Well, what the heck is it all about?"

"I don't know."

"Well, I suggest you figure it out. Merry Christmas."

"Merry Christmas," Gabriel answered. He took one more look at his schedule, then stuffed the notepad into the pocket of his black leather jacket. Inside the deep inner pocket, the tissue paper crackled around Elvis's shirt.

Then he turned down Blues Street toward Beale, walking alone through the quiet streets toward the Peabody.

He couldn't remember who had recommended the Peabody Hotel to him, but the moment the doorman swung open the doors and admitted him to the grand lobby, he felt at home.

No, this wasn't the Original Heartbreak Hotel. This was a true, grand old hotel, classically beautiful, with soaring pillars and arches, sweeping staircases, and perfectly uniformed staff. It made him think of the Plaza in Manhattan—perfectly appointed, perfectly run. A tasteful Christmas tree, sparkling with a million white lights, soared into the air, almost to the balconies of the second floor. A sparkling fountain made a soothing noise in the refined and subdued quiet of the lobby.

The concierge greeted him with a polite smile, while he explained that he had missed his flight from St. Louis, and had been unable to keep his reservation.

"No, sir, that's not a problem at all. If you'll just sign here . . ."

He accepted the pen, hesitated, and then signed, *G. Charles Van Dusen*. There. Gabriel didn't exist anymore. He was Charles again, in a familiar and comfortable world.

This hotel was just what he needed, to forget about Bailey. Elegant and predictable, no paintings on velvet, no rumors of ghosts, a mecca of sanity in the Elvis-obsessed world of Memphis. He looked over at the little round tables surrounding the atrium fountain, set with gleaming silver and linen. He'd bet there were no fried peanut butter–and-banana sandwiches on this menu.

"Your luggage, sir?"

"Lost in St. Louis," he said briefly, accepting his room key and turning away. Even saying *St. Louis* reminded him of Bailey.

He started toward the bank of elevators. He felt like Charles again. Nothing unexpected would happen here, nothing to make him think of Bailey.

The elevator doors slid open, and he stopped dead in his tracks.

A uniformed bellman appeared, unrolling a length of red carpet across the shining marble floors, as if preparing for a visiting dignitary.

But behind him, from the elevator, emerged another bellman, who bowed, gestured, and escorted out a gaggle of ducks.

Ducks. He stopped still in his tracks, staring with disbelief as the gang of ducks, waddling and quacking, made their way across the red carpet, over to the fountain. One after the other, they hopped in, splashing and flapping their wings.

Their escort quickly rolled up the red carpet, tucking it beneath his arm, and started back to the elevator. "Going up, sir?" he asked Gabriel politely.

Gabriel looked back at the fountain. "Excuse me—did I just see that?"

The young man laughed. "Yes, sir. Those are the Peabody ducks. They're a tradition here. Every morning we escort them down from their suite, and every evening we escort them back up. They're quite famous, actually.''

Bailey would have loved it. She would have laughed. She would love that the humble ducks had their own suite, that they waddled over a red carpet to swim in a marble fountain.

He looked at the ducks, imagining it.

One of the ducks, poised on the edge of the fountain, looked directly at him, quacked loudly, and jumped into the water.

He gave a defeated sigh. "All right," he said to the duck. "All right. I give up."

He took out his schedule, and right after *Have lunch,* he carefully wrote, *Get Bailey to the Peabody. Show her ducks.*

He turned to the bellman, who was still standing and holding the elevator door for him. "Can you recommend a good florist in the area? Anyone who might be open today?"

By the time she had arrived back from church, the first three dozen roses had arrived—glorious, fragrant roses in jewel red. Each of them bore a card with the same inscription: *I'm sorry.*

She wanted to throw them out the window, but they were too beautiful.

Ignoring them, she went for a walk.

By the time she came back, another two bouquets had arrived—orchids, this time, pale pink and lavender, smelling of exotic tropical places.

The card said: *Perhaps you don't like roses. I'm sorry.*

She almost smiled. She thought perhaps she should pack and leave, but curiosity restrained her.

The flowers kept coming—every half hour. There were baskets of carnations, and jewel red poinsettias, white roses mixed with evergreen fronds, paper whites smelling of spring. Her room turned into an enchanted jungle.

Finally at five o'clock, when she was sure that he had emptied every florist shop in Memphis, the final tribute arrived—a five-foot, fully decorated tree, covered with tiny angels and strings of pearls. A paper rested in the branches, rolled into a scroll and tied with ribbons.

Unable to resist, she unrolled it. It was written like a ransom note, letters cut from newspapers and magazines and pasted together.

I am desperate. I have Elvis's shirt. If you ever want to see it again, meet me in the lobby of the Peabody Hotel at seven, or I will sacrifice the shirt to the ducks.

Puzzled, she read the note, and then reread it.

Finally, defeated, she collapsed on the bed, surrounded by flowers, and laughed.

For a while, he hadn't thought she would come.

But she did. She came walking through the front doors of the lobby, wearing the same black dress she had worn last night. She had twisted her black curls up again, but tonight they were decorated with red roses.

His heart lurched at the sight of her. Any doubts he'd had vanished. He leaped up from the settee where he'd been waiting, and hurried forward to meet her.

"Merry Christmas, Bailey."

She smiled hesitantly, her eyes wary as she looked around. "Some place," she said. "Is this the kind of hotel you usually stay at?"

He nodded, uncertain of how to proceed.

"Wow," she said softly, her eyes taking in the colonnaded staircases, the sparkling fountain, the candlelit tables. A string quartet was stationed by the foot of the towering tree, classical music wafting sweetly into the air. "Boy, the Original Heartbreak must have seemed like quite a dive to you."

"Actually, it was a delight," he said.

"This is a different world, though," she said.

He nodded. "Well, welcome to it." He led her to the fountain, where a waiter stood ready to pull out her chair. More flowers waited for her on the table—white roses, this time.

The ducks, paddling around the fountain, glanced at them with cursory interest.

He told her about the ducks, how they arrived by elevator

100

every morning, how they had their own suite, and watched her face relax, saw the laughter rise to her eyes.

The waiter arrived, silent and efficient, and opened a bottle of champagne. He poured two glasses, left the bottle in a silver bucket, and disappeared.

"Okay, where do I start?" Gabriel asked softly.

She said nothing, just looked at her champagne, her dark lashes brushing her pale cheeks.

"I'm sorry. You were right. The article was condescending and unkind, and I had no right to use your remarks out of context. Will you please accept my apology?"

She hesitated.

"I've trashed the article," he said. "Killed it. It will never see print."

"I accept your apology," she said softly. The hint of a dimple was beginning to show under the curve of her cheek.

"I thank you for that. Now, Merry Christmas." He offered her the tissue-wrapped package, and watched the color spring into her cheeks as she unfolded the faded shirt.

"Oh, Gabriel. I don't believe it." She ran her finger over the worn stitches in the arm. "Is it really mine?"

"Forever."

"Would you really have sacrificed it to the ducks?" she demanded, clutching the faded denim to her heart.

He considered. "Bailey, when I'm with you, I honestly don't know what I'd do. No, probably not. Not unless I was sure you'd jump in to save it."

"I would have," she said, and finally laughed. The sound sparkled in his ears, sweeter than all the Christmas bells in the world.

She lifted her champagne and took a sip, her eyes sparkling over the rim. "This is great. The best I've ever had."

"Well, wait until dinner. They tell me the chef here is one of the best in the country. Have you eaten yet?"

She nodded. "But I can always eat again," she assured him. "I only had two hound doggies."

He laughed. "For Christmas dinner?"

She shrugged and lifted her glass, watching the bubbles

101

Amy Elizabeth Saunders

swirl and dance in the pale gold. "Isn't that beautiful?"

"Bailey—you're beautiful."

She looked at him, tears in her eyes. "I didn't get you anything for Christmas. I mean, nothing like this . . ." She gestured around at the champagne, the faded shirt, the string quartet.

"Bailey O'Connor, you've given me much more. You've given me Christmas, to start with. And a new perspective on life. You've given me joy. I could never give you enough back. But let me try." He waited for the last, sweet notes of Bach to die out from the string quartet, and then nodded at them.

The violinist nodded back; then the quartet lifted their bows and started to play—Elvis, of course—"I Can't Help Falling In Love," the song he had heard her singing in the shower.

Her eyes glowed like Christmas stars.

"Where do I begin, Bailey? What do you want? Do you want me to move to St. Louis? I'll do it. Will you come to Manhattan? Let's do it. What do you want to do with your life? I'll help you. Anything. Hell, if you want to stay here in Memphis, we can do that, and never go home again."

"Are you nuts?" she asked him, laughing with tears in her eyes.

"Hey, that's my line. Maybe you are, maybe I am. But I mean it. And this is all I want from you—promise me that I'll never, ever have to spend another Christmas without you. For the rest of my life."

"Are you asking me to marry you?" she demanded, her eyes widening with shock.

"I believe I am. Yes, I am. Most definitely."

She put her champagne down on the table. "Gabriel, you can't propose to someone you've only known for two days."

"I just did," he said, and waited.

She sat still, one graceful hand over her mouth.

"Okay," she said, very softly. "Okay, Gabriel. Maybe only fools rush in, but I'll go with my heart on this."

"Thank you," was all he could think of to say. He stood, offering her his hand, and when she rose from her chair, he

102

gathered her against him, feeling her heart beat next to his.

They stood together like that, while the sounds of Elvis's love song floated sweetly through the pine-scented Christmas magic of the beautiful room, the lights on the tree twinkling like a million enchanted stars.

Gabriel knew that, as long as he lived, he would never forget that feeling—the Christmas that he quit living in the practical world, and reached out into the magic of the heart, and began living his life for the joy of it.

"Merry Christmas, Gabriel," Bailey whispered, her breath soft and warm by his ear.

"A thousand Merry Christmases," he whispered back. "Merry Christmas forever."

Linda Jones

Always on my Mind

*For Tom-boy and Tom, jazz musicians by deed and at heart,
and the best father and brother a girl could ask for.
Elvis Lives.*

Chapter One

This was going to be much harder than she'd imagined.

Laura closed her eyes, gathered her strength, took a deep breath, and said the words: "Michael, you have a daughter." The revelation sounded much too blunt to her ears. Speaking more softly, she tried again. "*We* have a daughter."

This was all wrong, too sudden, too abrupt, too damn late—about four years too late. With a sigh Laura opened her eyes and stared at her reflection in the mirror. If she couldn't confess in an empty hotel bathroom, how could she possibly confess to Michael?

But what choice did she have? When Megan had turned up those big green eyes and asked, after one of her very first days of preschool, where her daddy was, Laura knew everything was about to change.

Not that Laura hadn't thought a million times about telling Michael. As soon as she'd discovered she was pregnant she'd gone to the club where he played piano, only to be told that he and the band were off on a six-month tour as the opening act for some aging blues singer who was trying to make a comeback. The wind had gone out of her sails then, when she realized that he was gone. With Michael, the music always came first. Always.

That was what their last fight, Christmas Eve five years ago, had been all about. Laura had been ready for stability, commitment, picket fences and a mortgage and a minivan. Michael wasn't ready to give up his music. He couldn't promise her that he'd ever be able to give it up, that he'd ever be able to offer her what she wanted.

He'd chosen his music over her, and she'd known then that he always would. She loved Michael, she'd never stopped loving him, but how could she live with him knowing that she'd always come second?

Eight and a half months later Megan had been born.

One other time, when she'd come home for Christmas when Megan was two, Laura had heard that Michael was back in Memphis and playing in a Beale Street club. She'd left her mother baby-sitting and tearfully pleading that she not do this foolish thing, to drive into Memphis on Christmas Eve. On the short drive to Beale Street she'd envisioned a hundred possibilities. That he'd see her and run into her arms, that he'd never forgiven her, that he'd never stopped loving her. With every passing second she grew more anxious.

When she'd stepped into the club she'd seen him sitting at his piano, oblivious to her presence, lost in his music as always. He was playing something slow and sad and just slightly jazzy, his eyes closed as if that helped him to feel each and every note. Afraid to move forward, she'd stood there and listened and stared for a long moment. His hair had been a little too long, wavy and black and thick, falling over his cheek and hiding too much of his face from her. She wanted, needed, to see more.

She'd stood numbly just inside the doorway, wondering how she could tell him about Megan, until a woman left the bar to saunter toward the piano with a smile, to step up on the stage and sit on the edge of the piano bench and kiss Michael on the cheek. He'd lifted his head and smiled, then flashed that wide grin Laura had never quite been able to forget.

Without thinking she'd turned and run. Her mother was right, she'd told herself as she had run to her car. She had Megan, she had a good job and a wonderful apartment in Birmingham, and she didn't need the heartache anymore. Laura had convinced herself long ago that Michael Arnett was nothing but heartache.

But Megan deserved to know her father, and maybe Michael deserved to know he had a child. That didn't mean anything would change between them. His music would always come first. She needed stability, for herself and for Megan. How could they ever make something like that work? It was impossible, just as it had been five years ago. Heaven help her, exactly how was she going to tell Michael that he had a four-year-old daughter?

A soft knock on the door saved her from choking out the words again. "Mommy," Megan called softly, "are you finished? I have to go."

"Just a minute," Laura answered, her voice falsely bright as she checked her image in the mirror once again. She'd changed a lot in five years. The last of the baby fat in her face had finally fallen away, she'd learned how to style her fine hair and how to apply makeup, and there were more business suits and pumps than jeans and sneakers in her closet these days. She'd grown up in the past five years. What would Michael think of her?

She was about to find out.

As she opened the door Megan rushed in, smile wide and eyes bright, chubby cheeks pink from running around the hotel room and exploring every corner. "You look so pwetty," Megan said, turning her head up so that her strawberry-blond ponytail swung gently down her back. Her bangs needed trimming again—fine and coppery, they brushed her pale eyebrows. "Do you hab a business meeting?"

"Yes," Laura said, breaking her vow never to lie to her child. What if Michael didn't care anything about having a little girl? What if he didn't want to be a part of Megan's life? This way, if her father rejected her, Megan would never know it. She would do anything to protect her daughter—even lie.

Very gently, she used her fingers to brush her child's silky bangs to the side. "I have a meeting. Jennifer will stay with you, and I promise I won't be gone long."

Laura stepped through the open bathroom door to see Jennifer, her sixteen-year-old niece, sitting cross-legged on the hotel bed she'd claimed for herself. Megan very forcefully closed the door, and Jennifer's head popped up so that her newly cut dark hair bounced.

"Wow," she whispered, and a grin bloomed on her face. "You look gorgeous. Whoever this new client is, he doesn't stand a chance."

Laura very carefully touched the smooth curl of blond hair that touched her neck. Nearly thirty years old, and she was as nervous as a girl on her first date. She'd tried on three outfits before deciding on the blue dress and matching heels, and she'd taken a painfully long time to style her hair. Professional and cool, that was the look she was going for, but at the same time she didn't want to come off like a bitter, plain spinster. So the heels were a little higher than most of the sensible pumps she owned, and she wore a little more makeup than usual, and this dress was just a bit too snug. Not tight, of course, but more formfitting than she normally went in for. She could deny it to herself all night, but the fact of the matter was that she wanted to look good for Michael.

"Thanks," she murmured, the more cowardly part of her suddenly wishing she'd settled for the plain gray dress she'd originally pulled from the closet. "And thanks for coming with me. I . . . I can't take Megan with me to this meeting, and I didn't want to leave her with my mother. Mom's so busy with the holidays coming."

Jennifer fell back onto the bed. "I should be thanking you. I've had just about all the family time I can stand, and we just got in Friday. If I'd stayed at Grandma's she'd have me doing kitchen duty for the next four days, and the place is so crowded. I mean, *everybody's* there this year. I had to share a bed with Heather this weekend, and she *talks* in her *sleep*. And I hate to say this, but I really dread the next few years with Megan and Katie, the way they are together."

Katie was her sister Karen Marlow Gentry's little girl. A year younger than Megan, Katie had always been difficult. From the time she was a baby, the Marlow women had had to take turns walking, rocking, and entertaining her. Together, Katie and Megan were like a toddler version of Butch and Sundance.

Laura collected her black coat from the closet and slipped it on. The lightweight wool was just right for the unpredictable Memphis weather. Her eyes roamed over the odd hotel room as Jennifer listed the failings of her aunts and uncles and cousins, all of whom had descended upon the Marlow house for Christmas.

If only she'd decided to go through with this weeks ago, maybe she could have reserved a room in a nicer hotel. This place wasn't exactly a rattrap, but it was definitely unusual. There was a portrait of Elvis—bright colors on black velvet— hanging over the television. The bedspreads on the side-by-side double beds were a vivid crimson that matched the color of Elvis's jacket perfectly, and the drapes were a heavy and faded blue. The rest of the furniture looked like it was a mixture of old elegance and newer, cheaper additions. The red velvet chair by the window was the only comfortable piece of furniture in the room.

Megan came bursting from the bathroom, her arms spread wide as she barreled toward her mother. "Good-bye hug!" she shouted, throwing her arms around Laura's legs and squeezing tight. Laura dropped down for a real face-to-face hug, needing the strength and love her daughter gave her more than ever. This was turning out to be so hard.

"How many days until Christmas?" Megan asked for the third time on this very long day.

"Four," Laura answered, squeezing tight. "Four days that will fly by so fast, Christmas will be here before you know it."

"Don't forget what I asked Santa for," Megan whispered in Laura's ear. "I want my daddy."

* * *

"I'll Be Home for Christmas" again. Bad as it was, Michael knew it could be worse. If one more drunken fool asked him to play "Jingle Bell Rock," he was going to do someone bodily harm.

He let his fingers move automatically over the keys of his cherished Bösendorfer nine-foot grand piano, the familiar Christmas song coming to him so easily that he was able to study the respectable Monday-night crowd as he played. He positively hated Christmas music, but it was his job to keep the customers happy and drinking, and if it took a dozen renditions a night of "I'll Be Home for Christmas" to make that happen, well, that was the price he paid for this particular gig.

One of his producers—and something of a friend—Spencer Modine, was here with a new woman. He was seated at his favorite table. The cute and definitely distracted blonde he was with looked anything *but* comfortable, wearing a business suit and alternately babbling and playing with her chili. The uptight woman was definitely not Modine's usual type, but they seemed to be . . . involved.

Michael played the notes, but he'd much rather be working on the new song Modine was waiting for. Dammit, "Rainy Night" was so close to finished he could almost hear it. Almost. The end wasn't quite right, and when he sat there after hours and played the damn thing again and again it just didn't sound complete.

But for now he was on automatic pilot, keeping the patrons happy. The crowd had been requesting Christmas songs since just after Thanksgiving, but there were only four more days to go. Four more days, and Christmas would be over for another year. *Thank God.*

There had been a time, he remembered, when he'd liked Christmas. Memories of the years before his parents had died were vague and too few, but they were good memories. He had fewer fond recollections of the perfectly organized and stress-filled Christmases after he'd gone to live with his Aunt Dinah, the aging and unmarried great-aunt who'd decided a young man needed something constructive to keep him busy.

Something like piano lessons. At least for *that* he would always be grateful.

After he'd met Laura, he'd loved the holiday. It was their time. They'd met just two days before Christmas, and by Christmas Eve he had known that she was the one. She'd become the other part of himself, the one person in the world he could rely on . . . at least for a couple of years. And then everything had fallen apart. Now he couldn't play a Christmas tune or see a Christmas tree without thinking of her.

Other women had come and gone in the past five years, but he was always alone at Christmas. He found a way to drive them away, as if sharing the holiday with anyone but Laura was somehow unfaithful. Many a Christmas Day he'd sat alone and wondered if this was his way of punishing himself for not being everything she'd wanted him to be.

A couple of years ago he'd almost done it. He'd made it all the way to Christmas Eve with a fun kind of girl whose name now eluded him. He'd met her at a Halloween party, and she'd hung around until he thought he might actually make it through Christmas that year *with* someone.

But on Christmas Eve he'd done it again. His mind had played a trick on him, teasing him with a false glimpse of Laura out of the corner of his eye, a glimpse so real he'd chased the phantom out the door, leaving the nameless, beautiful girl sitting on the piano bench wondering why he'd lit out of the place like a bat out of hell.

There had been nothing on the street, of course. No Laura, no phantom, no nothing. He'd walked for blocks, just in case, looking around corners and in sunken doorways. Just in case. Before the clock struck twelve he'd managed to chase what's-her-name away. By sunrise "Only a Shadow" had been written. A few months later it was recorded by a well-established rock star, and less than a year later an up-and-coming country singer had put it on his CD. The checks had come rolling in, and the requests for more songs followed.

It was a good gig. He got to play piano, write songs, and make a decent living, and very few people knew he was the man behind those maudlin love songs. There weren't even very many people who knew that he owned this club, Forever Blue. He liked it that way.

Tonight, it seemed, his mind had decided to play the same trick on him again. The woman who stepped through the club door moved like Laura—graceful, with a certain unique elegance that had haunted him for five years. No one else moved that way.

It was not a trick of his mind this time, he realized with a deep quiver as she turned her face to him. His hands continued to play effortlessly as he latched his eyes to hers. The years fell away, and it was just yesterday that she'd confessed how much she loved him. The smile came easily to his face, a smile of welcome and wonder and maybe even love.

Ah, but it wasn't yesterday, was it? He hadn't seen her for five years. She'd moved on, or so her mother had said on the occasion he'd foolishly worked up the nerve to make the short trip to their home in the suburbs. It had been two years to the day after Laura had left him. He'd never forget what Mrs. Marlow had said, would never forget the angry expression on her face. Laura was happy, and she didn't need a no-good musician showing up out of nowhere to screw up her life.

Michael knew too well what would make Laura happy. A husband, a home, a family. His smile faded and he turned his eyes to the keys beneath his hands. He'd stood there in the doorway of the comfy Marlow middle-class home and heard a baby's cry from upstairs. A moment later, looking over Mrs. Marlow's shoulder, he'd caught a glimpse of Laura at the top of the stairs. There was a baby in her arms, a tiny, squalling baby Laura had cooed at as she very carefully descended the stairs. A man came hurtling down the stairs behind her, to smile and take the baby from her arms. Michael had managed to whisper, "Hers?" and Mrs. Marlow had hesitated and then nodded once.

He'd turned away and not looked back. The door had closed quietly behind him, and still he didn't look back. So what the hell was she doing here now?

He looked up just in time to see the door swing shut, and Laura was gone.

Without thinking, he jumped from the piano bench in the middle of "I'll Be Home For Christmas" and headed for the door, ignoring the shouted "Hey!" from the drunk who'd requested this particular Christmas torture, and the surprised "Where are you going?" from the bartender, and the discordant ring of a song unfinished. Modine actually laughed, but Michael didn't even look his way. His eyes were on the door.

He wasn't going to let her get away this time. Maybe it was a mistake that she'd wandered into this particular club tonight. Chance, destiny, misfortune. Maybe she'd seen him sitting there and run away because she didn't want to see him ever again. And then again maybe it wasn't a mistake at all. Maybe she'd come here for him.

A blast of cold air hit him as he burst through the door, but he saw her right away. She was walking fast, but she wasn't running. Not exactly. Those heels she wore weren't made for running.

"Laura?" He called her name, and her steady gait faltered. But she didn't turn around. She didn't even slow down. He could make a fool of himself and run after her, or he could salvage his dignity and let her go. If he let her go he would always wonder. . . . He took off at a slow jog, following her, weaving past a couple of tourists and keeping his eyes on Laura's back. She passed through the light from a street lamp, and the stream of light shone on her golden hair. He increased his pace, just a little.

With every step, he gained on her. He whispered her name, and once again her step faltered. Heaven help him, he was almost close enough to reach out and touch her shoulder. Another step, and he reached out to take her arm and bring a halt to her flight.

She didn't fight him off, jerk herself free, and continue her escape. If she had, he would have let her go, he swore it. Her shoulders rose and fell with the deep, stilling breath she took, and then she turned to face him and he let his hand fall away.

God, she was as beautiful as ever. Big blue eyes in a pixie's face, hair gold as the sun, a mouth so ripe he itched to kiss it. She licked those lips nervously, blinked twice, and said, "Hi."

Where have you been? I missed you, I need you, don't ever leave me again. All that and more went through his mind in an instant, but his heart was rising and threatening to choke him and all he could manage was a weak "Hi" himself.

They stood there silently for a minute, maybe longer. He couldn't take his eyes off of her, couldn't think of anything sufficiently earth-shattering to say. Finally he gathered the strength to raise his hand and touch her cheek.

She didn't flinch, didn't turn away from his touch, and that was when he found the courage to smile. This was his Laura, showing up out of nowhere like a Christmas gift to end all Christmas gifts, coming to him when he needed her most. She was scared, a little; he could see the uncertainty in her eyes, the gentle quiver of her bottom lip.

His hand slipped to the back of her neck, and he lowered his mouth to hers for a brief kiss, for a caress he remembered, dreamed of, wrote love songs about, and she didn't hesitate in kissing him back.

It was a soft kiss, a gentle joining, and in that instant he was home.

Chapter Two

She didn't want the kiss to end, but of course it did. Michael drew away slowly, hesitantly, taking his mouth from hers and very slowly sliding his warm hand from her neck. She'd never been able to think clearly when he kissed her, and apparently that hadn't changed. Her brain was addled, and all she could think about was that kiss. She wanted another one. Now.

His hand rested on her arm, not too tightly but with a definite possessiveness. He leaned close, and his body, clad entirely in black as always, sheltered her from the too-cool breeze. Still, she'd only said the single word *hi*. He must think she was a complete moron.

"I thought I'd look you up while I was home for Christmas," she said indifferently, much too casually, given the situation. Maybe not so casually as she'd thought, since her voice had an uncustomary breathless quality.

Michael grinned. "Good," he whispered.

Her entire body tensed. "And then I thought maybe it wasn't such a good idea after all."

The fingers on her arm tightened ever so slightly. "You're not going to run again, are you?"

Laura shook her head, never taking her eyes from Michael's. Those green eyes were so much like Megan's that looking at them caused an unwanted jolt to her senses. It wasn't just the color; it was the shape, the clarity, a devilish twinkle. She needed to tell him why she'd come back, but not here, not like this. Not while they stood on the sidewalk, and not while her heart was pounding a mile a minute.

Michael slipped his arm through hers and led her back toward Forever Blue. Later, when she'd recovered from seeing and kissing him, she'd tell him about Megan.

"Let me play another song or two, and then I'll cut out early and we'll go somewhere for coffee."

Thirty years old, and he was still playing in juke joints. "They won't mind if you leave early?"

The grin he flashed was familiar and heartwarming. "What can they say? I work cheap."

Laura sighed. She couldn't help herself. Michael was talented, but music was a hard way to make a living. Very few aspiring musicians actually made it. He was so smart, he could do anything. With that smile and his natural charm he'd have made one hell of a salesman. When she'd mentioned that to him years ago he'd laughed at her. Michael Arnett a *salesman*? Maybe the very idea *was* laughable, she thought as she looked at him now.

He led her into Forever Blue, and all eyes turned toward them: the bartender and a beautiful cocktail waitress in a very short skirt, a man who had obviously imbibed too freely and a woman with big red hair, and all the rest. She didn't want to look too closely at the man who'd entered the club on crutches, since she'd almost barreled him over in her haste to escape. Still, she glanced at him out of the corner of her eye. He was now sitting with an attractive brunette, and didn't seem to be holding a grudge.

A fair-haired man wearing a Hawaiian-print shirt sat comfortably at a table they passed close by. The woman he was with was wearing a very nice navy blue suit, and would have been the very picture of decorum in this menagerie if she hadn't been singing at the top of her lungs—and rather badly.

Michael ignored them all. He placed Laura at a table near the stage and jumped onto the platform, and without a word he sat at the piano and began to play. She didn't know the name of the piece he played, but it was fast and bluesy and intricate. It was her turn to smile. Michael always went to the music when he was nervous. Some people smoked; some went in for a primal scream or a long run. Michael Arnett played the piano.

And what a piano it was, taking up nearly the entire stage. How many juke joints had a grand piano like this one? Not many, she was sure.

When the piece ended abruptly, Michael looked over the small audience. "One more number, folks, and then I'm out of here for the night."

" 'I'll Be Home for Christmas,' " the drunk called out sullenly. "You didn't finish last time, and I want my song."

"No!" The woman with the big red hair pouted. " 'Jingle Bell Rock.' That's what I want to hear."

For a couple of uncomfortable minutes, the two shouted at one another across the room. Their voices got louder, the insults became personal, and the redhead wickedly pitched a pretzel toward the drunk. Laura looked up to see Michael staring at the keys before him, lost in thought. If he heard the argument he paid no mind to the words.

When he laid his hands on the keys to play a silvery chord, there was silence from the dissenters, as they waited to see what he would play.

Bless his peacemaker heart, he played both—at the same time. The melodies intertwined into something beautiful and exotic and hauntingly entangled. No one in the place said a word. Even the bartender stopped what he was doing and leaned against the bar to listen and grin.

Laura listened, and smiled, and watched. He gave so much of himself to the music, and she could see it in his face and the set of his shoulders. There had always been something inexplicably erotic to her about watching Michael's hands as

119

he played, exquisite, strong, long-fingered hands that moved with ease over the keys. She'd fallen in love with those hands before she'd ever spoken a word to him.

When the unusual song was finished there was a long moment of stunned silence. Someone behind her let out a single whoop. The cheerful cry was followed by a burst of applause that went well beyond simply polite.

True to his word, Michael left the stage. He took Laura's hand as she rose, and together they headed for the door. They walked past the drunk, who placed his forehead on the table and muttered, "I'm confused."

When they passed the table where the singing woman and her companion sat, Michael nodded but didn't slow down. "I'll have that song ready for you next week, Modine."

The man named Modine just nodded in response, and the next thing Laura knew they were at the exit. Michael turned and waved to the bartender, who was a barrel of a man with a crew cut.

"Chuck, I'm taking off," Michael said easily. "How about a round of drinks on the—" He stopped in midsentence, glanced down at Laura, and after a moment of silence he finished. "How about a round of drinks on the piano player. Put it on my tab."

There was a smattering of applause, and the bartender raised his gruff voice. "On your tab?"

"Yep." With that short response, Michael ushered her from Forever Blue and onto Beale Street.

It wasn't fair, but then life wasn't fair, was it?

He wanted Laura back. There hadn't been a day in the past five years that he hadn't wanted her back, but right now the need was immediate and pressing. Knowing Laura, it wouldn't be easy. Beneath that reticent demeanor she was probably as stubborn as always, and there would no doubt be problems to work out.

One problem he wouldn't have to face: there was no wedding ring on her finger, and he knew his traditional, conventional, by-the-book Laura wouldn't be here if she were still a married woman.

Yes, he definitely wanted her back, but not with the confession that he was richer than he'd ever dreamed, that she'd been wrong when she'd said making it in the music business was impossible. He wanted her to take him as he was. For better or for worse, for richer or for poorer.

There was a coffee shop a couple of blocks up from Forever Blue that had recently reopened. No one there knew him, and that was where he took her.

They claimed a booth in the corner, and he ordered coffee for both of them. Regular, even at this time of night. He rarely went to sleep before dawn anyway, and caffeine had never bothered Laura. If he remembered correctly, and when it came to Laura he was sure he did, she could drink a pot of coffee and then slip into bed and fall immediately into a deep sleep.

How to begin? Dammit, this was much too awkward for his liking. Even after the waitress placed their large mugs of coffee on the table, Laura fidgeted. She bit her lower lip, briefly and just once, and she didn't look directly at him anymore. If he could just kiss her again the awkwardness would go away, he knew it.

He tried to think of something brilliant to say, and failed miserably. "Still a bean counter?"

At least that got a smile out of her. A small smile, but it was a start. "An accountant," she corrected. "Yes." She finally looked him square in the eye again, and the effect was immediate and powerful, as though he'd been punched in the gut, or the heart. "You're still the piano man, and better than ever from what I heard tonight."

It was an old joke, and not a very funny one. How had a bean counter and a piano man who had no beans ever gotten together in the first place?

"And writing," she added softly. "I heard what you said to that man as we left."

She didn't say more, but he could read Laura easily. People didn't make a living writing songs, not in her world. In his world, however, they did quite nicely. "I play with it a little bit," he admitted.

Laura nodded and gave him a noncommittal hum, and her eyes dropped.

"So," he said, anxious to change the subject. "You're home for Christmas. Staying at your mother's?"

She shook her head. "No. We're staying at a hotel nearby. The Original Heartbreak Hotel over on Blues Street."

We. It was a small word, casually thrown out there and weighing on his mind like a ton of bricks. He didn't even realize he was going to repeat the word aloud until he heard it coming out of his mouth.

Laura went pale and bit her lip again, but she didn't lower her eyes. "My daughter and me," she said very softly and quickly. "I have a daughter," she added unnecessarily. "We have . . ." She swallowed hard and blinked twice. "We have the most outrageous room in this odd hotel, and I swear there are Elvis impersonators everywhere I turn. In the elevator, in the lobby, in the café, on the street. Megan doesn't know quite what to think of it, but there wasn't a lot to choose from. I waited too long to make my reservations, you see, and this was all I could find." She went on, her words coming faster and faster until Michael was afraid she would explode. Did she take a breath? He didn't think so.

"Just you and Megan?" he interrupted. God help him, he had to know.

"And Jennifer," Laura added more calmly. "Elaine's oldest daughter. She agreed to come along and baby-sit."

No husband mentioned, Michael noted with what had to be a noticeable sigh of relief. He found that right now he didn't care what had happened to the smiling man who had chased Laura down the stairs three years ago to take the baby from her arms. He didn't care if they were divorced or separated or if the bastard was dead. Laura was his. She always had been.

Her hand was resting on the table beside her mug, and he reached across to cover that hand with his. He was different with Laura, better; his heart and his soul were stronger. No way was she getting away from him again.

122

* * *

They'd been at the coffee shop for hours, and as they talked the awkwardness fell away, crumbling a bit at a time until it was as if they'd never been apart. They'd talked about everything, catching up the way old friends do, worried one minute that they wouldn't have anything to talk about, worried the next that there wouldn't be enough time to say everything that needed to be said.

She'd learned that Michael lived in a room over Forever Blue, performed in the club six or seven nights a week, and played with writing songs on the side. Obviously his beloved music hadn't been financially kind to him in the past five years, but he seemed healthy and happy.

Yes, they'd talked about everything . . . well, almost everything. She still hadn't told him that Megan was his daughter. She almost had, but she'd chickened out and started babbling. What was she supposed to do? Interrupt one of his stories about playing piano for the news flash? Interject it into one of her spiels about her daily routine? *I have an apartment in Birmingham, my baby sister Karen got married the summer after we broke up, and, oh, yes, Megan is your daughter.*

She was such a coward.

The place was closing up before they left their booth, and there was still so much left to say. Laura tried to look at this meeting as a single step in a long journey. Maybe tomorrow, or in a couple of days, she'd tell Michael about Megan.

They walked toward the hotel slowly, arm in arm, close but never close enough. How had she survived without this, without the touch, the closeness, the knowledge that Michael lived inside her heart and always would? She could see the hotel just a little more than a block away, and she slowed her step. Late as it was, scared as she was of what came next, she wasn't ready to leave him.

As if he read her mind, he stopped in the middle of the sidewalk and faced her. He wrapped his arms around her, slowly, as if he were afraid she'd object, then tighter when she answered by wrapping her arms around his waist.

"It's still good, isn't it?" he whispered.

123

She shuddered from the top of her head to her toes. Good? It was magic, exquisite, perfect. Well, almost perfect. There was one tiny untruth that stood between them and perfection. "Yes," she answered.

"Tomorrow, I want to meet Megan," he said, and Laura nearly jumped out of her skin.

"Tomorrow?" she squeaked.

"For lunch," he said. "I'll meet you at the café where we had coffee tonight. We can—"

"Not lunch!" Laura interrupted.

"Why not?"

She sighed. Well, he would have to know sooner or later, wouldn't he? "Megan is a little warrior, and food and drink are her weapons of choice."

He laughed, loud and long. That was not the reaction she was expecting.

"It isn't funny," she insisted. "You want an example? I haven't dated much in the past . . . well, in a while." Michael's smile faded away, but he continued to hold her tight. "There was this one man, an accountant I work with, and he was sitting on the couch waiting for me to get ready, and Megan attacked him with . . . with grape juice."

The smile came back. "How do you attack someone with grape juice?"

"It was one of those box drinks with a bendable straw. She just very calmly and innocently aimed and squeezed. A stream of grape juice hit the poor man square in the face, squirted all over his glasses, and then Megan aimed at his shirt—his *white* shirt, I might add—and what was left ended up in his lap."

Michael's smile had always tugged at her heart; it was so warm and real. It was the hint of dimples, she supposed, or maybe the way his expressive eyes lit up. He wasn't just smiling now; he was laughing. "I'll have to thank her."

"It isn't *that* funny," Laura said, but she found herself smiling, too. "And you should see what she can do with a peanut butter–and-jelly sandwich. One poor unsuspecting man, a blind date no less, ended up with a slice of bread on either knee, gooey side down.'' Michael laughed. ''It was a new suit,'' Laura added.

''You don't usually date the same man more than once, do you?'' Michael asked as his laughter died.

''Never,'' Laura admitted. ''As a matter of fact, I finally just . . . gave up.''

He was going to kiss her again. She saw it coming, in the tilt of his head, in a slight change in the pressure of his arms, and heaven help her, she could hardly wait. When his lips hovered over hers he whispered again. ''In that case I'm really going to have to thank Megan.''

When Michael kissed her she forgot the mistakes she'd made. She forgot that she should have told him everything before it had gone this far, forgot that she was here for Megan, not for herself.

He reluctantly pulled his lips away, and with a shake of his head turned her about and they resumed their journey toward the hotel. ''Lunch,'' he said huskily. ''Tomorrow at noon.''

Chapter Three

A thousand things could go wrong. Megan could decide she didn't like Michael, and he'd end up with ketchup on his face or a French fry up his nose. She could make a real brat of herself, which she sometimes did, and Michael would hate Megan before he even knew she was his daughter. And then again Michael might look into green eyes so much like his own and know the truth. Would he forgive her for not telling him? Five years ago, last night, anytime in between . . .

With nervous fingers, Laura brushed Megan's bangs away from her eyes. Sometimes she looked at this little girl and her heart nearly stopped. Megan was a brat sometimes, sure, but she was also beautiful and bright. And hers. She'd never known what possessiveness was until she'd held her baby. The protective instincts hadn't faded with time, but grown.

"Remember what I said," she said gently. "I want you to be on your best behavior today."

Megan answered with a wide-eyed and innocent nod of her head. "I'll be good, Mommy."

Laura returned to the bathroom to finish with her hair and

makeup, leaving the door open so she could keep an eye on Megan. Jennifer was still sleeping, and had groggily decided to skip lunch with Megan and Laura and Laura's old friend. Just as well. If Jennifer mentioned the nonexistent client Laura had invented to explain away these days in Memphis, there would be a lot more explaining to do.

Megan seemed to be in a particularly good mood this morning, and she was especially darling in her green jumper and white tights and black patent-leather Mary Janes. If they could just survive this lunch, everything would be fine. She repeated that assurance to herself again and again as she darkened her eyelashes and tried to decide which lipstick to wear.

She applied a little Misty Mauve before the mirror, and when she was finished she looked herself squarely in the eye. "Michael," she whispered. "Do you remember how I always said I wanted kids . . . ?" Her voice trailed off into nothing. No, that wasn't quite right, either. "And speaking of sex, we were always so careful, except for that one night. . . ." Laura sighed as her voice died. *How pathetic.*

Megan's voice was soft, but she was definitely carrying on a conversation. Jennifer had been up late watching a movie and wanted to sleep a while longer, so she certainly wouldn't be happy with a chatty four-year-old at her side. Laura went to the door to shush her daughter, and found that Jennifer wasn't on the receiving end of this monologue after all. Megan was facing the red velvet chair by the window, talking softly and using her hands for emphasis, as she always did.

Laura sighed. It seemed Princess Babbette was back. She had just recently convinced Megan to send this imaginary friend back to her imaginary castle. Princess Babbette was the one who colored on the walls, and spilled drinks on the carpet, and encouraged Megan to do things she would never think of on her own. Like squirting Bill with grape juice.

"Megan," Laura said as she stepped from the bathroom. "I thought we agreed that there wouldn't be any more imaginary friends."

Megan spun around as though she'd been caught with her hand in the cookie jar. Her eyes were wide, her hands were clasped unnaturally behind her back, and she rotated one toe of her Mary Janes against the faded carpet. "But he's not 'maginary."

"Megan Michelle Marlow, you're talking to a chair." Why couldn't Megan be sensible, like her mother, rather than an idealistic dreamer, like her father? Why couldn't she be content to play quietly with dolls that didn't talk back?

"The King isn't 'maginary. Sometimes he's inbisible, but he's real."

"The king?" Laura leaned, defeated already, against the doorjamb. She recognized the sparkle in Megan's eyes, and knew this was a losing battle and had been from the start. "Princess Babbette's father, I assume. Don't tell me. Babbette came home with all sorts of bad habits, and the king's here to meet the young lady who taught his little girl to squirt juice boxes at people and use carrot sticks as swords."

Megan covered her mouth and giggled, and then she glanced over her shoulder. The King had evidently decided to stand, and he was also evidently quite tall. "Yes," she said to a spot high above her head. "She *is* funny."

She supposed it was all too much for Megan: the holidays, the weird hotel, the sudden craving for a father.

"He's not Babbette's daddy," Megan corrected. "He's a different kind of king."

"What kind of king is he?" Laura asked wearily.

Megan spun around on the soles of her new shoes and pointed to the Elvis on velvet above the television. "He's that kind of king."

"Elvis." Laura sighed, dismayed.

"Elbis Pwesley," Megan said as she faced her mother again. "*The* King."

She could rant and rave, which never did any good, or she could continue to play along. "Young Elvis or old Elvis?"

Megan pursed her lips and thought about the question for a moment before she answered. "Old Elbis."

Laura looked at the blank wall behind Megan. "Too bad."

"He has to be pretty old," Megan clarified, "because he said he has a little girl, and he's bery tall, much taller than me." She leaned forward slightly and lowered her voice. "And he's bery pwetty. I wouldn't squirt any juice at him, Mommy, I pwomise."

"Young Elvis," Laura muttered.

Once the subject had been broached, Megan had no further reservations about sharing her knowledge. "He sang me to sleep last night. Oh, he has the pwettiest voice I eber heard." She glanced over her shoulder and looked up again, so that her fine coppery ponytail danced down her back. "You're *welcome* bery much," she said seriously.

Laura stifled a groan. "What did he sing?"

"A song about a teddy bear, and a Christmas song, and the pwettiest song I ever heard." She looked up again. "What was that last song?" She waited a moment, and then looked at Laura once again. "Amazing Gwace."

Laura wondered if it was too late to cancel lunch with Michael. Of course it was. Would he be terribly disappointed if she showed up without Megan? Ah, but Megan was the reason she was here. She was turning into such a coward. "Tell Elvis good-bye. We have a lunch date to keep."

There was a different crowd on Beale Street by day, a crowd Michael rarely saw. Tourists mostly, mingling with shop owners and a few locals. The sun was shining and it was dreadfully bright out. The street before him bordered on ordinary, the neon signs waiting dormant for sundown. By daylight you could tell how old the buildings were, how badly in need of repair some of them were.

He'd be at the coffee shop ten minutes early walking at this rate—the safe, ordinary café where no one knew him. Unless Laura agreed right quick to stay and they got everything out and into the open, they were going to see an awful lot of that café.

A familiar face appeared in the doorway of a popular restaurant, Jackie's Place. It was Jackie himself who stepped onto the sidewalk, his bald head gleaming, his coffee dark face with its squinting eyes and grimace showing his displeasure, probably at a small infraction by one of his many employees. The look changed when he saw Michael, a wide smile blooming on his face.

"What on earth has happened," Jackie asked as he intercepted Michael, "to get Michael Arnett out of bed before the crack of three?"

Jackie was one to talk. A more than passable saxophone player, the successful restaurateur had spent many nights in Forever Blue, jamming until the sun came up.

"A date," Michael revealed in a lowered voice.

"Ahhhh," Jackie rumbled. "A new woman."

"An old woman."

Jackie raised his eyebrows, wrinkling his forehead.

"Not an *old* woman," Michael said quickly. "An old girlfriend. I hadn't seen her in five years, until last night."

"Ahhhh." The satisfied sound rumbled from his chest. "I see. She's come back to snare the newly successful songwriter with more money than he knows what to do with. I'll bet *she* knows what to do with all that money." Jackie was unfailingly pessimistic where women were concerned.

"Laura's not like that," Michael insisted. "She doesn't even know what's happened to me since she left."

"Right," was the drawled and disbelieving answer.

"It's the truth, and I don't want her to know. Not yet." The plan that suddenly came to him was brilliant. Well, maybe not brilliant, but since he hadn't had a plan at all until that point . . . "You could really help me out, pal."

"Why should I waste my time helping a skinny rich white boy?"

Michael flashed a smile to match Jackie's own. "I'll make it worth your while."

"I don't see how—"

Michael lowered his voice. "I'll let you touch my Bösendorfer."

Jackie raised a ham of a hand with surprisingly elegant fingers to his heart. "You can't mean it. You would allow a lowly saxophone player who only dreams of playing piano half as well as you do to touch your baby? The grand piano you personally dust and wax and tune so no one else will lay a finger on her?'' There was more than a touch of sarcasm in Jackie's voice, but then there usually was. "I can't wait to meet this old woman."

So far, so good. Megan hadn't mentioned speaking to Elvis in their hotel room, and she hadn't tossed any of her lunch in Michael's direction. *Yet.* Still, she was eyeing what was left of her fries as if she had great plans for them.

It would be simplest, the coward's way out, if Michael would look at Megan and see some of himself in her, the way Laura always did. Megan had Arnett eyes; the color was a soft green, and the corners, where Michael was showing the beginnings of very sexy laugh lines, were slightly turned down.

Ha! She should be so lucky. Michael was as charming with Megan as he was with her, smiling and laughing and including her in the conversation, but if he had even an inkling that Megan was his, he didn't show it, darn his hide.

They had talked about work, school, and Christmas, and so far there had been no disasters. Megan picked up a long French fry and studied it carefully before dipping the end in the small pool of ketchup on her plate. "I wonder if Elbis likes Fwench fwies. I could take him some of mine."

That got a slight eyebrow rise of out of Michael. "Elvis?"

Megan nodded and popped the end of the fry into her mouth.

"Finish eating," Laura said nervously. "We have to get back to the hotel and check on Jennifer." She gave in to the question in Michael's eyes. "It seems we have an invisible Elvis Presley sharing our room."

"He's a ghost," Megan informed them casually. "He told me so."

Laura closed her eyes and counted to ten. When she opened her eyes she saw that Michael had a huge grin on his face. Of course he wouldn't be disturbed by this revelation. His imagination had always been every bit as active as Megan's was.

"I've heard stories about that old hotel," he said, apparently delighted.

"Megan, there are no such things as ghosts," Laura said

sensibly, trying to paint the best possible picture of the situation for Michael. "This morning we were just pretending, remember?"

"I wasn't pwetending," Megan said firmly. "You were pwetending, but I wasn't."

Now was definitely not the time to spring the news. *She's seeing ghosts. She's yours. Uh-uh, no way.*

At that moment, a middle-aged woman in an Elvis sweatshirt plugged her quarters into the jukebox, punched in her selection, and a whirr and a heartbeat later, "You Don't Have to Say You Love Me" came over the speakers.

Megan stood in her seat. "That's him!" she shouted. "That's Elbis!"

"Sit down," Laura said softly. Everyone in the restaurant was watching as Megan jumped up and down on the padded vinyl seat of their booth. Maybe Michael and Megan liked being the center of attention, but Laura never had.

"But that's *him!*"

"Big Elvis fan, huh?" Michael asked with a smile, and Megan quit jumping and turned to face him, nodding her head vigorously so that her silky ponytail danced. "Then maybe I should ask your mother to dance with me to this song."

Laura was already shaking her head when Megan answered for her. "My mommy doesn't dance."

Michael's smile was unfailing, smug, satisfied as always. "Yes, she does. Watch this."

Laura's protests were quiet, and brief, and before she knew exactly what was happening she and Michael were dancing in the small space between their booth and the arrangement of small tables. Michael had one arm securely around her waist and one hand in hers. The dance was close, but not too close, easy, but not quite as easy as it would have been five years ago. They swayed with the languid grace of two people who knew one another so well they didn't have to think about how and when they danced. They just moved. And in a moment she forgot that people were no doubt watching and let herself enjoy being in Michael's arms.

It was hard to remember why she'd left, when he held her

like this. She closed her eyes and let herself drink in the sensation of being this close to Michael; his arms around her, his legs brushing against hers, the warmth of his touch and the pleasant scent of his skin. They were good together, and they had been from the moment they met.

She could so easily forget where she was, why she was here. Her eyes drifted open. Michael gave her a grin that was not as easy as she'd expected. She could see the strain there, in the set of his mouth and the slight narrowing of his eyes. He was usually so open, so easy to read, but right now she couldn't tell what he was thinking. She'd been away too long.

"What are you doing tonight?" he asked softly.

Laura shook her head. "Nothing." She could see the beat of his pulse in his neck, feel the fingers that moved ever so slightly at the small of her back. They were close, so very close.

"How about dinner?" he asked, and there was a flash of doubt in his eyes, as if he thought she might say no. "I made reservations at Jackie's Place. It's a lot nicer than this joint."

"I like this joint," she whispered. "But sure, Jackie's Place sounds great." Anywhere would be great. A peanut butter sandwich in an alley would sound great right now, if Michael was there.

The music ended, Michael dropped his arms, and just like that her reason returned. She hadn't come here to rekindle an old flame that was obviously still flickering. Flickering, hell— it was more like an inferno, and that could be very dangerous to her current state of mind.

Tonight, over dinner, she'd tell him about Megan. He'd probably hate her then, for having kept the secret for so long. She'd better enjoy his smiles while he was being generous with them.

Megan was standing on her seat and clapping as Laura and Michael took their seats. "Yeah!" she said as she plopped back into her seat. "Mommy *can* dance."

Michael winked at Megan, and his smile was easy once again. "You ain't seen nothin' yet."

Laura felt like the biggest coward in the world, watching

133

Michael and wishing with all her heart that he would look at Megan and see the truth, wishing that somehow he would just suddenly understand. Maybe he'd notice Megan's long fingers, or her Arnett eyes, or wonder how any child of Laura Marlow's could be blessed, or cursed, with such an imagination.

Anything to save her from the confession she was going to have to make.

Chapter Four

Michael was going to meet her in the lobby in fifteen minutes, and she wasn't nearly ready. She'd made a quick trip down the street this afternoon and bought herself a new outfit for the occasion, deeming everything she owned unsuitable. Now she was having second thoughts. Why had she chosen black when Michael rarely wore anything else?

But the classic little black dress did look better than any of the rest, and she was running out of time. It would have to do.

"Michael, I have something important to tell you," she whispered, practicing again. "Do you like Megan?" Goodness, what if he said no? Then what would she do? That was probably not the way to begin, either.

As Laura finished with her makeup and stepped into heels that were really too high for walking on Beale Street, she listened to the muffled sound of the television in the other room. Megan and Jennifer were munching on cheeseburgers from the Hound Dog Café, and she'd already told them that tonight's meeting might run a little late.

135

Wishful thinking?

When she opened the bathroom door, she was greeted by a cozy sight. Jennifer was sprawled across her bed, engrossed in a movie, her half-eaten cheeseburger in her hands and a canned drink on the table beside her. Megan had eaten most of her dinner, and was—dear God—talking softly to the red velvet chair again.

Megan spun around, and Jennifer pulled her eyes away from the movie as Laura stepped from the bathroom.

"I'll probably be late," Laura said as she grabbed her coat from the closet. Maybe if she said it forcefully enough and often enough it would come true. "Y'all get to sleep at a reasonable time."

Megan jumped up and down several times, her ponytail bouncing behind her. "Elbis says you're a knockout," she said when she stopped jumping.

"Tell Elvis I said thank you very much."

"He can hear you, Mommy," Megan said with an air of indignant toddler frustration.

Jennifer was so accustomed to Megan's imaginary friends she hadn't so much as blinked at the appearance of the ghostly Elvis in their hotel room. She scrambled from the bed, dropping her cheeseburger onto a napkin on the end table as she stood. As Laura passed her on the way to the door, Jennifer whispered, "There's no client, is there?"

Laura felt like a kid caught sneaking out of the house. "No," she admitted. "I'm sorry, I should have told you the truth."

Jennifer just smiled, apparently not at all distressed that Laura had lied about the reason for their Memphis trip. "I knew you wouldn't get dressed up like this for somebody who's looking for an accountant." She kept her voice low. "Good luck."

Laura sighed as she left the girls to their movie and cheeseburgers and ghost. *Good luck.* Those final words of loving kindness were more appropriate than Jennifer would ever know.

* * *

Laura had her arm through his as they walked toward Jackie's Place, her head down and tilted toward him to ward off the cold wind that whipped up all of a sudden. Soft hair, golden even in the glare of harsh streetlights and flashing neon, rose and fell gently with the breeze.

Tonight he would ask her to stay. True, she'd been back in his life for only one day, but it was long enough for him to be sure that he wanted—and needed—her back. If he'd been more sure of himself five years ago he never would have let her go. He would've chased her down and made her see that they could make it work. But he'd had doubts of his own, he had to admit. It wasn't until after she was gone that he'd realized living without Laura was much more difficult than living with her.

They stepped into Jackie's Place, a long, narrow restaurant crowded with tables and ferns. The lights were dim, the soft music that played in the background was jazz, and the place was packed, as always. Tables crowded the downstairs portion, and the more private, more exclusive tables were on the second floor on a wide gallery that looked over the main room.

The hostess, Jackie's sister Anita, smiled widely when she saw him. Michael crossed his fingers and hoped that Jackie had clued Anita in on the plan.

"Mr. Arnett," she said, her husky Southern accent more pronounced even than Jackie's. "Your table is ready."

He and Laura fell into line behind Anita, but they hadn't taken two steps before Jackie appeared out of nowhere, his scowl in place, his eyes narrowed.

"I'll show Mr. Arnett to his table," he said in a deep and somehow sinister voice. "We need to have . . . a word."

Jackie led the way to the narrow stairway, silent and imposing. When he had seated them at an upstairs corner table, possibly the most private in the restaurant, he leaned over the table with a menacing glower directed at Michael.

"Your checks are no good here, Mr. Arnett," he said softly, the soul of discretion. "Nor your credit cards. I hope you came prepared to pay cash this evening, because I cannot allow you to wash dishes for your supper again."

There was a twinkle in the big man's eyes that only Michael could see, a devilish sparkle, and the sight gave him a chill. Jackie was enjoying this immensely, and he was definitely taking the charade much too far. He was supposed to avoid mentioning anything that would give away too much, and to warn the staff to do the same—not make him out to be a beggar.

"I have cash," Michael said softly. "Do you want to see it?"

Jackie raised a stilling hand. "That will not be necessary. You're an honest man. A poor one, but honest, just the same. Your tips must have been particularly good this past weekend." He turned a brilliant smile to Laura. "What's a fine woman like you doing with a piano player who doesn't have two nickels to rub together?"

Laura's face turned red. For a moment, Michael thought she was blushing, perhaps embarrassed. Then he saw the spark in her eyes and knew it was anger that made her face flame this way. She didn't speak to Jackie, but turned to Michael. "Let's have dinner somewhere else."

"No," he said. "The food is good here. Let's stay."

There was a question in her big blue eyes. Did she wonder why he would allow the man who stood over their table to insult him? Maybe not. She'd always said he was too easygoing, too laid-back.

Jackie sighed deeply. "I have offended you." He raised a hand to his chest and stared down at Laura.

Laura raised her eyes to look at the big man squarely. "Yes, you have."

"My most sincere apologies," Jackie said with an unwavering grin. "It's one of my faults, that I am so outspoken. Let me make amends by giving you dinner on the house. My treat. The house special tonight is—"

Laura turned away from him and faced Michael across the table. "I'm not even that hungry."

"It would be my pleasure to make amends in this way," Jackie continued. "After all, it isn't every night that a man has such beauty"—he bowed to her—"and such talent"—he

138

gave Michael a nod of his bald head—"in his humble establishment."

Michael reached across the table and took Laura's hand. She was still angry, but now she simmered instead of boiled. "Let's stay. It's not Jackie's fault that he has no manners. The food here's great." He glanced up at a seemingly abashed Jackie. "Of course, *he* doesn't cook it." Maybe it was his smile that made her anger finally fade. The hand beneath his relaxed, and her face regained its normal color.

He ordered the most expensive thing on the menu for both of them, and Jackie answered with a harrumph and a scowl. On the house, my butt, Michael thought as Jackie walked away from the table. He'd end up paying for this dinner a hundred times over.

Laura didn't say much during dinner. Twice she seemed to start to say something, and then she changed her mind and gave her attention to the seafood on her plate. She seemed shy, nervous maybe. Had the charade embarrassed her? At least he didn't have to worry about prying eyes. The table Jackie had seated them at was exclusive, and Jackie himself served them—by way of absolution, perhaps. And then again, maybe he was just curious as to what would happen next. The saxophonist/restaurateur watched Laura closely throughout the meal, studying her, eyeing her every move closely. Once, from behind Laura's back, Jackie had winked and given Michael the thumbs-up; it was rare praise from the skeptic.

She was picking at her dessert, poking her spoon in an untouched chocolate mousse as she spoke. "We need to talk."

"I know."

"A lot has happened in the past five years that you don't know about," she said quickly, as if she had to force the words out. "There's Megan—" she began.

"I like her," Michael interrupted. Did Laura think he'd let her daughter come between them?

"Do you?" Her eyes widened, questioning, hopeful.

"She's a great kid."

Jackie appeared suddenly, interrupting to stare down at her dessert. "Is there something wrong with your mousse?" he asked with what appeared to be real concern. "I can take it away and bring you something else. The orange crepes with honey-butter sauce are fabulous."

"I'm really too full for dessert," Laura said, pushing the chocolate mousse away. "Everything was wonderful."

Jackie beamed.

Laura was right. They needed to talk, and this was not the place. Michael stood and took Laura's hand as she unfolded herself gracefully from her chair. When he reached for his wallet, Jackie stopped him with a raised hand.

"As I said earlier, this is on the house. It's always my pleasure to feed a talented, albeit starving, artist like yourself."

The big man was going to pay for this. "I was just fishing for your tip," Michael said, withdrawing a single dollar bill and slipping it into Jackie's shirt pocket. "The service was adequate, after all."

"You're most generous," the big man said softly.

When they were on the street, Michael took Laura's arm and headed in the direction of Forever Blue.

"You have to play tonight?" she asked as they walked slowly past lingering tourists.

"No. I took the night off." He didn't take many nights off, so he figured he was entitled. Besides, it was his place. He could do whatever he wanted. "But my apartment is above the bar and I thought, if you don't mind, we could go there and talk."

She shivered. The cold wind? Fear? Anticipation? It was impossible to tell.

The apartment was Michael, through and through. It was one big room, with a huge bed in one corner and a kitchenette in the other. There was a small bathroom off the side where the bed was located, and half a wall of closets.

It was big and neat and dark, and the most expensive items in the room were a massive stereo system and a very large, soft-looking gray chair.

Laura draped her coat over a hard-backed chair at a desk near the door and tossed her purse onto the desktop, while

Michael turned on the lights. She had to tell him—tonight—about Megan. Hard as it would be, it was the only reason she was here. Ah, but it was so easy to forget that when they were alone.

Michael came back to her, unsmiling, unnaturally tense. "We do need to talk," he said as he reached her.

"I know." Her voice wasn't much more than a whisper.

He wrapped his arms around her. "Stay," he commanded softly.

"I can't. Jennifer and Megan—"

"Not just for tonight," he interrupted.

"Michael—"

He silenced her with a soft kiss. Maybe he heard the protest in her voice, the uncertainty. When he pulled his lips from hers he whispered, "Believe in me this time. Have faith that what we have is enough."

Eyes closed, held tight in his arms, she wanted to say yes. Love should be enough, shouldn't it? She couldn't answer, so she kissed him again. She'd kissed other men in the past five years: friendly kisses, cold kisses, awkward kisses. But no one else had the power to make her feel this way. When Michael kissed her she felt as if she were glowing inside, and with every gentle move of his mouth over hers she wanted more.

He took his mouth from hers. "Stay," he whispered. "Forget how different we are and remember how good we are together." He ran a lazy finger slowly down her neck. "We are good together, you know. Surely you didn't forget."

"Michael . . ." she began, the protest clear in her voice.

"You're worried about where we'll be ten years from now, and I'm just wondering how I'm going to make it through another day without you." He laid his lips softly on hers. "Believe in me. Believe in us."

"I do," she whispered, and she meant it with all her heart.

They inched toward the big bed that was in the far corner of the room—a hundred miles away—shedding articles of unnecessary clothing as they slowly progressed.

She stepped out of her heels somewhere near the big gray chair, and they stopped their progress for a long, slow kiss.

They took a few steps toward the bed, and Michael reached around her to ease the zipper at her spine down. That done, he pushed the fabric aside so he could lay his mouth on her shoulder. Blindly, she unbuttoned his shirt so she could slip her fingers beneath the fabric and feel the heat of his skin in her hands.

The little black dress dropped to the floor about the same time his shirt did, and her bra followed soon after.

She had forgotten what a wonderful sensation this was, Michael's hands on her breasts, his mouth dancing on hers, her blood racing until she forgot everything but the mingled feelings of longing and love. She'd denied this part of herself since she'd left him, shutting down her need for love and touch, denying it as surely as she'd denied her love for Michael.

He brought it all back to life with his stirring kisses and exploring hands. His mouth on her breast almost made her cry out, the sensation was so powerful, and when he suckled gently her knees went weak.

They fell onto the bed, and with Michael's assistance she shed the only articles of clothing that came between her and him—her black silk underwear and panty hose. This was like the first time they'd made love—desperate and greedy and out of control. That was why, when Michael tossed what was left of his clothing to the floor, she opened her arms to him, ready for the joining she craved so much. He covered her, kissed her again, and made her wait, brushing newly patient fingers over her body as if he were touching her for the first time.

"I missed you so much," he whispered, sheltering her with his body, stroking her flesh with fingers that so easily brought to life a part of herself she'd denied for five years.

They came together with the ease of familiarity, and with the impatience of lovers who had been separated for too long. She needed this, the feel of Michael inside her, his body around and over and within hers. They found the rhythm that was theirs and theirs alone, the perfect harmony that they'd always had together.

The climax hit her with unexpected force, and she felt Michael give over to his completion as she did. It was too fast, over too soon, and she was left breathless.

"I missed you, too," she said belatedly, and Michael laughed lightly as he brushed his lips against her neck.

She lay there with her head on his shoulder, wondering why she'd left him all those years ago. He was a musician. It was in his blood, so much a part of him she was ashamed of herself for ever having asked him to give it up. If he'd given in to her all those years ago, if he'd given up this unstable business for something staid and respectable, he'd be miserable right now. And so would she.

"Stay," he said drowsily a few minutes later. They hadn't moved, and Laura was very sure she wouldn't be moving for quite some time. She was too happy, too drained . . . too scared of what came next. She still had to tell him about Megan.

"I want to," she whispered. "But we still have to talk." *But not now, not yet,* she pleaded silently.

Michael held her close. "We're terrible at talking. We're much better at this." He rolled her onto her back and kissed her, and the energy she'd thought gone came creeping back.

He held himself above her and gave her the most satisfied smile she'd ever seen on a man. "Have faith in us. Stay."

She was overwhelmed by the knowledge that he was right. She did believe in him, and in what they had. At this moment, love was more than enough. Together they could withstand anything . . . even the truth.

"Michael," she whispered, ready to confess all.

A pounding knock interrupted her, and it was all she could do to keep from screaming at the door.

Michael screamed for her. "Go away!"

An insistent female voice answered. "Sorry, boss, but Jimmy's on the phone. Chuck figured you'd want to take it."

"I know half a dozen Jimmys," Michael snapped. "And not one of them could roust me now."

"It's Jimmy Blue," the woman said. "What do you want me to tell him?"

Michael grumbled, but he left the bed and started grabbing his clothes. "I'll be right there," he shouted at the door, and

143

then he turned his attention to Laura, watching her as he dressed.

"You don't move," he ordered softly. "I'll be right back to pick up where we left off."

Laura was so wonderfully satisfied, so marvelously happy, that she didn't say a word as Michael quickly dressed and left to take his phone call. It wasn't until she was alone and growing cold in his bed that her senses returned to her.

Boss?

Jimmy Blue?

Chapter Five

Michael leaned against the bar, the receiver to his ear and his back to the Forever Blue patrons. The jukebox was playing, so he pressed a finger to his uncovered ear. *Elvis!* Chuck had been playing with the selections again.

Jimmy Blue had recorded one of Michael's first songs and made it a hit. The country singer was a nice guy and a great guitar player, and he and Michael had hit it off from their first meeting. He'd seen Jimmy and his wife, Jess, several times in the past year.

Michael hadn't purposely set out to write country songs. He was more into jazz, blues, a little rock and roll. But country was where the money was these days, and he'd discovered that what made a particular song work, country or rock, was all in the delivery.

"We're coming through Memphis in a couple of weeks," Jimmy said after their initial hellos and how-are-yous. "You'll be around?"

"Sure."

They made tentative plans to meet, have dinner, and get

together a few friends to have a jam session in Forever Blue after closing, before Jimmy changed the subject.

"Don't shoot me." His familiar Texas drawl became more prominent with this request. "But Jess has met this real nice woman who lives near Memphis, probably not an hour out of town, and she wants me to fix you two up while we're in town. You know how Jess worries about your love life, and you know I'll do anything to keep her happy. . . ."

"Stop right there," Michael said into the receiver with a widening smile he couldn't stop. "In two weeks I'll be married, if I'm lucky. Engaged, at the very least." He hadn't really asked her, not yet. "Involved, anyway."

"Sounds serious."

"It is."

"I'll have Jess put that girl on hold—"

"Have your matchmaking wife find her friend someone else," Michael interrupted, and then he lowered his voice. The jukebox had gone silent at last. "I'm not screwing up, not this time."

Jimmy wished Michael luck and got to the business at hand, a request for a song to be recorded in the spring for his next CD.

"I'd love to write another song for you."

The voice that came over the telephone was smooth and friendly with just a trace of that good-ol'-boy accent. "Glad to hear it. Jess says make 'em cry."

"Make 'em cry," Michael said. "That I can do." He shifted into a more comfortable position, turning to rest his back against the bar, and that was when he saw her.

Laura stood on the stairway that led to his apartment, watching, listening, her face pale. He didn't know how much of his conversation she'd heard, but it had obviously been more than enough.

"Jimmy, I'll call you next week," he said, dropping the receiver to its cradle with his eyes on Laura's face.

When she broke for the door, he went after her. He was slowed down because he had to get around the bar, around Chuck, around Susan and half a dozen small tables that got in

146

his way. By the time he reached the door Laura was gone, and even though she'd only stepped through the door a few seconds earlier, his heart damn near stopped.

It started beating regularly again when he saw her. She was stalking down Beale Street, and anyone who was in her path had sense enough to make way. It only took him a few seconds to catch up with her.

"You forgot your coat," he said as he reached out to grab her arm. It was a stupid thing to say, given the circumstances, but that was what came out of his mouth when he opened it.

Laura didn't jerk away but turned to face him defiantly. She did, however, shrug off his hand. "I'm not feeling particularly cold right now." Of course she wasn't. She was so angry she was practically steaming. "Did you think I wouldn't find out, *boss*?"

"Let's go back to my place and—"

"No," she snapped. "It really is your place, isn't it? Of course it is, *boss*. I should've known from the beginning. Who else but a piano player would have a grand piano in a juke joint?"

I was going to tell you would sound incredibly lame, wouldn't it? In the end it was all he could come up with. She all but snorted.

"And you wrote a song for Jimmy Blue. Not bad for a piano player who doesn't have two nickels to rub together."

She spun away, and he followed. "Okay, so I didn't tell you everything. It's not like I actually lied. . . ."

That stopped her dead in her tracks, and then she spun on him. "Didn't lie? What do you call that . . . that performance in the restaurant tonight? Dinner theater?"

"Jackie went a little further than I intended. . . ."

She snorted at him again and spun away in the middle of his inadequate explanation. He followed, of course. How could he have forgotten about her temper? He'd seen a hint of it earlier tonight at Jackie's Place, but she'd been able to keep it in check. Most of the time she was a sensible, levelheaded woman, but she had a volatile temper when it was roused. And it was definitely roused now.

147

She was at the corner of Blues Street and Beale, and she actually had a foot off the curb before she spun on him again. "Five years ago I left you because you were an impractical dreamer who refused to even think about settling down. Like a child, you always lived for the moment." She was seething, but he didn't back down when she poked him forcefully in the chest. "I didn't know you were going to turn into an insensitive jerk."

When she stepped into the street he was right behind her. "I wanted to know that we still had—"

"Wanted to make sure I wasn't after your money?" she snapped without turning her head to look at him.

It did look bad; he had to give her that. "No," he said, his voice softer than hers. She had to be able to hear him, he was so close. "I just wanted things to be the way they were, for a little while."

She shook her head but didn't answer.

"You want me to 'fess up? All right." She didn't even slow down. "Forever Blue is mine, the grand piano is mine, and I have more money in the bank than I ever thought I'd earn in my lifetime."

"Good for you."

"The club eats almost as much money as it makes, but a few of the songs I've written have done pretty well."

She snorted. Again.

"Won't you even stop and listen to me?" His own patience was wearing thin. "You know what your real problem is, don't you? You want everything and everyone in your life to add up nice and neat just like a column of numbers." His anger was coming close to matching her own. Lord, she gave up so easily! "Well, relationships don't always add up. They're messy and complicated and they change without warning. We don't add up on your mental calculator, so you run at the first sign of trouble."

He was the one who stopped suddenly on the sidewalk. The hotel was straight ahead, and Laura was headed unerringly for it. He was wasting his time; she'd never listen to reason when she was in this kind of mood.

"Make 'em cry, Michael," she said bitterly as she walked away. "Make 'em cry."

Her temper hadn't cooled by the time she knocked on the hotel room door. Dammit, the room key was in her purse, and her purse was in Michael's apartment. After a very short wait, the door swung open.

"Did you look through the peephole?" she asked too severely.

Jennifer took a step back. "Yes."

Laura closed and locked the door, putting the chain in place.

"It didn't go well?" Jennifer asked tentatively, and it was all Laura could do to keep from bursting into tears.

"No, it didn't go well," she snapped. "He's *rich*." Her voice broke, just a little.

Jennifer resumed her position on the bed. "And," she drawled, "this is bad?"

It changed everything. How could she tell him about Megan now? He'd think she was after his precious money, the fortune he'd lied so well about. She was glad he'd done well, she really was, but he'd lied to her, played a game she didn't even understand. "This is bad," she whispered, more to herself than to Jennifer.

Megan was sitting on the floor cross-legged and engrossed in a game that involved little people and little cars and a little house. As Laura watched, Megan lifted her head and spoke softly to the empty air before her.

This Christmas was a nightmare. Megan was talking to ghosts, Michael had played a game with her, and, worst of all, Megan was not going to get what she wanted most for Christmas: her daddy. How was she going to explain that away?

Laura paced for a few minutes. It was a frustrating effort, as she tried to stay out of Megan's way and not cross in front of the television Jennifer was watching. Finally she decided to seek refuge in the bathroom, telling the girls she was going to take a shower. A nice, long, cold shower.

* * *

149

Michael practically ran back to Forever Blue, and with every step he grew angrier. Laura hadn't listened to him, any more than she'd listened five years ago. When she was angry she was unreasonable, pigheaded, distant. . . .

He didn't respond to Chuck's or Susan's greetings, but stormed up the stairs to his apartment. It wasn't until he was inside with the door closed, studying the bed with its rumpled sheets and the black stockings on the floor, and the neatly discarded coat and purse, that he wondered if maybe she was right. He should have played her straight. Maybe tomorrow he could talk to her and make things right. . . .

The truth hit him with sickening clarity. She was going to run again. By tomorrow morning she'd be gone, dammit; he knew her well enough to know how she'd react. She'd write off her coat and purse as an acceptable loss, and be out of that hotel well before checkout time.

He should let her go. Maybe she'd been right when she left the first time. They didn't have the same dreams; they didn't see the same future. But dammit, he couldn't stand another five years without her, another five years of wondering when— if—she was going to come back.

He scooped up the small purse and opened it. There was a small wallet containing her driver's license and forty bucks and a picture of Megan. A lipstick and small comb were in the bottom of the purse, as well as a hotel room key. There was nothing here that couldn't be easily replaced, and Laura would write off the losses rather than face him again, if she had her way.

He plucked the key from the bottom of the purse and breathed a sigh of relief when he saw that it was one of those old-fashioned heavy keys attached to a triangular key chain with the room number stamped into the plastic.

Chuck and Susan ignored him this time, as he rushed down the stairs and toward the exit. He ran most of the way to the Original Heartbreak Hotel, afraid that Laura would pack up and leave tonight rather than chance seeing him again. There hadn't been time for her to pack and check out, but still he felt a touch of disquieting panic. Laura had always been one to run and hide from trouble, and he didn't imagine this time would be any different.

Once he was in the lobby, he headed not for the elevators but for the stairs. She was, after all, just on the fourth floor, and there were only two elevators. He wasn't in any mood to wait. By the time he reached Laura's room, he was breathless. He needed to start jogging or something, he told himself as he stood before a suddenly imposing door. He had to catch his breath, and maybe while he was standing here he could think a little bit about what exactly he was going to say to Laura. At least he told himself that was the reason he stood in the hallway and took a few deep breaths before he knocked on the door. His hesitation had nothing to do with fear, certainly.

The door was opened but the chain stayed in place. A dark-haired girl stared at him through the narrow opening.

Michael tried a smile. "You must be Jennifer. I'm Michael Arnett. Laura left her coat and purse behind." He held them up as evidence.

"So you're the rich guy," she said evenly as she slipped her fingers though the door to take the offered items. Michael drew them back slightly, out of her reach.

"I want to talk to Laura."

"She's in the shower."

The girl's expression told him nothing. She was slightly curious, but he had the feeling she was more interested in the movie that was playing in the background than in his floundering love life.

"Can I wait?" His patience was wearing thin, but he didn't think it would be wise to break past the chain and into a room where a woman and two little girls were staying. He really didn't want to spend this Christmas in jail. "Please?"

Jennifer was obviously trying to make up her mind. She looked him up and down judgmentally, and he wasn't sure that he could pass this particular test.

And then Megan, adorable in pink flannel pajamas, squirmed into the picture, working her way past Jennifer's legs and looking up. "Michael!" Her greeting was exuberant. "Elbis said it was you.'' She tugged on Jennifer's jeans. "Let him in. Elbis says let him in!''

Jennifer rolled her eyes. "Well, since you and Elvis recognize him I guess it's okay.''

With obvious reluctance Jennifer closed the door, unlatched the chain, and then opened it again to admit Michael to the room. He held on to Laura's coat and purse, afraid that once he relinquished the items he'd be ushered from the room.

He could hear the roar of the shower, and in spite of everything that had happened he pictured Laura there and wished he could join her. She'd listen to him, then, wouldn't she? If he could only hold her and make her understand . . . It didn't matter. The ever-vigilant Jennifer wasn't likely to allow him to make his way past that bathroom door.

So he carried Laura's purse and coat with him and headed toward the only inviting place in the room, a plush red velvet chair by the window. Jennifer plopped down on the bed and directed her attention to the television, and Megan bent over to pick up a couple of little plastic people from the floor.

As he lowered himself toward the chair she bolted straight up. "No!''

He jumped to his feet and looked behind him to the empty seat of the chair, searching for a cherished toy he'd been about to squash. The chair was empty.

"Elbis is sitting there,'' she said with an air of impatience. "You almost sat on him!''

There was a draft in this old room. A cold wind touched him as he stood there looking at the empty red chair, an unexpected chill that came and went quickly.

"Okay,'' Megan said, calm again. "He moved. You can sit down now.''

Michael lowered himself cautiously into the chair, and deposited the coat and purse on the floor beside it. Minutes ticked past, excruciatingly slow minutes, and the shower roared on. He had so much to say, and even though he wasn't sure how to put his feelings into words, he was anxious to see Laura face-to-face. Dammit, how long was she going to stay in there?

Forever, evidently. Jennifer, sprawled on her stomach across one of the beds, watched her movie and ignored him completely. A contented Megan played with her toys, on occasion making a comment to the space before her. Once, she even laughed for no reason at all. Michael found his foot pumping nervously as he waited.

Megan glanced up, her eyes focused on the expanse of nothing before her, and said, "Now?" She actually seemed to wait for an answer before placing her plastic people carefully on the floor and rising. She didn't only face Michael then; she very purposely climbed into his lap, elbows and knees landing in all the wrong places until she was settled comfortably on his lap, squarely facing him.

"Elbis says you need some Bwylcweem," she said seriously, reaching little hands up to push strands of hair gently away from his face.

"Oh, he does, does he?"

"Yes." She seemed to enjoy playing with his hair, so he let her. She pushed it back and pulled it forward and lifted it straight up. As she entertained herself by running her fingers through his hair, he watched her face. Megan was a beautiful kid, with chubby cheeks and a wide mouth, and that fine hair just short of being truly red. Her skin was so soft and flawless it was amazing. He could see Laura there, in the way she turned her head and in the little button nose. They were so beautiful. They were both fragile, too, though neither was likely to admit it.

Megan pushed his hair back and finally let it go, and then her warm little hands settled gently on his face and she placed her nose on his and stared into his eyes.

His heart lurched and he held his breath. Was he imagining this? Looking into Megan's eyes was like staring into a mirror, and the truth hit him like a thunderbolt. This was the reason Laura was back. Megan was his daughter. It couldn't be a coincidence that her eyes were so much like his, could it? But why had she waited until now?

"Megan Michelle Marlow," Jennifer said in what had to be an imitation of a frustrated Laura. "Get out of that man's lap. I'm sure he doesn't want you crawling all over him."

Megan Michelle Marlow. "It's all right," Michael muttered. This little girl was his daughter, and as the truth settled in he didn't know whether to be happy or angry or indignant. Right now, all he really wanted to do was cry, and he wasn't quite sure why.

"How many days until Christmas?" she asked, evidently not recognizing the importance of this moment.

"The day after tomorrow's Christmas Eve." His voice was deceptively calm and even.

She jumped up and down a little, but her face stayed close to his. "Goody! I hope I get what I asked for. Mommy said we'll see, and that usually means no, but sometimes it means yes."

He didn't want her to crawl down and start playing with her toys and talking to her imaginary friend Elvis. He wanted her to stay right where she was, for now. He wanted her close. "What did you ask for? A new doll? Some more little people?"

"No," she said with pursed lips. "I didn't ask for toys this year."

"What did you ask for?"

She settled her nose on his again and stared into his eyes. "My daddy."

His heart nearly thudded to a halt.

"Caitlin and Stephanie and Emily, they're my bestest friends in my class at school, they all have daddies," she said, her voice fast and high. "Justin has two daddies, but one is his real daddy and one is his stepdaddy, and I don't think it's fair that he has two daddies and I don't even have one."

"Not fair at all," he said numbly.

"Mommy said we don't *need* a daddy, but I think we do, so I asked Santa to bring me my daddy for Christmas." She took a deep breath. "Do you think Santa will leave him under the tree at Grandma's house? That's where he usually leaves my pwesents, at Grandma's house."

"You never know."

The roar of the shower ceased suddenly, and it was all Michael could do to keep from carrying Megan to the bathroom door and asking Laura how she could accuse him of lying when she'd told the biggest lie of all. But Megan clambered down off his lap and returned to her little people, and Michael rose slowly.

He wasn't going to let another argument separate them. Not now, when he had everything he'd ever wanted waiting before him. All he had to do was claim it. He was downright calm as he approached the bathroom door and knocked.

"I'll be right out," Laura called. Her voice was oddly thick, and he wondered if she'd been crying in the shower.

"No rush," he answered calmly.

There was dead silence for a long moment, and then he heard the brush of her hand against the other side of the door. "Go away," she whispered, plenty loud enough for him to hear.

"No. Not until you promise me that you're not planning to leave here tomorrow morning."

"It's best—"

"Don't run away again," he pleaded. "Give me . . . give me tomorrow to change your mind."

"I won't change my mind," she insisted.

"Then you've got nothing to lose." He, on the other hand, had everything to lose. "One day, Laura. Think of it as a Christmas present to make up for all the Christmases we missed."

"It's not a good idea," Laura insisted, but her voice, and maybe her resolve, had softened.

"I'm not leaving until you agree," he said to the door. "It's the least . . . you owe me that much."

He held his breath through the silence that followed. What would he do if she said no? What would he do if she said yes, and then decided to sneak out early in the morning anyway?

No. Laura was volatile when she was angry, but she was true to her word. If she said she'd be here in the morning, she'd be here.

"All right," she whispered. "One day."

Chapter Six

She should've left before dawn, breaking her word and escaping from Memphis while she still could have. Why had she agreed to this ridiculous proposition? What kind of torture did Michael have planned for her today?

And it would be torture, no matter what they did, no matter how pleasant he tried to make the day. She still loved him, liar that he was, but there was no way they could make this work. She couldn't even tell him about Megan; not now. Could she?

Her jeans and baggy sweatshirt were intended to put him off. There would be no primping before the mirror before meeting Michael today, no critical examination of her makeup and hair, no slinky dress and high heels to impress him.

Her heart lurched at the realization that this was so final. It was good-bye at last, and this time she wouldn't be coming back. This time, when she returned to her apartment, she'd have to give up her too-frequent daydreams of reconciliation and happily ever after. Heaven help her, she didn't want to let those daydreams go.

He knocked on her door right on time, twelve o'clock on the dot. Megan and Jennifer were playing on the floor, and she'd left them money for lunch in the Hound Dog Café. Elvis was conspicuously absent this morning, and Laura said a silent prayer that the King was gone for good.

As Laura reached out to open the door, Megan proved that her prayers were in vain. "Elbis says you look mighty fine," she said nonchalantly, her eyes on her little people. "But he liked the black dress better."

"Everyone's a critic," Laura mumbled as she opened the door.

Michael had outdone himself, but then what should she have expected from a man with his theatrical nature? He held a bouquet of red roses in one hand, and a huge box of chocolates in the other. His hair didn't hang limply around his face, but had been carelessly styled and combed back. He stepped into the room, and his eyes went immediately to Megan. With a finger on the hand that held the chocolates he pointed to his head as he whispered to her.

"Brylcreem."

Megan was delighted with this bit of trivia, and after an enchanting giggle she answered. "Elbis says . . ." And then she popped her thumb up in an encouraging salute.

Laura knew it was best to get this over with as quickly and painlessly as possible. She placed the roses in a plastic pitcher she found in the bathroom, and as she set the pitcher on the end table she gave the girls instructions on how much of the candy they could eat.

Michael looked great, as always, even though he wasn't any more finely dressed than she was. There was something about a tight pair of black jeans that did things for the man. As she passed the dresser mirror she caught a glimpse of herself and wished she'd picked something a little more flattering to wear. For him, for this one last time. What a fool she was, still.

Michael didn't take her arm and escort her into the hallway, but walked over to the girls and placed his hands on his hips as he looked down at their play family and Lego house. "Well? Aren't you ladies ready to go?"

Megan looked up, eyes big and bright. "We can go, too?"

"Of course," Michael said as if he couldn't believe they would assume otherwise. "You can even bring Elvis, if you'd like."

Megan shook her head slowly. "He just left. Sometimes he has other things to do, you know."

"Too bad. Can you call him back? I'd love to have him come along."

Laura sighed loudly, hopefully loud enough for Michael to hear. How dare he encourage her fantasies like this? If he heard her, he didn't show it.

"No," Megan said, standing and beginning the search for her shoes. "I don't think he's in the hotel right now."

Michael flashed a smile in Laura's direction. "Did you hear that? Elvis has left the building."

Jennifer and Megan were very pleased to be invited along for the day's adventure, and Laura was glad of the buffer between her and Michael. Things weren't likely to get out of control with the girls along.

He had planned a walking tour of Blues Street and Beale, starting with a stop at a live Nativity scene next to the hotel. Megan was delighted with the animals, but she was even more fascinated with the Elvis-like wise men in their spangles and sculpted hair, and she squealed over the real live baby who was playing the role of baby Jesus.

Michael squinted as he stared at the scene. "Is that Annie Fallon and her little brothers?" A smile broke across his face. "I'll be damned! What are they doing out here?"

Laura glanced to the side, wondering why Michael was smiling so widely. "You know an entire family of Elvis impersonators?" She took in the Nativity scene again, noting with a sinking heart that this Annie was obviously a very attractive woman beneath the hair and makeup. In fact, she looked a little familiar. Laura was almost certain she'd seen Annie Fallon in Forever Blue on Monday night. Michael hadn't noticed her then—but he certainly noticed her now. "Complete with Priscilla?" she finished.

"They're not Elvis impersonators; they're farmers."

"Farmers?" she repeated incredulously.

Michael's smile faded. "What, do farmers rank even lower than musicians on your list?"

"No," she said horrified. "It's just that they don't look like farmers."

After a few minutes of rapt wonder, Megan wondered aloud why Mommy couldn't have hair as big as the "Birgin" Mary's. Megan would have watched the Nativity scene all day if Michael hadn't hurried her along. Before they left he dropped a fifty-dollar bill in the pot at the front of the Nativity scene.

They walked through shops and an art gallery or two, playing tourists and browsing through Elvis memorabilia, listening to Michael's recited history of Beale Street. The tour ended nearly an hour later at Forever Blue. The shades were down, and the sign said CLOSED, but someone had been busy in the club. Tables had been pushed together and were piled high with barbecue, hamburgers, fried shrimp, hot dogs, French fries, onion rings, fruit salad, and four kinds of dessert. As she stared at the feast, Michael leaned near to whisper into her ear.

"I didn't know what Megan and Jennifer would like, so I told Jackie to bring a little bit of everything he thought kids would eat."

She saw the big black man, then, who'd been bending down behind the bar. Four different kinds of soft drinks and two kinds of juice were lined up before him. He smiled sheepishly at Laura, and raised one eyebrow in a rakish manner. She smiled back, and he seemed to be relieved.

"You can't close your business for this," she protested as Michael led her to her seat.

"We don't open until four."

"Four in the afternoon?" she asked, every business instinct within her appalled. "No wonder you don't make much of a profit here. You should open for lunch, maybe bring in some tourists with sandwiches and ice cream."

He shrugged his shoulders, unconcerned with money as always. "We do okay. This is a piano bar, not a restaurant. We

159

can come up with chili and sandwiches for a hungry customer, and Susan can heat up a decent frozen pizza. That's it.''

She resolved to stay out of his business, and gave him an unconcerned shrug of her own.

''But if you stay I'll let you count all my beans, and if you think we should open for lunch . . .''

''It's none of my concern.''

''It should be,'' he whispered. ''Everything I do and say and think should involve you.''

Laura ignored the provocative statement, and watched as Megan and Jennifer piled their plates high and found a table for two to the side. Jackie asked the girls what they wanted to drink, and it took them several minutes to make up their minds. Megan changed her mind four times within the space of two minutes, and the big man never so much as blinked. He was, she decided, a very patient man.

Michael ate, but Laura just picked at the food on her plate. Her stomach was one big knot. She should've run, she never should've come here, she was a complete and total idiot for sitting here like nothing had happened! Michael was blatantly trying to get to her through Megan, and maybe even through Jennifer, trying to show her what a great guy he was. *Ha!*

Megan was finished before anyone else, and her attention shifted to the grand piano that was the centerpiece of the room. She pointed a finger that was sticky with barbecue sauce toward the stage. ''Can I play with that?''

Jackie burst out laughing, for some reason, loud, maniacal cackling. His laughter died abruptly when Michael said, ''Sure.''

He did make her wash her hands first, and he was there to supervise, of course. Michael left the remains of his lunch to sit on the piano bench and lifted Megan into his lap. She laid one finger on the piano, and was elated by the resulting sound.

Within five minutes Michael had Megan playing simple scales, and neither of them seemed to notice that Jackie stared with his jaw dropping toward the floor, or that Jennifer was eating fries off her cousin's plate, or that Laura was doing her damnedest not to cry like a baby.

She'd dreamed of this moment, closed her eyes and imagined it in difficult times when she didn't know how she was going to make it to the next day. The man she loved and the child they'd created, together at last.

Like it or not, she *had* to tell Michael the truth, and once he knew he would want to be a part of Megan's life. That was the plan, right? Megan wanted a daddy; she wanted to be like the other little girls in her school. If Laura could give her that she had no right to refuse it. But how could she stand having Michael come in and out of her life?

When Megan tired of her lessons—about ten minutes after they started—Michael set her down and began to play a familiar song. Now he had Jennifer's attention.

"That's a Jimmy Blue song," she said when she'd finished chewing her barbecue. "It's one of my very favorites."

Michael smiled. "I wrote it."

Jennifer laughed out loud. "You did not."

Jackie was making the rounds, picking up dirty plates and glasses. He leaned over slightly as he passed Jennifer's table. "Yes, he did. Young lady, you are lookin' at the one and only heartbreak kid of Beale Street." He chuckled and whispered confidingly, "He hates it when I call him that."

Jennifer looked at Michael then with wide-eyed awe. "You actually wrote that?"

Michael kept playing, but he nodded once.

"Omigod," she said with a long exhale of breath. "You know him, don't you?"

"Know who?"

"Jimmy Blue," Jennifer said with very little evident patience.

"Sure."

Jennifer melted. Laura smiled. And Megan started to sing. She missed a few of the words, but she had the general idea and she got most of the song right. She had the chorus down pat.

It was a sentimental love song, all broken hearts and whispered promises, lost souls and lonely nights. When she listened to the words she could hear Michael, in the beat, in the phrasing. Even when Megan solemnly sang about "heartbeeps," Laura felt dangerously near tears.

Michael kept playing and locked his eyes to hers. "Listening to country these days?"

Laura shook her head. "You know me; I'm strictly a rock-and-roll girl. She must have heard it at a friend's house, or at school."

Megan stopped singing long enough to comment. "Elbis sang it to me. He said it's a pwetty good song."

The song came to an end, and Michael left his perch. "Next time you talk to him, tell him I said thanks. I'm glad he likes it."

Laura groaned. "Don't encourage her," she whispered when Michael sat beside her.

"Megan doesn't seem to need any encouragement."

It was a pleasant, safe afternoon, but somewhere along the way she remembered why she'd fallen in love with Michael in the first place: his smile that made her forget everything else, the soothing voice that made her heart warm, those eyes that looked right through her. All she had to do was look at him to know she wasn't alone in this world. She could deny it all she liked, but he was a part of her and always would be. Heaven help her, she didn't need this now. She needed distance, stability, sanity.

Susan, the cocktail waitress who'd been present the night before, came in about three, letting herself in with her own key. She was an attractive woman, dark haired and dark eyed, with a come-hither smile, a short skirt, and heels that were much too high for a woman who had to remain on her feet for hours. Laura couldn't help but wonder, when she smiled at Michael, if there had ever been anything . . .

Like it mattered. Michael was handsome, rich, talented, and completely unencumbered. Laura knew, had always known, that there had probably been countless women in his life since she'd left it. It just didn't hurt so much when she didn't have to watch.

Susan looked with apparent surprise at the scene before her. "You want me to come back later, boss?"

Michael shook his head. "We'll be clearing out of here soon, and you need to set up. Hungry? We've got plenty."

The shapely woman wrinkled her nose at the fun but not necessarily healthy spread. "Trust me, there's nothing here I can eat," she muttered, and Laura suddenly felt guilty that there was a half-eaten sparerib on her plate.

Antsy and apparently unhappy with the situation, Susan had something to say. Laura recognized that fact, even if Michael didn't. Finally, after depositing her purse and coat in the office, the cocktail waitress wagged a finger at her boss, and Michael went without hesitation.

Laura didn't want to watch, so she picked at the strawberry shortcake before her. She could mull it over all she wanted, but her choices were limited. She could tell Michael about Megan, or remain a coward and light out of Memphis tonight like there was a fire on her tail.

Jennifer sidled into Michael's chair and leaned close. "Can you believe it? He *knows* Jimmy Blue! He probably knows other famous people, too—do you think? Oh . . ." A startling thought had obviously just occurred to Jennifer. "Do you think he knows Travis Tritt?"

"You can ask him," Laura said, still picking at her dessert. *But ask him soon because we won't be here much longer, and we're not coming back.* She couldn't make herself say that aloud.

Jackie was making the rounds, picking up the few remaining dishes. She really should thank him for the fabulous meal, but she was having a difficult time, after the stunt he'd pulled at his restaurant. When he arrived at her table, he winked at her. "You get hungry while you're in town, you come see me. Don't let Michael feed you any of the crap they serve here." It sounded like an order from a strict uncle, or a demanding teacher.

He lifted his head as he reached out to snag the plate that had once contained the best spareribs she'd ever eaten, and stopped dead still. "Ma'am?" he said softly. "Your little girl . . ." He nodded his head toward the bar, and then he grinned widely.

163

Laura didn't want to look, but heaven help her, she had no choice. She turned her head so she would be forced to see Michael and Susan deep in conversation. Susan was leaning in close—too damn close—and Michael was listening attentively and nodding his head.

And Megan was on the floor at Susan's heels. The woman had cocked her leg seductively and slipped one shoe half-off, a high-heeled black shoe that Megan was very silently, very deliberately, filling with ketchup from a red plastic squirt bottle.

"Megan!" Laura shouted, pushing her chair back as she stood. Megan stood quickly, Michael looked at Laura, and Susan stepped back and into her shoe.

Susan made a sound that was somewhere between a groan and a scream as she kicked off her shoe. Megan quickly moved the ketchup bottle to her back, where she held it tight with both hands, but it was much too late. She'd been caught.

The cocktail waitress looked as though she wanted to scold Megan, but she stood very still and said nothing at all. Michael had jumped in quickly, promising Susan ten pairs of shoes in return. Laura insisted that Megan apologize, and she did— with the utmost insincerity. Michael took it a step further. He told Megan to shake Susan's hand and apologize as if she really meant it.

Megan stepped forward as if she really might do as he asked, but her right hand came from behind her back with the ketchup bottle aimed right for Susan's white blouse. What followed was a deliberate and carefully planned maneuver, as Megan popped the bottle up, wrapped her other hand around it, and squeezed. Laura was shouting "No!" when a stream of ketchup flew up and landed smack-dab in the middle of the woman's two mountainous breasts.

Michael soothed a fuming Susan while Laura took the weapon from Megan. Most of the ketchup was gone. In order to do more damage, Megan would have had to reload.

They left the club, Megan securely bound with one hand in Laura's and the other in Michael's. She was silent, but definitely unrepentant. They were on the street before Laura spoke.

"You should be ashamed of yourself," she said in a hiss, leaning down slightly.

Megan, eyes forward, answered calmly, "I'm not 'shamed of myself," she said with her nose in the air. "I don't like her. She has a sneaky face."

Michael laughed, and Laura shot him a warning glare. His laughter died, but his smile went on.

"Whether you like someone or not," Laura said calmly, silently agreeing with Megan's assessment of Susan, "you can't go around squirting ketchup in their shoes and at their clothes."

"Well, the mustard was on your table, and the barbecue sauce was by Jennifer's plate. . . ."

Michael started to laugh again, and Laura had to bite her tongue. "You can't go around attacking people with condiments of any kind," she said calmly. "I've told you this before."

"Okay, Mommy," Megan said, easily putting the incident behind her. "Jennifer!" she shouted, glancing over her shoulder to her cousin, who followed behind. "Watch this!" She held on to their hands tightly and jumped, hanging in the air for a long, magical moment.

Megan was, for the moment, caught between the two people in the world who should love and protect her above all else, who should be there for her whenever she needed them. She was sandwiched safely between her parents, and no one but Laura knew it.

They had to stop to watch the living Nativity scene next to the hotel for a few minutes before returning Megan and Jennifer to the hotel room. Megan was entranced by the baby and the Elvis impersonators, though she voiced the observation more than once that the real Elvis was not in attendance.

Just inside the hotel door, Laura gave Jennifer the room key and sent the girls on their way. No doubt she planned to say good-bye here and now, in a busy hotel lobby with the Hound

Dog Café jukebox playing "Love Me Tender" in the background and a skinny bellhop in a uniform two sizes too big lurking nearby. She couldn't say good-bye yet; she still hadn't told him about Megan.

He preempted her. "I'll pick you up in two hours."

"I really should—"

"You promised me the whole day, remember?" he interrupted. "We'll keep it simple. Dinner and then back to the club for a while, if we feel like it." He smiled at her. "I can take tonight off, too, if I need to. That's what Susan was complaining about when Megan decided she looked sneaky and needed ketchup in her shoes. Her tips suffer when I'm not playing, and I've been gone the past couple of nights. I promised her a huge Christmas bonus to make up for this time off, so I plan to make the most of it."

Laura nodded. "All right, but I can't be out late. My mother will expect us tomorrow, and my sister will kill me if I keep Jennifer away on Christmas Eve."

It was a grudging acceptance, but he was almost sure he saw the light of something promising in her eyes.

Chapter Seven

Michael had tried to lose himself during the hours he had to wait, playing "Rainy Night" as early customers drifted in for a drink and a listen. No matter how hard he tried, though, the last stanza wouldn't come together. He didn't sing, but he heard the words in his head as he played, and no matter how hard he tried, the song remained unfinished.

Even the music couldn't take his mind off Laura tonight, and he was fifteen minutes early to collect her, fifteen long minutes he spent pacing in the lobby.

Laura had been right when she'd said this was a strange place. He hadn't noticed last night. The decor was a marriage of old elegance and Elvis-mania, and the clientele blended right in. In the lobby there were old ladies and Elvis impersonators, tourists who eyed the Elvis-on-velvet paintings that hung on every wall, and bellhops in once-proper uniforms that were now faded and too worn to be anything but dreary.

"They're thinking about closing this place, you know." The voice, an Elvis-like soft drawl, came from a man in a white

167

jumpsuit who had sneaked up on Michael while he'd been thinking about Laura.

"I didn't know that," he said, trying to look into the man's face. A bright light on the wall was directly behind the Elvis impersonator, so Michael's view was less than perfect. Still he had to admit an uncanny resemblance to the King.

"It's a shame, a real shame."

Michael nodded and waited for the man to move on. He didn't. Instead the Elvis impersonator began to sing "Are You Lonesome Tonight?" softly, but plenty loud enough for Michael and anyone else in the vicinity to hear. He was surprised no one stopped to watch. People walked past without so much as glancing at the singing man. Well, Laura had said this place was strange.

The soft words rang too true, and they reminded Michael much too clearly of the days and nights that had passed without Laura at his side—sad days, each and every one. In two days it would be Christmas once more. Was he going to spend the day alone again, playing at his piano and blindly ignoring mistakes of the past?

The elevator doors opened and Michael held his breath and waited for Laura to get off, but he was disappointed. Instead it was a family who stepped into the lobby, a man and woman and three little boys who came off the elevator in a hurry. The mother scooted the smallest one along, straightening a cowlick as they rushed to the door.

They brushed so closely by Michael that he felt the breeze their rush created. When he looked back to the man beside him, he saw a smile on an uncannily Elvis-like face that remained indistinct thanks to the harsh backlight.

"You got kids?" the man asked.

Yesterday he would have said no. "Yeah," Michael said softly. "I do."

"Me, too," the man said softly. "A little girl."

"I have a daughter," Michael said, and it felt so right he grinned. He hadn't admitted it aloud until that moment. It sounded good.

"Don't let her slip away," the man in white advised, as if he knew more than he should.

Michael looked toward the elevators as the doors parted once again. This time Laura was there, and she didn't say a word as she stepped off the elevator and came straight to him. The expression on her face was one of determination, resolution, and perhaps just a little bit of fear.

He was relieved to find that the Elvis impersonator had made off silently. It wouldn't do for the man to ask about his daughter in front of Laura.

Beyond the hotel door all was dark, and the living Nativity scene had disbanded for the night when Michael led Laura past the deserted lot. He stopped before the quiet plot and stared at it for a long moment before saying anything. This was it; tonight was his last chance. If he couldn't convince Laura that what they had was too good to throw away, he was going to lose her for good.

Don't let her slip away. Hell, he was taking advice from an Elvis impersonator! He slipped his arm through hers. No matter who it came from, it was good advice.

"There used to be a photography studio here," he said, hanging on to Laura's arm as if she might decide to break for the hotel and safety.

"What happened to it?"

He glanced at her, at the golden hair she'd swept off her neck and the simple and flattering gray dress she probably thought was severe and plain, at the wary eyes and the stubborn mouth. *Now or never.*

"It burned down, oh, probably thirty years ago."

She looked over the barren lot as if she could see something he couldn't. Maybe she just didn't want to look at him. "Why didn't they rebuild?"

"I don't know what happened after the fire."

She watched him silently, waiting.

"I only know what happened before." There were ghosts here, dammit; he could feel them. They were in the shadows, in the soft moan of the breeze; they were in Laura's eyes.

"What?" she whispered.

169

He told her the story, the mixture of legend and rumor and romantic supposition, of Elvis and the lady photographer who'd died in the fire. She'd taken several photographs of the superstar over the years, and word had it that he was crazy about her. She was apparently just as crazy about him.

"Why is it that I never heard of this alleged romance? Everything concerning Elvis is public knowledge, and I never heard anything about any lady photographer," Laura said skeptically.

"There was no romance," Michael said as he turned her away from the spooky lot. "Evidently he never told her how he felt, and she never told him. They loved one another for years, but neither of them ever came clean about their feelings. They kept it locked inside, afraid, maybe, to confess all."

She shuddered; he could feel it in the arm he held. "That's very sad," she whispered.

"Yes, it is."

They began to walk, arm in arm, and had taken several steps before Michael spoke again. "It's just a story, one of a million stories about Elvis," he whispered. "Who knows if it's even true?"

Laura clung to his arm, and the fact that she held on so tight gave him hope. Then again, maybe she was hanging on because she knew she'd never have the chance again. That thought made his mouth go dry with fear. They were at Beale Street before either of them spoke again.

"What do you want for dinner?" he asked.

She stood very still beside him, clinging possessively to his arm. "I'm not very hungry."

"Neither am I."

The rain began then, one light, cold drop and then another. Surely they should run for cover, but they were both motionless on the corner while people rushed past to get out of the cold rain. Neon signs shone all around them, bright lights in a black night, garish colors breaking the darkness. The rain was steady and chilling.

"I don't want to make a mistake like that," Michael said, his eyes on the reflections of neon on a wet street. "I don't

170

want to play it safe and keep everything locked inside until it's too late.'' He faced Laura and placed his hands on her wet face. ''There hasn't been a day to pass in the last five years that I haven't thought about you. Some days I was angry with you for leaving, for not believing in me. Other days I wondered what I did wrong.'' He thought maybe she was crying, but with the rain on her face it was hard to tell. ''Most of the time I just missed you.'' He kissed her wet lips. ''I love you.''

Laura wrapped her arms around his neck and held on tight. ''I love you, too,'' she whispered against his mouth. ''I tried to find you,'' she said, and this time when he kissed her he could taste the tears. ''Believe that.''

''I do.''

Walking quickly in the rain, they hurried back in the direction they'd come from, back toward the hotel. Laura barely felt the cold rain, she was so elated. Michael loved her, still, and any doubts she might have had about her own feelings were gone.

She loved him, she belonged with him, and she had faith that no matter what happened, life would be better for both of them if they stayed together.

Soaking wet, they entered the lobby of the Original Heartbreak Hotel, the odd place that had, in the past two days, earned a warm place in her heart.

Michael didn't release her hand, but pulled her to the front desk. The very proper matronly manager, Mrs. Bloom, glanced at them with a disapproving lift of a single eyebrow and a chilling, ''May I help you?''

''We need a room,'' Michael said, ignoring her pursed lips. ''Preferably on the fourth floor.'' He looked down at Laura and smiled.

Mrs. Bloom was obviously hesitant. The Original Heartbreak Hotel might not be the nicest place in Memphis, but it hadn't yet degenerated to the point where they would rent rooms by the hour to a couple with no luggage.

Laura called up her most dignified smile. ''It's getting so crowded in our little room, we decided it would be best just to get another room and . . . spread out a little.''

The manager's eyes widened slightly. "Ms. Marlow? I didn't recognize you without the little one in tow." Her attitude changed, though she did glance suspiciously at Michael. "We have a room available just two doors down from yours, and then there's the Blue Hawaii Suite on that floor, which just became available this afternoon.''

Michael didn't even hesitate. "We'll take the suite.''

Beaming, Mrs. Bloom handed Michael, who had evidently just risen in her estimation, a key. "Harold can show you to your room.''

Michael draped an arm over Laura's shoulder and headed for the elevators. "No, thanks. I think we can find our way.''

The manager started to protest, something about a video and a tour of the suite, and Harold stepped forward.

Michael didn't even slow down. The elevator doors closed on Harold, a confused bellboy in an ill-fitting uniform who wasn't quite sure if he should tag along or not. Laura had a feeling Michael would have escorted Harold from the elevator if he'd tried to join them.

When the doors were closed Michael took Laura in his arms and kissed her, holding tight and kissing her as if it were the first time, or the last, as if they'd never get this chance again.

There was nothing quite so wonderful, she decided as the elevator moved smoothly upward, as a long, slow, deep kiss.

The doors opened on their floor, but they didn't know it until another couple stepped on to take the elevator down. If the man hadn't bumped into Michael as he reached for the lobby button, they might have made the trip down and back up again. Which wouldn't have been, Laura decided as Michael grabbed her hand and pulled her from the elevator just before the doors closed, such a bad thing. A kiss like that shouldn't be rushed.

The Blue Hawaii Suite was a testament to bad taste and, of course, to the fiftieth state. In the front room there were plastic and silk tropical plants, a distressing Polynesian mask against one wall, a pair of hula-dancer lamps complete with fringe shades bracketing a brightly colorful floral sofa, and—of course—Elvis on velvet. In this particular rendering he was wearing a Hawaiian print shirt and standing before a singularly vivid blue wave.

On the far wall there was a mural, so that a hotel guest might squint and pretend it was a wide window overlooking the surf and a towering volcano, and there in the corner was a working waterfall, with gently rushing water over smooth rock that emptied into a small pool.

The bedroom was no better, but once they were through those doors she didn't have time to take inventory. There was a king-size bed covered in a tropical-inspired spread of orange and red and turquoise and draped with what appeared to be mosquito netting—and that was as far as she got in her inspection.

"I love the rain," Michael whispered as he pushed her wet coat off her shoulders. Raindrops pattered against the windows, the sound seeming to buffer the two of them from the outside world, isolating them. He reached behind her to lower the zipper of her gray dress, and she stepped out of her shoes as he pushed the dress off her shoulders.

"Me, too," she said, standing on her toes to kiss him again, molding her lips to his. Surely she would never get enough of this, of the taste and the feel of Michael. "Do you remember," she said breathlessly as she unbuttoned his shirt, "that night . . . ?"

"After the concert."

"Yes," she said, stripping off his shirt for him.

"We got caught walking in the rain," he said, unfastening her bra and tossing it to the floor, where it landed on top of his shirt. He touched her breasts tenderly, tracing the soft globes and brushing his thumb over one hard nipple. "And we ended up at my apartment at two in the morning, soaking wet and laughing and . . . and undressing each other just like this," he said as he slipped his fingers into the waistband of her panties.

"So excited," she added as she unsnapped the top snap of his jeans, "that we didn't even make it to the bed, much less think of . . ."

173

Linda Jones

"Protection," he finished as they fell to the bed. "I still think about that night. Dream about it, close my eyes and hear the way you laughed and cried. I wake up with your scent in my nose and the feel of you on my hands as if I'd just touched you, but it never lasts."

"We made Megan that night," she said, the words coming so easily, so naturally after all her inept rehearsals.

He was very still for a moment, and then he kissed her neck, feathering kisses first and then sucking gently. When he lifted his head from her neck he whispered with a smile, "I know." She could see the twinkle in his eyes, and wondered why she'd ever worried about his reaction to the news.

"When did you figure it out?" She slipped her fingers into the waistband of his jeans and waited for her answer.

"Last night." His smile faded, and he lowered his head to kiss her thoroughly. There was nothing gentle about this kiss, nothing tender. It was pure heat, demanding hunger, a mating of their mouths that promised more.

There was a definite reluctance as he took his mouth from hers to speak again. "I looked at her and saw my eyes, and then I looked at her again and saw us."

They came together with a passion reminiscent of that rainy night five years ago, limbs entangled and bodies searching, touching, reaching. But there was something better now, something more. No doubts remained between them, and this time . . . this time Laura believed with all her heart that no matter what, they belonged together—now and always.

As Michael stroked her body with his, as he kissed her again and again, Laura heard the muffled strains of an old radio somewhere playing "Always On My Mind." It came to her softly, and yet it was very clear—muffled, and still so close she could hear every word distinctly. And then she was so lost in the way Michael loved her she didn't hear anything at all but his whispered "I love you."

174

Chapter Eight

After a short phone call it was decided that it would be best for Elaine to come to Memphis for Jennifer, rather than Laura driving her niece to Grandma's house. Facing her mother tomorrow, on Christmas Day, would be soon enough for Laura. More than soon enough. And Elaine wouldn't wait another day to have her eldest daughter with her. It was, after all, Christmas Eve.

Michael had left the hotel early, after suggesting that she and the girls move into the Blue Hawaii Suite. It hadn't taken them long to throw their things into suitcases and trudge down the hall.

Megan was delighted with the bigger rooms, with the hula lamps and the waterfall, and most especially with the Elvis on velvet, which she declared a better likeness than the one in the old room. Laura didn't argue with her. Not today.

Elaine came by to collect Jennifer well before noon. Jennifer was not happy to leave when they'd just moved into the very cool Blue Hawaii Suite, but she knew better than to argue with her mother for very long. Elaine had always been very

175

big on family and holidays. As they left, Jennifer with her small suitcase in hand and Elaine leading the way, Laura stopped her sister with a stilling hand.

"Tell Mom," Laura said softly, "that I'll be there tomorrow in time for dinner. And tell her . . ." She swallowed hard. This was not going to be easy. "Tell her if I'm lucky and I don't mess things up in the next twenty-four hours, I'll have Michael with me, and she'd damn well better welcome him with open arms if she wants Megan and me there."

Elaine bit one side of her lower lip, and then sent Jennifer to the end of the hall to get the elevator. When Jennifer was out of hearing range, Elaine leaned in close. "That won't be easy."

"I know she doesn't like Michael, and she never forgave him for . . . for Megan, but this is my life, and she can't make my decisions for me."

Elaine leaned against the wall. "She knows why you came to Memphis, you know. Last night she told me she was terrified you'd fall back in love with 'that piano player' and he'd break your heart again."

"It's my heart," Laura insisted.

Elaine smiled gently. "You have a daughter now. Wouldn't you do anything, including murder, to protect her heart, body, and soul?"

Laura nodded. "Sure, but—"

"Then forgive Mom for what she told me last night." Elaine hesitated before continuing, and Laura felt a cold chill shoot through her veins.

"Forgive her for what?"

Elaine's smile faded, and Laura didn't like the look that came over her sister's face. This was Elaine's most serious, I-hate-to-tell-you-this-but face. "Michael came looking for you one night a few years back, the Christmas after Katie was born, to be exact. Mom told him you were happy and didn't need him, and then he saw you with Katie and Wes and apparently assumed that they were both yours. Mom didn't feel compelled to tell him any different, and she didn't want to tell

Thrill to the most sensual, adventure-filled Historical Romances on the market today...

FROM  LEISURE BOOKS

As a home subscriber to Leisure Romance Book Club, you'll enjoy the best in today's BRAND-NEW Historical Romance fiction. For over twenty-five years, Leisure Books has brought you the award-winning, high-quality authors you know and love to read. Each Leisure Historical Romance will sweep you away to a world of high adventure...and intimate romance. Discover for yourself all the passion and excitement millions of readers thrill to each and every month.

Save $5.00 Each Time You Buy!

Each month, the Leisure Romance Book Club brings you four brand-new titles from Leisure Books, America's foremost publisher of Historical Romances. EACH PACKAGE WILL SAVE YOU $5.00 FROM THE BOOKSTORE PRICE! And you'll never miss a new title with our convenient home delivery service.

Here's how we do it. Each package will carry a FREE 10-DAY EXAMINATION privilege. At the end of that time, if you decide to keep your books, simply pay the low invoice price of $16.96, no shipping or handling charges added. HOME DELIVERY IS ALWAYS FREE. With today's top Historical Romance novels selling for $5.99 and higher, our price SAVES YOU $5.00 with each shipment.

AND YOUR FIRST FOUR-BOOK SHIPMENT IS TOTALLY FREE!
IT'S A BARGAIN YOU CAN'T BEAT! A Super $21.96 Value!

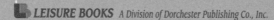 **LEISURE BOOKS** A Division of Dorchester Publishing Co., Inc.

GET YOUR 4 FREE BOOKS
NOW—A $21.96 Value!

Mail the Free Book Certificate Today!

Get Four Books Totally FREE — A $21.96 Value!

▼ Tear Here and Mail Your FREE Book Card Today! ▼

PLEASE RUSH
MY FOUR FREE
BOOKS TO ME
RIGHT AWAY!

Leisure Romance Book Club
P.O. Box 6613
Edison, NJ 08818-6613

AFFIX
STAMP
HERE

you that he'd come by because she was afraid you'd get involved and hurt all over again.''

Laura didn't know whether she wanted more to cry or to punch a hole through the wall. Michael had come back for her, and her mother had sent him on his way and never seen fit to share that information. It would have made a difference, Laura knew. She would have found the nerve to face him years ago if she'd known he still cared.

"Elevator!" Jennifer yelled impatiently.

Elaine took off down the hall, glancing over her shoulder once. "See you tomorrow?"

"Sure," Laura said, unable to move. "We'll be there."

No wonder it had taken Michael so long to realize that Megan was his daughter. Megan was a full year older than Katie, so he'd naturally assumed she was three years old, not four. He probably thought she'd found the stable, dependable man she'd been looking for and forgotten all about Michael. How could she ever forgive her mother?

The only reason she could even consider forgiveness was the one Elaine had offered. Megan had made her realize how far any mother would go to protect her child. When Megan hurt, Laura hurt; when Megan cried, Laura cried for her.

Maybe, in her own way, her mother had been trying to protect her. Laura had to take some responsibility for this. If she'd ever been brave enough to tell her mother the truth about the breakup with Michael, instead of resorting to tears and silence, that night three years ago might have turned out differently.

It was Christmas Eve, and Megan was so excited she literally couldn't sit still. She played with her toys, climbed over the green and yellow and red flowered sofa, and closely examined the hula girl lamps again and again.

Laura found herself pacing, as anxious as Megan. An hour passed, and then another. Where was Michael? What if her mother was right after all; what if he was going to break her heart all over again?

No, she refused to believe that. She had faith in him, had

faith in what they had. No matter what happened, they belonged together.

The knock on the door startled her, and she nearly jumped out of her skin.

She opened the door to face a Christmas tree decorated with white and gold satin ornaments and weaving precariously as the man who carried it swayed back under its weight. Beyond the branches, she saw Michael. His arms were full of packages big and small, and he was providing support, with one shoulder, for the bellhop who carried the tree.

Laura backed away from the door and let them in. Megan was delighted with the tree the weary bellhop placed by the window, and with the packages Michael placed beneath it. The bellhop seemed significantly cheered when Michael placed a hundred-dollar bill in his hand and wished him Merry Christmas.

"Sorry I was gone so long," Michael said as Megan examined the packages beneath the tree, fingering the bows and looking for her name. She squealed when she found that several were designated for her.

"Do we have to wait for tomorrow?" she pleaded, throwing herself at Laura's legs.

"It's not Christmas yet," Laura said as she brushed Megan's bangs away from her face. "Tomorrow morning—"

"I can't wait until tomorrow morning." Laura had expected this statement from Megan, but it came from Michael. "My Aunt Dinah always let me open my gifts on Christmas Eve."

"It's Christmas Eve right now," Megan said, jumping up and down before them.

Outnumbered, Laura relented, and Megan grabbed the largest package and began to unwrap it. Laura almost groaned when she saw what it was: a small keyboard.

Michael leaned over and whispered in Laura's ear, "I thought maybe I could give her lessons."

Laura couldn't help but smile. The other packages contained more conventional gifts for a little girl. There was a doll, and a stuffed giraffe, and another doll, and lastly a T-shirt with a picture of Elvis on the front and the back.

"Bring that little package to your mother," Michael instructed when Megan had opened all her presents. She obeyed dutifully, and then threw herself into Michael's lap.

"Thank you," she said, and then she planted a kiss on Michael's cheek. Before it could become a truly touching moment, she climbed down, unknowingly kneeing him in the crotch as she made her way.

"We're going to have to have a talk." Michael groaned as Megan made her way back to her presents, heading straight for the keyboard.

He turned to Laura with a smile and directed her to open her present. The box was tiny, square, and she knew what was in that box before she ever touched the gold wrapping.

She hadn't, however, expected anything so dramatic. She thought she might find a small diamond to cement everything they'd talked about last night, or something unconventional like an emerald or a pearl. What she saw when she opened the box was a set of three rings—matching gold wedding bands and the biggest diamond she'd ever seen.

"Michael!" she blurted when she could speak. "This is too much. I can't—"

"Yes, you can," he said calmly, taking the engagement ring from the box and slipping it onto her finger. "And I'll have you know I'm not into long engagements," he added as he slipped his fingers through hers. "I figure we can get married next week."

"Next week?" She was surprised, but found herself smiling.

"Unless you think you might change your mind."

She leaned close and kissed him quickly. "No chance of that, piano man. Next week it is."

Contented, Michael leaned back against the couch and turned to the tree and his daughter. "Megan," he said softly, "you have one more present."

"I do?" She jumped up, forgetting her keyboard for the moment to come to the sofa and stand before Michael with her hands on his knees and wonder in her eyes. "Really?"

Michael held up a finger, indicating that she should wait a

179

moment. He reached into his pocket and pulled out a large white tag and a smashed gold bow. The sticky-backed bow he slapped to his chest, and the tag he slipped over his wrist. Megan furrowed her brow and bent over the tag.

"I can see my name, but I can't read all that writing." She gave him a slightly censuring glance. "I'm only four, you know."

"Maybe Mommy can read it for you."

Laura's heart was in her throat as she turned the tag her way and began to read aloud. "For Megan. One daddy, slightly imperfect and gently used. Needs hugs and kisses daily to thrive. Must share with Mommy."

Megan's eyes got big, and then a wide smile grew, spreading across her face until she wore a full-blown grin. "Yeah!" she said, jumping into Michael's lap and throwing her arms around his neck. "Oh, you'll make the best daddy, I just know you will."

"I'm gonna try," Michael said softly, wrapping his arms around his daughter. "I'm gonna try."

Laura leaned her head on Michael's shoulder and placed a hand on Megan's back, and for a long, wonderful moment, they were all perfectly still. Laura drank in the perfection of the moment, reveled in the touch of the two people she loved most in the world.

With Megan, the cherished moments of warmth and silence and stillness never lasted long, and this was no exception. She scrambled off Michael's lap—without injuring him this time—and planted herself before him with her chin in the air.

"I hab a pwesent for you, too," she said smugly. "Elbis and I hab been working on it for days."

Megan looked up and to her left, as if someone tall stood there. She giggled, then looked at Michael and wrinkled her nose. "He's wearing a Santa hat today." Then she nodded once, and began to sing.

It was a song Laura had never heard before. Beautiful and sad, it was a love song about cold rain and lost love. She didn't think much of it—after all, it might have been a song Megan heard on the radio or on CMT while she'd been with Jennifer.

It wasn't until she looked at Michael, who had gone deathly pale, that she knew something was wrong.

Megan sang, looking up occasionally to her invisible partner. She even lifted her hand into the air, where it hovered as if someone were holding it gently.

When she finished, apparently in the middle of the song, there was a moment of complete silence.

"That was very good, Megan," Laura said. "Where did you learn that song?"

"Elbis taught it to me."

"Megan—"

"Maybe he did," Michael whispered, and Laura turned to see that his face was still much too pale.

"Don't encourage her."

Michael shook his head. "I'm not. Laura, that's my song, the one I'm writing for Modine. The tune's written down and locked in a safe in my office, and the words are here"—he tapped his temple—"and nowhere else. I've been having trouble finishing it. And just now while they . . . she was singing, the ending came to me in a flash, the way it sometimes does." He looked thoroughly confused. "Megan just helped me finish my song. It's not the sad ending I usually end up with, but it's right."

Megan placed her hands on his knees. "Elbis said you were . . ." She looked up and waited for inspiration or instruction. "Blocked. He said you need to remember that sometimes wainy nights are happy. And he also says that girl who's supposed to sing it needs another key."

Megan turned her head to look at her mother. "Why does she need a key to sing? I can sing without a key."

Laura tried to think of a logical explanation for all this, but nothing came to her offhand.

Megan climbed into Michael's lap again, and laid her hands on his face. "Elbis says you can make 'em cry, but you hab happy songs in your heart, too."

"Did you tell her . . ." Michael began, his eyes firmly planted on his daughter.

"No," Laura said softly, and then she took a deep breath.

There had to be a logical explanation . . . but she couldn't think of one. Her eyes searched the room for a sign, a ghostly image in white polyester, maybe, or levitating blue suede shoes. She saw nothing, but all of a sudden she heard the same radio that had been playing last night—"Always On My Mind," haunting and distant, and yet somehow very close. "Do you hear that?" she whispered.

"Hear what?" Michael asked.

"Music." Laura swallowed hard. " 'Always On My Mind.' Please tell me you hear it."

Michael shook his head. "I don't hear anything. If this is your idea of a joke . . ." He looked into her eyes and apparently saw that she was definitely *not* joking. "I talked to this guy in the lobby last night, and he was . . . he was . . . singing." She could almost see the working of his mind in the narrowing of his eyes and the set of his mouth. "Amazing. Do you know what this means?"

Instinctively, she leaned close to him, searching for comfort and security. She found both. "I don't know. Another plane? Ghosts? Life after death?"

Michael shook his head slowly. "It means Elvis sang one of my songs." Impossibly, he smiled.

The music died away, fading gradually until she heard nothing. For a second, just a split second, she was certain she saw a shimmering of something gold and blue and insubstantial beside the tree. And then it was gone.

Megan touched her pert little nose to Michael's long one, and smiled the smile of a child who had just received the gift she wished for with all her heart. "Mewwy Cwistmas, Daddy."

"Merry Christmas, baby," he whispered back.

Megan narrowed her eyes and cocked her head first one way and then another, studying her new daddy as if searching for faults. Apparently satisfied after a short inspection, she turned to her mother with a grin. "Next year," she said softly, "I want a sister."

Sharon Pisacreta

All Shook Up

For my cousin Cheryl Hanson,
who listened to all of my stories long before anyone
else did.

Chapter One

Kim Hanson had arrived in Memphis only an hour earlier, but she suspected either the city or her cough syrup was making her hallucinate. Crammed in the elevator with her were a police officer, two Elvis impersonators, an elderly woman clutching a thermos, and three nervous white poodles. And somewhere—hopefully—her bellhop and luggage. She couldn't move her neck enough to see. For all she knew, there was a partridge in a pear tree in here, too.

One of the poodles began gnawing on her ankle just as the elevator mercifully rattled to a stop.

"Please let me off."

No one moved.

"Let the little lady out!" The police officer had a voice as piercing as a smoke alarm. His bellow set the dogs to barking, startling the elderly woman, who dropped her thermos, which one of the Elvis impersonators stooped to pick up, allowing Kim just that little window of opportunity to fling herself out of the elevator.

Sharon Pisacreta

When she opened her eyes once more, the elevator had rattled onward and upward.

"You coming?" Her bellhop stood about ten feet away, his
little cap askew on his head. Somehow that cocked hat made
the wizened face beneath it that much more jarring.

Before she had a chance to appreciate the flocked wallpaper
or the gilt-framed paintings of Elvis lining the hallway, her
bellhop was already on the move. For an older fellow, he
seemed quite spry. She found herself breaking into a jog just
to keep up.

"I didn't know the hotel allowed pets."

"The Original Heartbreak Hotel don't permit pets, ma'am."

"It's just that I noticed the poodles in the elevator."

"Like I said, this here hotel don't permit guests to bring in
animals. Back in 1966, Mr. Amos Jackson from Helena, Arkansas, brought in two ferrets that caused no end of damage
to the fourth floor. No pets since then." They stopped in front
of Room 320.

"So what are the poodles doing here?"

He shrugged. "Couldn't say, ma'am. That's not my business."

The large key jingled in the lock as he turned it. He mo-
tioned for her to precede him.

Kim entered the suite only to stop dead in her tracks.
"There's a roulette table in here!"

The bellhop bustled past her. "Just a coffee table, ma'am.
But the wheel does move if you push it hard enough. Even
so, don't get carried away and start gambling. If the front desk
hears that guests are laying bets up here, I'm afraid they'll call
the law." He disappeared into the next room with her luggage.

She approached the roulette table cautiously, as though it
were a living creature that might harm her.

The table was so big, it took up nearly the whole sitting
area. What little space remained was swallowed up by gold
fabric chairs and glittering lamps shaped like slot machines.
She looked around in wonder. Dice and playing cards be-
speckled the pale yellow wallpaper, while two life-size pho-

tographs of Elvis and Ann-Margret water-skiing stood framed on each side of the bedroom door.

She sniffed. The room smelled faintly of gasoline.

The bellhop emerged from the bedroom. "In there is a king-size bed with a water mattress. Only three of them in the hotel, so you're a lucky one."

Piles of poker chips decorated the desk in the corner; above the desk hung laminated instruction sheets for baccarat and blackjack. And most bizarre, a glass case on the wall held a waiter's white jacket.

Kim plopped down in the nearest chair, her legs suddenly unsteady. The pillows on the sofa across from her had the words LUCKY LOVES RUSTY embroidered on them.

"What is all this?"

"Didn't they tell you downstairs? This here is the Viva Las Vegas Suite. Real popular with our honeymooners. If the Blue Hawaii Suite is booked, they always ask for this one."

It took a moment before she could tear her gaze from the car engines that served as tables for the slot-machine lamps.

He grinned widely at whatever bill she had fished out of her wallet. How large a tip had she given him?

"Who are Lucky and Rusty?" She pointed to the pillows.

"Like I said, this is the Viva Las Vegas Suite."

"Oh."

"Every suite in the hotel is named—and decorated—after an Elvis song or movie. You even got the video to watch in that cabinet there, and music from the movie in here." He pressed a button on the nearby tape player/radio.

The sound of Elvis belting out the words "Viva Las Vegas" filled the air.

He straightened his cap. "Well, hope you enjoy your stay in the hotel. Coffee shop downstairs is open twenty-four hours. Best restaurant cooking in Memphis, long as you don't eat there on a Tuesday. And don't get worried at night if you think you see something you shouldn't."

She shot him what she knew to be a very worried expression.

"The Original Heartbreak Hotel is haunted." His wrinkled

face took on a somber expression. "I thought everyone knew that."

"Haunted?"

The old man nodded. "I suppose you can guess by who."

Kim glanced over at the keno-pad calendar hanging on the speckled wall. "The decorator?"

"Nah, she's still alive." He leaned closer. "Folks swear that the ghost of Elvis lives in the hotel. I don't want to be scaring you none, but I've seen things with my own eyes that don't bear repeating. Stories I'd best keep for guests who look like nothing would rattle 'em. But I wouldn't fret if I was you." He gestured to her suite. "Seems Elvis ain't too fond of this room. Don't know why. Maybe it's that dang awful air freshener. Smells just like motor oil."

The door shut behind him, leaving her alone with Elvis still singing "Viva Las Vegas" on the tape player. Above her she could swear she heard dogs barking.

"But who are Rusty and Lucky?" she wondered aloud.

She felt as though she'd just gotten on a roller coaster, and the ride of her life was about to begin.

Kim hadn't flown all the way down here to be bested by Elvis, poodles, or slot-machine lamps. She'd even thrown away her cough syrup. If her nervous cough returned, she'd just tough it out. Like her Swedish forebears, like her mom. Like she knew she could.

"Yes, I'm still here," she said when someone at last came back on the line. "I don't care if it is Saturday; I know Mr. Modine is in today. His assistant told me that he meets with his vice president of commercial sales every Saturday morning."

Hadn't she thrown caution to the wind on that very slim bit of hope by packing a bag and flying out here? Fugitives from justice probably moved slower than she had these past twenty-four hours. She certainly felt as desperate as an outlaw.

It was now or never for Kim. If she didn't snag a lucrative client by the New Year, she'd end up in bankruptcy court. And the public relations firm she had worked so hard to build these past five years would be dissolved in weeks unless she could find a client so celebrated, so financially secure, that just by association her company would have a chance at a second life.

Now here she was in Memphis six days before Christmas, ready to do her best to impress Spencer Modine. The industry grapevine claimed Modine was looking for fresh new talent for his many business ventures in Tennessee. A former Silicon Valley computer genius, Modine had designed incredibly successful software, retiring rich at the tender age of thirty-one. Three years later, he was back in his native Memphis, working hard to revitalize the city's economy with his sizable fortune.

Kim's sights were set on Modine Music. Their first PR firm had not worked out so, for one heart-stopping moment, Modine Music was up for grabs. If she could just convince Modine to let her handle his record company's public relations, her own business had a chance to survive.

"No, don't put me on hold again, please." She paced the room, the phone cord yanking her back whenever she wandered too far. "I've been most persistent these past four weeks trying to set up an appointment, and I was given to understand—"

Kim tripped and landed in a heap on the floor. Looking for the dropped phone, she noticed it lying beside an overturned bucket of toy cars.

"Yes, I'm sorry, the phone must have slipped. I must insist on speaking to someone else if you can't help me." She paused. "Thank you. Thank you very much. Two o'clock."

She hung up, stunned. Spencer Modine had agreed to meet with her in two hours. She fell back on the carpeting, hoping her heart wouldn't start racing from anxiety now. Above her, Elvis and Ann-Margret water-skied happily, while scattered about her were little metal racing cars. And she had just noticed that not only did a poster of a Las Vegas swimming pool hang over the bed, but the words POOL MANAGER were stenciled on the wall above it.

She didn't understand this movie at all.

* * *

This was his favorite part: when the tenor sax cut loose, and he and the lead guitar leaned way back in the melody, riffing and trading licks. A person could feel the heat just radiating off the CD. Spencer shut his eyes, letting the music wash over him like a hot summer rain. Yes, this was his favorite part.

The rear door of his car opened suddenly. He looked up in surprise as a young woman hurriedly got in. She was so intent on closing her briefcase that she didn't even spare him a glance.

"Why won't this ever stay shut?" she muttered.

"Excuse me, miss, but can I help you?" Spencer sat up straighter. He could see only the top of her head—which was all blond, tousled hair—and the black business suit that made her petite frame look even slimmer.

He turned down the CD player. "Is there something I can help you with?"

"What?" She looked up at him as if *he* were the one to invade *her* car. At least now he could see her face. Such a nice face, too. Pert little nose, a wide mouth that probably held the silliest grin if it ever allowed a smile, and very big brown eyes—just about the same shade of brown as his favorite Gibson guitar. And she smelled intoxicating, like apple cinnamon and vanilla.

"Oh, I'm sorry. I'd like you to take me to Modine Music on Winchester Road. The street number is—"

He laughed. "I know where it is."

She sat back, arranging her purse and briefcase neatly on her lap. "Then could you drive me there, please? I have a two o'clock appointment that I can't be late for."

Spencer pulled off his baseball cap and scratched his head. "Miss, are you sure?"

"You are a cabdriver, right?" She pointed out the window at the curbside sign that read TAXIS ONLY. "They told me at the front desk that gypsy cabs were safe to take as long as I used only those that normally came to the hotel."

He hadn't even noticed where he'd parked. Not that there were ever all that many cabs in front of the Original Heartbreak Hotel. But still, who could imagine that his vintage 1957 purple Thunderbird was a cab? This distracted young lady, apparently.

"And you want to go to Modine Music for a two o'clock appointment?" He faced her now, letting her see him with the baseball cap off.

She nodded. "Is that a problem for you?"

"Oh, no problem, miss." He sat back and shoved his cap back on. "Just flew in from out of town?"

"Yes, Minnesota. Could we go, please? I can't be late."

It had to be her. After all, how many young businesswomen from Minnesota had a two o'clock Saturday appointment with Spencer Modine? Only one.

So this was Kim Hanson. He'd been curious about this persistent young woman from St. Paul. Never had any other company—especially one so small—tried so doggedly to get an appointment with him. After the second week, his people had checked into both the woman and her public relations firm in Minnesota. He'd read the report an hour ago, and been impressed with both her résumé and her fierce determination to land the account.

Even though he doubted a firm as small as hers could handle Modine Music, he thought it would be a friendly gesture if he went early to the hotel and met her in the lobby. That way he could find out more about her in a relaxed setting. But she hadn't recognized him.

She's too anxious to see clearly, he thought, looking at the grim set of her jaw. *All she can see is a funny purple car, and a man wearing a baseball cap and a faded high school letter jacket.* She was the type who did all her research using spreadsheets. Too bad. Spreadsheet types never did well working for him. They couldn't relax enough and accommodate what his people called—fondly, he hoped—the Modine Madness.

"Anything you say, miss." He swiveled the cap so it faced backward. This might be fun.

Spencer shifted his T-bird into gear, the tires burning rubber. He turned up the volume on his CD player so that the blues guitar riffs of "High On the Hog" thundered through the car.

"Course, there's no reason we can't shoot around the corner to Beale Street first, just to give you a look at some of the best clubs in the South."

"Absolutely not. I told you I have an appointment."

"But you'll want to see B. B. King's club. Do you know B. B. and I wear the same size shoe? Well, we do. Once we even switched shoes. Fit as perfect as Cinderella's glass slipper."

"Excuse me, sir."

He ignored her. "And maybe a fast turn down to Graceland. You can't go to Modine Music before you've even caught a glimpse of Graceland. Otherwise you might as well be in Toledo. While we're there, you can take a gander at some of the graffiti. The graffiti on Graceland's wall is world-famous. If you want, I can stop at a convenience store, pick up a few markers, and you can write something on the wall yourself. Won't take more than ten or fifteen minutes. Twenty minutes tops."

"I told you that I was in a hurry!"

"This baby here can hit ninety miles an hour; you won't even know it." He turned and gave her a half wink. " 'Cept when we make a turn. Then there's a chance we just might roll.'"

"I want to get off here." She pointed to the next street corner. "Let me out right now or I'll press charges."

"Now calm down; I'll take you straight to where you want to go, miss." Maybe this wasn't the sort of woman who enjoyed a practical joke.

He shot through an amber light. Probably it was best to get her to his office as quickly as possible. She looked positively frantic. "Okay, miss, I'm taking you to Modine Music. I promise. I won't even mention B. B. King or his feet."

She flung open her briefcase, rummaging through it. "I'm going to write down your number and report you to the gypsy cab people, or whoever is responsible for a madman like you being out on the road."

"Look, I should have told you." Spencer suddenly found

this whole charade completely absurd. "I mean, I'm not a cabdriver."

"What!" Her face turned white in the rearview mirror.

"Okay, okay, we're almost there." Good thing he was driving his Thunderbird. It was the only car that could possibly have gotten them to his office at roughly the speed of light.

"Who are you then?" Her voice sounded thin and shaky. Damn, he could kick himself for scaring her like this.

He squealed to a stop in front of the chrome-and-glass exterior of Modine Music. "I really thought you'd recognize me at some point."

Swiveling around, he saw only the top of her head as she dug feverishly in her purse. "Guess it's time for formal introductions. Miss Hanson, I'm Spencer Modine, and I'd like—"

He never finished the sentence. All he saw was mist from a small bottle being sprayed into his eyes before everything became one burning, stinging blur.

Kim felt terrible. Beyond terrible. She looked at the clock. Nearly ninety minutes had gone by since she'd attacked Spencer Modine, and still no one had come to reassure her. Or arrest her.

How could she not have recognized him? She had a copy of *Money* even now in her briefcase with Modine on the cover. It was just that he looked so different in the baseball cap and moth-eaten jacket. Not to mention all that light, sandy hair that kept falling into his eyes.

She groaned. His eyes. Right before she'd sprayed them, she noticed they were a lovely shade of blue. And now he would probably never see again. She'd maimed the very man she hoped would save her business.

A fit of nervous coughing overcame her. "I've blinded him," she wailed between coughs. "I just know I've blinded him."

She grabbed at the pewter flask on the desk, pouring herself a glass of water. No more losing control. She'd already done that once today, and now the Boy Wonder of Memphis was probably doomed to blindness or disfigurement. Could perfume squirted directly into the eyes cause permanent scarring? She swigged down the water. Why hadn't she grabbed her plastic bottle of eyewash instead? He could have the cleanest eyes in the building right now instead of the most inflamed.

Breathe deeply, she told herself, sitting back and trying to remain calm. She looked around the room. If this was Spencer Modine's office, then she clearly had the man pegged wrong. Although the teak desk in front of her was stacked neatly with leather-bound portfolios, the rest of the office resembled nothing more than an overgrown boy's bedroom. Shelves displaying everything from toy trains to G.I. Joes lined one wall, while at least a dozen guitars hung—some crookedly—from the opposite wall. The glassed-in bookshelves held comic books, and along the window ran a long showcase table containing an endless array of sheet music and vinyl records.

She bit her lip. "And now he may never see any of this again."

"Oh, it takes more than a spray of Apple-Spice Mist to blind a man, Miss Hanson." Spencer Modine walked in, his eyes red and a bit swollen. "That is what this stuff is called, isn't it? Lucky for me, it was only perfume, although it will do until you buy that can of Mace." He dropped the tiny spray bottle into her lap.

"You can see!" She felt giddy with relief.

"As well as any eagle at Reelfoot Lake. You gave it a good shot, though. I'd lay odds on you any day if a taxi driver tries to make off with you again."

What a wonderful crooked grin he had. Comforting, yet seductive, she thought. Like his voice, warm as honey, with a hint of a drawl.

He walked around to the other side of his desk. The letter jacket and baseball cap were gone, but he still didn't look like a businessman. Odd, but she never pictured the celebrated Mr. Modine in a black T-shirt and faded blue jeans. His sandy hair kept falling into his eyes—his very red eyes—and a wave of remorse washed over her once more.

"I'm so, so sorry, Mr. Modine."

"No, please, I'm the one who should apologize. Stupid thing for me to do anyway." He flung himself down in his burgundy leather chair. The muscles in his shoulders and arms filled out his T-shirt quite nicely. "The whole thing is my fault. I should have sent a car to pick you up, but I finished a jam session early and thought it might relax both of us if I just tooled down to the hotel myself." He rubbed at his eyes and laughed. "When I saw that you didn't recognize me, I couldn't help trying to play around a bit. Never had a woman mistake me for a cabbie before. One or two have told me I look like Kevin Costner, but never a cabbie."

"You do look a bit like him."

"Don't see it myself. Anyway, my mama would have my hide if she knew I was still teasing the girls like when I was in first grade. So my apologies, Miss Hanson. But I'm not known for conducting business like a proper businessman." He winked. "Can't say it's hurt me any."

"You were coming to pick me up?" Two hours ago, the prospect of such a powerful man playing chauffeur would have been unthinkable. But apparently anything might be possible with Spencer Otis Modine. "I feel so guilty now."

He nodded. "Maybe a little business talk will distract you."

"You still want to talk business?"

"I think it's the safest thing for both of us." He opened a leather portfolio. "Although I don't usually conduct business on Saturdays."

"But I was told you had a standing Saturday appointment with your vice president of commercial sales."

"You mean my jam sessions with William Stowe? Willie and I have been jamming every weekend since we met at Stanford. Don't think there's a vice president in the country who plays drums as wicked as Willie. If I'm in town, we always get together Saturday morning with some musicians in one of the studios downstairs. I wouldn't normally have told my assistant I'd see you, but since we're closed next week for the holidays, I didn't see the harm in squeezing you in for a few minutes this afternoon."

He chuckled. "Besides, I noticed in your paperwork here

195

that one of the contact people at Hanson Productions is your secretary, Gladys L. Smith. Now how can a good ol' Memphis boy like me not be curious about a woman who has a secretary named after Elvis's mother?''

Kim felt totally disoriented, as if she were back in the Viva Las Vegas Suite again. "Gladys is named after who?''

"Just a little thing that caught my eye. Shouldn't have mentioned it." Modine looked up at her, and for some strange reason, she suspected that she had disappointed him. "Gladys Love Smith was the maiden name of Elvis Presley's mother. Don't suppose your secretary's middle name is Love?''

She shook her head. "I think it's Lynn."

"It's not important. Anyway, I agreed to see you today because I'd hate to have you fly home with nothing to show for it."

"I'm willing to stay as long as it takes, Mr. Modine." She straightened in her chair. "All week and next, if need be."

He gave her a curious look. "You must have a better way to spend Christmas week than chasing after appointments with me. And people you'd rather spend it with.''

Her boyfriend's face briefly flashed before her. Jon Karl had said the same thing before she left. Well, she had risked destroying their relationship to come down here. And she was willing to risk humiliation and failure if only Modine gave her a chance to make her case.

"Nothing is more important to me than convincing you that my firm can handle Modine Music."

He looked at her. Even inflamed, his eyes were a soft blue. For all his wealth, power, and good looks, Spencer Modine seemed a kind man. *Let him be kind now. Please let him give me a chance.*

As if he heard her silent plea, Modine nodded.

"Okay, Miss Hanson. I'm listening." He leaned back in his chair. "Convince me you're the person for the job."

How hopeless. And sad. He simply couldn't give her what she so desperately wanted. Not that her credentials weren't impeccable. Boasting an MBA from the University of Minnesota, the twenty-eight-year-old woman pleading her case before him had obviously worked hard for a very long time, both to get through college and to set up and run her own public relations firm.

He'd already read her portfolio. Hanson Productions had flourished until the past year—largely due to Miss Hanson's efforts—but now it was failing, and she didn't know how to plug the leaks. He didn't hold it against her. He had his own ideas about why her firm was failing, but that wouldn't be enough to keep him from hiring her.

It was that he knew she wouldn't be happy working for him or his corporation. First off, he wanted his PR firm to be based in Memphis, and he just couldn't see this grimly intent young woman being happy here. Tiny worry lines showed around her eyes, as though she didn't sleep enough. And she had all sorts of nervous mannerisms, like a cough she worked hard to suppress.

He found her touching, like a pretty little bird that had forgotten it could once fly. If she lived in Memphis, he'd make sure to pick her up every Saturday morning in his favorite purple car and see that she ate plenty of gravy and biscuits. Then he'd take her to his jam sessions and let her kick her shoes off, lie on the floor, and feel the music filtering through her pores. Kim Hanson needed music, warmth, and more silly surprises in her life. A shame it wasn't his place to give them to her. Wasn't there anyone up in Minnesota trying to make her happy?

Spencer listened closely to her voice, so tight with tension. He suspected no one had tried to make her happy for a long time. Least of all herself. He closed the portfolio. He just had to make certain to let her down easy. Clearly she'd flown down here as a last-ditch effort to save her company, and she would be flying back knowing she had failed. But better to hurt her now rather than drag out the inevitable. Kim Hanson could never accommodate herself to the Modine Madness.

"You've made a fine presentation, Miss Hanson." He hated sounding so formal and businesslike, but he sensed that was what she expected.

Her eyes opened very wide. She looked like a frightened owl.

"I reviewed your firm and its record earlier. You have much to be proud of, and I'm certain you're capable of handling an account as large as Modine Music. But I'm afraid that logistically and personally, it wouldn't be a happy fit for either of us."

He went on quickly. "Now, I see that your firm is having problems, and I think I can advise you on how to rectify some of them. But other than that, I feel that handing over my Memphis record label to Hanson Productions would be unfair to both of us."

Please don't let her cry, he thought.

Instead, she sat as still as a stone. That was even worse.

"Miss Hanson?" He started to get up. "Are you okay?"

"You're turning me down?" Her voice came out in a croak.

"Well, yeah, I'm afraid I am." He ran his fingers through his hair in frustration. Maybe he could find something else for her to do. He didn't know what. Anything to prevent her from looking so stricken. "Look, I know what this means to you—"

"You can't know!"

He sighed. "You're probably right, but I have a lot of people and money riding on Modine Music. I won't jeopardize their future, no matter how much I might like to help yours."

"But I know I can do it. Please, Mr. Modine—" She broke off in a fit of coughing.

"Miss Hanson, don't do this to yourself."

"I can do it," she cried. Suddenly she grabbed the arms of the chair and turned even whiter. "Oh, no!"

"What?"

Her breathing became erratic and shallow, and she began wheezing like an old Chevy engine.

He raced around the desk and grabbed her by the shoulders. "What's wrong? Should I call 911?"

Gasping for breath, she shook her head. "Panic attack!" she managed to get out.

Damn, but he'd sent his doctor home as soon as his eyes

had been cleaned out. And there was no one else on this floor; even the janitors had left.

She clutched his shoulder. "Paper bag! To breathe into!"

He nearly dropped her in his hurry to find a paper bag. All he could come up with was a tennis sock in his desk drawer.

"Will this help?"

She clutched her chest. "I need a paper bag."

"Sit down. Calm down!" He had to stop shouting or he'd be having a panic attack next. "You've got to try to calm down. C'mon, you have to try."

She nodded, tears filling her eyes. But the wheezing and gasping continued.

Maybe some sort of distraction would help. He looked wildly around the room. The toy train wouldn't do it, nor a Spider Man comic. *Wait a minute!*

He ran to a corner cupboard. "Hold on. Keep breathing! Well, try not to think about breathing. I mean, just hold on."

She was a coughing, wheezing mess when he finally returned.

"Here!" He placed the one-foot-tall mechanical monkey on the desk before her and flipped the switch. It sprang to life, jerking and twitching, its metal lips moving. A second later, the monkey began loudly singing "All Shook Up." It was his favorite toy and his favorite song. If this didn't work, he'd have to club her.

"Miss Hanson, are you breathing? Kim?"

She suddenly grew still, her breathing slowing, her gasps becoming hiccups. The color slowly came back to her cheeks, and he leaned in relief against his desk. He gave her another moment to quiet down.

"Do you like him?" he finally asked.

Kim pressed a hand to her chest and nodded. Then she smiled.

Oh, Lord, what a smile—like sunshine after a month of storms. A man couldn't resist a smile like that, any more than he could resist a woman who came back to life because a toy monkey knew how to sing Elvis songs. Maybe he should give her a second chance. Certainly she deserved at least a ray of hope.

"Well, seeing as how you and Jim Bob have hit it off, I can't very well just turn you down flat."

"What?" Her voice came out in a ragged whisper.

"The first step in appreciating how we operate is appreciating Jim Bob, here. And you passed the first test."

Her big brown eyes lit up.

"Now, it's just a first step, and I can't promise anything, but, well, I ought to at least give you a fighting chance. You said you're willing to spend Christmas week down here."

She nodded.

"Let me take you around town—strictly business—and show you music and the way Memphis responds to it. Show you what made Elvis and what will make Modine Music. If by Christmas you can convince me that you understand Memphis, music, and what my employees call the 'Modine Madness,' then I'll give the account to your firm."

Even for him, this was a rash thing to do. Still, her public relations background was solid, and Lord knew, she would work hard enough for the corporation. She'd just about stopped breathing because of it.

"Thank you. Thank you so much, Mr. Modine." She tried to stand up but was still too shaky.

She smiled again, and for one moment Spencer felt his own breathing grow irregular.

Thankfully the monkey kept singing, distracting them both.

Chapter Two

After viewing *Viva Las Vegas* last night, Kim at least knew who Lucky and Rusty were now. Maybe she hadn't learned enough to convince Modine to give her the account, but she felt she'd accomplished something these past twenty-four hours—aside from making a fool of herself. Walking through the hotel lobby, Kim tried hard not to stare when she noticed two guests sporting Elvis sideburns, one of them a woman.

It was breezy and sunny outside, and the cool air felt good on her face. She'd dressed casually today: gray wool slacks and cardigan, peach turtleneck, penny loafers. After seeing what Modine had worn for their business meeting yesterday, she doubted his Sunday attire would be especially formal.

Two tour buses stood out front, along with a real cab. But there was no sign of Modine yet.

He's only doing this because he feels sorry for you, she told herself. *Going berserk in his office so he had to bring out a singing monkey!* Well, she didn't care if pity or guilt was keeping her in the game. She was still *in* the game, and that was all that mattered.

A Santa stood near the curb, ringing a bell for charity. She blinked when he turned around. Long dark sideburns showed beneath the white wig, while his Santa costume included both blue suede boots and a blue suede belt buckle. Another Elvis impersonator, but at least this was for charity. She dropped money into the red bucket beside him. As impersonators went, he looked quite authentic: tall, young, good-looking, and with the prettiest dark eyes she'd seen since . . . well, since Elvis.

"Merry Christmas, ma'am," he said in a low Southern drawl. With a shake of his bell, he began singing "Earth Angel."

The day was colder than expected. She considered running back to her room for a jacket, but was afraid to miss Modine's arrival. Still, compared to what she had left behind in Minnesota, the day seemed almost balmy. Long accustomed to icy northern winters, Kim found December in Tennessee a strange proposition—stranger still if she factored in all the Elvis wanna-bes. If it weren't for the bell-ringing Santa, she could easily forget it was Christmas.

Her boyfriend Jon Karl wouldn't forget, however; they'd fought bitterly about her coming down here for the holidays. Right before he stormed off, he had accused her of being a crazed workaholic. Not a fair accusation either. Jon Karl had made at least four business trips to Chicago since Thanksgiving. Why was it always different when *she* had a business trip? Sometimes she wondered why she still thought of him as her boyfriend. Increasingly, he seemed more like a business associate than a lover.

Determined to keep her mind on impressing Modine instead, she paced in front of the hotel. The Elvis Santa's rendition of "Earth Angel" sounded remarkably like that of the real Elvis. As she hunted around in her purse for another bill to drop in the bucket, a young boy began singing "Silent Night." His clear voice seemed as angelic and lovely as sunlight on the snow; even the Elvis Santa stopped in midverse to listen.

But the sweetly sung "Silent Night" was suddenly marred by the harsh braying of a donkey. Kim spun around. First poodles, now donkeys. She was either becoming delusional or

Memphis was one big menagerie. A small crowd milled about the vacant lot next to the hotel. Curious, she hurried over for a look. Just as she pushed her way through the gawking tourists, the donkey brayed again. This time, however, he was drowned out by the bleating of sheep.

"What in the world?"

The vacant lot held a living Nativity scene—rather touching, too—only Joseph and the wise men were all costumed as Elvis, and Mary seemed a dead ringer for Priscilla. Kim had never seen so much hair on a woman. It was a wonder she could hold her head up under the weight of all that lacquered hair. The young boy singing "Silent Night" was outfitted as a shepherd, even if his sheepskin robe did clash with the cowboy boots he wore.

The song ended and everyone clapped. Kim raised her hands to applaud but was diverted by movement in the rough-hewn manger. Good Lord, there was a real live baby in there! And from what she could tell, the child's hair was twisted into a curl that hung over its forehead, Elvis-style. What sort of place was Memphis? Did everyone have an Elvis gig? If she went to Sunday service, could she expect to see the minister garbed in a white Vegas jumpsuit and the whole congregation decked out in spangles and sideburns?

Just as the sheep baaed again, one of the wise men winked at her. Kim couldn't help laughing. This was all so absurd. No one back home would ever believe a word of it.

As she turned to go, a tall man in a dark business suit stalked onto the lot. He wore an angry expression, one clearly directed at the members of the living Nativity. That looks like trouble, Kim thought as she beat a hasty retreat. Behind her, she heard raised voices and that donkey braying again. *What an odd place.*

Once back on the sidewalk, Kim rubbed her forehead, trying to avoid the tension headache that was roaring her way. So everyone dressed as Elvis and Priscilla down here to celebrate the holidays. So the bellhop swore the ghost of Elvis haunted her hotel, and her room looked like the keno lounge at Caesar's Palace. So what? She could handle public relations for anyone or anything. And she was going to handle it for Modine Music, come what may.

When Spencer's shiny purple T-bird pulled up, the car suddenly seemed like the most conventional thing on the block. She hurried to get in.

"You know I can walk into the hotel to pick you up, Kim."

He called her Kim, not Miss Hanson. For some reason, that pleased her.

"I don't mind waiting for you outside. Besides, I couldn't wait to see if I'd overdressed today."

He did have the sweetest smile she'd ever seen on a man. Maybe it was the Mickey Mouse cap that gave him that endearing quality. She couldn't resist grinning back.

"All you need for Memphis is the right hat." He shifted gears and smoothly pulled away from the curb.

"I was afraid of that. I left my football helmet and Mickey Mouse ears back home." She amazed herself by making a joke. Did she feel that easy in his presence? It didn't seem possible.

His eyes crinkled in amusement. "I'll have you know this is my Sunday brunch best." He pointed to his feet. "See, new shoes. Very formal."

His blue running shoes did indeed seem new, and his jeans looked just washed. If not for the bright red sweatshirt proclaiming the sentiment I LOVE GUMBO, Kim might consider him well dressed enough for a genteel game of touch football.

"Very fashionable, too. Only I think both of us might get a little chilled as the day goes on."

He gave her a concerned look. "Are you cold?"

"Just a bit." She shouldn't have said anything. Now he would feel obliged to drive her back to the hotel for a coat, and she really didn't want to return to Blues Street. For all she knew, a herd of elephants was checking into the hotel at this very minute.

"Hold on a sec." Modine reached into the backseat. "Here, this should keep you warm."

He handed over a brown leather bomber jacket.

"Go ahead. Put it on." Modine dropped the heavy jacket

into her lap. "I'm not going to be needing it. My gumbo sweatshirt is warmer than three layers of flannel."

Kim slipped her arms into the large jacket. The lined interior felt smooth and luxurious; she settled back within its heavy folds, engulfed by the sudden warmth and the scent that permeated the jacket. And such a wonderful scent: a heady mixture of leather and whatever soap Modine used. Putting on this man's clothing suddenly seemed a shockingly intimate gesture, as if she had instead slipped into his arms.

She looked over at Modine. His hair spilled messily beneath all sides of his Mickey Mouse cap. If she lifted the cap, she wouldn't have been surprised to see a cowlick.

A very disarming gentleman, but he could be putting on an act, trying to get her to lower her guard and expose any potential weakness. He was even chewing bubble gum. No one was this quirky without effort. She wished now she'd worn something equally offbeat, like the pearl-studded blue gown just glimpsed on the living Nativity's Mary, or the sequined satin robes sported by the three wise men.

"I see you like Mickey." She gestured to his hat. Yesterday he'd worn a San Francisco Giants cap.

"I like how happy he makes kids." For a second she thought he actually blushed.

Modine seemed to sense how puzzled she was.

"Every week, I try to arrange for some kids to fly down to Disney World. You know, children who don't have the money to go or maybe not much time left to enjoy it." He did blush now, obviously uncomfortable talking about his good deeds.

After reading up on Spencer Modine, Kim had been amazed by how much philanthropic work he undertook, not only in Memphis but around the country. The newspaper reported only last month that he'd sent massive relief to the flood victims along the coast.

"You should be proud of helping so many people. Especially children."

He shook his head. "Charity is something that should be kept private, otherwise your reasons for doing it are suspect. Let's just say there are few things that make a man feel so good as helping people out and listening to good music."

She settled back in the seat. A fuzzy troll doll swung from the rearview mirror, while Ray Charles's "Hit the Road, Jack" came softly from the CD player. Why in the world did she suddenly feel so comfortable? She preferred Vivaldi and men who smelled of designer cologne, not whatever pine-scented soap Modine had been using. Yet for some inexplicable reason, she felt as though she and Modine had known each other a long time, shared high school memories perhaps, or swapped marbles as kids. She had expected to be impressed and intimidated by him when she flew down here. With a success story as dazzling as his, who wouldn't be?

But she had never expected to like him so much.

"You mentioned something about brunch?"

"Brunch and music." He looked over at her. Now that the inflammation was gone, those eyes were bluer than she could have imagined. "Hope your throwing arm is good."

"My what?" Maybe they *were* going to play touch football. She had no athletic skills at all. If this job depended on how well she played sports, she had just lost the account.

"Your throwing arm. We're going to Huey's."

As if that explained it.

"Now don't start looking worried again. I thought today we'd just kick back and relax, not worry about business. Thinking about it too much yesterday got you a tad nervous."

She felt herself grow crimson. How mortifying to have a panic attack in front of a prospective client.

"I'm so sorry about what happened, Mr. Modine."

"Spencer, please. Anyone who's gotten close enough to blind me with perfume has earned the right to dispense with formality." His infectious grin refused to let her get anxious.

"I left the perfume bottle in my room today."

"You still smell of apple pie and ice cream. Never met a woman who wore a fragrance like that. Reminds me of warm country cooking, spicy and sweet. Even the doctor who washed out my eyes wanted to know what smelled so good."

"I hope you can forgive me for losing control like that."

"You call that losing control? Last July I partied a little too hard for my birthday. Wound up in the ER and almost got my stomach pumped.''

"How much did you drink?"

"Just two beers. Nah, it was the hot dog–eating contest that did me in. Ate twenty-eight of them, with mustard and relish. The three pork sandwiches didn't help much either. I thought my great-aunt was going to strangle me." He laughed, a nice, masculine sound that filled the car. "Aunt Mae is a vegetarian."

He glanced over and seemed relieved she was smiling. "Feel like having fun today?"

What an odd idea. She hadn't deliberately set out to have fun in years. "We're going to have fun?"

"I mean to. And if I see you're about to get even the tiniest bit anxious, I came prepared."

He pointed to the backseat. There, sandwiched between a duffel bag and a stack of CDs, sat the mechanical monkey. Sunlight bounced off his little sunglasses, while the black leather pants and jacket he wore gleamed as though he were under a spotlight.

Kim burst out laughing. At that moment, the car hit a bump in the road and the monkey toppled over. She reached back to prop him up, straightening his glasses. Suddenly, she faced forward, her breathing uneven. Whoa, she was definitely letting her anxieties get the upper hand here.

For one crazy moment, she could have sworn the monkey had winked at her!

Was it possible to get a woman drunk on silly games, good jazz, and thick chocolate shakes? Judging by Kim Hanson, it certainly was.

She sat across from him, biting her lower lip in concentration. With a steely look, she flung her toothpick at the ceiling, then burst into applause. "Right on target!"

He smiled and swigged back the rest of his root beer. "And it's only taken three boxes of toothpicks."

They'd been at Huey's for hours now. The restaurant was his favorite Sunday hangout, serving up juicy hamburgers while live jazz bands blasted away. He introduced her to the Huey pastime of throwing toothpicks into the ceiling, and she practiced at it until she became nearly as proficient as he was. If this was any indication of how hard she worked on a project, she must be an indefatigable businesswoman.

Or did he just think that because he loved the way her short tousled hair shook when she laughed? She'd laughed a lot since they got here, as if she had years of laughter bottled up within, bursting to escape at the slightest opportunity.

He'd known the winters in Minnesota were cold, but the summers must be frosty as well. She reminded him of a delicate houseplant that craved warmth and attention, but until today had been shoved instead into a cold, dark corner. And without food, too. She was such a slim woman, he had been amazed to see her polish off two cheeseburgers, an order of steak fries, and two milkshakes. He felt like his mother, absurdly pleased to be fattening up a ravenous little guest. What would Kim make of a real Tennessee barbecue? Suddenly Spencer had the urge to show her so much, anything to see her laugh and open up like a flower discovering the sun.

It was unsettling how protective he felt about her. Funny feeling for him to have, especially about a pretty young woman. She didn't need anyone's pity either; she was intelligent, well-read, witty. Their conversation had bounced from the Dow Jones closing on Friday to the trout fishing in Minnesota lakes to the intricate plot of an Elvis movie called *Viva Las Vegas*. Apparently she'd watched it last night, and was quite pleased that she understood her hotel room now. He didn't ask her to elaborate. He was just happy that she seemed so much more relaxed today.

Suddenly he was the one who was anxious. He didn't want to say the wrong thing or make the wrong move, not with this woman. And he didn't want to examine his reasons too closely for fear he would be the one to panic. Not even the blues band playing Otis Redding could get his heartbeat down to normal.

He pushed away his empty glass. All that tousled hair and bubbly laughter was affecting him. He had a business decision to make by Christmas, and it wouldn't be fair to either of them if he let his healthy attraction for her get in the way of making the right choice.

What a way to spend the holidays, he thought with wry amusement as she shot yet another toothpick at the ceiling. He only hoped his own nerves would hold out.

She turned the wheel as if her life depended on it. The wind whipped through her hair as she took the curb at what felt like eighty miles an hour. How fast did go-carts go? she wondered. And when was the last time she had driven one? From behind her, she heard the buzz of another engine. Spencer was gaining on her. Any moment now he'd overtake her and win. But that was only if she played it safe. And tonight on this go-cart, Kim felt as foolhardy and audacious as any stock-car dare-devil.

"Let me pass!" she heard him shout behind her.

Giggling like a child on her first roller-coaster ride, Kim leaned her head back, reveling in the brisk wind blowing against her. If she went any faster, she'd be flying. The lights and sounds of the amusement park whizzed past, a loud, kaleidoscopic blur.

"Eat my dust!" She floored the accelerator and took the next corner so quickly, she swore the go-cart lifted onto two wheels.

Behind her, Spencer hooted with laughter. Funny how she had started thinking of him as Spencer these past few hours, instead of as Modine.

Well, maybe it wasn't so strange. Spending the evening riding bumper boats and playing putt-putt golf tended to put everything on an informal basis. Somewhere along the way— possibly during that zany hour spent in the batting cage—Kim had lost her fear and nervousness around him. She went for long periods of time without even remembering why she had come to Memphis. And it was Spencer who had put her so much at ease.

As she sped across the finish line, Kim let out a whoop of joy. Winning the Daytona 500 couldn't have felt any more exhilarating.

A moment later, she ran over to where Spencer squealed his go-cart to a stop.

"Now does that make up for losing all those putt-putt golf games to me?" he teased. His Mickey Mouse cap had long since flown off; his sandy hair was so windblown, it looked like it had been backcombed and lacquered.

"Don't even try to pretend you were letting me win." She helped him out of the vehicle. "I caught the look of terror on your face when I passed you on the fourth turn."

"Can you blame me? All I could hear was you cackling as you tried to run me off the track. If you had a go-cart back home in St. Paul, I'd have your racing license stripped from you."

"What a sore loser." She tried to smooth down his hair. "Look at these snarls. You'll never get a comb through it."

With a grin, he pointed at her own hair.

When she ran her fingers over the bird's nest that was once her hair, she let out a scream. The birthstone ring on one of her fingers got stuck in the knot of curls. "Oh, no. I can't get my hand out. Spencer, help me."

But he had collapsed onto the track in laughter. She pulled hard, but the ring remained caught in her hopelessly tangled hair. In another moment, she, too, had dissolved in helpless laughter beside him.

"Do you think there's a barber anywhere in the park?" Spencer asked.

"One teeny pair of scissors is all we need."

"I don't think scissors will do the job." He peered at her windblown hair, then gave a futile tug to the hand still stuck amid the curls. When he tried to pull his own hand away, his watchband snagged onto another tangled curl.

"Ouch! Be careful."

"Oh, no, I think we're both stuck now." He pulled again and got only a shriek in return.

"What are we going to do? We can't stay like this."

"Don't worry; I'll get us loose." He whistled at the manager of the go-cart track. "Hey, mister, I'm going to need

210

something to cut with here. Anything you got: Swiss Army knife, cleaver, ax.''

"An ax!"

"I'm sorry, Kim, it's the only way. Off with your head!"

The two of them fell back on the track, screaming with laughter.

Elvis gave a courtly bow as she passed, his haunting voice warbling "Love Me Tender." Wasn't that a sweet way to end a glorious day? she thought. And what a magical place Memphis had turned out to be. A city where amusement parks were open year-round—at least the Putt-Putt Golf and Games Park was—and Santas sang for charity until late into the night.

Spencer held open the door of the hotel for her. She walked through feeling like a princess, albeit one who held the strings to a half dozen helium balloons, now bobbing above her.

"Why do I feel like a bachelor uncle bringing his little niece back from the circus?"

"I've never been to the circus," she said dreamily.

He didn't look surprised, but only nodded. "If a circus was in town, I'd take you tomorrow. And I'd make sure the clowns squirted seltzer water right into those big brown eyes."

He reached out, but she laughed and turned aside so his hand instead brushed against her cheek. How she would have liked to feel his hand stroke her face again, feel him run his fingers over her lips. She must be tired. Too much stress yesterday, and too much laughter and fun today. Certainly she wasn't accustomed to such extremes in her life, at least not the fun part.

"Thank you, Spencer." It didn't matter that she felt bone-weary from swinging a baseball bat for close to an hour. Or that her face felt chapped and windburned, and her scalp was sore from all the tugging. The lightness singing through her was worth it. "I had such a wonderful time today."

"You had fun?"

"It was even worth losing my hair over."

"You're just lucky no one at the park could find that ax."

Suddenly she couldn't find her voice, and only smiled.

She'd be hard-pressed to explain rationally why a day spent throwing toothpicks and racing go-carts could translate into such happiness, such simple joy. Yet she was happy. What an astounding revelation to have while clutching red and purple balloons and listening to "Jailhouse Rock" waft through the lobby.

Spencer's blue eyes darkened suddenly, and he reached over and squeezed her shoulder. "I had a fine day myself, Kim. But—but you should try to get some sleep."

He looked at his watch, which startled her. He hadn't glanced at his watch all day, except for trying to untangle it from her hair.

"I forgot. I have a meeting tomorrow at seven; at least I think I do. Anyway, don't listen to me; I'm just tongue-tied tonight. Maybe we rode around that go-cart track one too many times."

"Are you feeling okay?" Kim's grip tightened around the balloon strings.

"Hey, I'm fine; it's just been a long day. So how about if I pick you up tomorrow about one? Maybe we'll drop by Sun Studio, and see how conversant you are with some Memphis music legends." He didn't wait for an answer. "Great, I'll see you tomorrow then. Glad you enjoyed yourself, Kim."

He paused before stepping outside. This was the most serious she'd seen him all day. She felt a nervous cough coming on.

"I had fun, too. You're quite a girl." He looked at her intently, as though searching for something in her eyes. She didn't know him well enough to tell if that was good or bad. "Well, good night. And take care of those balloons."

After he left, Kim stood there for several minutes, feeling all the childlike joy start to seep away. Had she made some fatal error today? Maybe she wasn't supposed to forget about business and throw toothpicks and ride go-carts if she really wanted this account. Maybe it had all been a test and she had failed miserably.

And he'd called her a girl. It sounded affectionate, almost like an endearment. But wouldn't he have said "woman," at least to the person who was going to handle public relations for a major recording label?

What a fool she was. She was lucky he hadn't called her "child." Wasn't that how she had behaved all day, with not even a word slipped in about public relations or what she was capable of doing for the company? Well, tomorrow would be different. Tomorrow she would dazzle him with her business acumen and her knowledge about the most arcane legends of Memphis music—even if she had to stay up all night, studying her music magazines and books.

Even if she had to call upon the ghost of Elvis himself to help her. "If you're here, Elvis, I'm asking for a little aid and assistance," she whispered, her gaze traveling about the lobby.

An Elvis impersonator walked past; he looked like one of those Flying Elvises she'd heard about, long cape fluttering behind him. This one wasn't a ghost though. She could smell the Old Spice cologne from twenty yards away.

The whole situation suddenly struck her as ludicrous. What was she doing? She'd been in Memphis only two days and she'd already tried to blind a man, been rescued by a singing monkey, and now she was *praying* to Elvis!

She trudged toward the elevator, balloons floating overhead. Heaven knew what Memphis and Spencer Modine had in store for her tomorrow.

Chapter Three

"Kim, how long are we going to stand out here in front of the Holiday Inn?" Spencer peered over his sunglasses.

He was definitely worried. And the bus exhaust fumes coming from Union Avenue were starting to make him nauseous.

She turned around, a smug expression on her face. "It's a hotel now, but this used to be where the office of one of the shrewdest country music promoters in Memphis was located. He was only a disc jockey at WMPS, promoting a show at the Overton Park Shell in which Elvis happened to be appearing, but this man was so savvy that he became Presley's manager in December 1954. He may not be as famous as Colonel Parker, who took over Elvis's management the following year, but this promoter—"

"Bob Neal."

Her mouth fell open. "You've heard of him?"

"Yeah. Just like I've heard of Chips Moman."

Ten minutes ago, he had been forced to stand at the corner of Thomas Street and Chelsea Avenue, while Kim expounded at length on the history of American Sound Studio and its

214

founder, finishing her lesson by listing—Lord help him—all one hundred and twenty hit songs that were produced there from 1967 to 1971. It didn't deter her in the least that the studio was long demolished. She seemed as comfortable lecturing in front of the day care center that now stood in its place as she was in front of this Holiday Inn Select.

She was like the Energizer Bunny, and picking up speed. She'd ordered him around the city like he was her rookie driver and she was the longtime native. And such a wealth of facts and figures she possessed. He knew she was sharp, but he'd never suspected she had a photographic memory. How else could she possibly remember all of the hit songs produced at Sun Records by Sam Philips? Or that in 1956 Elvis had gone to the O. K. Houck & Company Music Shop to swap his 1942 Martin D-18 guitar for a new one? Too bad the government hadn't discovered Miss Hanson's talents and made her the head of the CIA.

"Kim, maybe we should cut short the lecture tour around Memphis. It's getting late, and there's a musician I want to see tonight at the Forever Blue club. Let's say we just forget about who promoted what and when—"

"We can't forget." She shook her head. Uh-oh, he recognized that anxious glint in her eyes. "How can any person who hopes to promote Memphis music ever forget the great legacy of these men who have gone before us?"

"Maybe if we try real hard." He shot her a smile, hoping to get one in return. No luck. "Okay, maybe we could try for just an hour or two. Look, you haven't eaten a thing all day. Let's at least stop for a burger or some barbecue."

"Elvis didn't care for barbecue, you know."

He groaned. "You're not going to describe the menu items of Culpepper's Chicken Shack again?"

She looked temporarily crestfallen. "Well, Elvis did love to eat there when he was a young man. And so did Bobby Blue Bland."

Spencer felt defeated, taken down in two rounds by a mere slip of a female who smelled like apple pie and could outtalk Don King himself. He shoved his sunglasses back onto his nose, watching her pace before him. She was a nervous wreck again. All the easy, relaxed fun they had shared yesterday seemed to have happened to another woman. And he had no one to blame but himself.

He'd been so shaken by how much he liked her—how wildly appealing she was to him—that he'd reared up like a skittish horse last night in the lobby and spoiled the good work he'd accomplished that day. Making those fool comments about discussing the music business when next they met. It was the only thing he could think of. Anything to prevent him from blurting out how much he loved her silly laugh, and the way she tousled her already windblown hair with her hands when she was thinking hard. Or that little wiggle in her walk, difficult to discern today beneath yet another navy blue business suit.

He knew they were in trouble when she went back to wearing dark tailored jackets and skirts. Hell, he should have just kissed her last night in the Heartbreak Hotel's lobby—grabbed her and all those balloons and kissed her until neither of them could think straight. Instead, he'd dashed cold water on her dreamy happiness yesterday, and all because he—of all people in Memphis—*he* had lost his nerve. He could name a dozen women who would hoot and holler in disbelief if they heard about such a thing. The Spencer Modine he showed to the world was confident, glib, and invulnerable. Especially with women. Too many women looked at him and saw only dollar signs. They were the ones who were easy to handle. But here was a woman so intent on business that today she barely looked at him at all.

She snapped her fingers and a smile finally lit up her face. "Oh, and I learned B. B. King's shoe size!"

Spencer fell back against the rear bumper of the T-bird, his face in his hands. Now he knew how Dr. Frankenstein felt. Only why did the monster he created have to be so damn adorable?

How could everything go so terribly wrong?
Kim empathized with those poor people who went down on

tne *Titanic*. She knew she'd hit an iceberg hours ago, but she couldn't see any way to save herself. So she just kept talking. And talking. For an hour now, she'd been praying laryngitis would set in. Someone had at last heard her prayers. Not that her voice had grown hoarse; it was just that she had run clean out of facts about Memphis music. Mercifully silent, she could only stare exhausted at the bowl of chili steaming in front of her.

Spencer laughed beside her.

"That's the second time that drunk has asked for 'I'll Be Home for Christmas.'" He shucked off his brown leather jacket. "If Michael gets another request like that, we're likely to see a helluva barroom brawl."

Apparently, Michael was the pianist playing the requested Christmas tune at the longest piano Kim had ever seen. At least Spencer seemed amused by the situation. Thank heaven, she hadn't destroyed his sense of humor, although she suspected she'd come pretty darn close.

She shouldn't have insisted that he drive to that tortilla chip factory, memorable only because Elvis had skated at the roller rink that once stood there. It was the only time Spencer had really seemed irritated. Only she wasn't certain if it was at her or himself. Either way, staying up all night and memorizing music trivia had clearly backfired.

She tried to eat some chili, anything to prevent physical and emotional collapse. Why did every moment spent trying to impress this man only take her farther away from her goal? Maybe his first instincts were right; she'd never be able to understand Memphis, music, or him. She'd never be able to save her business—or look Jon Karl in the face when she flew home a complete failure. And that was assuming Jon Karl even wanted to see her again.

"It's Christmastime." She tried to rouse herself to make normal conversation, something she hadn't done all day. "Why wouldn't the hired musicians expect to play holiday songs?"

Spencer tore his attention away from the music. "That's Michael Arnett; he owns the place. Damn good songwriter, too. In fact, he's writing a song for one of my artists. I was hoping he'd be finished by now, but I think drunks and Christmas are getting in the way."

She tensed. Should she have heard of him? Probably. No doubt this was a test. That was why he'd brought her here. Her spoon clattered to the bowl as her mind raced through every current songwriter on the Memphis music scene. This was impossible. She must have been mad to think she could figure out what a man like Spencer Modine wanted from his people. Where she came from, respected businessmen wore three-piece suits and conducted meetings in wood-paneled offices. What hope did she have of trying to understand a record mogul who wore a flowered Hawaiian shirt beneath his leather bomber jacket, and preferred to close business deals in hamburger joints and vintage Thunderbirds?

Kim grabbed Spencer's arm. "I don't know who he is," she said brokenly.

His expression grew concerned. "I think you're pushing yourself too hard." He covered her hand with his own. It felt so warm and reassuring. "You've been babbling all day like you're afraid I'll gobble you up if you stopped. I want you to relax and enjoy yourself, like you did on Sunday. I don't need you to impress me with all this music trivia. That's not what I'm looking for in my PR person."

Tired and stressed out, Kim could barely understand what he was saying. She was only vaguely aware of her surroundings; she knew she was in a jazz club on Beale Street and that some Michael person was playing piano. Beyond that, reality was fading fast.

"Kim, how much sleep did you get last night?" His lovely blue eyes looked genuinely worried. She was being a bother to him again. And no doubt he'd forgotten to bring the singing monkey.

"I had some papers to look over. And I don't need a lot of sleep. I'm used to cramming. That's how I got through college."

She heard him chuckle, and the soothing sound of it made her close her eyes. For a moment, she thought she felt his lips brush against her forehead, but it had to be her disoriented state. Spencer Modine would have no reason or desire to kiss a wreck like her.

"I'm not a college exam, little one," he whispered.

She must be drifting in and out of consciousness. He couldn't possibly be using endearments to her. Especially after the tedious spectacle she'd put on today.

"No wonder Michael's been late with my song," she heard him say in amusement. "One too many distractions."

She forced her eyes open in time to see Spencer pointing behind her. A young blonde in a blue dress stood near the entrance to the club; she was staring intently at the piano player with a worried expression on her face. A second later, the woman turned and bolted out the door, nearly knocking over a man tottering on one crutch beside her. The dark-haired musician broke off his song in midphrase and ran after her, following her right out of the building. The man with the crutch and his companion, a lovely young woman in a flowered skirt, stared in obvious bewilderment after the fleeing pair.

Spencer grinned. "Now you know why Michael writes the best love songs in the business. Plenty of stormy experiences with pretty blondes." He turned his smile on Kim now. "Can't say as I blame him. I've a weakness for golden-haired ladies myself."

At last, the name registered. Michael Arnett.

"He wrote 'Only a Shadow'!" she cried in triumph.

Spencer sat back. "Yes, he did. I wouldn't have been surprised if you hadn't heard of him. Michael works hard at keeping a low profile."

As tired as she was, she could manage this. She could show him, Memphis, and Jon Karl that she was the only PR person for the job. It didn't matter that she felt dizzy from exhaustion and worried sick about being bankrupt next week. She was here now with Spencer Modine, and this was her last chance. If she was going down, then by heaven, she'd go down in flames.

"I do remember the song. I could sing it for you."

"No, really. I don't want you to do any of this for me. You are just knocking yourself out for no good purpose—"

Closing her eyes, she reached back for the memory of the country-and-western star who'd recorded "Only a Shadow." "You're only a shadow in my dreams at night," she sang out. "I cry out your name, 'cause it just ain't right."

"Kim, honey." Spencer's hand gently covered her mouth. "I believe you."

She forced her eyes open. "I know the whole song, Spence. Even the bridge."

He leaned close, and for a wild, dizzying, improbable moment, she thought he'd kissed her eyes shut.

Then everything went black.

What in the world was he going to do with her?

Her head had fallen to the table so rapidly, Kim had barely missed plopping right into the bowl of chili. With anyone else, he would just assume they'd fallen asleep, but he already knew this intense young woman didn't do anything in half measures. He feared—rightly—that she'd passed out.

"Kim, honey!" He shook her. Her head lolled back and forth on the tabletop.

A few tables away, another drunk cried out for someone to play "Jingle Bell Rock."

Spencer tried pinching her. Nothing. Considering how tense and overwrought she could make herself, he wouldn't be surprised if she'd up and died from the effort of trying to impress him.

Desperate, he grabbed her hair and pulled her head upright. "Kim, come back to me, Kim! C'mon, honey, you're making old Spence here nervous!"

He gave her head another shake. Maybe he should try to perform CPR. He was about to fling a glass of root beer in her face when she groaned and those lovely brown eyes fluttered open.

"Oh, lordy, woman, you are aging me by the minute." He propped her back up against the booth. "Here, sit up, sweetheart. C'mon, you can do it. I know you can."

220

She suddenly sat up straight and tall, seemingly oblivious to the fact that she'd just passed out cold. Her eyes focused on him and he wanted to hug her in relief. With a shake of her head, those blond tousled curls fell even more haphazardly about that lovely face.

"Kim, you gave me such a scare. I am ordering you here and now to get some rest and to stop worrying about this stupid job. You are making yourself sick over a damn public relations account!"

She held up her hand sternly, as though he had interrupted her. Baffled, he waited for what she was going to do next.

"Yes, only a shadow, a trick of the light," she belted out with gusto. "I can search all night long, but my lonely arms can't hold a shadow . . ."

Spencer was either going to start laughing uncontrollably— or kiss this maddening woman senseless. Even the bellowing drunk stopped to listen as Kim wailed away as if she were Loretta Lynn herself.

Watching her sing out of tune, he realized that whether he hired her or not was unimportant. No doubt she could handle the job, but even if she was the most incompetent PR person in the world, he knew now he wanted her by his side.

No, he *needed* her by his side. He needed to see that wonderful wide grin every morning; he needed to watch those intelligent brown eyes light up whenever she grew excited. He needed to hear her rapid, funny conversation and—God help him—he needed to touch her, hold her, and breathe in that delicious heady fragrance that was partly perfume, but was mostly Kim.

The hell with public relations and Modine Music. He'd just made the only decision that really mattered to him.

He was going to marry Kim Hanson.

And he didn't care how many singing monkeys it took to convince her.

221

Chapter Four

"You'll have to speak up," she shouted into the phone. "The poodles are making too much noise."

This announcement stopped even Jon Karl in his tracks. "What poodles?"

Kim fell back against the pillow, the water bed undulating gently beneath her. "Actually I'm not certain it's the poodles that are barking in the room above mine, but they're the only dogs I've seen so far in the hotel."

"You're staying in a hotel that allows pets?" His voice dripped with disdain.

"Of course not. I was assured this hotel doesn't permit pets of any kind." She wished now she'd kept quiet about the poodles.

"So what are the dogs doing there?"

"Aside from barking every morning, no one seems to know." She craned her neck, trying to see the neon clock by the dresser. She must have been exhausted to have slept nearly thirteen hours.

In fact, she had only the haziest memory of anything that

had happened after they arrived at the piano bar. She vaguely recalled being escorted to the hotel elevator by Spence, then collapsing alone onto her water bed. But why did her hair smell of chili?

"I'm glad you called, though." The sooner she directed his attention away from the poodles, the better. "I hated leaving after that terrible fight we had."

"You should have stayed here with me, Kim."

Guilt washed over her again. Jon Karl had been her only real confidant this past year, the only one whom she trusted. Running her business had eaten up her life, leaving no energy or thought for fun or romance. Until Jon Karl. Yet it was Spencer Modine's face that appeared before her suddenly, and that made her guilt even greater.

"I had to exhaust every possibility to try to save my company. What's a few days compared to keeping the firm from bankruptcy?"

"It's Christmas week. Remember the holidays? When people who care about each other are supposed to want to be together."

"But I asked you a hundred times to come with me so you could help present my case to Modine."

"Insane, ludicrous idea. What's the matter with you? Why would someone like Spencer Modine even consider letting a tiny PR firm in Minnesota handle his record label?"

"Because I've built Hanson into a top-notch firm. I'll match us against any company in the country."

"You should be home in St. Paul trying to salvage the few clients you have left, not sitting in some fleabag hotel, hoping to catch a glimpse of Modine as he drives by in his limousine."

"It's a Thunderbird." She almost wished now he hadn't phoned.

"What are you talking about?"

"He doesn't drive around in a limousine. Well, he may have a limousine, but every time he picks me up, he's always driving a purple Thunderbird."

"You've actually met with Spencer Modine?" He sounded

so shocked that Kim couldn't help but feel insulted.

"Of course. I've seen him every day since I arrived."

"Every day? Why would he want to meet with you? I don't believe this!"

"Why is that so unbelievable? I came down here to land this account, not sit around talking to his secretary. I wouldn't have badgered the man's office for all these months if I wasn't going to insist on seeing him."

Suddenly restless, she sat up, throwing off the yellow satin blanket. "Maybe you've forgotten that I started Hanson Productions when I was fresh out of grad school. Long before I met you, I built it up into one of the most aggressive PR firms in the Midwest. I'm a businesswoman, Jon Karl, and until very recently, quite a successful one. I know how to go after accounts."

Of course, there was no need to tell him about the anxiety attacks or the mechanical monkey. And he'd never understand the toothpick throwing or the evening spent at the putt-putt amusement park. Nor the fact that she'd passed out last night in a bar. At least she thought she'd passed out. She'd been so tired, maybe she'd just taken a short nap on the table.

"You have to trust me when I say I'm doing whatever is necessary to secure Modine Music. I'm spending every spare moment with him. I'm even meeting him at his home this afternoon."

"You're going to his home? Alone?"

"Why not? We're almost always alone."

He was so silent on the other end, she grew uneasy. "Are you there? Is something wrong?"

"What exactly are you doing to land this account, Kim?" He sounded as cold and angry as on the day she had left St. Paul. "My God, are you sleeping with the man?"

She slammed the phone down. Her hands were trembling.

Storming over to the dresser, she began brushing her hair with furious strokes. "When I sleep with Spencer Modine," she said aloud, "it's going to be for my pleasure alone! And not for any blasted account."

A moment later, she realized she'd said *when* she slept with

224

him, not *if*. The brush clattered to the floor. She was losing it: her mind, her morals, her business edge. Worst of all, she didn't know if she even cared anymore.

And why did she have this uncontrollable urge to sing "Only a Shadow"?

The light wasn't playing tricks on her. She stood only a foot away from a Monet painting. The colors were so lush and vibrant, she could easily imagine that she was the lady in the picture, surrounded by a garden of red and violet flowers. Breathless, Kim couldn't resist running her fingers over the heavy carved frame.

"It's magnificent," she said in an awestruck voice.

Indeed, the whole room was magnificent, filled with Impressionist masters, glorious even in the ebbing light. None of this was what she had expected from a man who kept comic books in his office and drove a purple car.

"So you're impressed." He sounded as pleased as a little boy showing off his frog collection.

She nodded. She'd been impressed to learn he had a pilot's license and that he raised Arabian horses. Impressed by his philanthropy, which was far more extensive than she could have guessed. And impressed by how he lived outside Memphis, in a wonderful sprawling house filled with sunlight, music, and aromatic home cooking. She still felt sated from the extravagantly delicious lunch created by Marcel, his smiling and gifted chef.

Spencer had taken her up to the second floor for the view. And what a view, inside and out. Wide windows flooded the long room with light, showing an expansive outdoor scene of green pastures and grazing horses. Inside, the scenery was just as stunning.

The walls were hung with the most spectacular artwork she'd seen outside of a museum, yet the room didn't feel like a gallery. An enormous hooked rug covered the polished oak floor, vases of yellow flowers and irises decorated the hand-carved tables, and the couches and chairs looked stylish but comfortable, plumped high with chintz-covered cushions.

Sharon Pisacreta

Spencer Modine lived like a country gentleman.

"I've never seen anything like it." She pointed to a large framed jigsaw puzzle of a giant pumpkin. "Especially that one. Very interesting use of color. What do you call it?"

"Three years of hard work."

She couldn't help laughing. "It took you three years to finish a jigsaw puzzle?"

"Why do you think I had it framed? I designed a dozen software packages in half that time, so imagine how this puzzle was getting to me." He looked at it accusingly. "Six thousand pieces! All of them the same color. It nearly gave me an ulcer. I still can't wear orange, and it used to be my favorite color."

"Somehow I can't imagine anything giving you an ulcer." She said this in fun, but his expression grew serious.

"That's because you didn't know the Spencer Modine who worked like a maniac in Silicon Valley for all those years. Spending my youth hunched over a computer screen, never taking a vacation, never taking a weekend off. Squandering what little leisure time I had putting together an orange puzzle in my third-floor apartment, with its wonderful view of a parking lot."

He gestured for her to sit down. After she did, he threw himself down in an overstuffed chair beside her.

"Never making time to read a book that wasn't business related. No time for pleasure trips or practicing my guitar. Lord help me, I didn't make time for music. Now that's unforgivable. A person can't live without music."

Even if she hadn't already guessed how he felt about music from the past few days, the hours spent at his sprawling home confirmed it. Each room had a sound system from which music softly played: never obtrusive, but constant and soothing as water splashing over stone or birds singing overhead in hidden greenery. The entire house seemed alive with music, each room vibrating.

Just now, the strains of a Spanish guitar sounded seductively from hidden speakers.

"But wasn't the result worth all that work? It gave you the

means to surround yourself with Monets and Arabian horses.''

"I don't know. What if I missed an opportunity for something even greater while I was so intent on those microchips? Wonderful adventures, perhaps. A moment of joy and discovery in the mountains. Or love." The room had grown too dark for her to read his expression. "But maybe I didn't miss that. Maybe love comes when we're ready for it. When we need it most."

Kim shifted uncomfortably in her seat. The man seemed as multi-faceted as a jewel, but no matter which side he displayed, they all dazzled her.

Had that been part of the reason for her overwrought state all this time? Maybe she'd been trying to fight back this growing attraction for him. If she let herself grow calm for too long, she might see that what she wanted more than anything was not the Modine Music account, but the man himself.

She longed for the courage to lean over and run her hands through his sandy hair, which looked as soft as corn silk to her. Or to nuzzle his neck, just like the prize horse in his stable had done earlier. And to feel what it would be like to have his arms hold her close, so she could hear the beating of his heart. They looked like strong arms, too. The blue pullover sweater he wore today accentuated his wide chest, while beneath the sweater's pushed-up sleeves, his forearms were tanned and muscular.

"Running my own business doesn't leave room for much else," she said, nervous beneath his steady gaze. "I know I work too hard, but it's the only way to succeed. Sometimes I regret the sacrifices; I don't see my family or my friends as often as I would like, and as for romance . . . ."

"As for romance?" Spencer prompted.

The angry voice of Jon Karl sounded in her ears once more. But he wasn't *always* mocking and contemptuous, she reminded herself. Jon Karl could be understanding and attentive; he'd certainly been supportive this past year when everything had started to crumble in the company. And there were those fleeting times they'd shared a bed. In retrospect, however, she couldn't honestly call any aspect of their relationship romantic.

She had never raced go-carts with Jon Karl or fallen helpless to the ground in laughter. She'd never sat with him in a room of flowers and paintings, while Spanish music played above and her heart beat out a wild, uncontrolled rhythm. She'd never played silly games with him or found his smile endearing.

"I make time for romance when I can," she said lamely.

Spencer shook his head.

"Anyway, it won't be forever, these long hours, this crazy worrying about the balance sheet. I know things will change one day, and I'll be able to relax, ease up a bit, enjoy myself."

"And then what?"

She glanced over at the Monet once more. "Then I'll have time to look at paintings of summer gardens."

"It's better to wander through those gardens yourself, Kim."

"I will one day." She turned to him. "I will." Was she trying to convince him or herself?

"You remind me of the old Spencer Modine. The man I was back in California, ruining my health and happiness, thinking success in business was all that mattered." He paused. "Before I learned to get my priorities straight, I even had anxiety attacks."

Kim's mouth dropped open. She couldn't picture this self-assured, relaxed man ever being so anxious and afraid that he would lose control.

"*You* had anxiety attacks?"

He nodded. "And much worse. I spent half my life trying to control my fear."

"What were you afraid of?"

"The same as everyone else. The same as you, Kim. I was afraid of failure, afraid of loneliness. Pretty universal stuff."

She sat back. Since she'd arrived in Memphis, Spencer Modine had endlessly fascinated her, charmed her. Now, with this latest revelation, he had disarmed her completely.

"That's why I feel like I know you. I understand you only too well. I wish I could teach you to enjoy life again." He paused. "But I don't think you'll let me."

The sun had set and he and all that glorious artwork were slowly becoming lost in the darkness. Around them the haunting strains of Spanish love songs still played. She felt tears well up in her eyes, and she wasn't sure why. Was it regret for the years spent without joy or love—or gratitude and relief to have stumbled upon someone who at last understood her?

Or maybe it was more. Something she had never felt before and couldn't put a name to. Excitement suddenly raced through her. She knew she had courage, at least the courage to appear a fool. She'd proved that a dozen times over.

Getting up from her chair, she slowly walked over to him. Yes, she had the courage to touch him. Because if she didn't, she felt as though her heart would burst inside her. Better to touch him and live, she thought wildly.

"Kim?" he asked. His voice held hope . . . and desire.

Leaning over, she did indeed run her hands through his hair. Silky, as she suspected. She bent her head, trying to nuzzle his neck and find that pulse throbbing so seductively.

She never got the chance. He pulled her to him with strong arms, crushing her to his chest. A sigh of contentment escaped her lips, and she hugged him in return, burying herself against him, holding him, reveling in the sensation, in his masculine smell, the muscles straining in his back, the way he kept murmuring her name.

Suddenly he reached for her chin, lifting her face to him. This close, she caught a final glimpse of his eyes just before the light completely disappeared. His lips were soft and tender against her mouth, then growing stronger and more insistent.

She was too impatient—too greedy—to wait. Like a hungry child, she clutched him and kissed him back. If nothing ever happened after this moment, it didn't matter. As long as she could cling to him, explore his mouth with her tongue. Shameless, she pulled back and ripped away her blouse. She heard buttons pop off and land on the wooden floor. Let him think her as brazen as she indeed was being. She needed him. She needed this.

"Kim, you're beautiful," he said huskily. "So beautiful."

He unhooked her bra and flung it away into the darkness.

She caught her breath as he cupped her breasts and kissed first one, then the other.

When she pulled off his sweater, she was amazed at how her hands trembled. But at the feel of his smooth, muscular chest, she forgot everything but how much she desired him. She rained kisses over his bare skin, her hands and mouth exploring him, seeking him.

Spencer pulled away for a moment. She lay back with her eyes closed, enjoying his hands on her body as he slipped off her jeans and panties. When he lay on top of her again, he was naked as well.

She burrowed into the couch's deep cushions, excited by the feel and the smell of his heated flesh. She wrapped her legs about his thighs, pulling him close.

He was hard, erect. She reached for him. Gratified to hear his loud moan of pleasure, she wrapped her fingers about him and stroked. He arched his back and an expression of bliss crossed his features.

She stroked him quicker until he pleaded, "Kim, stop. Not too quickly."

Then she felt his hand caress her thighs, seeking her own wetness. Now it was her turn to moan, as his fingers stroked, explored, caressed. She pressed her legs tightly about his hand. "Not too quickly," she teased.

"I want you, Kim." His voice was ragged and hoarse.

She opened her legs, ready, eager for him. When he entered her body, they both cried out in satisfaction. She wrapped her legs tightly about his back, pulling him in even deeper.

Basking in the hot pleasure of feeling him inside of her, she cried out as he began to move. Neither could wait any longer. They moved feverishly, time running out for both of them. She felt unrestrained, as wild as any erotic dream she'd ever had. Suddenly they were on the floor, she now on top, he still inside her.

Then they rolled again, knocking over a table. She was barely aware of the hard floor beneath her, or the sounds both of them were making. The night suddenly became hot and wet, while a Spanish guitar thrummed madly in the background until it seemed as though *they* were the music, moving in rhythm, moving faster, always together. She felt as if they were dancing, flying, until the music could go no faster, no higher.

She felt him stiffen, then cry out, and while he did, her own pleasure finally shattered through her. Clutching him even tighter, she leaned back and whispered his name. He whispered hers in return, both of them murmuring to each other until it sounded like a prayer.

No, Kim thought, not a prayer. It sounded like music. The most beautiful music she had ever heard.

She didn't know how long they slept, but the windows outside showed pitch-black. At least they'd gotten back onto the couch before drifting off. She smiled, contented. A gentle rain fell against the wide windows, making the room even cozier. And guitar music still played; this time, however, it sounded classical.

"Vivaldi," she said aloud.

"Try Weiss, Peretti, and Creatore," came the answer out of the darkness.

She sat up, wrapping the quilt around her. "Who?"

He replied with that wonderful, husky laugh. "It's a Presley song, darling. Blame my playing if it sounds a little stiff."

Reaching behind her, she turned on the lamp. The soft light revealed Spence sitting cross-legged on the floor, barefoot and wearing only his jeans. He strummed expertly on a shiny guitar, his hair falling into his eyes. His grin warmed the chilly air about her bare shoulders. She drank in the sight of him.

"You play beautifully."

He raised a skeptical eyebrow. "So beautifully you didn't recognize 'Can't Help Falling in Love'?"

She stood up, the quilt held loosely against her naked body. "Well, it sounds as perfect as Vivaldi." Kim walked over and kissed him.

He kept on playing, even as he returned her kiss with growing urgency. It was she who finally broke it off.

"Give me a minute to warm my feet." She dove back onto

the couch and burrowed beneath the quilt. "Keep playing, though. It sounds lovely."

He winked. "As soon as I stop playing, I'll warm you all over."

She smiled back. "Where did the quilt come from?"

"It was hanging on the wall by the door."

"What?

He strummed a few moments, as though improvising the song and enjoying it tremendously. "It's nineteenth-century Amish. Very prized by collectors."

"You shouldn't be using it for a blanket." She looked at it worriedly; just wrapping it around her may have damaged it somehow. "This must be quite valuable and precious."

He looked up at her, his blue eyes intense and serious. "So are you."

She felt suddenly shy, naked and exposed beneath the quilt.

He seemed to sense her awkwardness. "Don't worry. A hundred years of use hasn't hurt it." He grinned. "Although my new PR person is certainly worth a dozen prize quilts, I'd say."

"Your new PR person?" She felt disoriented. In the dreamy afterglow of their lovemaking, the farthest thing from her mind had been business.

Yet that had been the first thing *he* had thought of after having sex. A queasy, sick feeling overcame her.

"Spencer, are you telling me that you've made your decision?" She took a deep breath, trying not to panic.

He nodded. "You're obviously the best person for the job. I'm certain you'll do splendidly handling the Modine Music account." His fingers played over the guitar strings.

Now her heart felt as cold as her feet. In fact, she felt cold all over. What a stupid, idiotic person she was.

"Well, I guess my special skills were the clincher, weren't they? Maybe if I'd gone to bed with you on the first day, I would have gotten the job even sooner."

His playing stopped with a discordant twang. "What the hell are you saying?"

Flinging off the quilt, Kim began grabbing her clothing

where it lay scattered about the floor. "My résumé, my record, my five years of success as a public relations businesswoman didn't convince you. No, you were ready to send me back to St. Paul." She pulled on her clothes in a frenzy, not sure if they were on backward or forward. "But an hour spent rolling around naked on the floor gets me the job!"

"Are you out of your mind?"

He tried to stop her from dressing, but she pulled away.

"Where are my shoes? Please, Spencer, don't insult me any longer. I think you've done enough for one night."

"Listen to me! I did not offer you the job because we had sex."

"Oh, right. Sure." She heard the tears in her voice and prayed she wouldn't start crying.

"Damn it, I should have told you before." He raked his hand through his hair. "In fact, I'd made my decision last night, but you were so exhausted that I didn't think that was the best time to give you the good news."

"I've been here all day, Spence. All day! You could have told me at lunch, when we saw your horses, when we had a tour of the house, when we saw your damn collection of Looney Tunes cartoons downstairs. But isn't it funny that you waited until just after we made love! And where are my shoes?"

Just as she said this, she stumbled over them. "Actually, it's not funny at all. It's sad. Sad to realize that I'm this stupid. And how cruel of you, Spencer, to do it to me."

"I will not have you believe I'm offering you the job because we had sex." His voice shook with emotion. "The job has nothing to do with it."

"You're right. The job has nothing to do with it." She tucked in her blouse. "Nothing at all. That's because I'm turning it down."

"What? Kim, don't be a fool. You need this account to save your company."

"No, I've been fool enough already. I can't help being a fool. But I'm not a whore, Spence. I don't trade sex for business favors, even if it means my company goes bankrupt. I

233

couldn't look at myself in the mirror if I took the account now, not after knowing what I'd had to do to get it.''

He turned away. "I can't believe how everything can go wrong so quickly. I knew I should have said something sooner."

"You've said enough, Spencer. Now please call a cab for me." She crossed her arms, fixing her gaze on a Monet seascape.

"Damn it, no," He grabbed her by the elbow, forcing her to look at him. "You're the best person for the job. That's the truth. I'm not lying. I didn't expect to make love to you tonight, although Lord knows, I wanted to. I think I've wanted you from the moment I saw you."

"So much for my business presentation that first day." A large tear rolled down her cheek. Furious, she wiped it away.

He shook his head. "I can't say what it is I'm trying to say. You get me so flustered, I do everything wrong. I didn't mean for business to get so mixed up with, with—"

"Pleasure? Well, congratulate yourself, Mr. Modine. You've finally learned how to be successful at business *and* have fun. I wish I could say the same. Instead I just feel humiliated. And ashamed."

"Oh, honey, please, there's no need." He tried to take her in his arms, but she jerked away.

She walked toward the door, stopping just short of leaving. "I don't blame you, Spencer. After all, I'm twenty-eight years old, a grown woman. I should have seen this coming."

Spencer groaned loudly.

"Funny thing is, I hung up the phone on a man who dared to suggest the very thing today." She winced at the memory. "Jon Karl will get a good laugh out of hearing just how right he was. Although since he's supposed to be my boyfriend, I doubt he'll laugh too much at the sex part of the story."

"Your boyfriend?"

"Yes, doesn't that make this all the more sordid? I leave behind a man for the Christmas holidays—sacrificing the time we would share together—and all because I wanted to come down here to save my company. At any cost, or so I believed.

234

Well, there are some things in life that cost too dearly. So find yourself another PR person. I'm sure the business is filled with women who'd love to share your bed for a chance at the account.''

"I love you, Kim," he said quietly.

She leaned her head against the closed door. "Don't lie to me any more. Don't do this to me. It won't help."

"Kim!"

"It won't help. I refuse to take the job, no matter how many pretty lies you choose to tell me."

"I'm not lying. You know I'm not."

She shook her head. "I only know that Jon Karl was right."

"Who the hell is this Jon Karl?" Spence kept his distance as if wary of her expression, but his voice betrayed his frustration. "I thought you had no time for love or romance."

"I may not love him, but at least I can trust him not to lie to me. He's been a friend, my only real supporter left in the company. Jon Karl Jones may not be as celebrated and successful as the great Spencer Modine—"

"What's his name?"

"It doesn't matter. Please, just call a cab."

"No, wait." He seemed even more agitated than before. "How do you spell his name? With a *C* or a *K*?"

"I'm leaving." She turned to him one last time, although the sight did indeed cause the tears to flow unrestrained down her cheeks. "Thanks for the tour of the city. It's been most educational, but I think I've learned far more than I want to know about Memphis, music—and you."

It was fitting that the rain was coming down in a cold, steady mist. Why shouldn't the city itself seem melancholy when she herself could barely keep from sobbing?

At least Spencer had respected her wishes enough to send her home alone in a cab. In fact, he had seemed quite distracted as she left, as though he had already dismissed her from his mind—and life. No doubt he had. He'd made a mistake and offered the job to the wrong business bimbo, but he would soon find another willing and eager female to do whatever it took to get the job.

She couldn't allow herself to think about it anymore or she'd have a panic attack for sure.

"Here we are, miss," the cabbie announced from the front seat. "The Original Heartbreak Hotel." He swiveled around. "I hear it's supposed to be haunted."

"Ghosts don't frighten me," she said wearily. Blue-eyed men who strummed guitars in the dark frightened her. Frightened her and made her weak with desire. Well, weak, certainly.

The rain felt cool and refreshing on her face when she got out, like a cold shower bringing her back to reality.

A bell jangled.

Even for charity, this seemed going above and beyond the call of duty. It was long past midnight, and the street was deserted. What sort of charity kept their Santas out at such a time?

He seemed oblivious, however, his bell ringing, his dark sideburns showing wet and slick along his face.

"Excuse me."

He turned toward her. Under the street lamp, he was a dead ringer for Elvis. This one should be in Vegas, billed as the best Elvis look-alike ever.

"Merry Christmas, ma'am," he said in that soft drawl.

"Don't you ever go home?"

He only smiled.

"I see you every morning when I leave and every night when I return. When do you eat and sleep?"

In response, he began singing. Maybe he was insane, although his blue-eyed gaze seemed clear and steady. After a second, she realized he was singing "Can't Help Falling in Love." The image of Spence strumming that same song only an hour ago in the darkness came back to her. Such a haunting, wonderful image, now such a painful memory.

She marched toward the hotel, trying to outrun that infernal song.

"I'll forget him," she said aloud. "I'll forget him and soon, too."

The lobby seemed quiet, not an Elvis impersonator or poodle in sight. She sighed in relief. Now to quickly get to her room and go hysterical for an hour or two.

Someone grabbed her arm as she hurried past the Christmas tree in the lobby. Nerves already jangled, she flinched and let out a small scream.

"So now you scream when you see me?"

Jon Karl stood before her, looking angrier than she had ever seen him.

"What are you doing here?" She couldn't have been more surprised if the ghost of Elvis had just accosted her.

"Never mind about me." He looked pointedly at her blouse, now missing all of its buttons. "Where the hell have *you* been?"

Chapter Five

Kim struggled to open the window, desperate to get some fresh air. It was stuck tight. Probably a good thing, too. After five straight hours of arguing with Jon Karl, she might have had the urge to jump.

Suddenly the song "Viva Las Vegas" blared through the suite.

"You hit the wrong button again." She stormed over to the tape player and shut it off. "And if you're thinking of calling the front desk about the dogs, forget it. They're just going to say there are no pets allowed in the hotel."

"All they have to do is send someone up and they'll be able to hear them barking through the ceiling."

Behind his wire-rim glasses, Jon Karl glared at her with bloodshot eyes. His blond hair stuck out messily in all directions, while the loosened necktie about his collar gave him the appearance of a prisoner one step from the hangman.

"How is anyone supposed to get any sleep around here?"

"I've been begging you to calm down and get some rest all night."

She was too tired and exasperated to have an anxiety attack, but she was angry enough to take on Jon Karl and the barking poodles. It had been a long time since she'd felt this angry— angry at Spence for thinking she was here to trade sex for a business deal, angry at Jon Karl for yelling at her as though she were a wayward child. Most of all, she was angry at herself for getting involved with either man.

"You know, you're a fine one to be acting the injured party," Jon Karl grumbled from the love seat. "I fly out here to lend moral support, only to discover you waltzing in past midnight with no buttons on your blouse and missing panty hose."

She sat down on the sofa across from him, tucking her terrycloth bathrobe tighter about her bare legs. "I explained how that happened."

"Yes, you told me you had sex with Spencer Modine!"

"Did you want me to lie?" She leaned her head back on one of the embroidered pillows. In another minute, she was going to fall asleep, even if Elvis himself walked in and started swiveling his hips. "I had sex with him. I'm sorry. I feel terrible and guilty about it. But after all, it isn't like you and I are in love or even have an understanding. . . ." Her voice trailed off. It probably wouldn't help matters to be too honest.

"So betraying me only counts if we're in love?" Jon Karl looked at her with a disgusted expression.

"But we *don't* love each other," she said gently. "Not even close. We've been friends more than anything else. Business associates who got along well and felt comfortable with each other. Oh, we slept together a few times, but we both know this isn't the great passion for either of us."

He stared at her with narrowed eyes. "And Modine is?"

She looked away, not wanting to call up Spencer's memory, the way he laughed, the silly baseball cap worn backward, the lovestruck way he listened to music, the feel of his body moving in unison with hers.

"Well?" Jon Karl asked impatiently.

"I made a great mistake by going to bed with a prospective

239

client. I didn't intend for it to happen, but there's nothing I can do about it now. I was an idiot."

"Yes, you certainly were."

He didn't have to sound so pleased.

"Anyway, it's over. I've turned down the Modine account."

"You told Modine you're refusing his offer?"

She covered her eyes with her hand, trying to shut out Jon Karl's accusing gaze. "Yes, I made my refusal clear and unconditional. I've said this a hundred times already. I will not be handling the Modine Music account. Now is honor satisfied all the way around? I am, after all, going to be punished for my great transgression."

"There's no need to get so sarcastic."

"Sorry if I'm a little testy this morning, but I have to fly home and declare bankruptcy. The company I sacrificed for, the company I banked my future on, is about to disintegrate. Excuse me if I sound sarcastic or frustrated enough to tear my hair out!"

Even he looked a bit sheepish. They both knew how much Hanson Productions meant to her. Up until now, the business had been the most important thing in her life, the only thing that gave it meaning and purpose. Until a madman in a purple T-bird had driven up and overturned all of her carefully laid plans.

"It may still be possible to save the company, Kim. Right after the New Year, I can set up meetings with those clients we have left and try to convince them not to pull their accounts."

"I'm so far in debt now, it makes no difference. I've lost too many other clients too quickly—like rats deserting a sinking ship." She shook her head. "And I don't even know why I'm sinking. If I don't know that, maybe I deserve to fail."

The phone rang, making her jump.

Jon Karl reached for it quickly. "Hello, yes, she's here. What do you want?"

"Who is it?" she said in a hiss.

"I don't think she has anything to say to you, Mr. Modine."

Kim scrambled off the couch. "Let me talk to him."

Jon Karl turned away. "We're both returning to Minnesota this afternoon, so I'm afraid a meeting is out of the question."

"Give it to me." She reached for the phone, but Jon Karl held on with a death grip.

"No, she doesn't want to talk to you. And I think you know why. By the way, having sex with a woman who has come down here to talk business is highly unethical and probably constitutes sexual harassment."

She grabbed the nearest LUCKY LOVES RUSTY pillow and pressed it over Jon Karl's face. While he gasped for air, she snatched the phone away and darted back across the room.

"This is Kim Hanson," she announced in a businesslike voice. "And I don't think we have anything further to discuss, Mr. Modine." Even as she said it, she felt her heart race when he began speaking.

She raised a warning finger to Jon Karl as he emerged, red faced and spluttering from beneath the pillow. "I have a four o'clock flight to catch, so I don't see how we could possibly meet. Nor do I see any reason to."

She curled up on the couch. Pressing close to the receiver, she let his voice wash over her, as though he were murmuring endearments instead of merely asking for a meeting. After last night, everything he said sounded affectionate and inviting.

"All right. Maybe for just a few minutes then."

"You are not going!" Jon Karl flung the pillow at her.

"Yes, I can bring Mr. Jones."

He shook his head furiously at her.

"One o'clock in the Hound Dog Café. I understand. Good-bye."

"I am not meeting with that man," Jon Karl said after she hung up.

"Why not? You weren't the one who had sex with him."

"That's not funny, Kim."

"He says he has something to show me. Strictly business. And since you'll be there, how can it possibly be anything else?"

The always straitlaced and proper Jon Karl looked even

more disapproving. "What's happened to you since you came down to Memphis? Have you lost every ounce of sense or morality you once had? You're not the woman I knew at all."

She got up and stalked over to the bedroom. "The woman you knew died from stress, worry, and lack of sleep. *This* woman is going to nap for a few hours. After that, I'm going to take a shower, pack, then meet with Spencer Modine. You can come if you want, or stay here and think terrible thoughts about me. Either way, you can find me in the Hound Dog Café at one o'clock. You can't miss it. Just turn right at the velvet paintings in the lobby and follow the first Flying Elvis you see."

Even before she shut the bedroom door, Jon Karl commenced yelling at her once again.

Luckily, the barking poodles drowned out the sound of his voice.

* Spencer cradled the phone long after Kim had hung up. She hadn't sounded angry. Of course, she hadn't sounded particularly friendly either. Jon Karl, on the other hand, had played the part of the aggrieved boyfriend very well. He hoped Jon Karl Jones would be at the Hound Dog Café. He preferred face-to-face confrontations; better to state your case, fight it out, and be done with it. And he intended to fight for Kim.

Even if he lost this first round and she flew back to St. Paul, he wouldn't give up. He'd use persuasion, pleas, and singing monkeys, if need be. Once a Modine took it into his head to get something, it was as good as gotten. His Grandpa Andy once spent six weeks tracking the meanest black bear east of the Tennessee River, and all because it had killed his favorite hunting dog. The bearskin rug had decorated his grandmother's living room floor for fifty years.

Not that he regarded Kim Hanson as someone he had to track and bring back by force. He knew enough of women— and that woman, in particular—to realize that Kim's feelings ran as deep as his own. It was his stupidity that had ruined everything last night. If only he'd told her she had the job two nights ago, or as soon as she arrived at his house yesterday.

Instead, he'd blurted it out just hours after making sweet love to her. And Lord, she was sweet. Like a song by Bobby Blue Bland that got under your skin from the first note, then settled in your very soul.

Kim was in his soul; that was a fact. He'd been a goner from the moment she'd defended herself in his T-bird with that apple-pie perfume—a real fighting woman his Grandpa Andy would have loved. From the beginning, he'd seen himself in her futile attempts to keep calm, her dogged determination to succeed no matter how desperate the odds. Above all, he recognized the same loneliness that had cursed him since he was a shy teenager, hiding away in his room with his computer and his music.

He leaned over his desk and stared at the little monkey sitting in front of him. "You rescued Miss Hanson for me once before, Jim Bob. I'm hoping you can pull it off again."

Kim paced up and down the long hallway. She couldn't stand waiting in the hotel suite another moment, not with Jon Karl raising a ruckus over those dogs. Unfortunately, the donkey and sheep had arrived at the vacant lot next door, and he was now on the phone to the front desk, screaming to high heaven about every animal living within the city limits. What did he imagine they were going to do? Send out hotel cowboys to round up all the resident livestock?

"I can't believe I went to bed with that man," she said aloud. Her eyes fell on a velvet painting of Elvis. This one showed Elvis in his early years, decked out in tight black leather, his face impossibly young and handsome.

"You'd never complain about a few dogs, would you?" she asked softly. "And a couple of adorable little sheep. Of course, you might not be too crazy about that donkey."

"Don't do no good talking to them paintings."

Kim jumped. She felt like an idiot. Just when she took it into her head to speak to velvet paintings of Elvis, her wizened little bellhop popped up around the corner.

"I was talking to myself, actually."

The old guy smirked. "I wasn't born yesterday, you know. In fact, I was born June twelfth, 1919."

She pointed to the closed door of her suite. "I'm out here waiting for my friend."

"He's the one on the phone complaining about the dogs, ain't he?"

"How did you know?"

He shrugged. "Word gets around the Heartbreak. No secrets here, none at all. That's why you don't need to be talking to those paintings. Elvis knows what's going on without being told. This here is his hotel."

Kim shot an anxious look at the door to her room. She hoped Jon Karl didn't come out anytime soon. A couple of words about Elvis from this strange little man, and Jon Karl would probably start strangling him. Or her.

"Well, I'm sure Elvis doesn't know what's going on in my room. Even you said he didn't like the way it smelled."

He nodded. "I forgot about the air freshener in there. Got you mixed up with that mom and her daughter on the fourth floor. Now that little girl's been talking to Elvis just about nonstop. You got any questions for him, you should have given them to her."

"I don't have anything to say to Elvis." He didn't look convinced. "Really."

"You want him to get rid of that fellow in there?" he asked.

"So now Elvis is not only a ghost, he's a hit man, too?"

"Don't be silly. Elvis ain't no hit man. He just knows how to arrange things in the hotel. Gets people to say things they shouldn't. He gets people to open their eyes and realize what it is they really want." The old man jerked a thumb toward the door to her suite. "And what they don't want."

"Don't worry about that. Since being here, I've decided exactly what—and who—I don't want."

"You'd better thank Elvis for that. I mean it. Thank him."

She lifted up her arms. Better to surrender to the madness and be done with it. "Thank you, Elvis."

He patted her on the arm. "Everything will be fine from here on out. Don't you worry. Things might seem a tad rocky for a while, but that's just Elvis ironing out the wrinkles in your life."

"Maybe it would be better if he didn't take such a strong interest in my welfare."

"Don't be silly. Next to singing, that's what Elvis likes to do best."

He fiddled with the strap on his red cap. "And since you're a guest at Christmas, you can expect most anything to happen."

She sighed. "I think it already has."

"From what I hear, things are just starting to heat up for you. Today and tomorrow are really going to rock you back on your heels."

This sounded ominous. "Do you know something I don't?"

"Course I do. I told you I wasn't born yesterday." He seemed to have gotten the cap exactly where he wanted it, finally. "Well, got to get back to work. Can't spend all my time talking to you and Elvis."

The elevator behind them rattled to a stop. As soon as the doors opened, he hopped in, surprisingly quick and graceful.

"Wait a minute," she asked nervously. "What is going to happen?"

He stuck his head out just before the elevator doors slid closed. "You're about to get exactly what you want."

"Which is?"

"A hunk of burning love!" he yelled as the doors slid shut.

After a moment, she turned back to the velvet painting of Elvis. "I should have just kept talking to you."

Chapter Six

The waitress tapped her pencil on the Formica tabletop. "You take any longer to order, mister, and I'll have time to run out and get my hair permed."

Jon Karl slapped down the plastic-covered menu. "Do you have anything here that isn't laden with fat and cholesterol?"

Kim sat back, intent on watching the front door. They were on time, but Spencer hadn't arrived yet. Maybe he wasn't coming.

"There's the Earth Angel Food Cake." The waitress adjusted her turquoise skirt. "No fat or cholesterol in that."

"Okay, fine." He shoved the menu across the table to her. "Bring me the angel food cake."

"You got a heart problem?"

"No, I do not have a heart problem."

"Well, we only serve the angel food cake to customers who have a heart problem." She pushed the menu back at him.

Jon Karl looked ready to explode. "This is the most ridiculous restaurant I have ever had the misfortune to find myself in. If I want angel food cake, then damn it, that's what you'll bring me.''

"Sorry, mister, but this is house policy. That cake is reserved special for people with bad tickers.'' She shook her finger at him. ''And don't you be using any foul language to me either.''

Spencer walked through the café door.

Kim grabbed the menu and handed it back to the waitress. ''He'll have the same as me.''

"Two coffees and two fried peanut butter–and-banana sandwiches coming up.'' The woman walked away without a second look.

Jon Karl leaned over the table. ''Well, you can eat both of them, Kim, because I'll eat dirt before I try to choke down a fried peanut butter–and-banana sandwich. Who the hell eats peanut butter and bananas?''

"Elvis did,'' Spencer said. ''And if it was good enough for Elvis . . .'' He looked over at Kim and grinned.

Kim couldn't help but smile back, then sobered as she remembered that she was still angry at him from last night.

Yet he looked as appealing as ever, sandy hair falling into those wonderful blue eyes, baseball cap turned backward, a Frosty the Snowman sweatshirt visible beneath his bomber jacket. Jon Karl sat across from her in his designer three-piece business suit, hair slicked back, Gucci loafers on his feet. In comparison, he seemed as lifeless and dull as a department-store mannequin.

"Do you mind if I sit beside you?'' Spencer didn't wait for her answer, but plopped down next to Kim in the booth. The moment his leg brushed against hers, she felt the heat rise in her body.

"Well, I mind.'' Jon Karl looked at her. ''And I think Kim does, too.''

"It doesn't matter.'' She tried to keep her voice nonchalant, but having Spence this close was as heady as drinking champagne on an empty stomach.

Spencer gave her a searching look. ''Don't be upset with

me, Kim." His voice was so low and gentle, she wondered if Jon Karl could even hear him. "I should never have mentioned the job when I did. It was just that you'd made me so happy, I wanted to make you happy, too. I'm sorry if I hurt you. I never meant to. All I want is your happiness. I want to have you with me so we can make each other happy. I want you with me, darling, now and—"

Jon Karl tapped his signet ring loudly on the table. "Excuse me, but I thought this was supposed to be a business meeting."

Spencer ignored him. "The job offer has nothing to do with what I feel for you."

Kim shut her eyes. "Spence, please."

She didn't know what she felt anymore. Having this man beside her, pressed against her in the small booth, his eyes asking her questions she was afraid to answer, was overwhelming. It was like seeing the sun after being hidden away in the dark for an endless time. The effect was dazzling—but frightening as well.

She took a deep breath before facing him. He was achingly close. She could see the small mole on his right cheek and that he had nicked himself shaving this morning. And his eyes were red rimmed and tired; clearly she hadn't been the only one who didn't get any sleep last night.

He leaned closer, until his lips nearly brushed her cheek. She held her breath, waiting—hoping—that they would. "I love you, Kim," he whispered.

Her heart actually fluttered, like that of a young girl about to swoon.

"Here's your coffee, folks." The waitress set the mugs on the table. "Hey, I didn't see you come in, Mr. Modine. Like me to bring your usual?"

Kim reached for the mug quickly. Maybe scalding coffee would help her keep her wits about her. She peeked over at Jon Karl. He gestured to his watch. "Let's go," he mouthed silently.

Spencer sat back. "Not this time, Lou. I only came in to drop off some papers." For the first time Kim noticed the two large manila folders he had brought with him.

"Well, you change your mind, just give me a holler. I'll tell the boys to get a hound doggie on the grill." The waitress patted him on the shoulder.

"Hound doggie?" Jon Karl looked as though he'd just bitten into a lemon. "Dare I ask?"

At that moment, a cry from the kitchen went up. "Hound doggies for table nine."

Spencer cocked his thumb in that direction. "Watch."

Three waitresses, including Lou, headed for the kitchen. One of them picked up a round tray holding the most enormous hot dogs Kim had ever seen. They looked nearly two feet long and seemed to be topped with everything but whipped cream.

Suddenly all three waitresses began singing "Hound Dog" at the top of their lungs. As they slowly made their way around the counter and past the jukebox, the cooks and the cashier also chimed in. By the time the hound doggies were served to the couple at table nine, even the policeman at the counter was belting out the words of the Elvis tune. He stood up and threw in a few pelvic swivels. Kim laughed so hard she couldn't sip her coffee.

As the café's patrons brought "Hound Dog" to a rollicking conclusion, Spencer turned back to her. "I always like to order one when I have the time. Best floor show outside of B. B. King's Blues Club."

"You surprise me, Mr. Modine. This is not the sort of place I would have expected a Fortune 500 executive to frequent." Jon Karl glanced around at the aqua and white globe lights, the aqua linoleum and speckled tables, the golden star-shaped clock that read the wrong time.

"This café is famous among Elvis fans, Mr. Jones. On the back wall by the phone hangs some of the rarest Elvis memorabilia you'll find outside of Graceland."

"What about that?" Kim pointed to the white scarf framed in a shadow box near the register.

"Jeanine, the owner, caught one of Elvis's scarves at the nineteen seventy-four Memphis concert. That one's not so rare, though. My mother has three Elvis scarves framed in her living room. And Grandma Sue has four she caught at all the Vegas shows.'' He leaned toward her again. ''I was hoping to show them to you Friday.''

''Friday?'' she asked.

Jon Karl cleared his throat. ''We're leaving Memphis today.''

''I thought you'd like to have dinner at my parents' house on Christmas Day, Kim. You can meet the whole family. Be prepared though; there'll be at least forty of us, and that's a lot of Modines to encounter at one time.'' Spencer squeezed her arm. It was as if an electric current jumped between them.

''You're asking me to spend Christmas with your family?'' Kim felt absurdly honored—and intimidated—by the notion.

''Yes, I am. I want you there. I want to spend Christmas with the people I love best.''

''That's it.'' Jon Karl banged his fist on the table. ''Look, Mr. Modine, you said we were here to talk business. If not, Kim and I will get our bags and leave for the airport right now.''

She shook her head, trying to wake from a lovely but dangerous dream. ''Yes, Spence, I mean, Mr. Modine. I only agreed to meet with you because you said there was an important business matter you wanted to clear up.''

Mercifully, their peanut butter sandwiches arrived. She reached for hers and took a big bite. Anything to divert her from Spencer's gaze and his touch—and the irresistible things he was saying.

''Enjoy, folks.'' The waitress leaned over and kissed Spencer on the cheek. ''And you have a merry Christmas, Mr. Modine.''

Jon Karl waited until Lou left. ''So what is this meeting about?'' He took one look at his sandwich and pushed it aside. ''Kim said that you wanted me to be here as well, although I can't see why.''

''I'll make this short and sweet.'' Spencer slid a thick manila folder over to Jon Karl, then handed over a similar one to Kim. ''I think you'll both find this interesting.''

She opened up the folder nervously, not knowing what to

expect. Inside was a detailed spreadsheet covering the last fiscal year of Hanson Productions.

"How did you get this?" A fresh wave of anger and betrayal hit her. So he'd been spying on her as well.

"It's obvious, isn't it, Kim?" Jon Karl closed his folder and tossed it aside. "Modine here has been sending his flunkies off to St. Paul to dig up dirt on your company."

She rifled through the next few pages. "This is confidential information. Maybe you think you're rich enough to break all the rules, but this constitutes corporate espionage in my book. How could you do this?"

"I didn't do a thing. All this and more was sent to me by one of your competitors in Minnesota—a competitor who obviously doesn't want you to snag Modine Music. Although if you look closely at page six, you'll see that your competitor is now based in Chicago."

"What are you talking about?" She flipped through the paperwork. "What competitor?"

"The public relations firm of J. K. Smith and G. L. Jones."

Baffled, she looked over at Jon Karl. "Smith and Jones? Have you ever heard of them, Jon?"

"He's bluffing, Kim. Doing anything he can to get you to stay with him." Jon Karl pushed himself out of the booth. "Come on; we don't need to watch more grandstanding from the great Spencer Modine. All the man cares about is getting you into bed again. Don't let him humiliate you like this."

"Oh, she has been humiliated, Mr. Jones, and for a long time, too. From what I can tell from these records, Kim's secretary has been undermining her accounts for at least two years."

Kim dropped the folder. "Gladys undermining me? That's impossible."

"This game has gone on long enough, Modine," Jon Karl warned. "Leave her alone."

"Check out the list of clients taken on this past year by Smith and Jones." Spencer pulled out a piece of paper. "Every one of them former accounts handled by Hanson Productions."

She felt sick, sick and bewildered. "I don't understand. It doesn't make sense. How could Gladys do all this?"

"Let's go, Kim," Jon Karl said. "We've heard enough from lover boy here."

Spencer ignored him. "Gladys had a lot of help, especially this past year. Trying to steal accounts by herself wasn't quite as effective as she'd planned. So her husband joined your firm a year ago and together they finished you off in record time."

"Her husband? But Gladys Smith isn't married." Kim held up another paper from the folder. "See here, it says G. L. Jones, not Smith, so it can't be Gladys." Her voice trailed off as she took a second look at the names.

"J. K. Smith," she murmured. "J. K. for Jon Karl?" One glance at Jon Karl's grim face told her all she needed to know. Her voice hardened. "G. L. Jones. Could it possibly stand for Gladys Lynn?"

Spencer touched her hand gently. "Do you remember that first day in my office when I told you what it was about your portfolio that grabbed the attention of a Memphis boy like me?"

Kim was so stunned she could barely focus on what Spencer was saying. "Yes, I think so. You said my secretary had the same maiden name as Elvis's mother."

"Elvis again," Jon Karl muttered.

"Well, Elvis's mother was Gladys Love Smith, not Gladys Lynn Smith, but the similarity was enough to catch my eye. Then last night when you told me your boyfriend was Jon Karl Jones, the association clicked. They've simply switched last names, which is academic because Gladys married Jones here six years ago."

"Married?" She felt the blood drain from her face.

At least Jon Karl had the decency to look embarrassed.

"Is this true? You've been married for six years?"

"Kim, it was strictly business. You had the best, most promising PR firm in Minnesota, but we knew you didn't have the capital to go really big. Gladys and I worked in the Midwest for years; we had the contacts, the access to money that

252

you didn't. We felt that if we could just move the firm to Chicago—''

"So your wife gave you permission to seduce the boss? How noble of Gladys."

He looked away, his jaw rigid, his face pale.

"My God, I must have been blind all this past year." She put her head in her heads, dizzy with despair.

Spencer squeezed her shoulder. "I wouldn't have pieced it together even now, Kim, except that last month while you were trying to arrange an appointment with me, I've been receiving calls from Smith and Jones. They've been asking to meet with me after the New Year about handling Modine Music. I turned them down flat since they couldn't adequately account for their business transactions the past year. Once he and his wife realized that you were determined to meet with me, they started to panic. An account as big as Modine Music would have saved your company, and probably lured your old clients back."

"But how could they do all this right under my nose?" she asked. "I would know if there was a rival firm in St. Paul."

"The firm is being run out of Chicago, Kim. It's been handling your former accounts there for at least four months. Smith and Jones informed my secretary they were closing their office in Minnesota, and that all business would be conducted from Chicago after the holidays."

"Right after I declared bankruptcy." She sat back, suddenly feeling a complete failure as a businessperson. And as a woman.

"If you could just let me explain," Jon Karl said.

"At this moment, I don't want to hear explanations from either of you."

"Kim, honey." Spencer tried to put his arm around her, but she shrugged it off.

"Please go, Spence," she said wearily. No matter how hard she worked, it seemed as if her best efforts were doomed. Last night, Spencer had unwittingly ruined her plans to take on the Modine Music account. Being with Spence today, hearing his apology *and* his declaration of love, Kim forgave him for foolishly spoiling their lovemaking last night by offering her the account right afterward. Still, her professional pride was hurt. And now to learn that Jon Karl and her secretary had stolen the company out from under her!

"If you care about me, you'll do as I ask. Allow me the dignity of dealing with Hanson business problems on my own."

He sat silent beside her for a long moment. "Okay, you need to clear all this up yourself, but let me pick you up tonight."

"No, not tonight. So much has happened. Please."

He sighed audibly. "Get some rest then, Kim, and remember how much I love you. But tomorrow is Christmas Eve and I don't want to be alone. I don't want either of us to be alone."

She didn't respond. She couldn't. She needed time to think, to regroup, to get her emotional bearings.

Although she refused to look at him, Spence leaned over and brushed her cheek with a kiss. She heard him push Jon Karl out of the way. A moment later, the café door slammed shut.

"Well, thank God he's gone," Jon Karl grumbled. "If he hadn't interfered, Gladys and I would have disclosed our plans to you in a much more civilized manner. We never intended for you to find out like this."

"Shut up." She glared at him.

"I'm sorry, Kim. But this wasn't a personal attack on you. We simply wanted your company. You didn't have the resources to handle greater expansion, and if you had landed Modine Music, it would only have made this all drag out much longer. Eventually you would have been forced to sell, and that would just have cost all of us more time and money."

She grabbed the folders and her purse and slid out of the booth.

He blocked her way. "You have to let me explain."

"Please shut up. I asked you to shut up." She could feel anger boiling within her like lava rising to the top of a volcano.

"You listened to Modine. Why not listen to me for one

minute? We've been sharing a bed a lot longer than you and he have.''

Kim dropped the manila folders and her purse on the table.

"That's better," he said. "Now if you would just sit down and allow me to explain why all of this—"

Kim reached back and punched him in the jaw as hard as she could.

He went flying back, tripping over Lou the waitress and landing hard on table nine. Kim's hand stung from the blow, but a keen feeling of satisfaction welled up in her as she stared at Jon Karl lying dazed and covered with the smashed contents of four hound doggies.

"Hey, we're gonna need four more hound doggies here," Lou yelled to the kitchen. She turned to Kim and winked. "And let me get some ice for that hand, honey."

A moment later, Kim had a towel wrapped around her aching hand and was singing "Hound Dog" with the waitresses, as Jon Karl was thrown unceremoniously out the door.

Chapter Seven

The lobby's velvet paintings of Elvis were starting to look good to Kim. Or maybe they were just more appealing than the documents Spencer had given her, documents that proved she'd been betrayed by the man she thought was her friend. And who had been her lover.

Kim tossed the manila folder onto the empty chair beside her. Her company was gone. Hanson Productions was officially bankrupt, and the conniving Jon Karl and Gladys would go on spinning their all too successful web in Chicago.

So why didn't she feel devastated? Why wasn't she having another anxiety attack? She'd been on the verge of having one every five minutes for the past few months. Now, when failure was staring her in the face, she felt suddenly at peace.

Stretching out her legs, Kim leaned back in the chair to observe the fanciful comings and goings of the Original Heart-break Hotel. The oddly dressed guests, the Elvis souvenirs, even the poodles she glimpsed walking toward the elevator: all of it suddenly seemed endearing and comfortable. Like home.

Maybe it was because Spencer lived in this city—a man who had offered her hope, not only for her company, but for her. If she wanted, she had only to call him up and accept his offer of the Modine Music account. Hanson Productions would get a reprieve, if not downright salvation. Yet she didn't want business to tarnish their feelings for each other. Not now. Not when she was as shaky as a newborn lamb.

His whispered "I love you" still rang in her ears. Could he fall in love with her in just six days? Could anyone fall in love that quickly? And what did she feel for him? Maybe the trembling and uncertainty she felt was not because of Jon Karl's treachery. Maybe the Modine Madness had overtaken her at last.

"Don't get too comfortable. You still got a lot to do today."

By this time, Kim recognized the voice. The spry little bell-hop stood beside her chair, smirking as usual.

"Excuse me?"

"No time for putting your feet up. I got a message for you."

She sighed. "Let me guess. It's a message from the King."

"Don't be silly. These are phone messages. Elvis don't need to use the phone." He held out a stack of pink papers.

She took the sheets, then sat bolt upright. All of them were from Spencer! Apparently he'd been phoning her every hour since nine o'clock. A glance at the lobby clock told her it was nearly five. She'd gotten up early and spent most of the day walking restlessly through the streets of Memphis, trying to piece together her life, trying to come to grips with what Jon Karl had been doing to her this past year—and what Spencer had done to her these past few days. All this time, he had been calling her.

"Where's the phone?"

The bellhop pointed to a pay phone in the corner.

She tried phoning his office, then his home. Nothing. Only an answering machine. He probably thought she'd been here all day, stubbornly refusing to talk to him. Her heart sank. And it was Christmas Eve. He didn't want to be alone on Christmas Eve. He wanted to be with her.

Where was she going to find him? Maybe he'd gone to his

family's home, but she had no idea where they lived. Perhaps this was for the best. How foolish to think that either of them could trust their feelings, not after less than a week. After all, her last decision in romance had been worse than foolish: Jon Karl. And she'd known him for a year. It would be unfair to both Spencer and her to rush things, to let their emotions lead them into making a great mistake.

Kim went back to retrieve her business papers. Her serenity vanishing, she felt anxious again. "What's this?"

On the seat of her chair, someone had placed a parcel wrapped in Christmas paper. FOR KIM HANSON read the gold foil gift tag.

She looked around. The bellhop caught her eye as he walked past carrying a bulging suitcase.

"Package arrived for you a while ago. We left it inside your room, but seeing as how you're not even picking up your messages . . ." He disappeared out the hotel door.

The package had to be from Spencer. After all, Christmas Eve was a time for exchanging gifts. A wave of guilt crept over her. She'd been so busy she hadn't thought of buying presents for anyone, let alone a man she hadn't even met until last Saturday.

Curious, she tore away the paper.

"Oh, no!" She didn't know whether to laugh or cry.

The little singing monkey sat there in all his glory, dressed in black leather, sunglasses perched on his brown nose.

"Oh, Spence," she whispered. "You gave me Jim Bob."

She felt for the switch on his back. With a smile, she turned it on. She'd forgotten how loud the monkey was, its recorded voice belting out "All Shook Up" as if he were Elvis at the Las Vegas Hilton.

She placed the monkey on the table before her, then leaned forward to listen to him sing. The last time he had sung for her, she'd been in the throes of a major panic attack. Jim Bob had simply taken her by surprise and made her laugh. Now she actually paid attention to the words of the song.

Hadn't she been shaky and weak this past week? She'd blamed her nervous condition on the stress of having to land the Modine Music account, but maybe it was Spencer who caused her to act so crazy and wild. Then there was that sweet night at the amusement park when she'd felt as happy as a child in a field of buttercups. And maybe anxiety hadn't set her heart to pounding; maybe it was Spence. Heaven knew, she'd been feeling mixed-up since she arrived in Memphis, yet why did she feel so fine today when everything around her was crumbling?

If Kim Hanson wasn't shook up, then no one was. And Spence. The night he'd brought her home from the Putt-Putt park, he'd been tongue-tied, stuttering about having to leave right away because he had an early meeting. That wasn't the Spencer Modine who wore Frosty the Snowman sweatshirts and picked up business associates in a purple T-bird. That was a man as "shook up" as she was.

Kim listened to the monkey with tears in her eyes. "Sing it, Jim Bob. Sing it for us."

After the next chorus, she was going to go out and find Spencer. If she had to hunt through every piano bar, jazz club, and amusement park in Memphis, she'd find him. Tonight was Christmas Eve, and neither of them was going to be alone.

Spencer had waited all day. All night, too, if he included the long hours spent pacing in the room where they'd made love. Was it only two days ago? It seemed a lifetime since he'd held Kim in his arms, felt her warmth and sweetness, been overwhelmed by a wild hunger he hadn't known existed in him. And now he felt even more alone than before. Alone, abandoned. He'd called her suite, left numerous messages—and nothing. At least she hadn't checked out; the front desk said she was still registered. But apparently she didn't want to talk to him. Maybe she felt he had betrayed her just as Jon Karl had.

At one point today, he'd even offered to buy the Heartbreak Hotel from the owner. Anything at all associated with Kim Hanson had become extraordinarily precious. At noon, he finally broke down and went to the hotel himself, but she wasn't there. He wanted to give her Jim Bob, wanted to see her expression when the monkey sang, hoping she would be touched, happy, pleased. He finally left the parcel for the hotel to give her. That was hours ago, and still not a word. Not even Jim Bob had worked his magic.

He zipped up his leather bomber jacket. The sun had set, and it was getting cold. Cold for Memphis, and colder still for him. That was why he had come to Graceland, the grounds all decked out for Christmas and filled with people, music, and lights.

Kim clearly didn't want to spend Christmas with him. So instead he had come to Graceland to spend Christmas with Elvis.

Elvis was a man who understood heartbreak.

"Merry Christmas," she said to the Elvis Santa as she dropped money into the red bucket. A bitterly cold wind blew about them, and still he rang his bell, humming "Return To Sender."

"Whatever charity you work for should be very grateful."

"Thank you, ma'am," he said softly.

Tucking the little monkey under her arm, she walked over to the waiting taxi at the curb. "The Forever Blue club, please."

"He's not there, ma'am."

"What did you say?"

The Elvis Santa stopped ringing his bell. "The man you're looking for isn't there."

She wasn't sure what was more startling: the fact that this fellow was finally engaging her in conversation or that he was presuming to tell her where Spencer was.

"But you don't know who I'm trying to find." Kim stepped back onto the curb.

"Excuse me, are you coming or not?" the cabdriver asked.

"In a moment."

"The man is lonely, ma'am. He's been waiting for you a long time, and he thinks now maybe he's lost you." The Santa's haunting dark eyes stared intently into hers. For one startling moment, he almost reminded her of Spence. How silly. Spencer didn't have dark sideburns or wear Santa suits.

This was getting more absurd by the minute. Kim didn't know why she was even continuing this conversation.

"Well, I've been out all day and missed his calls."

"He's been looking for you much longer than just today, ma'am." The Elvis Santa started ringing his bell, the sound as clear and beautiful as a choir of angels. "He's been looking for you his whole life. And you've been looking for him, too."

She stood there, her mouth open.

"If you go wandering around Memphis for hours, you'll only waste this night." He shook his head. "He doesn't want to be alone on Christmas Eve, Kim. Go to him as soon as you can. Before his heart breaks."

"What did you call me?" She clutched the monkey to her as if for support.

But he only rang his bell louder in response.

"How did you know my name?"

"He's at Graceland." The Elvis Santa smiled. "Merry Christmas, ma'am."

"But—but how did you—"

He smiled wider. "Graceland," he repeated, then broke out into the loveliest rendition she had ever heard of "It's Now or Never."

"Where to, miss?" The cabbie turned an exasperated face to her when she finally slid in and closed the door.

She glanced over at Elvis, singing away on the curb. Then she looked down at Jim Bob. "Graceland," she said. "And step on it."

Where did so many people come from? Shouldn't everyone be home on Christmas Eve? Maybe everyone was, everyplace but Memphis. Kim pushed her way through a throng of people oohing and ahhing at the lavish Christmas display on the grounds of Graceland. How would she ever find Spencer in this crowd?

Glad she'd worn her wool coat, Kim felt that winter had finally arrived. Somehow the cold and the darkness, the twinkling colored lights, the festive atmosphere all made Christmas seem like a reality to her. But without Spencer to share it with, it would be the loneliest Christmas she had ever spent.

"Now all we have to do is find him," she told the monkey cradled in her arms.

An hour later, she found herself leaning against a wall, out of breath, chilled. She'd been everywhere: the car museum, the visitors center, the graffiti-strewn wall. Not a sign of Spencer. Her reason told her to leave. If she simply drove to his house and waited for him there, he had to turn up eventually. Yet her instincts told her that he was at Graceland, that she had been right to believe the Elvis Santa. Spencer was here, feeling alone, and the longer it took to find him, the more he would feel his heart was breaking. She knew that because she felt her own heart breaking, too.

But the grounds were so noisy and crowded. They could be within three feet of each other, and still not know it.

She tried to get out of the way as yet another Japanese tour group jostled past her. Their tour guide gestured for them to stop as he mounted a small step. Kim knew she was trapped until the group decided to move again, and she resigned herself to waiting.

The tour guide caught her attention, however, when he began speaking through what looked like a small karaoke machine. A microphone was attached to a black amplifier strapped about his shoulder. Even over the din of the surrounding crowd, his voice carried easily.

"That's it, Jim Bob," she whispered to the monkey.

She pushed her way through the tourists, most of them grumbling in Japanese as she stepped on toes.

The guide looked alarmed when she climbed up next to him.

"Excuse me, please, but could I borrow your microphone?"

He frowned and said something in Japanese.

"I'm sorry, but I really need it." She grabbed for the microphone. He grabbed back.

"I'll give it right back." She tore the microphone out of his grasp, and when he reached for it again, she switched on Jim Bob.

The mechanical monkey broke out into "All Shook Up,"

and the tour guide jumped down from the step. He obviously thought she was mad. Well, maybe she was. She held up the monkey to the microphone.

The entire Japanese tour group took several steps back, then several more as Kim herself joined Jim Bob in singing. If Spence couldn't hear the monkey, then she'd make certain he at least heard her.

She was well into the fourth verse when she spied a security guard making his way toward her. *Not much more time left.* She belted out the chorus, singing as if her life depended on it. And from the looks of the security guard, perhaps it did.

Neither she nor Jim Bob finished the chorus. A second later she switched off the monkey and dropped the microphone. Spencer was running across the lawn, waving his hand, his baseball cap flying off his head.

"Spence!" She pushed her way through the tourists, ignoring their stares and grumbling. "Spence!"

He grabbed her up in his arms, holding her so tight she feared he would crush Jim Bob.

"You're a madwoman, you know that, don't you?" He kissed her.

"I guess I caught the Modine Madness," she said when they finally came up for air. "You didn't tell me it was contagious."

Cupping his hands about her face, he looked searchingly into her eyes. "Then we're both mad. That or we're the sanest people in Memphis."

They kissed tenderly. Kim felt happy enough for tears, for shouting, for singing. "I didn't want to be alone on Christmas Eve," she murmured. "I didn't want either of us to be alone."

He kissed her again. "I love you."

She snuggled closer, the monkey still pressed comically between them. "And I love you, Spence. I love you."

They were about to kiss once more when Kim let out a cry.

"Look!" She held out one hand. Snowflakes fell through the night air, landing soft and delicate against her outstretched palm.

"Snow!" She laughed at the wonder of it. "I didn't know it snowed in Memphis."

Spencer smiled and caressed her cheek. "It does that sometimes."

"Really?" She stared up at the snow falling softly from the sky. Christmas carols played in the distance. "I thought it was a miracle."

"You're the miracle," he said in a husky voice. "You're *my* miracle."

They kissed for a long time, then held each other close, ignoring the crowds, the noise, even the snow.

"How did you know I was here?" he asked finally.

Kim rested her head on his shoulder. She doubted even Spencer would understand if she explained that Elvis had told her.

"Oh, I just knew."

"You knew because we're meant to be together." Spence hugged her tighter. "You knew because we love each other so much."

Kim glanced down at Jim Bob, nearly hidden between their two bodies. No need to spoil the mood, she thought. Let it be a secret between her and Elvis. With any luck, the monkey wouldn't talk.

She started to laugh. Then Spence kissed her again, and she could feel only wet snowflakes, dizzying joy.

And all shook up.

Sandra Hill

Fever

To my Aunt Catherine Conklin, who passed away last year:
Oh, the Christmas memories she brings to mind.
Angel hair on the tree, children's laughter, delicious scents
from her warm kitchen, but most of all, love.

I will always miss you, Aunt Catherine, but especially at
Christmas.

Chapter One

"Oh, my gawd! It's George Strait."

"Where? Where? Ooh, ooh! I swear, Mabel, I'm so excited I'm gonna pee my pants."

Clayton Jessup III, was about to enter his hotel suite when he heard the high-pitched squeals of the two blue-haired ladies in matching neon pink ELVIS LIVES sweatshirts.

He glanced over his shoulder to see who was generating so much excitement and saw no one. *Uh-oh!* In an instant, he realized that they thought he was the George person . . . probably some Memphis celebrity. Even worse, they were pep-stepping briskly toward him with huge smiles plastered across their expectant faces and autograph books drawn and at the ready.

"Open the damn door," he snarled at the wizened old bell-hop, whose liver-spotted hands were fumbling with the key.

"I'm tryin', I'm tryin'. You don't wanna get caught by any of these country music fanatics. Last week over on Beale Street, they tore off every bit of a construction worker's clothes for souvenirs, right down to his BVDs, just 'cause they thought he was Billy Dean.''

"Who the hell is Billy Dean?"

"You're kidding, right?" the bellhop said, casting him a sideways once-over of disbelief.

Clay grabbed the key out of the bellhop's hand and inserted it himself. Just before the women were ready to pounce, gushing, "Oooh, George. Yoo-hoo!" the door swung open and they escaped. Leaning against the closed door, he exhaled with a loud whoosh of relief.

He heard one of the women say, "Mabel, I don't think that was George. He wasn't wearing a cowboy hat, and George never goes anywhere without his trademark wide-brimmed cowboy hat."

"Maybe you're right, Mildred," Mabel said.

"Besides, he was too skinny to be George. He looked more like that Richard Gere."

Richard Gere? Me? Mildred needs a new set of bifocals.

"Richard Gere," Mabel swooned. "Hmmm. Is it possible . . . ? Nah. That guy was taller and leaner than Richard Gere. Besides, Richard Gere is more likely to be off in Tibet with the Dolly Lay-ma, not in Memphis."

"At least we saw Elvis's ghost at Graceland today."

Their voices were fading now, so Clay knew they were walking away.

Dropping his briefcase to the floor, he opened his closed eyes . . . and almost had a heart attack. "What is this?" he asked the bellhop.

"The Roustabout Suite," the bellhop said proudly, shifting from foot to foot with excitement. The dingbat looked absolutely ridiculous in his old-fashioned red bellhop outfit, complete with a pillbox hat. "It's the best one in the Original Heartbreak Hotel, next to the Viva Las Vegas and the Blue Hawaii suites, of course. Families with children love it."

"I do not have children," Clay gritted out.

"Aaahh, that's too bad. Some folks think the spirit of Elvis lives in this hotel. Seen 'im myself a time or two. Maybe if you pray to the Elvis spirit, he'll intercede with the good Lord to rev up your sperm count. Or if the problem is with the little lady, you could . . . uh, why is your face turnin' purple?''

"I do not have children. I am not married. Mind your own damn business.''

"Oops!'' the bellhop said, ducking his head sheepishly. "Sometimes I talk a mite too much, but I'm a firm believer in Southern hospitality. Yep. Better to be friendly and take a chance than . . .'' The fool blathered on endlessly without a care for whether Clay was listening or not. Really, he should be home in a rocking chair, instead of parading around a hotel like an organ grinder's monkey. Another "to do" item to add to his itinerary: check the hotel's retirement policy.

Clay turned his back on the rambling old man . . . and groaned inwardly as he recognized that his view from this angle wasn't any better. *The Roustabout Suite. Hell!*

The split-level suite had a miniature merry-go-round in the sitting room. As the carousel horses circled, a pipe organ blasted out carnival music. A cotton candy machine was set up in one corner, and the blasted thing actually worked, if the sickly sweet odor was any indication. Candy apples lay on the bar counter beside a Slurpee dispenser in the small kitchenette. The walls were papered with movie posters from the Elvis movie *Roustabout,* and the bed was an enlarged version of a tunnel-of-love car. On the bedside table were a clown lamp and a clock in the shape of a Ferris wheel. Up and down went the clown's blinking eyes. Round and round went the clock's illuminated dial. Mixed in with this eclectic collection were quality pieces of furniture, no doubt from the original hotel furnishings.

If Clay didn't have a headache already, this room would surely give him the mother of all migraines. "You can't seriously think I'd stay in this . . . this three-ring circus.''

"Well, it was the best we could do on such short notice,'' the bellhop said, clearly affronted.

"Hee-haw! Hee-haw! Baaaa! Baaaa! Hee-haw!''

For a moment Clay lowered his head, not sure he wanted to know what those sounds were coming from outside. Walking briskly across the room, he glanced out the second-floor window . . . then did an amazed double take.

"Oh! Aren't they cute?" the bellhop commented behind him.

"Humph!" Clay grumbled in disagreement. Pulling his electronic pocket organizer from his suit, he clicked to the Memphis directory, where he typed in his observations, punctuated by several more "Humphs." It was a word that seemed to slip out of his mouth a lot lately . . . a word his father had used all the time. *Am I turning into a negative, stuffy version of my father now? Is that what I've come to?*

"Hee-haw! Hee-haw! Baaaa! Baaaa! Hee-haw!"

"Oh, good Lord!" The headache that had been building all day finally exploded behind his eyes—a headache the size of his bizarre "inheritance" he'd come to Tennessee to investigate. Raking his fingers through his close-clipped hair, he gazed incredulously at the scene unfolding on the vacant lot below . . . a property that he now happened to own, along with this corny hotel. Neither was his idea of good fortune.

"Hee-haw! Hee-haw! Baaaa! Baaaa! Hee-haw!"

"What the hell is going on?" he asked the bellhop, who was now standing in the walk-in closet hanging Clay's garment bag.

"A live Nativity scene."

"Humph!" Clay arched a brow skeptically. It didn't resemble any Nativity scene he'd ever witnessed.

"Did you say humbug?" the bellhop inquired.

"No, I didn't say humbug," he snapped, making a mental note to add an observation in the hotel file of his pocket organizer about the attitude of the staff. *What does the imbecile think I am? A crotchety old man out of a Dickens novel? Hell, I'm only thirty years old. I'm not crotchety. My father was crotchety. I'm not.* "I said 'humph.' That's an expression that denotes . . . Oh, never mind."

He peered outside again. The bellhop was right. Five men, one woman, a baby, a donkey, and two sheep were setting up shop in a scene reminiscent of a Monty Python parody, or a bad "Saturday Night Live" skit. The only thing missing was a camel or two.

Please, God. No camels, Clay prayed quickly, just in case. He wasn't sure how many more shocks he could take today.

The trip this morning from his home in Princeton had been uneventful. He'd managed to clear a backlog of paperwork while his driver transported him in the smooth-riding, oversize Mercedes sedan to Newark Airport. He'd been thinking about ditching the gas guzzler ever since his father died six months ago, but now he had second thoughts. The first-class, airline accommodations had been quiet, too, and conducive to work.

The nightmare had begun once he entered the Memphis International Airport terminal. Every refined, well-bred cell in his body had been assaulted by the raucous sounds of tasteless music and by the even more tasteless souvenirs of every conceivable Elvis item in the world . . . everything from "Barbie Loves Elvis" dolls to "authentic" plastic miniflasks of Elvis sweat.

The worst was to come, however.

When Clay had arrived at the hotel to investigate the last of his sizable inheritance, consisting mostly of blue-chip stocks and bonds, he'd found the Original Heartbreak Hotel. How could his father . . . a conservative Wall Street investment banker, longtime supporter of the symphony, connoisseur of old master paintings . . . have bought a hotel named Heartbreak Hotel? And why, for God's sake? More important, why had he kept it a secret since its purchase thirty-one years ago?

But that was beside the point now. His most immediate problem was the yahoos setting up camp outside. He hesitated to ask the impertinent bellhop another question, which was ridiculous. He was in essence his employee. "Who are they?"

The bellhop ambled over next to him. "The Fallons."

"Are they entertainers?"

The bellhop laughed. "Nah. They're dairy farmers."

Dairy farmers? Don't ask. You'll get another stupid non-answer. "Well, they're trespassing on my property. Tell the management when you go down to the lobby to evict them immediately.''

"Now, now, sir, don't be actin' hastily. They're just poor orphans tryin' to make a living, and—''

"Orphans? They're a little old to be orphans," he scoffed.

"—and besides, it was my idea.''

"Your idea?'' Clay snorted. Really, he felt as if he'd fallen down some garden hole and landed on another planet.

"Yep. Last week, Annie Fallon was sittin' in the Hound Dog Café, havin' a cup of coffee, lookin' fer all the world like she lost her best friend. She just came from the monthly Holstein Association meeting across the street. You know what Holsteins are, dontcha?''

"Of course I do," he said with a sniff. *They're cows, aren't they?*

"Turns out Annie and her five brothers are in dire financial straits," the bellhop rambled on, "and it occurred to me, and I tol' her so, too, that with five brothers and a new baby ... her brother Chet's girlfriend *dropped* their sweet little boy in his lap, so to speak ... well, they had just enough folks fer a Nativity scene, it bein' Christmas and all. I can't figure how the idea came to me. Like a miracle, it was ... an idea straight out of heaven, if ya ask me.'' The old man took a deep, wheezy breath, then concluded, "You wouldn't begrudge them a little enterprise like this, wouldja, especially at Christmastime?''

Clay didn't believe in Christmas, never had, but that was none of this yokel's business. "I don't care if it's the Fourth of July. Those ... those squatters had better be gone by the time I get down there, or someone is going to pay. Look at them," he said, sputtering with outrage. "Bad enough they're planting themselves on private land, but they have the nerve to act as if they own the damn place.'' Hauling wooden frames off a pickup truck, they were now erecting a three-sided shed, then strewing about the ground hay from two bales.

That wasn't the worst part, though. All of the characters were made up as Elvis versions—*What else!*—of the Nativity figures, complete with fluffed-up hair and sideburns.

The three wise men were tall, lean men in their late teens or early twenties wearing long satin robes in jewel-tone colors, covered by short shoulder capes with high stand-up collars. Their garish attire was adorned with enough sequins and glitter to do the tackiest Vegas sideshow proud. They moved efficiently about their jobs in well-worn leather cowboy boots, except for the shepherd in duct-taped sneakers. Belts with huge buckles, like rodeo cowboys usually wore, tucked in their trim waists.

The shepherd, about thirteen years old, wore a knee-high, one-piece sheepskin affair, also belted with a shiny clasp the size of a hubcap. Even the sleeping baby, placed carefully in a rough manger, had its hair slicked up into an Elvis curl, artfully arranged over its forehead.

Joseph was a glowering man in his mid-twenties, wearing a gem-studded burlap gown, a rope belt with the requisite buckle, and scruffy boots. Since he kept checking the infant every couple of minutes, Clay assumed he must be the father.

"Hee-haw! Hee-haw! Baaaa! Baaaa! Hee-haw!"

Clay's attention was diverted to an animal trailer, parked behind the pickup truck, where one of the wise men was leading the braying donkey and two sheep, none of which appeared happy to participate in the blessed event. In fact, the donkey dug in its hooves stubbornly—*Do donkeys have hooves?*—as the now-cursing wise man yanked on the lead rope. The donkey got in the last word by marking the site with a spray of urine, barely missing the boot of the Wise Man who danced away at the last moment. The sheep deposited their own Nativity gifts.

Clay would have laughed if he weren't so angry.

Then he noticed the woman.

Lordy, did he notice the woman!

A peculiar heat swept over him then, burning his face, raising hairs on the back of his neck and forearms, even along his thighs and calves, lodging smack-dab in his gut, and lower. *How odd!* It must be anger, he concluded, because he sure as hell wasn't attracted to the woman. Not by a Wall Street long shot!

Sandra Hill

She was tall—at least five-foot-nine—and skinny as a rail. He could see that, even under her plain blue, ankle-length gown . . . well, as plain as it could be with its overabundant studding of pearls. In tune with her outrageous ensemble, she sported the biggest hair he'd ever seen outside a fifties-movie retrospective. The long brunette strands had been teased and arranged into an enormous bowl shape that flipped up on the ends—probably in imitation of Elvis's wife. *What was her name? Patricia? Phyllis? No. Priscilla, that was it.* She must have depleted the entire ozone layer over Tennessee to hold that monstrosity in place. Even from this distance he could see that her eyelids were covered with a tawdry plastering of blue eyeshadow and weighted down with false eyelashes, à la Tammie Faye Baker. Madonna she was not . . . neither the heavenly one, nor the rock star with the cone-shaped bra.

Still, a strange heat pulsed through his body as he gazed at her.

Does she realize how ridiculous she looks?

Does she care?

Do I care?

Damn straight I do! he answered himself as the woman, leader of the motley biblical crew, waved her hands dictatorially, wagged her forefinger, and steered the others into their places. Within minutes, they posed statuelike in a Memphis version of the Nativity scene. The only one unfrozen was the shepherd, whose clear, adolescent voice rang out clearly with "O, Holy Night."

Already tourists passing by were pausing, oohing and ahhing, and dropping coins and paper money into the iron kettle set in the front. It was only noon, but it was clear to Clay that by the end of the day this group was going to make a bundle.

"Not on my property!" Clay vowed, grabbing his overcoat and making for the door. At the last minute, he paused and handed the clearly disapproving bellhop a five-dollar bill.

For some reason, the scowling man made him feel like . . . well, Scrooge . . . and he hadn't even said "Humph!" again. It was absurd to feel guilty. He was a businessman . . . an in-

vestment banker specializing in venture capital. He had every
right to make a business decision.

"Thank you for your service," he said coolly. "I'm sure
I'll be seeing you again during my stay here in Memphis."
Clay intended to remain only long enough to complete ar-
rangements for the razing of the hotel and the erection of a
strip mall on this site and the adjoining property. He expected
to complete his work here before the holidays and catch the
Christmas Eve shuttle back to New Jersey on Thursday. Not
that he had any particular plans that demanded a swift return
to Princeton. On the contrary. There was no one waiting for
him in his big empty mansion, except for Doris and George
Benson, the longtime cook/housekeeper and gardener/driver.
No Christmas parties he would mind missing. No personal
relationships that would suffer in his absence.

Clay blinked with surprise at his out-of-character, maudlin
musings. This hokey Elvis-mania that pervaded Memphis must
be invading his brain, like a virus. *The Elvis virus. Ha, ha,
ha!*

The bellhop's eyes bored into him, then softened, as if seeing his thoughts.

Clay didn't like the uncomfortable feeling he got under the
bellhop's intense stare.

"You really plannin' on kicking the Fallons off your property? At Christmastime?" the bellhop inquired in a condemn-
ing tone of voice.

"Damn straight."

"Even the iciest heart can be melted."

Now what the hell does that mean? "Yeah, well, it's going
to take a monumental fever in my case, because I have plans
for that property." *This is the craziest conversation in the
world. Why am I even talking to this kook?*

"You know what they say about the best-laid plans?"

"Am I supposed to understand that?" *Shut up, Jessup. Just
ignore him.*

"Sometimes God sticks out his big toe and trips us humans.
You might just be in for a big stumble."

God? Big toe? The man is nuts. "Lock up on your way

out,'' Clay advised, opening the hallway door. *Time to put a stop to this nonsense . . . the bellhop, the hotel, the Nativity scene, the whole freakin' mess.*

But damned if the impertinent old fart didn't begin humming "Fever" as Clay closed the door behind him, thus getting in the last word.

"This is the dumbest damn thing you've ever conned us into, Annie."

"Tsk-tsk," Annie told her brother Chet in stiff-lipped sotto voce. "We're supposed to be statues. No talking. Furthermore, St. Joseph should *not* be swearing."

A flush crept up the face of her oldest brother, who was handsome even with the exaggerated Elvis hairdo. Chet was the kind of guy who would probably make a young girl's heart stop even if he were bald.

Good looks aside, her heart went out to Chet. He was twenty-five, only three years younger than she, and so very solemn for his age. Well, he had good reason, she supposed. He'd certainly never hesitated over taking responsibility for raising his baby, Jason, when his girlfriend Emmy Lou abandoned the infant to his care a month ago. Even before that, he'd tried hard to be the man of the family ever since their parents had died in a car accident ten years ago, changing overnight from a carefree teenager to a weary adult.

Well, they'd all changed with that tragedy. No use dwelling on what couldn't be helped.

"There's no one around now," Chet pointed out defensively.

That was true. It was lunch hour and a Sunday, so only a few people had straggled by thus far. But tourist sidewalk traffic past their panorama on Blues Street, just off the famous Beale Street, should pick up soon. Yesterday, their first day trying out this enterprise, had brought in an amazing $700 in tips between eleven A.M. and five P.M. Annie was hoping that in the five days remaining before Christmas they would be able to earn another $3500, enough to save the farm, so to speak.

276

"I feel like an absolute fool," Chet grumbled.

"Me, too," her other four brothers concurred with a unified groan.

"Wayne keeps trying to bite my butt," Johnny added. "I swear he's the meanest donkey in the entire world. Pure one-hundred-proof jackass, if you ask me."

"He is *not* mean," Jerry Lee argued. The only one Wayne could abide was Jerry Lee, who'd bred him for a 4-H project five years ago. "Wayne senses that you don't like him, and he's trying to get your attention."

"By biting my butt?"

Everyone laughed at that.

"I had a girl once who bit my butt—" Roy started to say.

Annie gasped. "Roy Fallon! If you say one more word, I swear I'll soap your mouth out when we get home. I don't care if you are twenty-two years old."

Everyone laughed some more. Except for Annie.

"Your sheep keep nuzzling this fleece outfit you made me wear," Johnny continued to gripe. He directed his complaint now at Annie. "I think they think I'm one of their cousins."

Ethel and Lucy were Annie's pets. She'd won them when they were only baby lambs in a grange raffle two years ago.

"Stop your whining, boys," she snapped. "Do you think *I'm* enjoying myself? My scalp itches. My skin is probably breaking out in zits like a popcorn machine. I'm surely straining some muscles in my eyelids with these false eyelashes. And I'm just praying that the barn roof doesn't cave in before we earn enough money for its repair. Or that the price of milk doesn't drop again. Or that we'll be able to afford this semester at vet school for Roy. And—"

"Don't blame this sideshow on me," Roy chimed in. "It's not my fault the government cut the student-aid program."

"Oh, Roy, don't get your sideburns in a dither," she said, already regretting her sharp words.

"Or get your duck's-ass hairdo in a backwind," Hank taunted.

Annie shot Hank a scowl, and continued, "No one's to

blame, Roy. Our problems have been piling up for a long time.''

"Well, I'll tell you one thing. If anyone from school comes by, I'm outta here, barn roof or no barn roof," Jerry Lee asserted. At fifteen, peer approval was critical, and dressing up as an Elvis wise man probably didn't score many points with the cheerleading squad.

"You're just worried that Sally Sue Sorenson will see you," Hank teased.

"Am not," Jerry Lee argued, despite his red face.

"Shhhh," Annie cautioned.

A group of tourists approached, and Annie's family froze into their respective parts. Johnny, her youngest brother—*God bless him*—broke loose with an absolutely angelic version of "Silent Night." He must have inherited his singing talent from their parents, who'd been unsuccessful Grand Ole Opry wanna-bes. The rest of them could barely carry a tune.

In appreciation, the group, which included a man, a woman, and three young children, waited through the entire song, then dropped a five-dollar bill into the kettle, while several couples following in their wake donated a bunch of dollar bills each, along with some change. Thank God for the Christmas spirit.

After they passed by, Roy picked up on their interrupted conversation. "Actually, Jerry Lee, don't be too quick to discount the appeal of this Elvis stuff. Being an Elvis look-alike could be a real chick magnet for some babes."

"You've been hanging around barns too long," Jerry Lee scoffed, but there was a note of uncertainty in his voice. Roy was a first-year vet student and graduate of Memphis State. Jerry Lee wasn't totally sure his big brother, at twenty-two, hadn't picked up a few bits of male-female wisdom.

"He's bullshittin' you," Hank interjected with a laugh, ignoring the glare Annie flashed his way for the coarse language. Hank was a high school senior, a football player, and the self-proclaimed stud of the family.

Jerry Lee gave Roy a dirty look for his ill advice. Obviously, Hank ranked as the better "chick" expert.

"What do you think, Annie?" Roy asked, chuckling at Jerry Lee's gullibility.

"How would I know what attracts women? I haven't had a date in two years. Then it was with Frankie Wilks, the milk-tank driver."

"And he resembles the back end of a hound dog more than Elvis," Hank remarked with a hoot of laughter at his own joke.

"That was unkind, Hank," Annie chastised, "just because he's a little . . . hairy."

They all made snorting sounds of ridicule.

Frankie Wilks had a bushy beard and mustache and a huge mop of frizzy hair. Masses of hair covered his forearms and even peeked out at the neck of his milk company uniform. *Hirsute* would be an understatement.

"You could go out with guys if you wanted to," Chet offered softly. "You don't have to give up your life for us or the farm. It was different when we were younger, but—"

"Uh-oh!" Roy said.

Everyone stopped talking and stiffened to attention.

A man was stomping down the sidewalk toward them, having emerged from the hotel entrance. He wore a conservative black business suit, so finely cut it must have been custom-made, with a snow white shirt and a dark-striped tie, spit-shined wing-tip shoes, and a black cashmere overcoat that probably cost as much as a new barn roof.

He was a taller, leaner version of Richard Gere, with the same short-clipped dark hair. He would have been heart-stoppingly handsome if it weren't for the frown lines that seemed to be etched permanently about his flaming eyes and tight-set mouth. How could a man so young be so disagreeable in appearance?

Despite his demeanor, Annie felt a strange heat rush through her just gazing at him. It was embarrassment, of course. What woman enjoyed looking like a tart in front of a gorgeous man?

Unfortunately, Annie suspected that the flame in his eyes was directed toward them. And she had a pretty good idea who he was, too. Clayton Jessup III, the new owner of the

Original Heartbreak Hotel and the vacant lot where they had set up their Nativity scene.

The kindly couple who managed the hotel, David and Marion Bloom, had given them permission for the Nativity scene when Annie had asked several days ago. "After all, the lot has been vacant for more than thirty years," Marion had remarked. "It's about time someone made use of it."

But when Annie and Chet had stopped in the hotel a short time ago, where David and Marion had also been nice enough to let them use an anteroom for changing Jason, they soon realized that everyone at the hotel was in an uproar. The new owner had arrived, unannounced, and he intended to raze the site and erect a strip shopping mall. As if Memphis needed another mall!

Didn't the man recognize the sentimental value of the hotel and this lot? No, she guessed, a man like him wouldn't. Money would be his bottom line.

Just before Mr. Jessup got to them, some tourists paused and listened with "oohs" and "ahhs" of appreciation, dropping more paper money and change into their kettle. The boys stood rock still, but Annie saw the gleam of interest in their eyes at a petite blonde in gray wool slacks and a cardigan over a peach-colored turtleneck who stood staring at them for a long time. There was a hopeless sag to her shoulders until Hank winked at her, and she burst out with a little laugh.

Drawing the sides of his overcoat back, and planting his hands on slim hips, Mr. Jessup glared at them, his lips curling with disdain upon getting a close-up view of their attire. At least he had the courtesy to wait till the tourists passed by before snarling, "What the hell are you doing on my property?"

The baby's eyes shot open, and he began to whimper at the harsh voice.

"We have permission," Chet said, his voice as frosty as Mr. Jessup's as he leaned over and soothed his child. "Hush, now. Back to sleep, son," he crooned, rocking the manger slightly.

Annie tried to explain, "Mr. and Mrs. Bloom told us it

would be all right. We'll only be here for a few days, and—''

He put up a hand to halt her words. ''You won't be here for even a few more hours.'' He peered down at his watch—probably one of those Rolex things, equal in value to the mortgage on their farm—and grated, ''You have exactly fifteen minutes to vacate these premises, or I'll have the police evict you forcibly. So stop fluttering those ridiculous eyelashes at me.''

''I was not fluttering.''

''Hey, it's not necessary to yell at our sister,'' Roy yelled. He, Hank, Jerry Lee, and Johnny were coming up behind Annie to form a protective flank. Chet had taken Jason out of the manger and was holding him to his shoulder, as if Mr. Jessup might do the infant bodily harm.

''Furthermore, those animals had better not have done any damage,'' Mr. Jessup continued, and proceeded to walk toward the shed where Wayne was hee-hawing and the sheep were bleating, as if sensing some disaster in progress.

''No! Don't!'' they all shouted in warning.

Too late.

Mr. Jessup slipped on a pile of sheep dung. Righting himself, he noticed Wayne's back leg shoot out. To avoid the kick, he spun on his ankle. Annie could almost hear the tendons tearing as his ankle twisted. His expensive shoes, now soiled, went out from under him, and the man went down hard, on his back, with his head hitting a small rock with an ominous crack.

''I'm going to sue your eyelashes off,'' Mr. Jessup said on a moan, just before he passed out.

Chapter Two

He was drunk . . . as a skunk.

Well, not actually drunk. More like under the influence of painkillers. But the effect was the same. Three sheets to the Memphis wind.

"Oh, I wish I was *not* in the land of Dixie," Mr. Jessup belted out. He'd been singing nonstop for the past five minutes.

Annie and the emergency room intern exchanged a look.

Annie tried to get him to lie down on the table. "Mr. Jessup, you really should settle—"

"Call me Clay." He flashed her a lopsided grin, accompanied by the most amazing, utterly adorable dimples. Then he resumed his rendition of "Dixie" with a stanza ending, ". . . *strange* folks there are not forgoooootten."

Geez!

"I wish I'd bought that t-shirt I saw at the airport." Mr. Jessup . . . rather, Clay . . . stopped singing for a moment to inject that seemingly irrelevant thought. "It said, 'Elvis Is Dead, And I'm Not Feelin' So Good Myself.' Ha, ha, ha!"

"He's having a rather . . . um, strange allergic reaction. Or perhaps I just gave him a little too much Darvon," the young doctor mumbled, casting a sheepish glance toward the other busy cubicles to see if any of his colleagues had overheard.

"No kidding, Ben Casey!" Annie remarked. Clay was now leading an orchestra in his own version of "Flight of the Bumble bee." She didn't think Rimsky-Korsakov had actual buzzing sounds in his original opera containing that music.

"You have biiiiig hair," he observed to Annie then, cocking his head this way and that to get just the right angle in studying its huge contours. "Does it hurt?"

"No."

"Does your boyfriend like it?"

"I don't have a boyfriend."

He nodded his head, as if that was a given. "A man couldn't get close enough to kiss you. Or other things," he noted, jiggling his eyebrows at her.

The man was going to hate himself tomorrow if he remembered any of this.

Annie was already hating herself . . . because, for some reason, the word *kiss* coming from his lips—*who knew they would be so full and sensual when not pressed together into a thin line of disapproval?*—prompted all kinds of erotic images to flicker in her underused libido. She pressed a palm to her forehead. "Boy, is it hot in here!"

"I'll second that. I'm burning up." Clay twisted his head from side to side, massaging the nape of his neck with one hand. Then, before she could protest, he loosened the string tie at the back of his shoulders and let his hospital gown slide to the floor. He wore nothing but a pair of boring white boxer shorts.

Boring, hell! He was sexy as sin.

Annie's mouth gaped open, and her temperature shot up another notch or two at all that skin. And muscle. And dark, silky hair.

Funny how hair on Frankie Wilks seemed repulsive. But with this man, she had to practically hold her hand back for fear she'd run her fingertips through his chest hairs. Or forearm hairs. Or—*lordy, lordy*—thigh hairs.

How could a man so stodgy and mean be so primitively attractive? She'd gotten to know just how stodgy and mean he could be on the ride over here. And how did a man who presumably worked at a desk all day long maintain such a flat, muscle-planed stomach?

Startled, she clicked her jaw shut.

"It's not warm in here," the doctor pointed out, intruding into her thoughts. *Thank God!* "Perhaps you both have a fever. But, no, I checked your temperature, Mr. Jessup. It's normal."

Normal? There's nothing normal about the steam heat rising in this room.

Clay glared at Annie accusingly. Was he going to blame her for a fever, too? To her horror, he broke out with the husky, intimate lyrics, "You give me fever." He was staring at her the whole time.

Oh, mercy! Who would have thought he even knew an Elvis lyric? It had probably seeped into his unconscious over the years through some sort of Muzak osmosis.

"The medication will wear off in a couple of hours," the doctor was saying. "After that, we'll switch to Tylenol with codeine. Considering his reaction, I would suggest you give him only half a tablet."

"Me? Me?" *Hey, I've got to get back to the Nativity scene. Without my supervision, who knows what my brothers are doing? Probably a Macarena version of "Away In a Manger." I wouldn't put it past Roy and Hank to be flirting with passersby, too.*

The doctor finished wrapping Clay's sprained ankle tightly and took on what he'd probably practiced in front of a mirror as a serious medical demeanor. "The goose egg on the back of your head is just a hard knock, but you should be watched closely for the next twenty-four hours. I don't like the way you reacted to the Darvon. Do you have family nearby to keep an eye on you?"

"I have no family," Clay declared woefully.

He's not married. Annie did a mental high-five, though why, she couldn't imagine. Her heart would have gone out to the man at that poignant comment if it weren't for the fact that he was back to glowering at her. She tried to understand why he directed all his hostility toward her. No doubt it stemmed from the fact that he'd been *really* angry about the accident and blamed it all on her family. "You and your crazy brothers are going to pay," he'd informed her repeatedly on the drive to the hospital, during the long wait in the emergency room, throughout the examination, right up until the painkillers had performed their miraculous transformation. Good thing she'd talked her brothers into manning the Nativity scene, minus a Blessed Virgin, till she returned. They would have belted Clay for his surliness!

She was hoping he'd meant the threat figuratively. She was hoping it had only been the pain speaking. She was hoping God listened to the prayers of Blessed Mother impersonators.

They couldn't afford a new barn roof *and* a lawsuit.

"Well, then, perhaps we should admit you," the doctor told him. "At least overnight . . . for observation."

"I'm going back to my hotel room," Clay argued, shimmying forward to get off the examining table and stand. In the process, his boxers rode high, giving Annie an eyeful, from the side, of a tight buttock.

And her temperature cranked up another notch.

Who knew? Who could have guessed?

"Ouch." He groaned as his feet hit the floor. He staggered woozily and braced himself against the wall.

"You could stay at the farm with us for a few days," Annie surprised herself by offering. The fever that had overcome her on first viewing this infuriating tyrant must have gone to her brain. "Aunt Liza can help care for you. . . ." *While we're in the city doing our Nativity scene.* "It'll be more comfortable than a hotel room." *And you wouldn't see us on your property.*

"That's a good idea," the doctor offered, obviously anxious to end this case and move on to the next cubicle.

"Okeydokey," Clay slurred out, the time-release medication apparently kicking in again. He was leaning against the wall, bemusedly rubbing his fingertips across his lips, as if they felt numb. Then he idly scratched his stomach . . . his *flat* stomach . . . in an utterly male gesture his lordliness probably never indulged in back at the manor house.

Her heart practically stopped as the significance of his quick agreement sank in. *Criminy! I'm bringing Donald Trump home with me. What possessed me to make such an offer? My brothers will kill me. But no. It really is a good idea. Get him on home turf where we can talk down his anger. Perhaps convince him to let us continue our Nativity scene the rest of the week. Take advantage of his weakened state. Heck, we might even persuade him to change his plans about razing the hotel.*

On the other hand, Elvis might be alive and living in the refrigerator at Pizza Hut.

"A farm? I've never been on a real farm before." A grin tugged at his frowning lips, and he winked at her. "Eeii, eeii, oh, Daisy Mae."

Holy cow! The grin, combined with the sexy wink, kicked up the heat in her already feverish body still another notch. Even worse, the man appeared to have a sense of humor buried under all that starch. It just wasn't fair. Annie didn't stand a chance.

"Uh-oh." His brow creased with sudden worry. "Do you have outhouses? I don't think I want to live on a farm if I have to use an outhouse."

Live? Who said anything about "live"? We're talking visit here. A day . . . two at the most. But Annie couldn't help but smile at his silly concern.

"Hey, you're not so bad-looking when you smile." Clay cocked his head to one side, studying her.

"Thanks a bunch, your smoothness," she retorted. "And, no, we don't have outhouses."

"Do you have cows and horses and chickens and stuff?" he asked with a boyish enthusiasm he probably hadn't exhibited in twenty-five years . . . if ever.

"Yep. Even a goat."

"Oh, boy!" he said.

As the implications of her impetuous offer hit Annie—Mr. *GQ* Wall Street on their humble farm—she echoed his sentiment; *Oh, boy!*

"Did you ever make love in a hayloft?" he asked bluntly.

"No!" She lifted her chin indignantly, appalled that he would even ask her such an intimate question. Despite her indignation, though, unwelcome images flickered into Annie's brain, and her fever flared into a full-blown inferno.

"Neither have I," Clay noted, as he stared her straight in the eye and let loose with the slowest, sexiest grin she'd seen since Elvis died.

At the sign, SWEET HOLLOW FARM, Annie swerved the pickup truck off the highway and onto the washboard-rough dirt lane that meandered for a quarter mile up to the house.

Tears filled her eyes on viewing her property, as they often did when she'd been away, even if only for a few hours. She loved this land . . . the smell of its rich soil, the feel of the crisp breeze coming down from the Blue Ridge Mountains, the taste of its wholesome bounty. It had been a real struggle these past ten years, but she prided herself on not having sold off even one parcel from the 120-acre family legacy.

"Oh, darn!" she muttered when she hit one of the many potholes. The eight-year-old vehicle, with its virtually nonexistent springs, went up in the air and down hard.

She worriedly contemplated her sleeping passenger, who groaned, then rubbed the back of his aching head. His eyelids drifted open slowly, and Annie could see the disorientation that hazed their deep blue depths. As his brain slowly cleared, he sat straighter and glanced at the pasture on the right, where sixty milk cows, bearing the traditional black-and-white markings of the Holstein breed, grazed contentedly, along with an equal number of heifers and a half dozen new calves.

"Holy hell!" Clay muttered. "Cows!"

Geez! You'd think they didn't have dairy herds in New Jersey.

Slowly, he turned his head forward, taking in the clapboard farmhouse up ahead, which must be a stark contrast to his own Princeton home. She knew she was correct in her assessment when he murmured, "The Waltons! I've landed in John Boy Central."

His slow survey continued, now to the left, where he flinched visibly on seeing her . . . still adorned in all her Priscilla/Madonna garishness.

His forehead furrowing with confusion, he loosened his tie and unbuttoned the top button of his dress shirt. Then his fingers fluttered in an unconscious sweep down his body, hesitating for the briefest second over his groin.

Annie understood his bewilderment, even if he didn't. For some reason, an odd heat—of an erotic nature, not the body-temperature type—was generated when they were in each other's presence. She empathized with his consternation. Clayton Jessup III was a gorgeous hunk . . . when he wasn't frowning, that was. He, on the other hand, would find it unbelievable that he could be attracted to a tasteless caricature of the Virgin Mary.

"Can you turn down the heat?" he asked testily.

"There is no heat. The thermostat broke last winter."

"Humph!" he commented as he rolled down the window on his side. "Pee-yew!" He immediately rolled it back up. "How can you stand that smell?"

"What smell? Oh, you mean the cows." She shrugged. "You get used to it after a while. Actually, I like the scent. It spells good country living to me."

"Humph! It spells cow crap to me."

Clay's condescending attitude was starting to irk Annie. She had liked him a whole lot better when he was under the influence.

"Am I being kidnapped?" he inquired hesitantly.

"What?" *Where did that insane idea come from? Oh, I see.* His gaze was riveted now on his far left, where Chet's hunting rifle rested in the gun rack above the bench seat. "Of course not."

"Where am I?"

"Don't you remember? You fell outside the hotel. I took you to the hospital emergency room. Oh, don't look so alarmed. You just have a sprained ankle and a goose egg on your head. The doctor said you need special care for a day or two because of the reaction you had to the Darvon, and I offered to bring you out to the farm. We're about a half hour outside Memphis.''

"I agreed to stay on a . . . *farm*?" His eyes, which were really quite beautiful—a deep blue framed by thick black lashes—went wide with disbelief.

"Yes," she said in a voice stiff with affront.

"Why, for heaven's sake?"

Yep, his superiority complex was annoying the heck out of her. "Maybe because you were under the influence of drugs.''

"I don't take drugs.''

"You did today, buddy.''

"Take me back to the hotel.''

She let loose with a long sigh. "We've already been through this before. You need special care. Since you have no family, I volunteered—out of the goodness of my heart, I might add—and do I get any thanks? No, sirree.''

"Who said I have no family?"

"You did!''

"I . . . did . . . not!" His face flushed with embarrassment.

Geez, why would he be uncomfortable over revealing that he had no family? It only made him appear human. *Ha!* Maybe that was the key. He didn't want to be human.

"I don't discuss my personal life with . . . strangers.''

Bingo! "Well, you did this time.''

His eyelids fluttered with sleepiness even as he spoke. "What elsh did I saaaay?''

The little demons on the wrong side of Annie's brain did a victory dance at Clay's question. Here was the perfect opportunity for her to get even for his patronizing comments.

"Well, you did a lot of singing.''

His eyes shot open. "Me? In public?''

"Hmmm. Do you consider the emergency room a public place?''

"That's impossible.''

"And, of course, there was your remark about haylofts . . .''

"Huh?"

Annie could see that the poor guy was fighting sleep. Still, she couldn't keep herself from adding, "... and making love."

"Making love in a hayloft? I said *that*?" Clay murmured skeptically. "With *you*? Humph! I couldn't have been *that* much out of my mind."

Before she could correct his misconception that he'd associated making love in a hayloft with her, his head fell back. Good thing, too, because Annie was about to give him a matching goose egg on his insulting noggin. "Did you say humbug?"

"No! Why does everyone think I'm a Scrooge?" he said drowsily, following with a lusty yawn.

"Maybe because you are."

"I said humph," he mumbled in his sleep. Then a small snore escaped from his parted lips.

"Humph you, you egotistical bozo."

Clay awakened groggily from a deep sleep to find it was dark outside. He must have slept a good four hours or more.

For several moments, he didn't move from his position on the high maple poster bed, where he lay on his stomach, presumably to protect the back of his aching head. He burrowed deeper beneath the warm cocoon of a homemade patchwork quilt and smiled to himself. *So this is how it feels to be one of the Waltons.*

By the light of a bedside hurricane lamp, he studied his surroundings. It was a cozy room, with its slanted dormer ceiling—hardly bigger than his walk-in closet at home. The only furniture, besides the bed, was a matching maple dresser and a blanket chest under the low double windows facing the front of the house. A well-worn easy chair of faded blue upholstery sat in one corner, flanked on one side by a floor lamp and on the other by a small sidetable on which sat a paperback book and a pile of magazines. A few photographs, which he couldn't decipher from here, a high school pennant, and some cheaply framed prints of cows—*What else!*—adorned the pink rose–papered walls.

It had to belong to the Blessed Virgin bimbo who'd brought him here. Unless the collection of teddy bears on the chest and the toiletries on the bureau belonged to one of her brothers. Somehow, though, he didn't think any of the strapping young men he'd seen in that wacky Nativity scene were gay farmers.

Clay should have felt outrage at finding himself in this predicament. Instead, a strange sense of well-being filled him, as if he'd been running a marathon for a long, long time, and finally he'd reached the finish line.

Slowly he came fully awake as the sounds of the house, which had been deathly quiet before, seeped into his consciousness. The slamming of a door. The clomp, clomp, clomp of boots on hardwood floors. Laughter and male voices. Water running. The never-ending blare of Elvis music, "You ain't nothin' but a hound dog . . ." *Good Lord! People have the nerve to call that caterwauling music. Humph!*

The cry of a baby emerged from down the hall—from one of the other second-floor bedrooms, he presumed—mixed with the soft crooning voice of an adult male, a mixture of lullaby and words of comfort. "Shhh, Jason. You've had a long day. What a good boy you were! Just let me finish with this diaper; then you can have your bottle. Aaah, I know, I know. You're sleepy." Gradually, the crying died down to a slow whimper, then silence, except for the creak, creak, creak of a rocker.

From the deep recesses of Clay's memory, an image emerged . . . flickering and ethereal. A woman sitting in a high-backed rocking chair, holding an infant in her tender embrace. He even imagined the scent of baby powder mixed with a flowery substance. Perfume? The woman was singing a sweet, silly song to the baby about a sandman coming with his bag of magic sleepytime dust.

A lump formed in Clay's throat, and he could barely breathe.

Could it have been his mother . . . and him? No! His mother had left when he was barely one year old. It was impossible that he could recall something from that age. Wasn't it?

With a snort of disgust, Clay tossed the quilt aside and sat up on the edge of the bed. He gritted his teeth to fight off the wooziness that accompanied waves of pain assaulting him from both the back of his head and his bandaged ankle. Once the worst of the pain passed, he took in the fact that he was clothed only in boxers. Had he undressed himself? No, it had been the woman, Annie Fallon, and her Aunt Liza, a wiry, more ancient version of the grandma on *The Waltons*. *God, I've got a thing about the Waltons today.* They'd helped him remove his clothing, then encouraged him to take half a pill before tucking him into the big bed.

In fact, Clay had a distinct recollection of the old buzzard eyeballing his near-nude body, cackling her appreciation, then telling Annie, "Not bad for a city slicker!"

He also had a distinct recollection of Annie's response. "Don't go there, Aunt Liza. He's an egotistical bozo with ice in his veins and a Scrooge personality disorder."

"Scrooge-smoodge. You could melt him down, sweetie. Might be a nifty idea for our Christmas good deed this year."

Annie had giggled. "I can see it now. The Fallon family Christmas good deed, 1998: bring a Scrooge home for the holidays."

I am not a Scrooge. Not, not, not! I'm not icy, either. In fact, I'm hot, hot, hot . . . at least when the Tennessee tart is around. Furthermore, nobody—especially not a bunch of hay-seed farmers—had better make me their good deed. I am not a pity case.

Clay wanted nothing more than to be back home, where his life was orderly and sane. He was going to sue the pants off these crackpots, but he had more important things on his mind right now. An empty stomach—which rumbled at the delicious scents wafting up from downstairs—and a full bladder.

First things first. Clay pulled on his suit pants gingerly, and made his way into the hall, using one crutch to avoid putting full weight on his injured ankle. Across the corridor, a boy of about thirteen—the one who'd been a shepherd in the Nativity scene—was propped against the pillows on one of the twin beds in the room, reading a biology book and writing in a class notebook. He wore jeans and a T-shirt that proclaimed, FARMERS HAVE LONG HOES. His hair was wet from a recent shower and no longer sported the high pouf on top or duck's tail in the back. It was from a stereo at the side of his bed where the Elvis music was blasting.

When he noticed Clay in the doorway, the boy set his schoolbooks aside and turned down the volume. "You're up. Finally."

"Where's the bathroom?"

"Gotta take a leak, huh?" the boy inquired. "My name's Johnny," he informed him cheerily. "You're Clay, right? Annie says you're gonna stay with us for a while. Cool. Do you like Elvis?" The boy never waited for answers to his questions, just chattered away as he led the way to the end of the hall.

By the time they got there, Clay was practically crossing his legs—not an easy feat when walking with a sprained ankle. Was there only one bathroom to serve more than a half dozen people? There were eight bathrooms in his home, and he was the sole inhabitant these days, except for Doris and George, and they lived over the old carriage house.

Clay soon found himself in the small bathroom with an old-fashioned claw-footed tub and porcelain pedestal sink. No shower stall here, just a showerhead and plastic curtain that hung from an oval aluminum rod, suspended from the ceiling and surrounding the tub on all sides. At least there was a toilet, Clay thought, releasing a long sigh of near-ecstasy after relieving himself.

He'd barely zipped up his pants when there was a knock on the door. "You decent?" a male voice called out.

Define decent. Hobbling around barefooted, decent? Wearing nothing but a knot on my head the size of a fist and a pair of wrinkled slacks, decent? Caught practically midleak, decent? Under the influence of drugs, decent? "Yeah, I'm decent."

The door creaked open and the oldest brother, the father of the baby, stuck his head inside. He apparently hadn't showered yet because he still had the Elvis hairdo, though the St. Joseph outfit was gone, in favor of jeans and a sweatshirt. "Hi. My name's Chet. Annie told me to give you these." He shoved a pair of jeans, a white undershirt, a blue plaid flannel shirt, socks, and raggedy sneakers at him. "You look about the same size as me."

Clay took the items hesitantly. He was about to tell him that he wouldn't need them, since he intended to go back to the hotel, ASAP. And call his lawyer. Before he could speak, though, the man—about twenty-five years old—asked with genuine concern, "How ya feelin'? Your body must feel like a bulldozer ran over it."

"Do you mean your sister?"

Chet threw his head back and laughed. "Annie does have that effect sometimes, doesn't she? No, I meant the boink to your head and your twisted ankle."

Clay shrugged. "I'll be all right."

Just then Clay noticed the black satin bra hanging on the doorknob. The cups were full and feminine to the nth degree. He was pretty sure the wispy undergarment didn't belong to Aunt Liza. Hmmm. It would seem the scarecrow Madonna was hiding something under her virginly robes.

"Hey, that's my sister you're having indecent thoughts about," Chet protested, interrupting his reverie.

"I was not," Clay lied, hoping his flushed face didn't betray him.

"Yeah, right. Anyhow, dinner's almost ready. Do you want me to bring a tray upstairs? Or can you make it downstairs?"

Clay debated briefly whether to eat here or wait till he got back to the hotel. The embarrassing rumble in his gut decided for him. Clay told him he'd be down shortly and went back to the bedroom to change clothes while Chet made use of the shower.

A short time later, he sat at the huge oak trestle table in the kitchen waiting for Annie to come in from the barn with two of her brothers, Roy, a twenty-two-year-old vet student, and Hank, a high school senior. They were completing the second milking of the day for the dairy herd. All this information was relayed by Aunt Liza. That was what the woman had demanded that he call her after he'd addressed her as "ma'am" one too many times.

Had he ever eaten dinner in a kitchen? He didn't think so.

Did he have a personal acquaintance with anyone who had ever milked a cow? He was fairly certain he didn't.

Aunt Liza wore an apron that fit over her shoulders and hung to her knees, where flesh-colored support hose bagged conspicuously under her housedress. She hustled about the commercial-size stove off to one side of the kitchen. Sitting on benches that lined both sides of the table, chatting amiably with him as if it were perfectly normal for him to be there, were Chet, Johnny, whom he had already met, and Jerry Lee, a fifteen-year-old. This family bred kids like rabbits, apparently. The baby was up in his crib, down for the night, Chet said hopefully.

A radio sitting on a counter was set on a twenty-four-hour country music station. *Surprise, surprise.*

"Do you people honestly like that music?" Clay asked. It was probably a rude question to ask when he was in someone else's home, but he really would like to understand the attraction this crap held for the masses.

"Yeah," Chet, Jerry Lee, Johnny, and Aunt Liza said as one.

"But it's so . . . so hokey," Clay argued. "Listen to that one. 'I Changed Her Oil, She Changed My Life.' "

They all laughed.

"That's just it. Country music makes you feel good. You could be in a funky mood, and it makes you smile." Jerry Lee thought about what he'd said for a moment, then chuckled. "One of my favorites is 'She Got the Ring, I Got the Finger.' "

"Jerry Lee Fallon, I told you about using such vulgarities in this house," Aunt Liza admonished. Then she chuckled, too. "I'm partial to 'You Done Tore Out My Heart and Stomped that Sucker Flat.' "

"I like 'I Would Have Wrote You a Letter but I Couldn't Spell Yuck,' " Johnny said.

"Well, the all-time best one," Chet offered, "is 'Get Your Tongue Outta My Mouth 'Cause I'm Kissing You Good-Bye.'"

Some of the other titles tossed out then by one Fallon family member after another were: "How Can I Miss You if You Won't Go Away," "I've Been Flushed from the Bathroom of Your Heart," "If I Can't Be Number One in Your Life, Then Number Two on You," "You Can't Have Your Cake and Edith Too," and the one they all agreed was best, "I Shaved My Legs for *This?*"

Despite himself, Clay found himself laughing with the whole crazy bunch.

Just then, the back door could be heard opening into a mud-room. Voices rang out with teasing banter.

"You'd better not have mooned any passersby, Hank. That's all we need is a police citation on top of everything else," Annie was chastising her brother.

"I didn't say he mooned the girl," another male said. It must be Roy, the vet student. "I said he was mooning *over* her."

There was the sound of laughter then and running water as they presumably washed their hands in a utility sink.

Seconds later, two males entered the room, rubbing their hands briskly against the outside chill, which they carried in with them. They nodded at him in greeting and sat down on the benches, maneuvering their long legs awkwardly under the table.

Only then did Clay notice the woman who stepped through the doorway. She was tall and thin. Her long, *looong* legs that went from here to the Texas panhandle were encased in soft, faded jeans, which were tucked into a pair of work boots. An oversize denim shirt—probably belonging to one of her broth-ers—covered her on the top, hanging down to her knees with its sleeves rolled up to the elbows. A swath of brunette hair lay straight and thick to her shoulders. Not a lick of makeup covered her clear complexion. Even so, her lips were full—almost too full for her thin face—and parted over large, even, white teeth. She resembled a thinner, more beautiful version of Julia Roberts.

Clay put his forehead down on the table and groaned.

He knew everyone was probably gawking at him as if he'd lost his mind, but he couldn't help himself. He knew even before the fever flooded his face and arms and legs and that particular hot zone in between . . . he knew exactly who this stranger was. It was, unbelievably, Annie Fallon.

He cracked his eyes open a bit, still with his face in his plate, and glanced sideways at her where she still stood, equally stunned, in the doorway. Neither of them seemed to notice the hooting voices surrounding them.

How could he have been so blind?

How could he not have seen what was happening here?

How could he not have listened to the cautionary voice of the bellhop who'd warned of destiny and God's big toe?

All the pieces fit together now in the puzzle that had plagued Clay since he'd arrived in Memphis. God's big toe had apparently delivered him a holy kick in the pants. Not to mention the fever He'd apparently sent to thaw his icy heart.

Clay, a sophisticated, wealthy venture capitalist, was falling head over heels in love with a farmer. Old McAnnie.

Donald Trump and Daisy Mae.

Hell! It will never work.

Will it?

He raised his head and took a longer look at the woman who was frozen in place, staring at him with equal incredulity. It was a sign of the madness that had overcome them both that the laughter rippling around them failed to penetrate their numbed consciousness.

He knew for sure that he was lost when a traitorous thought slipped out, and he actually spoke it aloud.

''Where's the hayloft, honey?''

Chapter Three

Clay felt as if he'd landed smack-dab in the middle of the Mad Hatter's party. It was debatable who was the mad one, though—him or the rest of the inmates in this bucolic asylum.

Love? Me? Impossible!

Music blared in the background—ironically, "Can't Help Falling in Love"—and everyone talked at once, each louder than the other in order to be heard. A half dozen strains of dialogue were going on simultaneously, but no one seemed to notice. Good thing, too. It gave him a chance to speculate in private over his monumental discovery of just a few moments ago.

I'm falling in love.

Impossible! Uh-uh, none of this falling business for me.

What other explanation is there for this fever that overtakes me every time I look at her? And, man, she is so beautiful. Well, not beautiful. Just perfect. Well, not perfect-perfect. Hell, the woman makes my knees sweat, just looking at her.

Maybe it's not love. I've never been in love before. How do I know it's love? Maybe it's just lust.

Love, lust, whatever. I'm a goner.
But a farmer? A farmer?

"How come you and Annie keep googly-eyeing each other?" Johnny asked.

"Shut your teeth and eat," Aunt Liza responded, whacking Johnny on the shoulder with a long-handled wooden spoon.

"Ouch!"

Meanwhile, a myriad of platters and bowls were being set on the table. Aunt Liza assured him this was an everyday meal, not a special spread on his behalf.

Pot roast—about ten pounds, give or take a hindquarter—cut into half-inch slabs. Mashed potatoes. Gravy. Thick noodles cooked in beef broth. Creamed spinach. Pickled beets. Succotash—whatever the hell that was! Chowchow—whatever the hell that was, too! Tossed salad. Coleslaw. Homemade biscuits and butter. Pitchers of cold, unhomogenized milk at either end of the table sporting a two-inch head of real cream. Canned pears. Chocolate layer cake and vanilla ice cream.

There were enough calories and fat grams on this table to fatten up the entire nation of Bosnia. Yet, amazingly, everyone here was whip-thin. Either they'd all inherited good genetic metabolisms, or they engaged in a massive amount of physical labor. He suspected it was a combination of both.

"Do you think it's a good idea to eat so much red meat and dairy?" Clay made the mistake of inquiring.

"Bite your tongue," everyone declared at once.

For a moment, Clay had forgotten that these were dairy farmers whose livelihood depended on milk products. Plus, they had about a hundred thousand pounds of beef on the hoof in their own backyard.

Clay rubbed a forefinger over his upper lip, pondering all that had happened to him so far this day. In the midst of the conversations swirling around him now, he felt as if he were having a personal epiphany. Not just the monumental discovery that, for the first time in his life, he was falling in love; it was much more than that. He'd never realized till this moment how much he'd missed having a family. He never would have described himself as a lonely man—a loner, perhaps, but not *lonely*. Now he knew that he'd been lonely for a long time.

And that wacky bellhop had been right this morning about his coldness. Over the years, he must have built up an icy crust around his heart. *Just like my father.* Little by little, it was melting now. Every time he came within a few feet of Annie, a strange fever enveloped him, and his chest tightened with emotions too new to understand. He yearned so much. For what exactly, he didn't know.

In a daze, he reached for a biscuit, but Chet coughed meaningfully and Aunt Liza glared stonily at him. Once he sheepishly put the roll back, Annie took his hand on one side, and Jerry Lee on the other. All around the table, everyone bowed their heads and joined hands, including Aunt Liza and Chet, who sat in the end chairs, on either side. Then Annie said softly, "Lord, bless this food and all the poor people in the world who have less than we do, and even the rich people who have less than we do. For this bounty, we give you thanks. Amen."

Everyone dug in heartily then, passing the bowls and platters around the table as they chattered away. Clay soon found himself with an unbelievable amount of high-cholesterol food on his plate, and enjoying it immensely. He practically sighed at the almost sinful flavor of melt-in-your-mouth potatoes mixing on his palate with rich beef gravy.

"Frankie Wilks called when you were in the barn." Jerry Lee bobbed his eyebrows at Annie. "Said something about wantin' you to go to the Christmas Eve candlelight service with him."

"Oooooh! Oooooh!" several of her brothers taunted, meanwhile shoveling down food like monks after a Lent-long fast.

"Who's Frankie Wilks?" Clay's voice rose with more consternation than he had any right to exhibit. *Yet.*

"The milkman," Annie said, scowling at Jerry Lee. She had a hearty appetite, too, Clay noticed, though you wouldn't know it from her thin frame. Probably came from riding herd on her cows.

Did they ride herd on cows?

Then Annie's words sank in. *The milkman? The milkman? I have a five-million-dollar portfolio, I'm not a bad-looking guy, attracting women has never been a problem for me, and my competition is . . . a milkman?*

Competition? Whoa! Slow down this runaway testosterone train.

"Don't you be sittin' there, gloatin' like a pig in heat, Chet," Aunt Liza interjected as she put another slab of beef onto Clay's plate, despite his raised hand of protest. His mouth was too full to speak. "You got a phone call today, too, Chet."

Everyone at the table turned in tandem to stare at Chet.

"Emmy Lou?" Chet didn't appear very happy as he asked the question.

"Yep. She was callin' from London. Said she won't be home before Christmas to pick up the baby, after all."

"Stupid damn girl," Annie cursed under her breath. Clay suspected *damn* was not a word she used lightly.

"You drove her away, if you ask me," Hank accused, reaching for his dessert, which Aunt Liza shoved out of the way, pushing more salad his way first.

"Who asked you, mush-for-brains?" Chet snapped.

"All you had to do was tell her you looooovvvve her," Roy teased. He waved a forkful of potatoes in the air as he spoke.

"I offered to marry her, didn't I?"

"*Offered?* Sometimes, Chet, you are dumber than pig spit," Annie remarked. "Have some pickled beets," she added as an aside to Clay.

Chet's face, which was solemn to begin with, went rigid with anger, but he said nothing.

"Is this Lilith?" Annie addressed Aunt Liza as she chewed on a bite of pot roast.

"Yep. Nice and tender, ain't she?" Aunt Liza answered. "Thank God we got rid of the last of Alicia in the stew Friday night. She was tougher than cow hide."

They name the cows they eat? Will they eat those two sheep that were in the Nativity scene, too? Or—God forbid—the donkey? Bile rose in Clay's throat, and he discreetly pushed the remainder of his pot roast to the side of the plate.

"Speaking of cows, I noticed this morning that Mirabelle's vulva is swollen and red," Johnny interjected. "We better breed her soon."

"I'll do it tomorrow night."

Clay choked on the pot roast still remaining in his mouth. A thirteen-year-old kid was discussing vulvae at the dinner table, and no one blinked an eye. Even worse, Annie—*his* Annie—was going to breed a cow. "Can I watch?"

"Huh? Oh, sure," she said and resumed eating. Clay liked to watch Annie eat. Her full lips moved sensuously as she relished each morsel, no matter if it was a beet or the chocolate cake. He about lost it when her tongue darted out to lick a speck of chocolate icing off the edge of her bottom lip. "If you're sure you want to. Some people get kind of squeamish."

"I can handle it," he asserted. Heck, he'd probably seen worse in Grand Central Station. But, hot damn, Annie had just-like-that agreed to let him observe her breeding a cow. And she wasn't even embarrassed.

"Are you rich?" Roy asked.

"Rooooy!" Annie and Aunt Liza chastised.

"Yes."

"Yes?" Everyone at the table put down their eating utensils and gaped at him. Except Annie. Her face fell in disappointment. Could she be falling in love with him, too? He didn't have time to ponder for long. He just kicked into damage control. "Well, not *rich*-rich."

"How rich?" Annie demanded to know.

Before he could respond, Hank commented, "Betcha draw a bunch of chicks, having heaps of money and all."

"At least a bunch," Clay said dryly.

Annie flashed Hank a glower, which the teen ignored, smiling widely. "Man, if I had a little extra cash, and a hot car, I would be the biggest chick magnet in the whole United States. I'm already the best in the South."

His brothers hooted in reaction to his high self-opinion.

"If you'd get your mind off the girls once in a while,"

Aunt Liza reprimanded, "maybe you'd pass that cow-cue-lust."

Everyone laughed at her mispronunciation of the word *calculus,* except Annie. "And, by the way, where is your second-term report card, Mr. I-Am-the-Stud?"

"Uh-oh," Johnny and Jerry Lee groaned at the same time.

"You had to remind her," Johnny added.

Clay's lips twitched with suppressed mirth. Being in a family was kind of fun.

But Jerry Lee was back on his case again. "Do you have a chauffeur?"

Clay felt his face turn red. "Benson—George Benson—doubles as my *driver* and gardener. His wife Doris is my cook and housekeeper."

"You have a gardener!" Annie wailed. You'd think he had told her he employed an ax murderer. "And a housekeeper!"

"Do you live in a mansion?" Johnny's young face was rapt with interest.

"No, he lives in a trailer, you dweeb," Hank remarked, nudging Johnny in the ribs with an elbow.

"No. Definitely not. Uh-uh. I do *not* live in a mansion." This was the most incredible conversation Clay had ever experienced. Why was he trying to downplay his lifestyle?

To make Annie more comfortable, that was why.

Annie's eyes narrowed. "How big is this nonmansion?"

"Tweytfllrms," he mumbled.

"What?"

"Twenty-two rooms. But it's not a mansion."

"Twenty-two rooms! And you live there alone?" She appeared as if she might cry. "You probably have caviar for breakfast and—"

He shook his head quickly. "Toast, fresh-squeezed orange juice, and black coffee, that's what I have. Every day. I don't even like caviar."

"—gold faucets in your bathrooms and—"

"They're only gold plated. Cheap gold plating. And brass. I'm pretty sure some of them are brass."

"—and date movie stars—"

"The only movie star I ever dated was Brooke Shields, and that was because she and I are both Princeton alumni. And it wasn't really a date, just brunch at—"

"Brooke Shields!" five males at the table exclaimed.

Annie honed in on another irrelevant fact. "He eats brunch. *Brunch.* Oh, God! He must think he's landed on Welfare Row. *Better Slums and Gardens.*"

"Who's Brooke Shields?" Aunt Liza wanted to know. "Is she one of those *Melrose Place* hussies Roy watches all the time?"

Before anyone could explain, Annie sighed loudly and declared, "Maybe I'd better take you back to your hotel tonight."

"Annie!" Johnny whined. "You promised we would put up the Christmas tree tonight."

"Yeah, Annie," Jerry Lee chimed in. "We would have had it up by now if it wasn't for your dumb Nativity scene idea."

"Well, actually . . . uh, I'm not feeling so good," Clay surprised himself by saying. He was in a sudden panic. If he went back to the hotel, he'd have no opportunity to study this fever thing with Annie . . . or this falling in . . . uh, whatever. He could easily conduct business on his pocket cell phone from the farm, for a day or two anyhow.

"You aren't?" Annie was immediately concerned.

"Maybe coming downstairs was too much for you." Aunt Liza got up and walked to his end of the table, then put a hand to his forehead to check his temperature. "Yep, he's got a fever."

No kidding! What else is new?

"I'll help you back up the steps," Chet offered.

"No, that's all right. I think I could sit in a chair and watch you put up your tree." *I am shameless. Pathetic, even.* Then, before he had a chance to bite his tongue, he blurted out, "I've never had a Christmas tree."

Everyone stared at him as if he'd just arrived from Mars. Or New Jersey.

"My father didn't believe in commercial holidays," he disclosed, a defensive edge to his voice. *Put a zipper on it, Jes-*

sup. You don't want pity. You want . . . well, something else.

"That settles it, then," Aunt Liza said, tears welling in her eyes.

Yep, pity.

Annie reached under the table and took his hand in hers.

On the other hand, I can stomach a little pity.

Immediately, a warm feeling of absolute rightness filled him almost to overflowing. He knew then that he'd made the right decision in forestalling his return to the city. Besides, he'd just remembered something important.

He hadn't checked out the hayloft yet.

Annie Fallon had thought she had troubles this morning before she ever left for Memphis. Little had she known that her troubles would quadruple by nightfall.

In fact, she'd brought trouble home with her, willingly, and it sat big as you please right now on her living room sofa, with one extended leg propped up on an ottoman, gazing at her with smoldering eyes that promised . . . well, trouble.

Clayton Jessup III had looked handsome this morning when Annie had seen him for the first time in his cashmere overcoat and custom-made suit. But now, sporting a nighttime shadow of whiskers, dressed in tight, faded jeans, a white T-shirt, and an unbuttoned blue plaid flannel shirt that brought out the midnight blue of his eyes, the man was drop-dead gorgeous, testosterone-oozing, hot-hot-hot trouble-on-the-hoof, with a capital *T*.

"I need to talk with you . . . *alone,*" he whispered when Annie stepped close to get the popcorn and cranberry strings he'd been working on for the past two hours. When Aunt Liza had first suggested that he help make the homemade decorations, he'd revealed with an endearing bashfulness, "My father would have been appalled to see me performing this mundane chore. 'Time is money,' was his favorite motto. Over and over he used to tell me, 'You're wasting time, boy. Delegate, delegate, delegate.' " Then Clay had ruined the effect of his shy revelation by asking Aunt Liza the crass question,

"Don't you think it would be cheaper, timewise, to buy these garlands already strung?"

Clucking with disapproval, Aunt Liza had shoved the darning needle, a ball of string, and bowls of popcorn and cranberries in his lap. "You can't put a price tag on tradition, boy."

Along the same line, he'd observed, "I never realized Christmas trees could be so messy." Her brothers had just dragged in the seven-foot blue spruce from the porch, leaving a trail of fresh needles on the hardwood floors. "Wouldn't an artificial tree be a better investment in the long run?"

They'd all looked at him as if he'd committed some great sacrilege. Which, of course, he had. An artificial tree? Never! Couldn't he smell the rich Tennessee forest in the pine scent that permeated the air? Couldn't he understand that bringing a live tree into the house was like bringing a bit of God's bounty inside, a direct link between the upcoming celebration of Christ's birth and the world's ongoing rejuvenation of life?

"Think with your heart, not your brain, sonny," Aunt Liza urged.

Now the tree decorating was almost complete, except for the star—which had been in the family for three generations—the garlands, and the last of the handcrafted ornaments made by Fallon children for the past twenty-five or so years. And all Annie could think about was the fact that the man had said he wanted to talk with her, *alone*. About two thousand red flags of warning went up in Annie's already muddled senses. "If it's about your threat to sue, well, you can see we don't have much."

The Fallons were a proud family, but her brothers were trusting souls, and in the course of the evening they'd casually divulged their dire need for a new barn roof, the money crunch caused by lower milk prices, and Roy's tuition woes. They'd even discussed at length how every year at Christmastime the Fallons performed one good deed, no matter how tight they were for money. One year it had been a contribution to a local farm family whose house had burned down. Another year they made up two dozen baskets for a food bank in Memphis, complete with fresh turkeys, home-canned fruits, vegetables and preserves, crisp apples, and pure maple syrup. Still another year, when the till was bone-dry, they'd donated ten hours each to Habitat for Humanity. This year, they hadn't yet come up with any ideas. But they would before Christmas Eve. Tradition demanded it.

"You can sue us if you want, but it's obvious that we barely have two dimes to spare. I'll fight you to the death if you try to take our farm."

"What in God's name gave you the idea that I want your farm?" he snapped. Then his voice lowered. "It's not your farm I'm interested in, Annie."

Annie loved the way he said her name, soft and special. But there was no way in the world she would ask what he meant by that enigmatic remark. "Perhaps we could pay for your medical expenses over a period of time."

He shook his head slowly. "I'm insured."

Okay, he's insured, but he didn't say he wouldn't sue us. Should I ask, or assume that he won't? Hmmm. Better to let sleeping dogs lie. "I hope you're not going to stop us from doing our Nativity scene for the rest of the week. You've got to know it's our last chance. And—"

He put up a halting hand. "I'd rather you didn't go back to that sideshow again, but that's not why I want to talk with you."

"It's not?" Annie's heart was beating so fast she was afraid he might hear it.

"It's not."

"What do you want from us, then?"

"From your family . . ."—he shrugged—"nothing."

She reflected on his words. "From me?" she squeaked out.

A slow grin crept across his lips, causing those incredible dimples to emerge. Annie had to clench her fists against the compulsion to touch each of the tiny indentations, to trace the outline of those kiss-me lips, to—

A low, masculine chuckle emerged from said lips. "If you don't stop looking at me like that, Annie, love," he said in a husky undertone, "I'll *show* you what I want."

Annie, love? Mercy! "I don't know what you mean," she said huffily, and backed away before he could tell her exactly how she'd been ogling him and what he would show her.

"You know what I mean, Annie," he commented to her back. "You know."

She didn't know, not for sure, but her imagination kicked in big-time. It was the fever, of course—that strange malady that seemed to affect only the two of them when they were in the same room. Hadn't they complained of the heat all night? And they both knew it had nothing to do with the roaring fire in the fireplace. It was a fire of another kind entirely.

After that, in the midst of their decorating efforts, Clay helped Hank with his calculus homework. No one was surprised that a man with his financial background could actually perform the complicated equations. Then Jerry Lee expressed a curiosity about Clay's electronic planner gadget. He showed him its various gee-whiz functions and answered questions about the stock market. Annie had never realized that Jerry Lee was even interested in the investment world.

Throughout the evening, Aunt Liza coddled them all by bringing out trays of hot chocolate and her latest batch of Christmas sugar cookies. "Have another," she kept urging Clay, who swore his jeans were going to unsnap.

Now that was a picture Annie tried to avoid.

Finally, the tree decorating was complete.

"Turn off the lamps and flick on the tree lights," Aunt Liza advised. The darkened room looked beautiful under the sheen of the multicolored lights. There was a communal sigh of appreciation from everyone in the room, even Clay.

"Is everyone ready?" Johnny asked, reaching over to turn up the volume on the old-fashioned stereo record player. It had been pumping out Elvis Christmas songs all night.

Her family began singing along with "Blue Christmas" . . . a less than harmonic but poignant custom that always brought tears to Annie's eyes. It reminded her of her parents, now gone, and the yuletide rituals they'd started that would be carried on by Fallons forevermore. In some ways, it was as if, at times like this, their parents were still with them.

Annie glanced over at Clay to see how he was reacting to what he must consider a sappy custom. By the glow of the tree lights and the burning logs in the fireplace, she noticed no condescending smirk on his face. He seemed stunned.

Moving to the front of the sofa and leaning forward, she inquired, "What do you think of your first Christmas tree?"

Before Annie could blink, he grabbed her by the wrist and pulled her down to the sofa at his side. One of her brothers chuckled midstanza, but Annie couldn't bother about that. Clay had tucked her close with an arm locked around her shoulder and her hip pressed tight against his. Only then did he answer . . . a husky whisper breathed against her ear.

"This is a Christmas I will never forget, Annie, love."

They were alone at last.

And Clay had plans.

Big plans.

Aunt Liza had gone to her bedroom on the first floor off of the kitchen after wishing everyone Merry Christmas and giving each a good-night kiss on the cheek, including Clay, who felt a tightening in his throat at being included in the family. Hank had put another log on the fire for them, winked, then hit the telephone for a long chat with his latest girlfriend. Roy and Jerry Lee had gone out to the barn for a final check of the farm animals. Chet was upstairs giving his baby a last nighttime bottle. Johnny was probably asleep already, being among those who'd gotten up by four A.M. today to do farm chores before going into Memphis. Even Elvis had shut down for the night.

Clay turned to Annie, almost overwhelmed with all the new emotions assailing him. "What's happening here?" he asked in a hoarse voice that surely tipped her off to his sorry condition.

"I don't know," she answered, not even having to ask him what he meant, "but it scares me."

"Me, too," he said, nodding. "Me, too."

"I never really believed in all that instant-attraction stuff.

It's the kind of thing you see in sappy movies, or read about in romance novels. Not real life.''

''I thought it—the instant . . . uh, attraction stuff—was a woman thing . . . some half-baked idea women dream up to snare men.''

Neither of them said the word, but it was there, hovering between them . . . a wonderful-horrible possibility.

Then, unable to resist any longer, he relaxed the arm that had been wrapped around her shoulder, holding her immobile. His hand crept under her silky hair to clasp the bare nape of her neck. His other hand briefly traced the line of her jaw and her full, parted lips before tunneling into her hair, caressing her scalp.

She moaned. But she didn't pull away. She, too, must sense the inevitable . . . the impending kiss, and so much more.

''Oh, Annie, I've been waiting to do this for hours.''

''I've been waiting, too,'' she confessed, turning slightly so he could see her better. ''For a long, long time.''

He wasn't sure if she referred to a kiss or this bigger thing looming between them. By the expression of fear on her face, it was probably the latter. Hell, he was scared, too.

At first, he just settled his lips over hers, testing. With barely any pressure at all, he shifted from side to side till they fit perfectly. Then, deepening the kiss, he persuaded her to open for him. The first tentative thrust of his tongue inside her mouth brought stars behind his closed lids and another moan from Annie. He pulled back and whispered against her moist lips, ''You taste like candy canes.''

She smiled against his lips and whispered back, ''You taste like popcorn. All buttery and salty and movie-balcony naughty.''

Chuckling, he cut her off, kissing her in earnest now, long, drugging kisses that went on and on. He couldn't get enough. She seemed to feel the same way.

''Annie, love,'' he cautioned after what appeared an hour, but was probably only a few minutes, ''your brothers are back.'' The clomp of heavy boots could be heard on the back porch by the kitchen.

They both sat up straighter, their clasped hands their only body contact.

"G'night," Roy and Jerry Lee said as they passed through the living room on their way to the stairs. There was a snicker in Roy's tone, but thankfully he said nothing more.

"Were they kissin'?" he heard Jerry Lee ask in an undertone once they were in the upper hall.

"Do pigs grunt?" Roy answered.

"Annie? Our Annie? Yech!"

"What? You didn't think she knew how to kiss?"

"Sure . . . I mean, I guess so. It's just . . . I never saw her lookin' so pink and flustery. And Clay, he looks guilty as sin."

"Better not be too guilty, or too sinful," Roy growled.

Their muted voices faded to nothing.

Annie put her face in her hands and groaned. "Pink and flustery! I'll never hear the end of this. Never. By tomorrow morning, my brothers will be making pink jokes. 'What's pink and goes squawk-squawk?' 'A flustered Annie chicken.' Ha, ha, ha."

Clay barely suppressed a smile. Her embarrassment was endearing. "Annie, that's not a joke. It's not even funny."

She raised her head. "Since when do my brothers' jokes have to be funny? And don't think you're going to escape their teasing either. Uh-uh. You are in for it, big-time. How about, 'What's got a scratchy jaw and googly eyes?'"

"Annie," he warned.

"'A Princeton hog in rut.'" At his gaping mouth, she nodded her head vigorously. "See. That's what you can expect."

Is she saying I have googly eyes . . . whatever the hell googly eyes are? Clay lowered his lashes to half-mast and pulled Annie into his embrace again, fitting her face into the curve of his neck. He kissed the top of her head, murmuring, "Oh, Annie. It doesn't matter what they say when this feels so right."

She sighed, which he took for a nonverbal sign of agreement, and nestled closer. "I suppose you want to sleep with me."

Whoa! That got his attention. "Where did that come from?

311

We were just kissing, Annie." *Not that other parts of my body weren't headed in that direction. But, geez! Talk about getting right to the point!*

Annie put her hands on his chest and shoved away slightly so she could look at him directly. "Are you saying you don't want to make love with me?"

"Hell, no."

He reached for her, but she squirmed back, keeping her distance.

"Me, too."

Me, too? What does that mean? Oh, my God! Did she just say she wants to make love with me? "Annie, this is going a bit fast, don't you think? I mean, I'm not sure it's a good idea making love on your living room couch where anyone could barge in at any moment." *Me, too? Son of a gun! I do like a woman who can make up her mind. No games with my Annie. No, sirree.*

She made a snorting sound of disgust, waving a hand in the air. "That's not what I meant, you dolt."

His spirits immediately deflated. *Damn!*

"I'm just trying to tell you that . . . uh . . . um . . ."

"What?" he prodded. This was the most disarming, confusing conversation he'd ever had with a woman, and if it got any hotter in this room he was going to explode.

As if mirroring his thoughts, Annie wiped her forehead with the back of one hand and began to unbutton her flannel shirt, revealing a tight white T-shirt underneath.

He refused to look *there*.

He was not going to look.

He was looking.

Man, oh, man!

That had been her bra in the bathroom, all right. Her breasts pushed against the thin material, full and uptilted, the nipples puckered into hard peaks. It wasn't that she was big busted, but because she was so thin, it appeared that way. Good thing she didn't look like that in her Blessed Mother outfit or she'd have had men propositioning her right there in the Nativity scene. Or else she'd get some super tips.

"Stop looking at me like that."

"Like what?" he choked out.

"Like you're . . . like you're . . ."

". . . interested?" He couldn't stop the grin that twitched at his lips.

"Stop smirking. I'm trying to tell you something."

"Oh?" he said, trying his damnedest not to look at her chest and not to grin with pure, unadulterated anticipation. As a final measure, he clenched his fists at his sides to keep from grabbing for her.

"I'm a virgin."

That was the last thing Clay had expected to hear.

"A virgin?" he squeaked out. *A twenty-eight-year-old virgin?*

"Yeah, isn't that the biggest joke of all?"

She was actually embarrassed by her virginity. Well, it did put a new light on their making love. Not that he didn't still want her, but it sure as hell wouldn't take place on a sofa with broken springs in a houseful of gun-toting brothers and an aunt who wielded a wicked spoon. "Annie, why tell me this now?"

"You have a right to know . . . if I'm reading that glimmer in your eye the right way."

She is. Clay lowered his lashes and tried his best to curb that "glimmer" in his eye.

"You probably think I'm repressed or gay or ultrareligious. But it's just that I haven't had time for dating since my parents died. And Prince Charming doesn't come riding his charger down the lane to a dairy farm real often."

"So I'm the first prince to come your way?" he asked with a laugh.

She slanted him a Behave-yourself glare and went on, "Now that you know, I suppose you don't want me anymore." She glanced at him shyly and looked away.

He took her chin in his hand and turned her face back to him. Kissing her lips lightly, he murmured, "I still want you."

A slow, wicked smile spread across her lips. "Stand up, then," she ordered.

Huh? With his brow furrowing in confusion, he got up cautiously, bracing himself on one crutch. At the same time, the stereo suddenly came on with Elvis wailing, "It's Now or Never."

He jerked back at the unexpected noise and Annie laughed.

"The stereo does that sometimes. There's a short in its circuit, I guess."

He thought about telling her that was a safety hazard, but decided he had more important things on his mind right now. Like why she'd wanted him to stand, and why she was staring at him, arms folded across her chest, with that odd expression on her face. She was probably afraid, being a virgin and all. It was sweet of her, actually.

"Don't be afraid, Annie. I won't do anything to hurt you."

She laughed, a joyous, rippling sound mingling with Elvis's husky now-or-never warning.

That was probably nervous laughter, Clay concluded. Still, he tilted his head to the side, questioning. "Annie?"

"Take off your shirt, Clay. Please."

Her softly spoken words ambushed him. With a quick intake of breath, he almost swallowed his tongue.

"Reeeaal slow."

Chapter Four

Annie could see that she'd shocked Clay, but she didn't care. This was her big chance.

Just because she was a virgin didn't mean she was a dried-up old spinster with no needs. As she'd told him before, there weren't many princes who ambled on down the farm lane. And when one not-so-perfect specimen accidentally rode in, well, heck, she'd be a fool not to drag him down off his destrier and have her way with him.

"I have needs," she told him matter-of-factly.

"Needs?" he choked out. Geez, the man looked as if he were choking on his own tongue. Where was the suave, cool-as-a-hybrid-cucumber man who could cut a person off at the knees with a single icy stare?

Okay, sometimes Annie forgot that city people didn't understand the plain speaking of farm folks who lived with the facts of life on a daily basis. Those who worked with the land and animals tended to be more earthy, more accepting of the forces of nature. Sex was just another of the physical urges God gave all animals, nothing to be embarrassed about. At least, that was what she told herself. If she didn't justify her behavior in that way, she'd have to admit she was a lust-driven hussy with a compulsion to jump this poor prince's royal bones.

"Yep. Needs," she answered with more bravado than she really felt. If he rejected her, she was going to crawl in a hole and never come out. "So shuck that shirt, honey. I've been having indecent thoughts ever since I saw you in the emergency room in those cute little boxer shorts."

Stains of scarlet bloomed on his face at her mention of his boxers. Or was it her needs turning up his internal thermometer?

"This is a joke, right?" Clay said, backing up a bit.

Oh, swell! I'm scaring him. Slow down, Annie. Play it cool. Pretend he's just hairy old Frankie Wilks.

Ha!

"No joke, Clay. You have a chest that would cause a cloistered nun to melt, and I already have a fever to begin with. So take off the darn shirt, for crying out loud." Her voice had turned shrill at the end.

"All right, all right," he said, raising a palm in surrender. "Let's backtrack to step one. You want me to take off my shirt because you like my chest?"

"Yes."

He smiled then, one of those glorious affairs that bared his even white teeth and caused those irresistible dimples to play peekaboo with her heart. "What if someone walks in . . . like your aunt?"

She pooh-poohed that idea. "Do you think Aunt Liza hasn't seen a man's chest before? In a house with five males?"

"But Annie," Clay explained with exaggerated patience. "If you want me to take off my shirt, I'm pretty sure I'll be wanting you to take off your shirt." He flashed her a So-there grin.

"Oh." Delicious images swam in Annie's head at that suggestion. "Well, I guess I forgot to mention that Aunt Liza is dead to the world once her head hits the pillow. Her alarm clock, set religiously for four A.M., is the only thing that will awaken her now.''

''Yes, you did forget to mention that fact.'' His grin didn't waver at all. ''And your brothers?''

''The same. Besides, there's an unwritten rule in the Fallon house. Nobody walks in unannounced on a courting couple . . . not that you and I are courting, mind you. Don't get your feathers all ruffled in that regard. I'm not out to trap you.''

''My feathers aren't ruffled,'' he protested indignantly. Then, understanding that they wouldn't be interrupted, he immediately pulled off the flannel shirt and raised the T-shirt over his head. Superman couldn't have done it faster. After that, standing still, he waited for her to make the next move.

He wasn't smiling now.

He was so beautiful. Wide shoulders. Narrow waist and hips. A thin frame, but not too thin. Muscles delineating his upper arms and forearms and the planes of his chest and abdomen—not a muscle-builder's puffed-up flesh, just healthy, fit male muscle. Dark, silky hairs peppered his chest, leading down in a vee to the low-riding jeans.

Under her sweeping appraisal, he never once lowered his eyes. Women faltered under such close scrutiny, but not men . . . not this man.

''Can I touch you?'' she whispered.

She saw the hard ridges of his stomach muscles lurch.

Heat curled in her stomach.

At first, he closed his eyes and a low, strangled sound emerged from his lips. He appeared to be out of breath, panting. When he lifted his eyelids, Annie almost staggered backward under the onslaught of blue fire. ''If you *don't* touch me, I think I'll go up in smoke,'' he whispered back.

Well, that sounds encouraging. She stepped closer and put her hands on his shoulders. He tried to take her in his arms, but Annie swatted his hands away. She wanted to do this herself, with no distractions. ''Let me . . . I want . . .'' she murmured, her brain reeling with feverish urgency. ''I want to do things to you. So many things.'' *Things? What things? Where are these outlandish thoughts coming from? And how am I getting up the nerve to say them aloud?*

"Annie . . ." he started to say, then paused, lost for words. "You take my breath away."

"Don't move," she ordered, and ran her fingertips down both sides of his tension-corded neck, over his shoulders, skimming over the light fur on his arms to his hands, where she twined their fingers for one brief moment, raising the knuckles of one hand, then the other for a brief kiss. She released his hands then, setting them back at his side.

Smoothing the palms of her hands across his chest, she felt his heartbeat thud. She watched in fascination as the flat male nipples hardened and elongated.

Clay gritted out one crude word between clenched teeth.

Annie decided to take the expletive as a compliment.

She couldn't resist then. Lowering her head, she licked one nipple, sucked it into her mouth, rolled it between her lips.

"Omigod, omigod, omigod!" Clay exclaimed, snaking out a hand to grasp her nape, then lifting her into an embrace where her hips cradled his erection. Alternately kissing her with a devouring hunger and growling into the curve of her neck, he ended up cupping her buttocks and rocking her against him. All the time he was overcome with a violent shiver.

Incredibly, Annie felt herself approaching climax. It was way too soon for that, and not the way she wanted it to happen.

It was Clay who slowed the action. Setting her away from him, he said in a gravelly rasp, "Do you know what I want, Annie, love?"

She cocked her head to the side. "I think so."

"Not *that,* silly girl. I mean, yes, I want *that,* but not now. What I really want is to feel your skin against mine."

It took several moments for his words to sink in. When they did, Annie felt a thrill of excitement ripple through her already oversensitized body. She jerked off her flannel shirt, then drew the T-shirt up and over her head, leaving only a plain, white nylon bra. Through its thin fabric, her small nipples stood out with stiff, pale rose peaks, aching for his touch.

His eyes studied her with apparent appreciation. He licked his lips as he waited for her final unveiling. When the wispy bra fell to the floor, his eyes seemed to water up. "Oh, Annie, you are so beautiful."

She wasn't beautiful; Annie knew that. But it was nice that he found her appealing. She wanted to be beautiful for him.

"It's your turn now, sweetheart. Don't move," he said then, giving equal attention to her body, murmuring compliments to each part examined by his tantalizing fingers and feathery kisses. When he came to her breasts, Annie's heart stood still. First he raised them up in the palms of his hands, then skimmed both nipples with the pads of his thumbs. By the time he angled his head down to wet one, then the other with his lips and tongue, and finally suckled rhythmically, Annie was mewling in an increasing frenzy.

Recognizing her spiraling passion, Clay eased backward toward the couch, taking Annie with him. But he lost his balance and fell onto his back, half reclining, with one leg extended out to the floor. Annie tripped, too, and ended up plopped on top of him. When she raised herself up, she found herself, amazingly, straddling him, jean-clad groin to jean-clad groin.

Clay groaned, a long, husky sound of pain emitted through clenched teeth.

Immediately, Annie remembered Clay's injuries. It was a sign of her fevered brain that she'd forgotten to begin with. "Oh, my God! Did I hurt you? Is it your head? Or your ankle?"

Clay tried to laugh, but it came out strangled. "That's not where I'm hurting, Annie." He rolled his hips from side to side against Annie's widespread thighs, and Annie felt the clear delineation of the ridge pressing against her with an urgency that matched her own.

"Oh," she said.

Clay chuckled. " 'Oh' about says it, darling." Then he chucked her under the chin.

"I've shocked you, haven't I?" she asked, belatedly shy.

Shocked would be the understatement of the year, Clay decided. *Who knew when I woke up this morning, a cold, dreary day in Princeton, that my evening would end with such unexpected manna from heaven? But wait a minute.* He didn't like the look creeping onto Annie's face. "Don't go shy on me now, Annie."

"I've never behaved this way before . . . so forward and uninhibited," she confessed, hiding her face in her hands.

"Your eagerness excites me. Tremendously. Don't you dare stop now," he said in a suffocated whisper, prying her fingers away. "I have plans for you that require a major dose of forwardness and uninhibitedness."

"You do?"

Was that hope in her voice? "Absolutely. Are you afraid?"

"No. Are you?"

He laughed outright. God, how he loved her openness.

"Listen, Annie—stop, you witch . . . I can't think when you do that." She was leaning forward, her hair a thick swatch curtaining his face, as she still straddled him. Back and forth, she was brushing her breasts across his chest hairs.

"That's the point, isn't it? Not to think?"

He leaned up and gave her a quick kiss. "You don't act like any virgin I've ever known." *Not that I've known very many . . . or any, for that matter, that I can recall.*

"Just because I didn't do *that,* doesn't mean I didn't do anything," she said, meanwhile kissing a little line from one end of his jaw to the other.

Clay fought against the roil of jealousy that ripped through him at the thought of any other man touching his Annie in any way. Had it been the milkman, or someone else? How many someone elses? "Annie, you're driving me mad. Be still for one moment. Please."

Surprisingly, she did as he asked. Of course, when she stilled, she also sat upright, square on his already overeager, overengorged erection. He closed his eyes for one second, to keep them from bulging clear out of his head. Finally, when he managed to speak above a squeak, he said, "We're not going to make love tonight, Annie."

She stiffened at once, and her face went beet red. "You don't want me?"

"Of course I want you, but I refuse to make love with you on an uncomfortable sofa, out in the open, with a houseful of people . . . no matter what you say about sleeping patterns or rules for . . . uh, courting."

She pondered his words, then seemed to accept their logic. "So, we're not going to make love *tonight*? Will we ever?"

"Oh, for sure, darling. For sure."

She smiled widely at that.

"And there's another thing, Annie, love. We have to talk about this thing that's happening with us."

"It is . . . strange."

"Strange, overpowering, confusing. I have an idea, Annie. Let's go out tomorrow night. Slow down this runaway train. See where this relationship is going."

"I like the sound of that."

He took a breast in each hand then and admired the contrast of the firm, white mounds against his darker skin. "I love your breasts. I love the way they aren't big, but appear to be so because of your thin frame." He stretched his head forward to savor one of them with his mouth.

She made a keening sound low in her throat, halfway between a purr and a cry for mercy. "I thought we weren't going to make love," she gasped out.

"True. We're not going to make love. But we can make out. A little."

"Oh, goody," she cooed. Before he knew what she was about, Annie slid a hand between them and caressed his tumescence. "Does this count as making love or making out?"

He about shot off the couch. And all he could think was, *Who the hell cares?*

"Whoa, whoa, whoa, Annie." Very carefully, he dislodged her grasp and placed both her hands at her sides and held them there. "You've been running the show for much too long in your family. It's time for you to sit back and let someone else take over."

Her chin went up.

"All right?"

After a long pause of hesitation, she nodded.

He proceeded then to unbutton her jeans.

Her eyebrows shot up in surprise, but she didn't protest.

"Lift up a little, honey, and lean forward," he advised. When she did, he slid a hand inside the waistband of her panties, down between her legs. The warm wetness he met there caused him to sigh with pleasure. "Oh, Annie, love, you feel so good."

"Clay," she cried out, unsure whether she wanted him to touch her there.

Before she had a chance to think further, he inserted a long middle finger inside her tightness and rested a pulsing thumb against the swollen bud. "Now, Annie," he encouraged her with a guttural hoarseness, "you ride . . . you set the pace."

"I . . . I don't think I can," she whimpered.

"Yes, you can, darling."

And she did.

With each forward thrust, she brushed the ridge of his erection. They were separated by denim material, but the sensation was still intense. With each withdrawal, that part of his body yearned for her next stroke. It didn't last long. Probably only minutes. But when Annie began to spasm around his finger and melt onto him, he held her fast by the hips, leaned forward to kiss her with a devouring hunger, and bucked upward . . . once, twice, three times.

"Annie, love," he whispered into her hair a short time later. She was nestled at his side, both of them stretched out full-length on the sofa.

"Hmmm?" She was half-asleep and sated.

Clay couldn't have been prouder if he'd pulled off a million-dollar investment deal. You'd think he was personally responsible for having made the world move. Well, he had, actually. For both of them.

"Clay?" she prodded.

"I think I'm falling in love with you," he disclosed. He hadn't intended to tell her . . . not yet. But his senses were on overload, brimming with so much joy. He couldn't contain it all.

"I already know I'm in love with you. I think I fell the minute I saw you storming across that vacant lot looking like Scrooge himself."

He poked her playfully in the ribs at that insult, but inside he felt such a triumphant sense of elation. *Annie loves me. Annie loves me. Annie loves me.* It was all so new and strange and confusing. Not what he'd come to Memphis to find. It would pose all kinds of problems in his life. But what a wonderful, wonderful thing. *Annie loves me.*

Annie worried her bottom lip with her teeth then. Obviously, she had something on her mind. Finally, she blurted out, "When will you know for sure?"

Clay chuckled and said, "Maybe after we check out the hayloft."

I love her.

It was Clay's first thought when he awakened the next morning to bright sunlight warming the cozy bedroom. You'd think it was springtime, instead of four days before Christmas. But then, Clay recalled, he was in Tennessee . . . almost the Deep South.

With an openmouthed yawn, he stretched widely, becoming immediately aware of the ache in his ankle and at the back of his head. He glanced to the side, saw the bedside clock, and jolted upright, causing the dull pain to intensify. *Ten o'clock!* He hadn't slept beyond six A.M. in the past twenty years.

Oh, well! First he would take a shower. Afterward he had at least a dozen calls to make, first to check with his office in New York, then to set the hotel sale in motion here in Memphis.

But there was only one thought that kept ringing through his head. *I love Annie.* Clay was not a whimsical person. If anyone had told him a few days ago that he would believe in love at first sight or romantic destiny, he would have scoffed heartily. He didn't know how it had happened or why, though he suspected, illogically, that it involved that dingbat bellhop and God's big toe and Elvis's spirit. He'd been fated to come to Memphis. Not to sell the blasted hotel, though he would do that as soon as possible, but to find Annie. *Amazing!*

It would take some doing to get Annie moved to Princeton. Probably they'd have to wait till after the holidays. Oh, he knew it would be hard for her to leave the farm, but she had Chet and her brothers here to take over for her. And her Aunt Liza would care for the boys. Hell, he'd hire a live-in housekeeper to help Aunt Liza if necessary. Or the whole gang could come live with him, though he couldn't imagine that ever happening. It would be like the Clampetts moving to Princeton. All he knew was that it was time someone took care of Annie, and Clay thanked God it was going to be him.

Would they get married?

Of course. There was no way her family would allow her to live with a man without the bonds of matrimony. And Annie would want that, too, Clay was sure.

How did he feel about marriage? *Hmmm.* A few days ago, he would have balked. But now . . . Clay smiled. Now the idea of marrying Annie seemed ordained. Perfect.

So everything was all set. He and Annie would go out tonight on a date. He would propose. She would accept. They'd make plans for the wedding and the move to Princeton. And a honeymoon . . . they'd fit a honeymoon in there, too. Perfect.

The only problem was that Clay kept hearing the oddest thing. Somewhere in the house, a radio was playing that old Elvis song, "Blue Suede Shoes," but every time Elvis would belt out a stanza that was supposed to end in a warning not to step on "my blue suede shoes," Clay kept hearing, ". . . don't you step on *God's big toe.*"

If Clay was a superstitious man, he would have considered it a premonition.

"You've got to be kidding!"

Clay had showered and shaved with a disposable razor he'd found in the bathroom. Then he'd unhesitatingly entered Chet's room, where he borrowed a clean set of clothes, including a pair of new underwear straight from the package.

This family owed him that, at least. Okay, he owed them a lot, too, he was beginning to realize . . . like a new life.

But now, Aunt Liza had forced him into a chair at the kitchen table, where she'd placed in front of him a half dozen platters heaped with bacon and sausage, hotcakes dripping with butter and maple syrup, scrambled eggs and leftover biscuits from last night (also dripping with butter), slices of scrapple (which he feared contained pork unmentionables, like noses and things), black pudding (which Aunt Liza told him without blinking was blood sausage), coffee, orange juice, and a glass of cold milk with a head of pure cream.

"All I ever have for breakfast is coffee, juice, and an English muffin or toast," he demurred.

"Well, you ain't in New Jersey now, boy. So eat up. I got some oatmeal cookin' on the stove, too, to warm up your innards."

He groaned. "If I eat all this, I won't be able to move."

"You ain't goin' anywhere anyhow, sonny. You're stuck here on the farm with a gimp leg, in case you hadn't noticed."

"But I have work to do . . . calls to make—"

She slapped a couple of pig-nose slabs on his plate and glared at him till he finally gave in. He pushed the pig-nose slabs to the side, though, and gave himself modest helpings of eggs and biscuits, one sausage link, two slices of bacon, and one hotcake, but before he knew it his plate was overflowing.

Despite all his protests, the food was mouthwateringly delicious, and he told Aunt Liza so. She smiled graciously at the compliment and sat down at the table with him, sipping a cup of coffee.

"When did everyone leave for Memphis?" he asked as he ate . . . and ate . . . and ate.

" 'Bout nine," Aunt Liza said, nibbling on a buttered biscuit slathered with strawberry jam, while she continued to drink her coffee. "They wanted to get an early start today . . . hopin' the Christmas shoppers and tourists will be out early."

Clay nodded. "Why didn't they leave Jason here with you?"

Aunt Liza's shoulders slumped, and her parchment cheeks pinkened. "I can't be on my feet too long. Gotta take lots of naps. And sometimes I don't hear the baby when he cries."

Clay wished he hadn't asked when he saw the shame on her wrinkled face. He decided silence was a better route to take . . . to shut his big mouth. So he tentatively tasted a piece of the black pudding, which was surprisingly palatable.

"So when you gonna make an honest woman of our Annie?" Aunt Liza asked unexpectedly.

His milk went down the wrong pipe and he sputtered. He probably had a cream mustache, to boot. "I haven't done anything to make Annie *dis*honest," he asserted, wiping at his mouth with a napkin.

Aunt Liza gave him a sidelong glance of skepticism. "That whisker burn she was sportin' on her cheeks this mornin' didn't come from a close shave, honey. Besides, Roy and Jerry Lee was sayin' somethin' 'bout 'pink and flustery' and 'guilty as sin.' Don't suppose you know what they was talkin' about?"

Clay hated the fact that his face was heating up, but he wasn't about to cower under the old buzzard's insinuations. He raised his chin obstinately and refused to rise to her bait.

"We got one loose chick hatched on this place, and I don't want no more," Aunt Liza went on. "Randy roosters and footloose hens are runnin' rampant these days."

Clay didn't have the faintest idea what she was talking about. Roosters and hens and chicks?

"Now I don't countenance loose behavior none, but you'd best be keepin' these," she said, pulling a small box out of her apron pocket and shoving it his way, "just in case the devil sits on your shoulder sometime soon."

"Wh-what?" Clay stammered as he realized that Aunt Liza had handed him a box of condoms. *Oh, man! A woman old enough to be my grandmother is giving me condoms.* "Where did you get these?"

"The supermarket."

"You . . . you went into a supermarket and bought condoms?"

"Yep. Durn tootin', I did. 'Bout caused ol' Charlie Good, the manager, to swallow his false teeth."

"You bought condoms *for me*? But . . . but I just got here yesterday." Clay's head was reeling with confusion.

"Don't be an idjit, boy. 'Tweren't you I bought those suckers for." Aunt Liza took another sip of coffee, ignoring the fact that he was waiting, slack jawed, for her next bombshell. "Chet learned his lesson good, I reckon, with that little chick of his. But I was figurin' on havin' a talk with Hank. That boy's headed on the road to ruination sure as God made Jezebels and hot-blooded roosters."

Hank? She bought the condoms for Hank? That makes sense. I guess. Whew!

"This whole generation's goin' to hell in a handbasket, if you ask me." Aunt Liza made a *tsk*ing sound, piercing him with a stare that included him in the wild bunch. "I blame it all on the tongue business."

The tongue business? Don't ask. Don't ask. "What tongue business?"

"Tongue kissin'. What tongue business didja think I was gabbin' about?" she answered tartly, as if he should have known better. "When courtin' couples start tongue kissin', the trouble begins. Next thing ya know they're buyin' Pampers by the gross."

She narrowed her eyes at Clay, and he just knew Aunt Liza was going to ask him if he'd been giving Annie tongue. Before she could speak, he put up a halting hand. Time to put some brakes on this outrageous conversation.

"Aunt Liza," Clay said in the calmest voice he could muster, without breaking out in laughter, "Annie and I have not had sex." *Yet.* "But even if we had, whatever happened or didn't happen or is about to happen is between me and Annie."

"Well, that may very well be, Mr. Hoity-Toity City Feller, but if there's a weddin' to be planned, I gotta commence makin' a menu, and preparin' food. Everyone in the whole county will wanna come to Annie Fallon's weddin', that's for sure. I don't wanna be goin' to all that trouble for a bride with

327

a belly what looks like she swallowed a watermelon seed nine months past.''

I'm going insane. I just discovered I'm falling in love, and already she has me making babies and walking up the aisle, in that order. And, good Lord, does she think we would get married in a farmhouse? With pigs' noses and cows' blood and other equally distasteful stuff on the wedding menu?

Now that was unkind. She's only being concerned. You really are being hoity-toity, if that means the same as poker-up-your-butt snobbish. C'mon, Jessup, stop acting like you're in Princeton.

"Aunt Liza, if and when Annie and I decide to marry, you'll be the first to know."

"Oh, I know, all right," she said, leveling him with a scrutiny that saw right through his facade. "I knew the minute Annie brung you through that door yesterday. I knew when the radio kept bopping on and off all day with Elvis's music that his spirit has come into the house. I knew when you gawked at Annie all durin' dinner last night, and couldn't keep the love out of your eyes. I knew—"

"Enough!" he said with a laugh of surrender. "Pass me the pigs' noses."

Chapter Five

Clay was waiting on the front porch when Annie got home at five.

She felt the now familiar feverish heat envelop her the minute he came into view. It was the strangest, most wonderful, scariest feeling in the world to drive up in the pickup and see this man she'd come to love in such a short time, just standing there waiting for her to come home.

Leaning against a porch post, he was dressed in his neatly pressed suit, the sides of his jacket pulled back over his slim hips by hands that were tucked into the pockets of his slacks. One crutch was propped beside him. It was a casual pose, but Annie could see he was as nervous and excited as she was.

"Hi," she said breathlessly, coming up the steps.

"Hi," he said back, his eyes crinkling with amusement as they skimmed over her, from bouffant hair to Blessed Mary robe.

She stopped midway up the steps, an attack of timidity overcoming her. All day she'd been thinking about him, the wicked things he'd done to her last night, how he'd made her feel.

Now, all the thoughts she'd wanted to share with him stuck in her throat. What if he'd changed his mind? What if his heart wasn't racing as madly as hers? What if he didn't really want to take her out tonight? What if he didn't love her?

Clay uncoiled himself from his leaning position and stepped forward, slowly. One hand snaked out to grasp her by the nape and draw her closer. "I missed you," he said in a husky voice.

"Oh, God, I missed you, too. But I look awful," she said, waggling her fingers in a flustery fashion to indicate her caricature appearance. *Flustery? I'm probably pink, too. Roy and Jerry Lee were right. Flustery and pink.*

Clay chuckled. "Just shows how far gone I am. You're beginning to look good even as a sixties Madonna." He dragged her close and lowered his head toward hers. Annie watched, mesmerized, as his eyelids fluttered closed and his lips parted.

Then she forgot everything, too engrossed in the kiss, which seared her already feverish body to her very soul. When he slipped his tongue inside her mouth, she felt his heat, and knew the fever had overtaken him as well.

She moaned against his open mouth.

He moaned back.

A sharp rapping noise jarred them both from their kiss, ending it far too soon. It was Aunt Liza, using her wooden spoon to knock a warning on the kitchen window, which looked out over the porch. "There'd better not be any tongue business goin' on," Aunt Liza called out. "Remember what I told you, young man."

Annie leaned back, still in the circle of Clay's arms, and peered questioningly up at him.

He laughed. "You don't want to know."

"Hey, Clay," Chet greeted him. Still dressed in his Elvis/St. Joseph gear and high, duck-tail hairdo, Chet had just come from the pickup truck, where he must have been gathering the baby's paraphernalia, which was looped over one shoulder. The baby, which he held in the other arm, was wide-awake and gurgling happily, swatting at Chet's nose with a rattle. Chet must have heard Aunt Liza, because he waggled his eyebrows in commiseration and commented, "Aunt Liza gave you the tongue lecture, right?"

"Oh, no!" Annie groaned, putting her face in her hands.

"We made eight hundred dollars today," Johnny informed him cheerily as he skipped up the steps, Elvis hair bouncing up and down. His sheepskin shepherd outfit was in sharp contrast to his duct-taped sneakers. "Annie says I can get a new pair of athletic shoes for Christmas if we keep going at this clip. And see, Annie? I didn't say one single word about 'pink and flustery,' just like you warned."

"Where do you think you're going?" Annie asked Johnny. "There's milking to be done."

"I know, I know. Don't get your dander up. I have to go to the bathroom first. They can start without me," he whined, pointing at his brothers.

Roy, Hank, and Jerry Lee, still dolled up as Elvis wise men, were unloading the donkey and two sheep from the animal van, alternately smirking toward him and Annie and trying to get the stubborn donkey to move. At one point, Roy and Jerry Lee were shoving the donkey's butt while Hank pulled on a lead rope. The only thing they accomplished was a load of donkey manure barely missing their feet.

"I swear, Annie, I'm butchering this donkey come Christmas," Roy vowed.

Clay tasted bile rising in his throat. They wouldn't really eat donkey, would they? Hell, they ate beef blood and pigs' noses. Why not donkey? "Hurry and shower so we can go out," he whispered to Annie. "I have big plans for tonight."

"Big plans? Oh, my! I certainly hope so."

"Before you shower, we'd better go out to the barn and breed Mirabelle. She's not gonna be in heat much longer. I don't think we wanna wait another twenty-one days for her to go in heat again." Clay hadn't realized that Chet still stood on the porch, behind them. "Here," Chet added, handing the baby to Clay, "take him in the house for me. We'll be back in a half hour or so."

"What? Who? Me?" Clay said, staring at the wide-eyed baby who gaped at him as if his father had just delivered him to King Kong. Clay was holding the kid gingerly with hands under both his armpits. Just when Clay thought the baby was going to let loose with a wail of outrage, Jason gave him a slobbery smile and belted him on the forehead with a rattle.

Clay could swear he heard Aunt Liza giggling on the other side of the kitchen window. She probably considered it just payment for tongue.

A half hour later, Annie hadn't returned to the house. Aunt Liza had changed baby Jason after Clay had performed the amazing feat of feeding him a bottle. The kid, who was really quite precious, was now cooing contentedly from his infant seat in the kitchen, where he was pulverizing a piece of melba toast.

Clay decided to check out this cow-breeding business.

What he saw when he entered the huge barn stunned him. First of all, there was the overpowering smell: cow manure, the hot earthy scent of animal flesh, and fresh milk. A cow belched near him and he almost jumped out of his wing-tips. The sweet reek of the cow's breath that drifted toward him on the wake of the bovine burp was not unpleasant, but strange. Very strange.

There was a center aisle with about sixty black-and-white cows lined up in stalls on both sides. Jerry Lee was washing down cow udders and stimulating teats, while Roy was hooking the teats up to automated milking contraptions, six cows at a time.

Hank was shoveling feed in the troughs for the big cows, which must have weighed about 1500 pounds, at the same time ministering to the sixty or so young stock at the far end of the barn. The whole time he was addressing the cows by name. Florence. Sweet Caroline. Aggie. Winona. Rosie Posie. Lucille. Pamela Lee. On and on, he chatted with the cows. How he ever remembered all the names, Clay didn't know.

Johnny was sitting off to the side, bottle-feeding a half dozen baby calves. "Hey, Clay, wanna help me?" he asked.

"Uh . . . I don't think I'm dressed for that," he declined. Besides, he wanted to see what Annie was doing at the other end of the barn. She and Chet were in a separate, larger stall with one humongous cow about the size of a minivan. That must be the breeding section.

"Where's the bull?" he inquired casually, as if he strolled through barns every day to view cow sex.

Chet and Annie jerked to attention. Apparently they hadn't heard him come up behind them. Well, no wonder. With all these cows mooing, he could barely hear anything himself.

"We don't have any bulls," Annie answered. "We butcher or sell off all the male stock."

"Why?"

"Bulls are too darn ornery, that's why," Chet answered. "They're not worth the trouble, believe me."

"But . . . but how do you breed the cows then?"

"Artificial insemination," Chet informed him. "This is the nineties, man."

It was only then that he noticed Chet was holding the cow still, even though it was tied by a loose rope to the front of the stall. Annie, on the other hand, stood there with a big brown apron covering her Virgin Mary gown. On one arm, she wore a plastic glove that reached all the way to the shoulder. In the other hand, she held a huge syringe-type affair, more like a twenty-inch caulking gun. *My Lord!*

"You'd better step back," Chet warned him.

Clay's eyes bugged and his mouth dropped open at what he saw then. Almost immediately, he spun on his heels and rushed outside . . . where he proceeded to hurl the contents of his stomach, which Aunt Liza had taken great pains to stuff all day long.

I wonder where this ranks in the God's-big-toe category?

Clay had almost botched things, big-time.

At first, it had seemed as if their blooming relationship had been slam-dunked back to step one, or zero, with his disastrous reaction to that scene in the barn. He still shivered with distaste at what he'd seen, but he was doing his shivering internally. The sooner he could erase that picture from his mind, the better. In time—maybe ten or twenty years—he would, no doubt, forget it totally.

Annie had appeared crushed when she'd followed him out. He could understand that. Farm work, in all its crude aspects, was what Annie did for a living—her identity. It had been obvious that Annie thought he was repulsed by *her*. But it wasn't her, it was what she'd been doing. But Clay hadn't dared say that. Instead, he'd lied, "My stomach has been upset all day. It must be the aftereffects of those painkillers, or something I ate."

She'd stared at him dubiously. "Maybe it's not such a good idea for us to go out on a date. Things have been happening too fast. We haven't stopped to consider our differences. It's probably a good idea for us to slow down and count to ten—"

Reconsider? Count to ten? No way! We're not even counting to two. Oh, God! She's going to dump us. He'd backpedaled then and convinced her to give him another chance. At what, he wasn't sure. He only knew he loved her, cow breeding or no cow breeding. And he didn't want to blow the best thing that had ever happened to him.

Now, strolling down Memphis's famous Beale Street, he was getting yet another view of his Annie. This one he liked a whole lot better than all the rest. So far, he'd had the Priscilla Virgin Mary, the jeans-and-flannel farm girl—he was still waiting for the Daisy Mae outfit, darn it!—and the cow breeder to the bovine stars. Now Annie wore an ankle-length floral print skirt of some crinkled gauze material over a satin lining. It was robin's egg blue with gold flowers. On top was a long-sleeved, matching blue sweater of softest angora, which reached to her hips and was belted at the waist. The gold flowers of the skirt were picked up in embroidery around the sweater's neckline. On her legs she wore sheer stockings and old-fashioned, lace-up ankle boots. Her lustrous brown hair was pulled off her face by gold clips and hung in disarray to her shoulders. She'd even used some makeup for the first time since the day Clay had met her—a little blush, mascara, and lip gloss, as far as he could tell. She looked smart and sexy.

Sort of like Julia Roberts, but better, to his mind. No wonder he'd fallen head over heels in love with her.

Clay couldn't stop looking at her.

And she couldn't stop looking at him.

She smiled at him.

He smiled back.

He was using one crutch to keep his full weight off his sprained ankle, which was almost better today. With his free hand, Clay twined Annie's fingers in his.

She swung their clasped hands.

Clay couldn't understand how he got so much pleasure from just holding hands with a woman and hobbling slowly down the street. Annie had been giving him a running commentary on the history of Memphis.

"Are you sure you don't want to eat yet?" she inquired. "It's almost eight o'clock."

He shook his head. They'd already passed up hot tamales and greasy burgers at the Blues City Café, where Tom Cruise had filmed a scene for the movie *The Firm,* as well as ribs, catfish, and world-famous fried dill pickles, the specialties at B. B. King's club.

"How about this?" Annie had stopped in front of Lansky Brothers/Center for Southern Folklore. "This museum is dedicated to preserving the legends and folklore of the entire South, but especially Memphis. They have an excellent photography collection here."

"My mother was a photographer," Clay revealed. *Now, why did I mention that? I never talk about my mother.*

"Really? Did she use her maiden name or her married name?" Annie was already tugging him by the hand to enter the small museum, where a plaque informed him it was the site of the former Lansky Brothers Clothing Store where Elvis, B. B. King, Jerry Lee Lewis, Carl Perkins, and others had purchased their clothes. *Well, that impresses the hell out of me. I'd want to buy my boxers in the same store as Elvis, for sure. Geez!*

But Clay knew he was dwelling on irrelevant garbage to

avoid thinking about Annie's question. Finally, he answered, "Her maiden name. Clare Gannett."

"Clare Gannett? Clare Gannett? Why, she's famous, Clay."

"She is—was—not!" he said with consternation.

"Well, not Annie Leibovitz famous, but she has a fame of sorts here in Memphis."

It doesn't take much to be famous in Memphis. Just be a store that sold Elvis a pair of boxers. Or the barber who gave him a haircut. Or the playground where he scraped his shin.

"Annie, my mother was not a famous photographer. For one thing, she died when she was only twenty-five—Whoa . . . wait a minute—what are you doing?" Annie paid for two tickets, and was pulling him determinedly past the exhibits into another room.

"See," she said, pointing to one wall where there were a series of photos of Elvis Presley. Casual shots . . . leaning against a car, strumming a guitar, standing in front of the Original Heartbreak Hotel. A framed document explained that Clare Gannett was one of Memphis's premier photographers, documenting on film many of the city's early music performers during the sixties—not just Elvis, but many rock and blues personalities who later went on to fame.

Oh, great! My mother knew Elvis. First I find out my father owned a hokey hotel named after one of Elvis's songs. Now I find out my mother must have known the King. What next?

"Legend says that Elvis loved Clare Gannett—"

Clay put his face in his hands. He didn't want to hear this.

"—but she fell in love with some Yankee who came to Memphis on a business trip one day. They say the Yankee bought the hotel and next-door property where her studio was located as a wedding present for her. The studio later burned down, and Clare Gannett died in the fire. The hotel owner, your father, refused to erect anything else on that site. Isn't that romantic?"

"Annie, that is nothing but propaganda, a silly yarn spun for gullible tourists."

"Maybe. But legend says Elvis was heartbroken over losing Clare Gannett. It was after that he decided to marry Priscilla.

Some people even think he wrote 'Dreams of Yesterday,' better known as 'I Can't Stop Loving You,' in her memory."

Clay turned angrily and stomped as fast as he could on one crutch out of the building. He was breathing heavily, in and out, trying to control his rage.

"Clay, what's wrong?" Annie asked softly. She came up close to him and put a hand on his sleeve.

He waited several seconds before speaking, not wanting to take out his feelings on Annie. "Annie, my mother abandoned me and my father when I was only one year old. So your telling me she had a relationship with that hip-swiveling jerk doesn't sit too well with me."

"I'm sorry, Clay. I didn't know. But maybe you're wrong about her. The legend never said that anything happened between them. In fact, she supposedly broke Elvis's heart when she married your father. Maybe—"

He leaned down to kiss her softly, the best way he could think of to halt her words. "It was a long time ago. It doesn't matter anymore."

She gazed at him with tears in her eyes. *Tears, for God's sake!* Not for a moment did she buy his unconcern.

"Hey, let's go in this place," Clay suggested cheerily, coming to a standstill in front of Forever Blue, a small jazz club. He desperately sought a change of mood. "It doesn't seem as crowded as some of the other joints."

As they entered the establishment, Clay accidentally jostled a woman standing transfixed in the doorway.

"Sorry," they both mumbled.

A short blonde in a formfitting blue dress and matching high heels was staring at the piano player as if she'd seen a ghost. Her face was taut with some strong emotion as she clenched and unclenched her hands at her midsection. Suddenly the piano player seemed to notice her. He faltered slightly, then stopped playing his rendition of "I'll Be Home for Christmas." Before anyone in the audience could fathom his intent, he jumped off the small stage and rushed after the woman who had spun on her heel and run out the door onto busy Beale Street.

Clay and Annie looked at each other and shrugged as the man rushed past them, obviously in pursuit of the mysterious woman.

"That was Michael Arnett, the owner of this club," Annie informed him. "He's a famous songwriter, too. Did you ever hear 'Only a Shadow'?"

"The Jimmy Blue hit?" Clay wasn't a fan of popular music, but he'd have to be dead not to be aware of that song and its phenomenal success.

"Yes. That was one of Michael's songs."

Michael? She calls him by his first name? "You know this guy?" Clay hated the wave of jealousy that knifed through him. He hated the possibility that he might have a milkman *and* a musician as competition. He hated the fact that the dark-haired piano man was tall, slim, and probably considered handsome by some myopic women.

"A little. Michael and I went to the same high school, but he graduated a few years ahead of me."

Okay. So maybe I overreacted a little. "It looked as if something serious was going on with that woman."

Annie nodded. "Yeah. I hope it works out."

He smiled at Annie's whimsy as he guided her in front of him into the club. At the table next to theirs, a beautiful woman with short, tousled, honey-colored hair, in a dark, conservative business suit, was talking a mile a minute to a guy in a Hawaiian shirt and baseball cap. The guy was leaning back lazily in his chair, clearly amused by her nonstop chatter. It sounded as if she was reciting the tourist directory of Memphis, and every fact and figure ever compiled.

Suddenly, the woman began belting out the lyrics to "Only a Shadow." Her date didn't appear quite so amused now. In fact, his face went white with concern. With good cause, it would seem. Within seconds, the woman pitched forward, her face almost landing in her bowl of chili, but for a last-minute rescue by her male companion.

Clay shook his head at Annie. "Nice bunch of people here in Memphis." He flinched as the woman began to sing again.

"They are nice," Annie insisted. "In fact, that man is Spencer Modine, one of Memphis's financial success stories. He made his money in California, but he returned here to start up a record company."

"Spencer Modine?" Clay rubbed his chin thoughtfully. "Hell, are you talking about the Bill Gates of Silicon Valley? The computer whiz kid who made a killing in computer software?"

"Uh-huh."

"Did you go to high school with him, too?" he grumbled.

Annie laughed. "No, I didn't."

They settled back then to order drinks and a mushroom-and-sundried-tomato pizza. A short time later, Arnett and the woman he'd pursued came back into the club. Arnett seated her near the stage, and he resumed playing. Clay moved his chair close to Annie and fiddled with the ends of her hair, nervous as a teenager on his first date.

"Annie, love," he whispered, kissing the curve of her neck. She smelled of some light floral fragrance . . . lilies of the valley, maybe. As always, there was that delicious heat ricocheting between them.

"Hmmm?" she purred, arching her neck to give him greater access.

"I don't want to go back to the farm . . . yet."

"Me neither," she said softly, turning to stare directly into his eyes.

"Will . . . will you come back to my hotel room with me?"

Annie continued to stare into his eyes, unwavering. She *had* to know what he was asking. Finally, she nodded, leaning closer to place her lips against his, softly. "I have to go back to the farm tonight, though. There's the four A.M. milking before we come back into Memphis for the Nativity scene."

He stiffened at the thought of the woman he loved demeaning herself in that ridiculous sideshow. "Annie, stay home at the farm tomorrow. Give up the Nativity scene venture. Let me help you—and your family—financially."

She immediately bristled. "No! The Fallon family doesn't accept charity."

He should have known she'd balk. But, dammit, how was

she going to reconcile accepting his money after they were married? "Whatever you say, sweetheart. It was only a suggestion," he conceded, for now.

She softened at his halfhearted apology. "I want to be with you, Clay," she whispered.

"Not half as much as I want to be with you."

The piano player had just finished up a blues song, so fast and intricate that his talent was evident. Next, in reaction to the loud requests from two ends of the club for "I'll Be Home for Christmas" and "Jingle Bell Rock," Arnett played a skillful blending of both yuletide classics. When he finished, silence reigned briefly, followed by thunderous applause.

Clay barely noticed the piano player and his girlfriend leaving the club once again. All he could think about was Annie and the fact that they were going to be together tonight. It appeared as if it would turn out all right, after all. No more celestial big toes.

He hoped.

Annie was nervous, but exhilarated, as they entered the foyer of the Original Heartbreak Hotel.

It was only ten o'clock, and the hotel lobby still buzzed with activity, its guests coming in for the evening, or just going out, in some cases. As myriad as Memphis itself, the guests ranged from sedately dressed businessmen to a group of Flying Elvi. But mostly there were tourists come to view the spectacle that was Memphis, the adopted home of Elvis . . . like those two middle-aged women over there in neon pink ELVIS LIVES sweatshirts who were eyeing Clay as if they thought he might be someone famous.

"They think I'm George," Clay informed her dryly, noticing her line of vision.

"George who?"

Clay shrugged. "Damned if I know. Straight, or Strayed, or something like that."

Annie burst out in laughter. "George Strait?"

"Yes. That's the one."

Annie hugged the big dolt. "How could anyone in the mod-

340

ern world not know George Strait? Clay, you are too, too precious.''

He grinned at her calling him precious, then took her hand and led her around the massive Christmas tree in the center of the lobby. It was decorated with sparkling lights and priceless country-star memorabilia left by the various musicians who'd stayed in this hotel over the years. A gold-plated guitar pick from Chet Atkins. Guitar strings tied into a bow from Hank Williams. A silver star that had once adorned the dressing room of Eddie Arnold. Pearl earrings from Tammy Wynette. ''Have you ever seen such a gaudy tree in all your life?''

''Clay, you need a major attitude adjustment.''

''And you're the one to give it to me, aren't you, Annie, love?'' he said, flicking her chin playfully. ''Come on. I need to pick something up from the desk.''

David and Marion Bloom, the longtime managers, nodded at Clay as he approached, and then at Annie, too. The refined couple, who resembled David Niven and Ingrid Bergman, right down to the thin mustache and the neatly coiled French twist hairdo, respectively, were probably surprised to see Annie with their boss, but they didn't betray their reactions by so much as a lifted eyebrow.

''Did an express mail package come for me today?'' Clay asked.

''Yes, sir,'' David Bloom said, drawing a cardboard mailer out of a drawer behind the desk.

''And I have all those tax statements you asked me to gather together when you called this afternoon,'' Marion Bloom added.

Clay took the mailer, but waved aside the stack of papers. ''I'll examine those tomorrow.''

Annie could see that the Blooms looked rather pale, their faces pinched with worry. Heck, everyone at the hotel was alarmed, from what Annie had heard when in Memphis earlier today. The possibility of imminent unemployment once the hotel closed had them all walking on tenterhooks, especially with the holidays looming. Annie would have liked to tell them that Clay would never close the hotel now that he knew what a landmark it was to Memphis, not to mention the connection with his mother. But it wasn't her place.

"We'll meet tomorrow at one with the accountant, right?" Clay asked the couple. When they nodded solemnly, he concluded, "Good night, then," and led Annie toward the elevators.

Once the doors swished shut, Annie leaned her head on Clay's shoulder and sighed. But he set her away from him and stepped to the other side of the elevator, staring at her with a rueful grimace. "If I touch you now, sweetheart, we'll be making love on the elevator floor."

She smiled.

"You little witch. You'd like that, wouldn't you?" Clay observed with a chuckle.

Soon he was inserting the key into the lock of his hotel room. Once they entered, Clay flicked on the light switch, and Annie was assaulted with a dozen different sounds, sights, and smells. A carousel—*a carousel, for heaven's sake*—was turning in one corner of the massive suite, churning out calliope music. A television in another corner clicked on automatically, playing a video of that old Elvis movie *Roustabout*. A popcorn machine began popping, and a cotton candy machine began spinning its weblike confection. Hot dogs sizzled on a counter grill, where candy apples were laid out for a late-night snack. And the bed— *holy cow!*—the bed was in the form of a tunnel-of-love cart with high sides, and what looked like a vibrating mechanism on the side to simulate a water-rocking motion.

"Clay!" She laughed.

"Did you ever see anything so absurd in all your life?" A delightful pink stained his cheeks.

"Actually, it's kind of . . . uh, charming."

"Please." He begged to differ. Then, tossing his crutches aside, he leaned back against the door and pulled her into his embrace. "At last," he whispered against her mouth.

When he kissed her, openmouthed and clinging, Annie could taste his need for her. What a heart-filling ego boost to know she could affect this man so!

With clumsy haste, they pulled at each other's clothes.

"Slow down, honey," Clay urged raggedly, then immediately reversed himself. "No, hurry up, sweetheart."

"I can't wait, I can't wait, I can't wait. . . ." she cried.

Soon they were naked, he with nothing but a bandage wrapped around one ankle, she with nothing but two gold barrettes, which she quickly tossed aside.

She saw his arousal, and felt her own throb in counterpoint. Leaning forward, she pressed her lips to his chest, breathing in the clean, musky scent of his skin.

Clay gasped.

"You are so hot," she blurted out.

He grinned. "I know."

"Oh, you! I meant you throw off heat like . . . like an erotic bonfire."

Clay laughed. "So do you, Annie. So do you," he whispered, holding her face with the fingertips of both hands. He gazed at her with sheer adulation, which both humbled and exalted her. Tears filled her vision at the admiration she saw in his wonderful blue eyes.

"I love you, Clayton Jessup. I don't know how it's possible to fall in love with someone so fast and so hard, but it's the truth. I love you."

"I feel as if I've been walking through life with a huge hole in my heart, and now, suddenly, it's been filled. You make me complete, Annie. I know, that sounds so corny—"

"Shhh," she said, putting a forefinger against his lips. "It doesn't sound corny at all."

He led her to the bed then and they climbed over the ridiculously high side frames, laughing. It was an awkward exercise, with Clay's injury.

"At least there's no danger of us falling out of bed if you get too rambunctious," she teased.

In response, he swatted her on the behind, which was raised ignominiously in the air before she plopped down next to him.

Turning serious, Clay rolled onto his back and adjusted her so she lay half over him. Then he took her hands, encouraging her to explore him.

And she did.

Oh, Lord, she did.

She told him things she'd never imagined were in the far reaches of her fantasies. She used words . . . wicked words that drew a heated blush to her cheeks, and a chuckle of satisfaction from Clay.

Clay told her things, too, in a voice silky with sex. He spoke of erotic activities that made her tremble with trepidation. Or was it anticipation?

"I never expected that a man's hands could be so gentle and aggressive at the same time," she confessed.

"Who knew you'd be so passionate!" Clay said as he performed magic feats on the many surfaces of her body. "I love the soft sounds you make when I touch you here. And here. And here."

Clay nudged her knees apart and lay over her, weight braced on his elbows. He teased her nipples with his fingers and lips and teeth and tongue—plucking, sucking, fluttering, and nipping—till Annie ached for more. It was hard to believe that the staid businessman could be such an inventive lover.

Finally, finally, finally, he penetrated her, and there was no pain, just a stretching fullness. Clay went still, his body taut with tension as he watched her.

"I love you, Annie," he whispered.

Her inner folds shifted around him in response, allowing him to grow even more, filling her even more.

"I love you, too, Clay. With all my heart."

Only then did he begin to move, long strokes that seemed to draw her very soul from her body. Then he surged back in again. Over and over, he took her breath away, then gave her new life.

She drew her knees up to give him greater access.

His heart thundered against her breast.

"Come for me, Annie," he gritted out painfully. "Let it happen, love."

But Annie fought her climax till she saw Clay rear his head back, veins taut in his neck, and let loose with a raw animal sound of pure male release as he plunged fully into her depths. Only then did Annie allow herself to spasm around him in progressively stronger reflexes till she, too, cried out with pure pleasure-pain.

Annie wept then—not from physical soreness, or emotional distress. It was the beauty and rightness of what they shared that drew her tears. There was a dampness in Clay's eyes, too.

After that, they made love again, a slow, serious exploration of each other's bodies, their likes and dislikes.

Then they made love a third time . . . a joyous, rib-tickling affair, involving mattress wave machines and carousels and sinfully sweet cotton candy.

Chapter Six

It was two o'clock in the morning, and she and Clay were sitting on the floor watching *Roustabout*. She wore only Clay's dress shirt; he wore only a pair of boxers. She'd never enjoyed a movie more.

They were eating candy apples and chili dogs. He'd balked at the food choice at first, but Annie noticed that he'd then scarfed down two of both in record time, washed down with a Coke.

"We have to go back to the farm soon," she said regretfully. "We don't want to arrive when everyone is already waking up for the day. Talk about 'pink and flustery'! I'd be more like red and catatonic . . . with mortification."

"You aren't having second thoughts, are you?" Clay stood up and was taking their empty plates and glasses over to the kitchenette counter. He stopped and stared at her with concern.

"No, sweetheart, I'm not ashamed of anything we've done together. I just don't want to broadcast it to the world yet."

"Good," he said. "Because I have something for you." Clay went over to the hallway where he'd placed the express

346

mailer that Mr. Bloom had handed to him earlier. Pulling the string zip, he took out a small box and handed it to Annie.

She raised her brows with uncertainty, then stood up and opened the small cardboard box. Inside was a velvet box. Annie felt a roaring in her ears, and she began to weep before she even opened the tiny latch to see an old-fashioned diamond in a gold setting, surrounded by diamond chips.

"It belonged to my grandmother. I called my office this morning and had my secretary take it out of the safety-deposit box and mail it to me. If you don't like it, we can buy a new one, whatever you want." Clay was rambling on nervously while Annie continued to weep.

"It's beautiful," she sobbed.

"Will you marry me, love?"

"Of course I'll marry you," she said, and continued to sob.

"Here, let me put it on for you," Clay urged, a tearful thread in his voice, too.

It was dazzling. Not too big. Not too modern. Ideal.

"Oh, Clay, I love you so much."

"I love you, too. More than I ever thought possible."

They kissed to seal their betrothal.

Then they sealed their betrothal in another way.

"How soon before we can get married, do you think?" Clay asked much later. "I've got to get back to my office sometime soon, and I hate the thought of leaving you behind."

"I don't know. Aunt Liza will want to have a big wedding, but we can do something small, for family only."

"Is that what you want?"

"I'm not sure. I always pictured myself walking down the aisle in a white gown . . . the works. But now . . . well, I want to be married to you as soon as possible."

"We'll have a big wedding, if that's what you always wanted, Annie, love. But we'll set a new time record for arranging a big wedding. Okay?"

She nodded, unable to stop staring at the beautiful ring on her finger.

"Will you be able to come back to Princeton with me for

a while? Would that be too scandalous for Aunt Liza?''

Annie laughed. ''Oh, I think we could convince her that your housekeeper is chaperon enough, but I couldn't stay for more than a week. It's too much to ask Chet and the others to take on my work for much more than that.''

''But, honey, at some point they'll have to pick up your slack. When you move up north, they'll have no choice but to—''

The small choked sound Annie made caught Clay midsentence.

''Annie . . . Annie, what's wrong?''

Stricken, she could only stare at him. ''You think I'll move to New Jersey permanently?''

A frown creased Clay's forehead. ''Of course. You didn't think I would be moving here, did you?''

''Yes,'' she wailed. ''You didn't think I'd give up the farm, did you?''

''Yes.''

They were both gaping at each other with incredulity.

''How could you think that you and I would marry and live in that farmhouse? It's too small for your family as it is.''

Annie shrugged. ''I guess I wasn't thinking that far. At some point, Chet will probably marry Emmy Lou, once he gets his head together. And I would imagine they'll live at the farmhouse. But we could always build a house somewhere else on our land. There's plenty of acreage.''

''Annie, I'm not a farmer.''

''Well, I am,'' she said stormily then softened her voice, putting a hand up to cup Clay's rigid jaw lovingly. ''Clay, isn't there any way you could do your work from Memphis?''

''Annie, my business has been operated from the same Manhattan office by three generations of Jessups. My family home has been in Princeton for almost a hundred years.''

''You didn't answer my question.''

''I am *not* moving to Memphis, and that's final.'' He pleaded with her to understand. ''That farm of yours is a money drain, pure and simple. This afternoon I read some of the farm magazines sitting around your house. You don't have to be a rocket scientist to know that eventually you'll have to sell off some land to developers or use hormones in your cattle feed. You're about twenty years behind the times, babe.''

"How dare you . . . how dare you presume to tell me how to run my farm? And you know nothing about me at all, if you think I would ever sell off even a shovelful of Fallon land."

"It's an unwise financial decision, Annie. Believe me, this is what I do for a living. This is my expertise."

"You can shove your expertise, Clay Jessup. And you can shove this, too," she said, taking off the ring and handing it back to him. The whole time tears were streaming down her face.

"Annie, don't. Oh, God, don't leave like this," he said, watching with horror as she snatched up her clothes and began to dress as quickly as possible. "Let's talk about this. You're not being rational." He began to dress as well.

"You're not coming back to the farm with me."

"I don't want you driving alone in the middle of the night."

"I'm a big girl, Clay. I've been doing it for a long time." Dressed now, she stared at him for a long moment. "Tell me one thing, Clay. Do you still intend to raze this hotel?"

"Of course. What would ever make you think otherwise?"

Annie tried, but couldn't stifle the sob that rose in her tight throat. "Call me crazy, but I thought you were developing a heart."

"You're being unfair."

"Life's unfair, Clay." She grabbed her shoulder bag and headed toward the door, anxious to be out of his sight now, before she broke down completely.

"I love you, Annie."

Her only response was to slam the door in his face.

Clay gazed at the closed door with abject misery.

How could I have made such a mess of things? How will I survive without Annie? What should I do now?

And somewhere, whether it was the television or inside his head, Clay couldn't tell for sure, Elvis gave him the answer: "I'm so lonesome I could cry . . ."

Truer words were never sung.

And Clay was pretty sure this qualified as a God's-big-toe stumble.

Two days later, on Wednesday, a despondent Clay stared out his hotel room window as Annie and her brothers dismantled their live Nativity scene for the day. Tomorrow was Christmas Eve, so it would probably be their last day on the site.

Clay had no idea if he'd ever see Annie again after that.

Oh, he'd tried to reconcile their differences, but Annie wouldn't budge.

"Are you still selling the hotel?" she'd demanded to know yesterday when he'd confronted her in the hotel café. She and her family had managed to deflect all his phone calls before that. She'd even threatened to give up their live Nativity scene yesterday, despite her family's need for money, if he didn't stop coming out and "bothering" her. "Well, answer me. Are you still selling the hotel?"

"Yes, but it has nothing to do with us, Annie. It's a business decision."

She'd made a harrumphing sound of disgust. "Would you move to Memphis?"

"Well, maybe we could live here part of the time . . . have homes in New Jersey and Tennessee." *See, I can compromise. Why can't you, Annie?* "Would you be willing to promise to never . . . uh . . . to never stick your arm up a cow's butt again?"

Annie had looked surprised at that request. Then she'd shaken her head sadly. "Clay, Clay, Clay. You just don't get it, do you? I've bred a hundred cows in my lifetime. I'll breed hundreds more before I die. If you think cow breeding is gross, you ought to see me butcher a pig. Or wring a chicken's neck, cut off its head, gut, and feather it, all in time for dinner. Believe me, cow breeding is no big deal."

It is to me. And I refuse to picture Annie with a dead chicken or cow. She's just kidding. She must be. "Don't you love me,

Annie?'' He'd hated the pathetic tone his voice had taken on then, but the question had needed to be asked.

''Yes, but I'm hoping I'll get over it.''

No! his mind had screamed. *Don't get over it. You can't get over it. I won't. I can't.*

That had been the last conversation he'd had with the woman he loved and had lost, all in the space of three lousy days in Memphis. Then today he'd discovered a card table in the lobby with the sign HEARTBREAK HOTEL EMPLOYEE FUND. Apparently, Annie and her family had donated two hundred dollars of their hard-earned money to start a fund for hotel employees who would soon be out of work, due to him. Annie had found a way, after all, to make him, albeit indirectly, involved in the Fallon family Christmas good deed for 1998. And it didn't matter one damn bit to anyone that he'd dropped five hundred dollars in the box.

A knock on the door jarred him from his daydream. It was the elderly bellhop. ''Mr. and Mrs. Bloom said to tell you the lawyers'll be here any minute. Best you come down to the office to go over some last-minute details for the sale.''

The bellhop glared at him, then turned on his heel and stomped away, not even waiting for Clay to accompany him. Hell, the entire hotel staff, except for the Blooms, had put him on their freeze list. You'd think he was Simon Legree. Or Scrooge.

Minutes later, Clay was in the manager's office, doing a last read-through of the legal documents. The attorneys hadn't arrived yet, and David had gone out front to register a guest.

''Mr. Jessup, I have some things that belong to you . . . well, they belonged to your mother, but I guess that means they belong to you now.''

''What?'' Clay glanced up to see Marion lifting a cardboard box from a closet shelf.

''When the fire occurred at the photography studio next door all those years ago, I was on duty. I managed to save a few scraps of things from the fire,'' she explained nervously.

''Why didn't you send them to my father?''

''I tried to give them to him when he came to Memphis to

351

bury your mother, but he refused to take them . . . said he wanted nothing to remind him of her. It was the grief speaking, of course.''

No, it wasn't the grief speaking. That's how my father regarded my mother his entire life.

Hesitantly he opened the box. On top was an eight-by-ten photograph, brown on the edges.

"It was their wedding picture,'' Mrs. Bloom informed him.

Clay felt as if he'd been kicked in the gut. His father— looking much younger and more carefree than he'd ever witnessed—was dressed in a dark suit with a flower in the lapel, gazing with adoration at the woman standing at his side carrying a small bouquet of roses. Their arms were linked around each other's waists. She wore a stylish white suit with matching high heels, and she was staring at her new husband with pure, seemingly heartfelt love. They were standing on the steps in front of a church. The date on the back of the picture read *August 10, 1967.*

"How could two people who appear to have loved each other so much have fallen out of love so quickly?''

Marion gasped. "Whatever are you talking about? They never stopped loving each other.''

Clay cut her off with a sharp glower. "My mother abandoned me and my father less than two years after this photo was taken.''

"She never did so!'' Marion snapped indignantly. "Clare came here to tie up some loose ends with her business, and to give her and your father some breathing room over their differences. But they never stopped loving each other.''

He started to speak, but Marion put up a hand to halt his words. "You have to understand that there's something about the air that comes down from the Blue Ridge Mountains. It gets in a Memphian's soul. Your mother was Memphis born and bred. She had trouble adjusting to life in Princeton, and your father was a stubborn, unbending man. I think he feared the pull of this city on your mother—jealousy, in a way—and so he became dogmatic, unwilling to be flexible.''

"She left my father,'' Clay gritted out.

Marion shook her head vigorously from side to side. "Clare wasn't giving up on your father. She had every intention of returning home. If it hadn't been for the fire . . ." Her eyes filled with tears as she spoke. She swiped at them with a tissue and pointed to an envelope in the box of miscellany.

Clay picked it up and immediately noticed the airline logo on the outside of the envelope. Inside was a thirty-year-old one-way ticket, Memphis to Newark. It was too much to digest at once. Clay stood abruptly and headed for the door.

"Mr. Jessup, where are you going? We have a meeting soon."

He waved a hand dismissively. "I'm going for a walk. I need to think."

"But what should I tell the lawyers?"

"Tell them . . . tell them . . . the deal is off . . . for now."

It was Christmas Eve, and Clay was driving a bright red Jeep Cherokee up the lane to Sweet Hollow Farm, more hopeful and frightened than he'd ever been in all his life.

Would he and Annie be able to work things out?

Would her brothers come out with shotguns in hand?

Would he fight to the death for her . . . a virtual knight in shining Jeep?

Would Annie still love him in the end?

There was a full moon out tonight, but Clay didn't need it, or the Jeep's headlights, to see. The entire barn and farmhouse were outlined with Christmas-tree lights. In the front yard was a plywood Santa and reindeer display, illuminated by flood lights. It resembled a farm version of the house in Chevy Chase's movie *National Lampoon's Christmas Vacation*. He wondered idly who had climbed up on the roofs of the house and barn to put up all those blasted lights. *Probably Annie. Or Aunt Liza. Geez!*

Clay was so nervous he could barely think straight, especially when he saw the front door open even before he emerged from the vehicle.

It was Annie.

Please, God, he prayed, *no big toes this time.*

"Clay?" Annie said, coming down the steps and walking woodenly toward him. She looked as if she'd been crying.

Who made her cry? I'll kill the person who made her cry! Oh! It was probably me.

"Where did you get the Jeep?" she asked nervously, as if that irrelevant detail were the most important thing on her mind.

"I . . . uh . . . kind of . . . uh . . . rented it." Clay's brain was stuck in first gear.

"You came back," she said then, surrendering to a sob. "I called the hotel all night and Marion said you were gone, and I thought . . . I thought you went home."

"I am home, sweetheart." Clay opened his arms to her and gathered her close. "I've done a lot of walking, and thinking, since you left me."

"I've been so miserable," she blubbered against his neck.

"Me, too, sweetheart. Me, too." He was running his hands over her back, her arms, her hair, her back again. He kissed the top of her head, her wet cheeks, her lips. He tried to show her with soul-deep kisses how much he'd missed her, and how important she was to him. He couldn't get enough of her. He was afraid to let go for fear this was all a dream.

Annie leaned back to get a better look at him. Cupping his face in her hands, she gazed at him, tears streaming down her cheeks, with such open love that Clay felt blessed.

"Annie, love, we're going to work this out. I've talked with my legal department in New York, and they see no problem with my setting up a satellite office in Memphis. Could you live with me in New Jersey part of the time, if I'm willing to live here?"

Her mouth had dropped open with surprise. "You would do that for me?"

"In a heartbeat." *It's either that, or suffer heartbreak. Easy choice!*

"How about the hotel?"

"Well, I'm not sure. I called Spencer Modine this morning. Remember, you pointed him out to me at Forever Blue."

"You called Spencer Modine? But you don't even know him."

He shrugged. "Modine certainly has the capital to finance a purchase of the hotel property, and he has the Memphis ties that would make such a landmark attractive to him. But I don't know if I'm ready to give up the hotel yet. Oh, Annie, I've learned some things this week about my mother and father that are going to take me a long time to understand."

She pressed a light kiss to his lips in understanding. "We don't have to decide all this right now."

"We?" he asked hopefully.

"We," she repeated.

"Will you marry me, Annie, love?"

"In a heartbeat," she said.

A short time later, they were heading toward the front steps, arms wrapped around each other's waists, their progress hampered by his limp and their constant stopping to kiss and murmur soft words of love.

Clay couldn't stop grinning.

"You're looking awfully self-satisfied, Mr. Jessup."

"Well, I'm a negotiator, Annie. It's part of my business as a venture capitalist. I figure I just pulled off the deal of the century. I got you, didn't I, babe?"

She laughed. "You had me anyhow, *babe*. I already talked to my brothers about taking over the farm so I could move to New Jersey. Why do you think I was calling you all night?" She tapped him playfully on the chin in one-upmanship.

"Well, you little witch, you," Clay said. But what he thought was, *Wait till you see what I bought at the mall. You haven't had the last word yet.*

Elvis was singing "Blue Christmas" on the stereo, a fire was roaring in the fireplace, the tree lights were flickering, and Clay was enjoying his first ever family Christmas Eve celebration. If his heart expanded with any more joy, it just might explode.

It was almost midnight, but already the family members were opening their Christmas gifts. Clay sat on the sofa with

Annie on one side, holding his hand. Aunt Liza was on the other side, keeping an eagle eye on his hands, lest they stray.

The gifts the Fallons gave to each other were simple items, some homemade, some silly, many downright practical. Who knew that people got socks and underwear for Christmas gifts? Johnny raved over his new athletic shoes ... the spiffiest in the store, according to Annie. Everyone received new shirts and jeans. The pearl stud earrings that Johnny had bought for Annie, probably from Wal-Mart, might have come from Cartier, for all her oohing and ahhing. And the boys exhibited just as much appreciation over cheap card games or music cassettes.

There were even gifts for Clay from the family, to his surprise and slight embarrassment. When Aunt Liza handed him a suspicious-looking small box, wrapped with Santa Claus paper, he almost choked. *She wouldn't!*

Aunt Liza *tsk*ed at him till he unwrapped it to find an audio cassette of *Elvis's Greatest Hits*.

"Whadja think I bought, you fool?" she said with a chuckle.

Chet, Roy, and Hank had pooled their money to get him a pair of low-heeled cowboy boots. Jerry Lee gave him a Wall Street joke book, and Johnny presented him with a tie imprinted with dozens of Holstein cows.

When it was Annie's turn, she made much ado over the homemade tree ornament with his name and date stenciled on the back, thus symbolizing his formal acceptance into her family. Finally, with much nervousness, she handed him what he sensed must be a special gift.

Tears filled his eyes, and he couldn't speak at first. Inside was a leather album. The words on the front, embossed with gold letters, said, THE WORKS OF CLARE GANNETT. Annie had somehow managed to gather together dozens of photographs taken by his mother. On the last page was a copy of an obituary from a Memphis newspaper, detailing her artistic talent and what she had contributed to Memphis and music history.

"Where did you get these?" he asked when his emotions were finally under control.

"I badgered the museum curator yesterday. When he heard your story, he helped me pull those photos made by your mother, and I duplicated them at a one-hour photo studio down the street."

"Thank you, love," he whispered against her hair. Then he decided it was time to reciprocate. "Can you guys help me get some gifts from the Jeep?"

There was a communal awed curse from Annie's brothers when they saw how the back of the Jeep overflowed with gaily wrapped packages, some in huge boxes.

Aunt Liza could be heard rapping on the kitchen window at that crude expletive. "I heard that, boys. You're not too old for soap, you know. That goes for you, too, Mr. Jessup."

After the boys had each made three trips, the living room was filled with his purchases. Hank closed the door with a shiver—it was turning cold outside, and snowflakes had just begun to flutter down in wonderful Christmas fashion—and he asked Clay, "Where'd you buy that spiffy red Jeep?"

"Oh, he didn't buy it," Annie explained. "It's a rental."

"That sure looked like a new car plate to me," Hank commented as he hung his coat on an old-fashioned coatrack.

"Clay?" Annie tilted her head in question to him. "Did you buy yourself a Jeep?"

"Well, no, I didn't buy a Jeep for *myself.*"

Everyone turned to stare at him then. Clay shifted uneasily, and his eyes wandered over to Hank.

There was a long, telling silence. Then Hank whooped. "Me? Me? You bought a car for me?"

"Clay Jessup! You can't go out and buy a car for someone you barely know."

"I can't?" he said. "Well, hell . . . I mean, geez, Annie, Hank distinctly said that first night I was here for dinner that if he had as much money as me, he would buy a fancy new vehicle and be the biggest chick magnet in the United States. I knew you'd be upset if I bought him a Jaguar."

"Holy cow! I wonder what I get if Hank gets a new Jeep," Johnny commented in an awestruck voice.

Annie made a low gurgling sound, which he figured was his cue to move on to the other gifts.

Chet's Adam's apple moved awkwardly as he studied Clay's gift . . . airline tickets for Chet Fallon and son, Jason, to London, dated December 26.

"At least you show *some* good sense," Aunt Liza observed. "It's about time someone pushed Chet in the right direction."

For the entire family, Clay had bought a high-tech computer system that would allow them to program in all the statistics on their milk production. Aunt Liza got a microwave, which she pooh-poohed at first, stating, "What would I do with one of those fancy contraptions?" But she was soon reading the manual, exclaiming, "Didja know you can do preserves in a microwave?" By the time Jerry Lee went ballistic over his laptop, Roy had gone speechless over the bank envelope showing a trust fund passbook covering his entire vet school tuition, and Johnny was in tears over a new entertainment system for his bedroom, complete with portable TV, CD player, and game system . . . well, by then Annie had given up on her protests.

"It's too much, Clay," she said on a sigh of frustration.

"No, it's not, Annie. Generosity is giving till it hurts . . . like you and your family do every Christmas. This is just money I spent here . . . money whose loss I won't even miss."

"But I still think you should take back—"

"Annie," Aunt Liza cautioned in a stern voice, "shut up." They all laughed at that.

"So what did you get for Annie?" Hank wanted to know. She gazed at the ring on her finger. "I have my gift."

But Hank ignored her. "With all the great gifts he gave us, he must have bought you at least . . . a new barn. Ha, ha, ha!"

Annie folded her arms indignantly over her chest at the teasing, and Clay's face heated up in a too-telling fashion.

"Well, actually . . ." he admitted, handing her a gift certificate from a local contracting firm.

"You didn't!" Annie scolded.

He did. It was a purchase order for a new barn roof.

She punched him lightly in the stomach, but he didn't care. He could see the love in her eyes.

A hour later everyone had gone to bed, except him and Annie.

"I love you, Annie," he said for what must be the hundredth time that evening.

"I love you, too, Clay . . . so much that my heart feels as if it's overflowing."

"It's hard to believe that so much has happened to us in the five days since we first met."

"Maybe you were destined to come to Tennessee . . . for us to meet. Maybe there is an Elvis spirit looking over Memphis."

Clay wanted to balk at the idea, but the words wouldn't come out. "Maybe you're right. Perhaps Elvis really does live," he finally conceded. "Oh, I forgot. There's one more gift I bought for you." He reached behind the sofa and handed her the package.

"Clay, this is too much. You've already given me too much."

"Well, actually, this gift is for me." He waggled his eyebrows at her.

Hesitantly, Annie unwrapped the package, which came from a costume shop in the mall. Annie laughed when she lifted the lid. It was a Daisy Mae outfit—a white off-the-shoulder blouse, and cut off jeans that were cut off *real* high on the buttock. "You devil, you."

"So, are you going to try it on for me tonight?"

"Here?"

"Hell, no. In the hayloft."

There was an old legend that said that on Christmas Eve on a farm, the animals talk.

One thing was certain. On Christmas Eve, 1998, on Sweet Hollow Farm, the animals in the barn, under the hayloft, had a lot to talk about.

Author's Note

If you believe the spirit of Elvis is still alive, you're not alone.

It's been more than twenty years since the King died, but almost six hundred Elvis fan clubs still flourish around the world. No one disputes the fact that Elvis had a profound impact on the music industry, but his magic lives on not only in his own songs, but in those of the many musicians influenced by his talent.

So, if you are one of those people who can't help singing along when an Elvis tune comes on the radio . . . or if a smile breaks out when you hear "Blue Suede Shoes" . . . or if you believe some people "live on" after death, then please look for my December 1998 release, *Love Me Tender*. In that book, there is a fake Spanish prince, a Wall Street princess . . . uh, *trader* known as "the Irish Barracuda," and a secondary character named Elmer Presley, who thinks he's Elvis reincarnated.

Maybe he is. And maybe he isn't. But one thing's for sure: the legend does go on.

Christmas Spirit

ELAINE FOX
LEIGH GREENWOOD
LINDA WINSTEAD

Three Heartwarming Tales of Romance and Holiday Cheer

Bah Humbug! by Leigh Greenwood. Nate wants to go somewhere hot, but when his neighbor offers holiday cheer, their passion makes the tropics look like the arctic.

Christmas Present by Elaine Fox. When Susannah returns home, a late-night savior teaches her the secret to happiness. But is this fate, or something more wonderful?

Blue Christmas by Linda Winstead. Jess doesn't date musicians, especially handsome, up-and-coming ones. But she has a ghost of a chance to realize that Jimmy Blue is a heavenly gift.

___4320-3 $5.50 US/$6.50 CAN

Dorchester Publishing Co., Inc.
P.O. Box 6640
Wayne, PA 19087-8640

Please add $1.75 for shipping and handling for the first book and $.50 for each book thereafter. NY, NYC, and PA residents, please add appropriate sales tax. No cash, stamps, or C.O.D.s. All orders shipped within 6 weeks via postal service book rate. Canadian orders require $2.00 extra postage and must be paid in U.S. dollars through a U.S. banking facility.

Name_____
Address_____
City_____State_____Zip_____
I have enclosed $_____ in payment for the checked book(s).
Payment __must__ accompany all orders. ❑ Please send a free catalog.

THE OUTLAW VIKING

SANDRA HILL

As tall and striking as the Valkyries of legend, Dr. Rain Jordan is proud of her Norse ancestors despite their warlike ways. But she can't believe her eyes when a blow to the head transports her to a nightmarish battlefield and she has to save the barbarian of her dreams. If Selik isn't careful, the stunning siren is sure to capture his heart and make a warrior of love out of the outlaw Viking.

___52273-X $5.50 US/$6.50 CAN

SANDRA HILL

Sweeter Savage Love. When a twist of fate casts Harriet Ginoza back in time to the Old South, the modern psychologist meets the object of her forbidden fantasies. Though she knows the dangerously handsome rogue is everything she should despise, she can't help but feel that within his arms she might attain a sweeter savage love.

___52212-8 $5.99 US/$6.99 CAN

Desperado. When a routine skydive goes awry, Major Helen Prescott and Rafe Santiago parachute straight into the 1850 California Gold Rush. Mistaken for a notorious bandit and his infamously sensuous mistress, they find themselves on the wrong side of the law. In a time and place where rules have no meaning, Helen finds herself all too willing to throw caution to the wind to spend every night in the arms of her very own desperado.

___52182-2 $5.99 US/$6.99 CAN

Dorchester Publishing Co., Inc.
P.O. Box 6640
Wayne, PA 19087-8640

Please add $1.75 for shipping and handling for the first book and $.50 for each book thereafter. NY, NYC, and PA residents, please add appropriate sales tax. No cash, stamps, or C.O.D.s. All orders shipped within 6 weeks via postal service book rate. Canadian orders require $2.00 extra postage and must be paid in U.S. dollars through a U.S. banking facility.

Name_____
Address_____
City_____ State_____ Zip_____
I have enclosed $_____ in payment for the checked book(s).
Payment <u>must</u> accompany all orders. ☐ Please send a free catalog.

Linda Jones

On A Wicked Wind

Hurled into the Caribbean and swept back in time, Sabrina Steele finds herself abruptly aroused in the arms of the dashing pirate captain Antonio Rafael de Zamora. There, on his tropical island, Rafael teaches her to crest the waves of passion and sail the seas of ecstasy. But the handsome rogue has a tortured past, and in order to consummate a love that called her through time, the headstrong beauty seeks to uncover the pirate's true buried treasure—his heart.

___52251-9 $5.99 US/$6.99 CAN

**"I loved *Rose*, but I absolutely loved *Fern*!
She's fabulous! An incredible job!"**
—*Romantic Times*

A man of taste and culture, James Madison Randolph enjoys the refined pleasures of life in Boston. It's been years since the suave lawyer abandoned the Randolphs' ramshackle ranch—and the dark secrets that haunted him there. But he is forced to return to the hated frontier when his brother is falsely accused of murder. What he doesn't expect is a sharp-tongued vixen who wants to gun down his entire family. As tough as any cowhand in Kansas, Fern Sproull will see her cousin's killer hang for his crime, and no smooth-talking city slicker will stop her from seeing justice done. But one look at James awakens a tender longing to taste heaven in his kiss. While the townsfolk of Abilene prepare for the trial of the century, Madison and Fern ready themselves for a knock-down, drag-out battle of the sexes that might just have two winners.

___4409-9 $5.99 US/$6.99 CAN